continued . . .

Clean

"I am addicted to this world, this character, and this writer. Alex Hughes spins stories like wizards spin spells . . . a stellar debut!"
—James R. Tuck, author of the Deacon Chalk series

"A fun blend of *Chinatown* and *Blade Runner*."
—James Knapp, author of *State of Decay*

"[A] tightly written futuristic detective story set in an alternate Atlanta. . . . This crisp debut marks Hughes as a writer to watch." —*Publishers Weekly*

"Really well done." —*USA Today*

"I didn't want to stop reading." —Smexy Books

"[A] fast-paced sci-fi yarn. . . . Reminds me very much (and very fondly) of Jim Butcher's Dresden Files."
—SF Signal

"An excellent start on a series . . . so many twists, turns, and double-crossings. . . . I'm going to be first in line for the next novel in this Mindspace Investigations series."
—Night Owl Reviews

"Fans will want more by Alex Hughes." —SFRevu

ALSO AVAILABLE BY ALEX HUGHES

MARKED

A MINDSPACE INVESTIGATIONS NOVEL

Alex Hughes

A ROC BOOK

ROC
Published by the Penguin Group
Penguin Group (USA) LLC, 375 Hudson Street,
New York, New York 10014

USA | Canada | UK | Ireland | Australia | New Zealand | India | South Africa | China
penguin.com
A Penguin Random House Company

First published by Roc, an imprint of New American Library,
a division of Penguin Group (USA) LLC

First Printing, April 2014

 REGISTERED TRADEMARK—MARCA REGISTRADA

ISBN 978-0-451-46693-8

Printed in the United States of America
10   9   8   7   6   5   4   3   2   1

To Sam, who makes it all possible.
Thank you, my love.

"Once a telepath or any person with Ability
is accepted by and accepts the Guild,
he belongs to the Guild for the remainder of his life.
He no longer pays taxes to any nation-state;
he is not subject to its laws, cannot be tried
in any court, and cannot accept employment
except by consent of the Guild."

*—Koshna Accords, section 33,
paragraph 4.3, sentence 1 (called the
"Once Guild Always Guild" section)*

CHAPTER 1

Lying in a society of telepaths was possible, but just barely. The key was not to think about the lie at all—something akin to spinning a plate on top of your head while standing on one foot and reciting multiplication tables—or to lie to yourself first, and often. The frightening thing was how often someone got away with it. The even more frightening thing was that lying well—and being caught at it—seemed to give a certain cache to the telepath involved, and more often than not came with job offers.

In the world of the normals this was also true, though lying wasn't as hard if you didn't have to do it mind-to-mind. Politicians seemed to get reelected more readily after a good lie, bureaucrats seemed to thrive on them, and in my job, contractor interrogator for the DeKalb County Police Department, a good lie to a suspect would get you anything you wanted. I was learning to lie well to the suspects. The trouble was, nearly everyone I met these days was suspect in one way or another.

Homicide detective Isabella Cherabino stuck her head in the door. "We have a murder, Adam."

"Oh, goody," I replied.

She looked at me.

"You realize I'm in the middle of an interview," I said. I

helped her out on murder cases, but I was technically employed as an interviewer. The interview rooms were supposed to come first.

"You have ten minutes," she said, and closed the door behind her as she left.

I turned back to the suspect, a thirtysomething house-wife accused of auto theft. "You know, I'm a Level Eight Guild–trained telepath," I said conversationally.

Exactly nine minutes later, she had just finished explaining how she subverted the cars' antigravity engine lock systems, and how none of the crew she used appreciated her. I made all the right noises, and she finished the confession with times and dates. Finally she looked up with bloodshot eyes and asked me quietly, "Do you think I need a lawyer?"

"I certainly don't know what to think," I said, the standard answer. I went to find a police officer to go sit with her. The empty spot in the room behind me, the spot that would have been Officer Bellury's if he were still alive, seemed to echo. Not only did I need another person to do paperwork if I wasn't going to be here, but it would be nice to have a witness who could testify in court. I was a convicted ex-felon (drug charges only, and more than three years clean out of rehab), and while a video of a confession would hold in court regardless of the interrogator, I certainly couldn't testify. Credibility and all that. Besides, any day that I spent with Cherabino was a good day. I even liked helping with the murders.

One of the secretaries found me on the way out and handed me a message slip.

Kara, it read. *Call Kara Chenoa immediately. Emergency.*

"Immediately" was underlined three times.

Kara had been my fiancée once upon a time, well, until she'd reported me to the Guild for the drug habit that had gotten me kicked out more than ten years ago. These days we were on decent terms—well, when I didn't think too hard about the past. She had moved up in the Guild since we'd been together, to the position of attaché to the city, and she helped me with the occasional case I needed Guild information from. In exchange I tried not to resent her new job and new husband. Kara wasn't given to hysterics. If she said emergency, it was.

"Are you coming or not?" Cherabino asked, literally tapping her foot in impatience.

"Yeah," I said distantly. "I'm going to need a phone."

"I need to get to the crime scene before Bransen docks me for overtime for the Forensics techs. There will be a pay phone close by. *After* you do your reading mumbo jumbo."

My attention turned back to her. "It's highly delicate, trained analysis of what the victim left behind in Mind-space, not mumbo jumbo."

"Don't be touchy."

I made a frustrated sound and trotted after her. She was in one of her moods, clearly.

Cherabino hustled down the main floor of the DeKalb County Police Department, the secretaries busy in the large pool to the left, the suspects screaming in a long line in front of Booking to the right, citizens waiting in front of Reception to the front, near the doors she was headed to. The ordered chaos was home. This job, even with all the stress and the budget cuts, was part of what kept me sane and on the wagon. It helped that they refused to give me pay directly, so I had nothing to buy my drug with.

"Where's Michael?" I asked. Michael was a wiry Korean guy with a calm personality and a close-cut haircut, a new detective she'd promoted up out of uniforms when he'd helped with a case. He'd proven invaluable, even if he and I

had tension sometimes. He was just so . . . nice. I didn't
know what to do with nice.

Cherabino held the door for me. "He's getting the car."
In that moment, I got a whiff of impatience along the mental Link between us. I'd established a bridge between our
minds by accident during an earlier case, and she still
wasn't quite comfortable with it. In fact, she wanted it gone
as quickly as possible, and told me so. Often.

"What?" she asked, as I stood there too long.

Michael landed the car up to the front of the station with a
small *squeal* of an abused anti-grav system. Cherabino's
method of driving must have been wearing off on him; he
used to be a great deal safer.

Moving quickly to get out of the cold November wind,
we piled in the car, Cherabino in the front, me exiled to the
back with the fast food wrappers.

Cherabino shielded mentally, using the technique I'd
shown her to block me out of her mind, long rows of bricks
going up between us. But she left one little brick unset, so
I could still feel the edge of her presence like a dim beam
of light landing on the floor of my mind.

I held on to that light like a lifeline. It hadn't been so
long ago that I had felt nothing but her mind over the Link;
I'd injured my mind in a life-and-death confrontation with
a suspect, and it had taken a couple of months to heal fully.
That is, if it was, in fact, fully healed.

I put my seat belt on. Michael flipped the sirens on and
accelerated. He obeyed most traffic laws most of the time,
and had lights and sirens on when he did not. I'd only
feared for my life once total when he was driving, and that
hadn't been strictly his fault.

To distract myself—a pillar of strategy in the Twelve

Steps—I asked Michael, "What do we know about the victim?" He was still connected to his old network as a beat cop; plus he had a knack for research and detail that wouldn't quit. If there was something to be known at this stage, he would know it.

Also, I added, "Thanks for driving."

"Just a second." Michael cut through smaller city streets, found a skylane entrance—an actual official entrance—and squeezed around a car stopped to let him by. He settled into the upper, mostly empty, skylane with plenty of room to spare for the floating anti-grav markers, and only *then* started to talk.

"Victim is Noah Wright, a sixty-seven-year-old white male, unemployed, found at home. First officer on the scene indicates extreme violence."

"Blunt-force trauma? Gun?" Cherabino asked. "What is 'extreme violence' exactly?"

I sighed. I hated the messy scenes.

"Officer at the scene indicates a small fire ax found on-site and no further details. I'm betting the violence was with the ax or she wouldn't have mentioned it. The ME is running late, so we'll likely have to make the initial call."

Cherabino huffed. "Why call for a senior detective?"

"The lieutenant didn't tell me," Michael said. "It could be the violence level."

They talked about that for a minute, and Cherabino asked another question about the scene.

"Adam!"

"What?"

"We're here," Cherabino said.

"Oh," I said, and started paying attention to the surroundings. Crime scene, after all. And I was still on the clock, still being paid for this, for better or for worse. I needed to do my job, especially since the budget crisis meant if I didn't, I'd be on the street. I might be anyway, if a miracle didn't arrive.

We were in a small driveway in a small lot on a row of identical small boxy brick houses. They had different-colored doors, and a few flags hung from doorposts, touting different political stances. Block parties must be interesting in this neighborhood.

The house had patchy grass, and a different-colored roof and door than the rest. Otherwise, it was the same boxy brick house with one window up front that everyone else had. This one didn't have bars on the windows.

We pulled in, a police cruiser parked crooked on the driveway in front of us, its undercarriage flashing with the occasional burst of orange light, the *whine* you could hear in the air saying its anti-grav hadn't been properly shut down. The officer would be lucky to get it working again with a good mechanic and a hefty bill; if not, he'd be grounded and his wages garnished until the department could afford to fix it.

Next to the cruiser was a huge metal structure, burnished bronze and discolored steel, what might have been a weather vane designed by an antiestablishment artist on a strong drug. It flashed in time with the cruiser's light. Maybe an electrical field at play or some kind of quantum property that entangled to the cruiser's engine and caused the mechanical trouble. Either way I stayed well clear.

"You okay?" Cherabino asked.

"Yeah," I said and got out of the car next to her.

Even though the wind was bitterly cold, the concrete pathway was warm, some kind of deicing setup I could feel even through the shoes. There were small metallic flowers holding lights along the walkway, and the overhanging roof was made out of some kind of supermaterial with an odd snakeskinlike grain. There was more money and thought put into this boxy brick house than was obvious. The door was patterned with overlapping metalwork, like a mosaic out of similar colors of metal, something you could only see when you got up close.

I noticed two camouflaged spy holes set into the door, and when I looked up, two small overhanging boxes. They could have been cameras, I supposed, but they had grates at the bottom. Delivery system for some kind of gas, perhaps, or fine-grade projectiles? Cherabino saw where I was looking and swallowed.

"Gotta love post–Tech Wars architecture," I said.

"Well, at least we know he knew his killer." Cherabino shrugged. "Either that or the killer broke in the back." She turned the handle and we went in, Michael trotting past the apparent kill zone in the doorway all too fast.

Inside was plush carpet and old furnishings, the wallpaper a graphic print popular twenty years ago, dated and old to my eyes. Faux aged-wood panels took up the entire covering of the hallway to the right, a kitchen ran off to the left, and ahead and in front between an outdated couch, a chair, and several small side tables. An ax lay to one side, the kind you'd cut firewood with, the handle stained with brown, something dried and leathery stuck to its edge. A puddle of fresh-smelling vomit sat a few feet outside the blood spray, near the couch.

I walked closer in. Sprays of blood and gore had splashed up on the furniture, a few hitting the walls—one on an abstract painting like an emphasis note. The body—I looked for a moment, then looked away.

We were here before Forensics. The blood was dry, but I didn't smell decomposition; he'd been dead a day or two at the most. I held my shields tightly; with this level of violence, it wouldn't be a fun scene to read mentally either.

The back door looked intact to me, but I was sure it would be checked and rechecked. I noticed a phone in an alcove in the kitchen. A phone I could use to call Kara later, if I managed to dodge Cherabino long enough.

Cherabino sighed and pulled out disposable booties. "Michael, why don't you start a sign-in sheet for the scene? And you," *Adam*, her mind echoed, "you see if you can find the officer who left the car out front and yet is not with the body."

"Oh. Yeah." I lowered my shield enough to skim the top layer of Mindspace—trying to ignore the death hole sitting in the middle of the room—looking for minds. I found one feeling very sick in the rightward direction. I followed the mind like a beacon and found myself outside a bathroom with an open door. A female cop in uniform knelt in front of the toilet.

She heard me and pointed a gun in my direction.

"Police telepath, DeKalb County." I raised my arms. "Authorized consultant. There's two detectives in the main area. I can produce ID."

"Please," she said, and lowered the gun back to the floor. She controlled the urge to heave again; she'd just flushed the toilet and didn't want to be seen doing this to start with.

I fished out my department ID—which I should already have clipped to my shirt—and handed it to her. "Who are you?"

"Briggs," she said, and swallowed again. She gave the ID a cursory look and handed it back.

I gave her space. She was upset; I could feel that along with the nausea.

"Did the scene get messed up?"

"So far as I know, we're the first ones here and it looked good," I said. Waited a moment.

"Could you leave now?"

"Sure."

"Where is the officer?" Cherabino asked.

I explained, then added, "From the feel of it, she'll be throwing up or trying not to for awhile."

Cherabino frowned. "I'll take care of her later." She was pissed, caught between her hard-line rule that officers didn't leave the scene and the knowledge that the officer had called it in properly and had avoided throwing up at the scene itself; the puddle was well clear. She'd had her own messy scenes, when she was a rookie. She'd give the woman space but chew her out later. "Let's handle the scene."

I nodded, like I had any understanding of how this all worked without the Forensics crew here.

Michael was doing something with a box of swabs, stand-up numbers, and plastic baggies around the perimeter. Getting ready for the photographer?

Cherabino held out a set of disposable booties, and I put them on.

"How closely do I have to look?" I asked.

She looked at me.

"No, really."

"This is not happy-fun time. This is time to figure out what happened."

I waited.

She sighed. "If the victim's mind left anything at all for us behind, you go over that with a fine-tooth comb. Twice. That's what you're here for. Do you have to study the exact damage? Yep. Nobody likes this stuff. We do it anyway so that the killer doesn't do it to the next guy."

I looked down. "Would be easiest to go ahead and read the scene before anyone else arrives."

"You want me to be your anchor again? We need to do it quickly. I'm going to have to administer the scene." As she looked over at the scene, her voice was flat. Too flat. Through the Link, I could feel a careful control, a not-think, a walling off of any possible reaction.

I stole shamelessly from that not-think, that dispassion, putting it on like a coat as I trudged over to the couch, looking into the space that had gotten most of the blood. It soaked the carpet in a long puddle; the human body held more blood than you thought it ought to, and that blood was everywhere.

The body was pretty damaged, an ax strike having shattered the collarbone, shredded part of the arm, impacted the clothes-covered back and buttocks in strikes covered with blood, and cut far too deeply into the skin in a way that made my stomach curl. He was facedown, and the major damage was to the back of the head—most of it was simply gone, some spread out over the room along with the blood, and some doubtlessly on the blade of that ax. One ear was completely missing, dried blood and flesh in its place.

I looked away, breathed deeply, and told myself I wouldn't vomit either. Even with Cherabino's borrowed dispassion, it was horrible. Really, really horrible. "Ready?" Cherabino prompted. Her voice was still too flat.

"Yeah," I said. If I waited to think about it, I wouldn't do it. And I had to do my job and get out of here. Now.

She held out the mental hand, the anchor that would help me find my way back to the real world. With all the times she told me to keep my hands and mind to myself, for a case, for safety, she'd do anything it took.

I established brutal mental control, and then took that mental hand, carefully, so carefully.

Reality faded as I moved deeper and deeper, the connection with Cherabino falling behind me like a long yellow scuba line, yellow where no yellow should be. Mindspace was a colorless space, a space in which vision was useless, like the inside of a totally dark cave. The landscape was more felt than seen, echoing back vibrations like I was a bat and the world my cave. Other creatures made waves in the space, and some left wakes behind.

Mindspace remembered. It held on to strong emotion and the leavings of human minds for days, sometimes weeks in a hot spot. Occasionally a spot forgot too soon. But here, in what was apparently a deep and wide container of human energy, I felt Mindspace along the edges of the room layered with the habitual feelings of the house's occupant.

He was a thinker, a planner, a wheels-within-wheels plotter with mathematics and problems and three-dimensional crafting. The space was littered with the spillovers of his thinking, like complex glyphs worn into a wall over time. Other, smaller, lighter presences left scents here and there, other people came and went, but the majority of his time, his life, was wheels-within-wheels.

In the center of the room was the collapsed "hole" of death, where the mind Fell In . . . to wherever minds went when they died. The hole left a distinct shape in Mindspace, a distinct residue and taste. Still very clear, but not fresh.

And around it—anger and violence and dark satisfaction layered with pain like red knives slicing through the very fabric of Mindspace. Layer upon layer of resentment and frustration and anger, leading to this final assertion of control.

And the victim—surprise and panic and anger and pain, so much pain. Hit after hit of damage, then nothing.

I'd have to dive deeper into the emotion eventually, but for now I tried to gauge how old the traces in Mindspace were. Always tough, but here, with the strength of these, it was tougher. I wasn't a newbie, though, and here, finally, I was in my element.

Time of death between twenty-two and twenty-six hours. I shaped the words carefully and sent them up the long yellow line behind me to Cherabino. *Assuming Mindspace here has the standard fading pattern.*

Insight on the killer? Her voice came back, faint and far away, like a missive sent around the world. *Grudge or random?*

Give me a second. I breathed.

I swam forward with my mind until I was right above the death place, until I could feel the time around it clearly, until I could interact as best I could with the memory. *Careful, careful,* I told myself. *Don't want to change the space so much I can't read it.*

But of course, thank Heisenburg and his Uncertainty, you couldn't read something without changing it somehow. You couldn't see without interacting, hear without being changed. Two particles—and two minds—necessarily interacted no matter what you did. Even with memories. Even with emotion-ghosts, no matter how strong they were; by reading them, you changed them. You had to.

Grudge or random? Cherabino's mental voice echoed down to me again. I hadn't replied.

I moved, and found myself drowning, drowning in anger and violence and pain. It turned me over and over like an ocean riptide, overwhelming and deadly, until I could tell what end was up.

I tumbled over and over, coughing up anger, coughing up pain, until finally—I found the connection to Cherabino. Two hands on it and I pulled against the tide, pulled up and out on the long yellow rope, emotions grabbing at me, hanging on like thick taffy.

I pulled with all my might, pulled again, and again, and finally popped free. Panic beat at me as I looked at the maelstrom below. That would have gotten me without her. It would have eaten me alive. Level Eight telepath or no, I would have been lost.

My heart beat hard with panic and pain, and I reached for training to calm myself by force and will. Guild training was the only thing that had saved me; the forcible drills through hell and back the only thing that kept my mind together. Strong emotions. Too strong.

When I could compose myself, I sent a line of thought right back up at Cherabino, who was sending a vague sense of concern.

Bad one, I said, *I don't think—I don't think it was planned. Got a strong picture of the ax by the fireplace; when he saw it, he snapped.*

I collected my thoughts, pushing for dispassion again. *The victim . . . calm. He's an ordered guy. But he was nervous. The killer . . . the killer was here to assert control and to prevent something. The violence was just the escalation. Calculating? He wanted the man dead, Cherabino. He wanted him well dead.*

Not a bad start for a profile, Cherabino told me. *Get on back here; Forensics is arriving and I need you out of the way.*

I swam up, slowly, from the depths of all that pain, into the shallower areas of Mindspace, following the yellow cord up to Cherabino's mind. When I reached it, I surfaced: into reality, into the presence of other minds and blinding sunlight. The cops and the techs were staring with hostility. I shielded, slowly, against that gaze.

"Have you swept the house for the missing pieces?" Jamal, one of the Forensics techs, asked Michael, while looking directly at me.

"Not yet," Cherabino said, letting go of the mental hand that had grounded me. "We've been processing the scene here."

"You think the back of the head is sitting on a bed somewhere?" Michael asked, looking very green.

"Stranger things have happened," Jamal said.

"Keep a lookout for that arm section," Cherabino said. "And the head."

"What arm section?" Michael asked.

"Can I go?" I asked.

If you must, she sent through the Link. For someone who claimed to hate the Link between us, she was getting awfully comfortable with speaking mind-to-mind. When I tried it, half the time she told me to keep my hands and mind to myself.

She added out loud, "There's a section missing from the right biceps. Maybe four inches? Could be under the body. Obviously there was a bit of a struggle. I just want it found."

Michael looked thoughtful. "Trophy maybe?"

"The arm?" Cherabino blinked. "Odd place to take a trophy, don't you think? More likely it just got thrown under the sofa or something. Just keep a lookout, Jamal, okay?"

He shrugged. "You got it."

I left.

CHAPTER 2

Near the drafty-cold back of the house I flagged down one of the Forensics techs, a woman with the focused look of someone in the middle of a critical portion of her job.

"Have you guys processed the bedrooms yet?" I asked.

She just looked at me.

"I need to make a phone call," I said. "Can I use the phone in the back bedroom without messing up the scene?" I was tired of getting screamed at for my prints being at scenes. With my drug felonies, I inevitably ended up as a suspect for a day or two until I got cleared.

"Um, we've processed for fingerprints, but . . ."

"Good," I said, and pushed past her.

I sat gingerly on the twin bed's faded bedspread. An old treadmill sat at the end, and a small bookcase of odds and ends took up the rest of the small room. The large phone sat on the nightstand, beneath a lamp with an ugly shade.

I had long since memorized Kara's number. The receiver felt heavy in my hand, the keys of the phone all too real.

She picked up on the second ring.

"How are you holding up?" I asked.

"I'm fine, thanks for asking," a man's voice replied. "Is this Adam?"

"Yes," I said cautiously. "Who is this?"

But the phone was already being passed to Kara.

"Adam?" Her voice was thick, as if she'd been crying.

"Yes. I'm sorry I couldn't call sooner," I said. I didn't like apologizing—it felt like rehab every time—but I also didn't like hearing her crying. Even all these years later. It stabbed me in the heart. "What's wrong? What's going on?"

"There was a death in the family yesterday morning," Kara said quietly, in a voice that shook just a little.

"I am so sorry. Do you need me to come over?" Crap, the husband wasn't going to be a fan of the old fiancé coming over. What else did you offer in these situations? "I can help with arrangements." Wait. That was even worse. Crap, I was terrible at this. "What do you need?"

A pause on the other side of the phone. "Aren't you going to ask who died?"

I took a breath. "Who died?"

"Uncle Meyers," she said. "They're calling it a suicide."

If I hadn't already been sitting, I would have sat down, hard. I'd known her uncle; we all had. He'd been surprisingly good to me when I'd been a self-righteous punk kid. I couldn't believe he was dead.

"How?" I asked.

"It's complicated," she said, and her voice broke. "I need your help."

"I'll help you however I can," I promised quickly, and realized I meant it. "Anything, Kara."

"I don't think it's a suicide," she said quietly.

My stomach sank. "Enforcement is investigating?" Enforcement was every telepath's worst nightmare: judge, jury, and executioner all in one, with absolute legal authority over telepaths. Since the Koshna Accords, they had absolute authority over telepaths, absolute. The Telepath's Guild had saved the world from the Tech Wars, but they'd scared most of the world doing it. In return, they'd asked for—and gotten—the right to self-police. They could shoot any telepath in broad daylight on a normal street, no trial, and have no repercussions other than a PR crisis. Normals wanted it that way, in the post–Tech Wars world. But the telepathy police were fair, or at least that's what we were taught, though my experience with the normal courts put some of that into question. Still, Kara was part of the system. She'd been taught since she was small that Enforcement represented the truth and the Guild as a whole. They got to the truth, no matter what it cost, even if it took steamrolling over you and your memories to do it.

"Why not just let them investigate?" I asked. "What's the problem?"

She sniffled, and didn't speak.

"Kara?"

"They put somebody junior on it, so I pulled to get Stone. He got reassigned to the case like I wanted, but now he won't talk to me."

"You trust Stone?" I asked. He'd seemed fair, when he was investigating me, but it was still an odd choice. He worked as a Watcher, not an investigator.

She sniffed. "Not enough—he's not talking, and they're pushing to do a full wipe on the apartment where Uncle Meyers died. They're trying to cover this up, Adam, and I don't know why. They're saying he's crazy. They're saying it's safest for everyone to lock it down and worry about what happened later. It could be a contagious madness situation."

"Madness?" I asked. Oh. Suddenly it all made sense. In a society of telepaths, that was Public Health Crisis Number One. Thought patterns and mental health issues could spread through a population of telepaths in scary ways. Madness, a particular kind of transmittable health issue, was worse. It destabilized a mind in unpredictable ways, was difficult to treat even at early stages, and if untreated was universally degenerative to the point of death—suicide, homicide, or both. Although madness never transmitted more than once or twice between people and its origin wasn't clearly understood, one person with madness could infect half the Guild if he wasn't shut down immediately. "You're sure it's not a real contagion of madness? You're absolutely sure?" Suicide was one of the indicators. On the other hand, suicide (and homicide) happened on their own pretty often. "Quarantine might be the right thing to do here, Kara."

"He's . . . he d-didn't kill himself. He wasn't upset. He wasn't mad. He wasn't— Adam, I need you to come down here and look at him. At . . . at the b-body. And the apartment where they found him. I want you to tell me if they're lying."

"Why would Enforcement lie?" And why would she want me to risk contagious madness? "Especially about a suicide?"

"It was *not* a suicide!" Kara said, and her voice broke. "He was not mad. No one else is having issues! Look, he was electrocuted with an iron. An iron, you know, an iron you iron with! They say it was tampered with, but . . ."

"An iron?" I asked. This was surreal. "They think he killed himself with a faulty iron?"

"It had some kind of failure and it electrocuted him. They thought it was an accident, but he's a Councilman. They had to investigate. And now they're saying it's a suicide, Adam. They're saying he did it to himself on purpose."

"With an iron?" I asked. I couldn't picture any man from Kara's hypermasculine family killing himself with an iron. Hanging or a gun, maybe. But an iron? Seemed . . . unmanly.

"That's what I said!" she nearly shouted at me. "I told them he'd never . . . not with an iron. But they say he went crazy after the divorce. He wasn't! I'd know. I need you to help me prove this was a murder."

Okay. Here was the real reason. "Where is the scene? Where did it happen?"

"In his apartment."

"In Guild housing?" I asked carefully.

"Yes."

"You want me to go into Guild jurisdiction and ask difficult questions of everyone. Potentially offend some very important people. Interfere in a quarantine proceeding." If I did that, no one in the police could save me— they could ask, sure, but they had no power whatsoever in Guild halls. "I take it the telepaths Meyers worked with are still very important people?"

"Well, yes, he's the Employment chair on the Council. Everyone he works with is a VIP." In other words, one of the dozen or so most powerful people in the Guild.

"The Council isn't going to interfere in quarantine even for one of their own, Kara. I'm not Guild. I'm not Enforcement." I wanted to help, at least do something, for her. I'd asked her for many things in the last year; I should be able to step up and give her something in return. But this, well, I kept picturing being dragged in front of the Council. Having Enforcement showing up en masse and wiping all of my memories. Either way I'd be lucky to be thrown in a holding cell. "Enforcement takes their job very seriously," I told her. "Especially for a Councilman. Why not let them handle it?"

A short pause, and a shuddery breath. "Tobias Nelson looked Uncle Meyers straight in the eye on Tuesday in open committee and told him he'd bleed. Four days later, he's found dead in his apartment."

"Who is Tobias Nelson?" I asked carefully, but with a sinking feeling I already knew the answer.

"Tobias Nelson is the executive chair of Enforcement. Everyone in the branch reports to him. Uncle Meyers was pushing for a budget cut for his department."

Great. Just great. "And you want me to take on the head of Enforcement, a man with an established interest against your uncle and possibly your family as a whole?"

She took a breath. "Tubbs—that's my boss—told the finance committee that Nelson can't be objective and that the job should be given to someone not associated with his chain of command. I'm pretty sure that your credentials with the police will translate into an answer the committee can accept. You'll find out who killed my uncle and they'll prosecute him."

"You're pretty sure?" I asked. "You're pretty sure! Tell me you've thought this through more than that, Kara." Pretty sure could get me killed, damn it.

Another shuddery breath. Another. Until she was crying, full out, deep sobs that wrenched at my heart. But there wasn't anything I could do for her, not on the end of a phone line. And she was crying harder now.

We'd been engaged once, and the Link was still there, too deep to lose. Like a hotel room with two locked doors, we'd closed it off. But it was still there. I found it, in the back of my mind, pulled the furniture from in front of it, and opened my side of the door. I knocked, gently. A Link was the only exception to the location-limited physics of telepathy; like two bound quantum particles, when two people were Linked they could contact each other halfway across the world.

Her crying paused, and I could almost hear the locks slide. The door came open in small, rusty spurts. And then she was there, in my head.

I was pulled headlong into hurricane-force grief and shock and anger and loss, so strong and deep and wide it shook the boundaries of reality. After a while, I pulled back enough, got enough distance to think about hanging up the phone, and decided against it.

My eyes might have watered too, with hers. Then I was able to send waves of warmth and shared sorrow over Kara. Her tears tapered off, and over the phone she made the snuffly sound that was Kara, and only Kara.

I pulled away then. She was married, I told myself. Married. I must have leaked it into Mindspace as well, because then the door was closing again.

"Hold on, I need a tissue," she said. The sound of someone riffling through papers and boxes came over the phone, then her cute little blowing-nose sound.

I closed my own side of the Link, lighter this time. I'd help if I could, but there was a reason why I kept my distance. A good reason. For my health, my sanity, and the debt I had outstanding from an earlier agreement with the Guild. I did *not* need to go into their headquarters and cause trouble.

"Will you help me?" Kara asked after a minute. "I don't have—well, I don't have anybody—"

"I'll help you if I can," I said carefully. "I'm not going to storm the Guild to do it. I'm not going to end up mind-wiped over this or interfere in a real quarantine. I'm not crazy. But I'll come and talk to you if you want me to. You need to make sure you jump through the right hoops and get me cleared. You know, so I don't get shot when I walk in the door."

"If I can get you cleared with security for an hour or so from now, will you come?" Her voice was small, and still heavy with tears.

She'd betrayed me once, long ago, when I'd been in the middle of my drug addiction. She'd reported me to Enforcement, the first domino in the chain that had sent me to the street. She'd betrayed me. But she was still Kara, still the

woman I'd lived with and loved with for years. And this
last year she'd moved mountains for me—and she hadn't
had to. I should be able to do the same for her. I should.

But I hesitated. I didn't want to go back. I didn't want to
face the Guild again.

"If I can get you safe passage to the Guild this afternoon,
will you show up?" she repeated, her voice more firm. "Soon?"

I sighed. Looked like I was going to do this. "Can I
bring Cherabino with me?" It seemed less likely I'd disappear with a normal cop in tow, somehow.

"No, that won't work. She's not on file with security."
Her voice quavered. "Just say you'll come."

I closed my eyes. For anybody but Kara . . . "I'll be there
in an hour and a half." It would take me at least that long to
take the bus to Buckhead.

"Thank you!" she breathed.

"This is not a promise about anything. I'll listen. We'll
talk. You might invite Stone to be there, if you trust him."

"I'll think about it," she said coldly. "I'll get you cleared.
Adam?"

"What?"

"Thanks for coming."

"I'm not promising you—"

"Even so . . . " She paused. "I appreciate it more than
you know."

One winter day some years ago, when I was still at the
Guild and still living with Kara, her uncle Meyers stopped
by the classroom where I was teaching just as the tone
sounded for end-of-school.

"I'm taking a walk in the gardens," Meyers had said.
"Care to join me?"

I'd met him at a few of Kara's family functions—she was

part of several politically important family groups who met regularly—but I hadn't ever spent much time with Meyers one-on-one. Still, if I was going to marry Kara, I was marrying the family, right?

"Let me get my coat," I'd said, curious but confident I could handle whatever he'd throw at me. Probably just another warning to treat Kara well; I'd gotten four of those already from various family members.

Outside, Meyers led the way along a small path of white gravel, quiet in both voice and mind. His breath, like mine, steamed in the chilly air.

I shivered but didn't complain. If he could take the cold, so could I.

I've never been in the gardens this late in the year, I said, mind-to-mind. It was true, the prickly green bushes and spare brown trunks of trees set in geometrical shapes looking very different without the blooming plants of the summer. It would be pretty in the snow, I thought, the one time a year we got snow in Atlanta.

The silence got long, and I started to fidget mentally.

Meyers noticed and finally spoke, oddly out loud. "You're one of our highest-rated teachers of advanced students."

"That's right," I said, wondering where this was going. The voice-speech was a distancing method sometimes, and I wondered why he needed the distance.

"You have Xavier's gift," he said.

"Yes?" What did that have to do with anything? Just because I could teach several students mind-to-mind at a time . . . well, it had gotten me the job. I remembered Meyers worked for the employment and training division of the Guild. "Am I in trouble? I'm up to date on all of my continuing education units. I've taken all the tests on time. Do I need more supervision hours?"

Be calm, he said. *There's nothing wrong.*

I subsided. A particularly cold burst of wind cut through my coat. "What's going on?"

He turned to regard me directly. "You were scheduled for a career at a psychological hospital before—"

I interrupted. "Before they caught me tutoring two kids at once, I know. What—"

"Don't interrupt me, please, Adam. I do have a point to this, and I'd like to make it in my own order."

I stuck my hands in my pockets. *Go ahead.*

"You were scheduled for a very lucrative career in resetting structures of the mind. You were, by all test scores, extremely qualified, and your essays showed real passion for the subject."

So? A pang hit me then, but I pushed it away. I was a teacher, and my students would go out and do all of that for me.

"Would you rather do that?" Meyers asked me.

I took a step back. "What?" In two years, no one had ever . . . *The decision was made,* I said. *It was made a while ago. Why bring this up now?* My heart was beating now, beating far too fast. How could he . . . ?

"I'm a senior fellow in Employment and Training, Adam. And my family—your family soon—has a lot of pull with the decision makers all over the Guild. You aren't just a member anymore. If you'd rather go out and work at the hospital, I can make that happen for you."

"But I can teach . . ." I trailed off. They'd told me over and over that my gift for teaching a room was too precious to lose. "I'm worth more to the Guild as a teacher," I said, but my voice was weak. "Why are you asking me to do something else?"

"Very few people anymore have the opportunity to do what they love. They get stuck in what they can do, or what they ought to do. I'm giving you a chance to ask a bigger question. What will make you happy, Adam? What will help you and Kara be happiest together?"

I doubted him, and didn't make a secret of it, but he opened up the public side of his mind and I walked in.

He was sincere. Utterly, unbelievably sincere. He wanted to give a gift, an opportunity, to someone who was joining his family.

"Can . . . can I think about it?" I stuttered in shock.

"Certainly," Meyers said, and started walking again, around the dormant garden.

My feet crunched on the gravel in time with the beating of my heart.

Three days later, I went back to him with my decision: teaching stirred something inside me I couldn't put into words. As much as I'd wanted to work in the hospital, I thought teaching would truly, truly make me happier.

"As you wish," Meyers said, and turned the talk to the latest political candidates for Council. I followed along, giving my own opinions, and the awkwardness was over.

The next Sunday he came for dinner at our apartment and Kara cooked a roast. He never spoke of the offer again.

But I never, never forgot.

I stared at the phone in the here and now, the receiver ringing with a dial tone from too long off the cradle. I set it back down with a *click*. I couldn't believe Meyers was dead.

I couldn't believe I was going to the Guild on lockdown. But this was Kara. And this was Meyers. To not show up . . .

I could at least try to talk Kara down. Be there for her. Figure out what was going on. Meyers deserved that much.

I could work with Stone, I knew that already. He'd been my Watcher, in and out of my head while passing judgment on my intentions a few weeks ago. He'd decided I wasn't a threat. I could spend the afternoon talking honestly, help Kara decide what to do, and then leave. Go in, go out, go home.

So why did I feel like I was going into the lion's den rubbed in steak sauce?

I sighed, picked up the phone and called the department.

"DeKalb County Police Department Headquarters Administration," the brass's receptionist answered, a young guy straight out of college with a smooth voice who could calm down a bleeding rabbit in the middle of the apocalypse.

I said who I was and where I was. "Is Paulsen free?"

"She's in a budget meeting at the courthouse. It's an all-day affair and she cannot be disturbed for any reason. I've been instructed to tell officers to consult their division and squad leaders, who are fully empowered to make decisions."

I *could* call Clark, who technically was the most senior of the interviewers these days, but he hated my guts. "Could you take a message?" I asked the guy.

"One moment," he said, and I heard the sound of shuffling papers. "Go ahead."

I repeated my name and job title. "I will not be back in the interview rooms this afternoon. You'll need to contact Clark so he can make arrangements. Tell Paulsen that an emergency has come up and that I will be back in the office tomorrow morning. I'll check in then."

The sound of a pen scratching paper. Then it stopped. "Anything else?" the guy said.

"No, that's it," I said. I paused, wanting to tell them that like an idiot, I was going into the middle of the Guild headquarters during lockdown. A Guild that, because of the

Koshna Accords, still had absolute authority over me if it wanted. "No, I guess that's it."

"Thanks for calling," the guy said, and hung up the phone.

Nervous as hell, I went to find Michael, who was observing the crime scene in the main living area. The ME's tech was currently packing up the body, and everyone else swirled around that central task like a whirlpool, chaotic and focused both.

"Did they ever find the missing pieces?" I asked, trying for a conversational starter.

"Not yet, and we've looked everywhere. They didn't by chance turn up under the bed in there, did they?" He looked almost hopeful.

"Not that I saw," I said, but I hadn't looked under the bed. Honestly, if there were body parts hidden like some insane game of hide-and-seek, I'd rather someone else find them. That was just creepy.

"Did you need something?"

"Can I get you to drive me somewhere?"

"I thought somebody else here in the department drove you around," Michael said. He paused. "I'm kinda in the middle of something. Where do you need to go?"

"Um, well." Bellury, my usual babysitter, had died a few weeks ago, killed by a suspect we were tracking down. Because I was stupid. Because I'd pushed us to rush in. Because . . . "I need to run an errand in Buckhead and I'd rather not take the bus if I can help it," I said. "Where's Cherabino anyway?"

"She's calling Electronic Crimes and letting them know she won't be able to help out this week. This is the fourth murder we've gotten since Tuesday."

"That's why I'm here," I realized. "She needs a way to solve the crimes faster."

"Yes, that's why we're both here," Michael said in the tone of voice you'd use to state the obvious while trying hard not to be insulting. "Um, can't you drive yourself? I'll loan you the keys to the cruiser. We can ride back in one of the vans." His mind flashed to his dad, and some complex feelings; the man lived two streets away, apparently.

I was very tempted to take the damn keys. "The department prefers that I not have control of any resources that might be construed as valuable." It also wouldn't let me handle my own money, but really, who was counting? "Look, it's just Buckhead. If I take the bus I'll spend three hours getting there and back."

Now I had his full attention. "You can't drive the department's cars? You lose your license?" His eyebrows pulled down. "DUI?"

"No!" I said. I'd never owned a car, and never had access to one when I was in my life on the street. DUI hadn't been an option for me, though I hoped I wouldn't have done it anyway. In the heat of the addiction, though, probably I would have. There was no pride, no shame, no anything in the heat of that addiction. "No, it's just they prefer me not to have a car unsupervised. You know what, never mind, I'll take the bus."

Michael looked at me oddly, the feeling coming off him in Mindspace . . . unsettled. "Does Cherabino know you're going?"

"Would you tell her?" I asked, and started walking down the street. I thought I remembered where the bus stop was.

The North American Guild Headquarters complex had three large buildings, which were the only non-anti-grav-assisted glass-and-chrome old-style skyscrapers in the business district of Buckhead; they were dwarfed by the hundreds-of-stories-high monstrosities that had used antigravity during construction. The newer buildings looked like tall, thin fortresses, which is what they were; this entire area had been flattened during the Tech Wars by a bomb, and those who rebuilt it valued security and defense over looks.

Except the Guild, of course. Their best security was the people inside, not only the ones who would see your attack coming and give warning, but the thousands of highly trained Abled who would defend the complex with their last breaths. The extra expense of three-foot-thick earthenworks seemed paltry in comparison, and the arrogant beauty of a mostly glass building stood on its own merits.

The Guild had much to fear after the Tech Wars, but what they feared most wasn't anything that a heavy building would protect them from.

Was I really here? Was I really intending to tempt my fate?

It was Kara asking, and I'd been here to see her at her office before. Either they'd turn me away or they wouldn't.

I walked into the relative heat of the main atrium, a huge circular place with marble columns and the Guild founders looking down on you, judging. On the right was a glass-and-chrome desk blocking the way, manned by a security guard. Today's guard was the small black woman I'd seen there before; she looked like she'd blow over in a strong wind, but anyone who did guard duty for the Guild could handle four armed normals with no backup.

"I'm here to see Kara Chenoa," I told her, taking off my coat and folding it over my arm. I was very polite to guards.

She looked me up and down in Mindspace, and I suppressed the sudden urge to check my fly.

"I'm—"

I know who you are, she sent mind-to-mind, on the lightest, politest level. Along with the words came the sense that I was infamous. Also that I was messy with public/private mental space these days. She'd recommend fixing both if I could.

I blinked, and settled my emotions down into the more acceptable Guild calm. Should have done that before walking in the door, but I appreciated the reminder. I'd been around normals a great deal the last few years.

I blocked off a polite, surface level of my mind and dropped all but the lightest shields around it, public space. The rest of my mind I locked up with barbed wire; I was in no mood to be more vulnerable than I had to.

She looked at me again. *Better.* She handed me a visitor's badge; Kara had me on her list for the day. There was no brain wave recorder, she sent into my mind, because I'd been vouched for, good or ill, but there was a small location pip. *No audio, no visual, just location.*

"Now," she said out loud, clearly in her official capacity as she leaned forward over the desk. "Don't you be wandering around today. Enforcement's got a lockdown on Personal Quarters seventeen and adjoining, and high-rise four is secure-access only. You're lucky; Ms. Chenoa's office is in this building, which is still public-access." She stared at me and added privately, *I catch you outside your allowed areas, I catch you acting up in any way, I practice Mindspace kata blows on your skull. Don't make me do that.*

"Understood." I looked at my coat; that was going to be a problem to carry around.

"I'll take the coat," she said, and I handed it over. "Now. Ms. Chenoa's office is down the main hallway, second right, third door on your left."

"Thanks," I said. *What's your name?*

"Turner," she said. *Ruth Turner, second-class permanent guard attached to Headquarters. Currently bored and will be monitoring.*

I forced a smile and a calm. "Nice to meet you, Turner."

She nodded. "Ms. Chenoa is waiting."

CHAPTER 3

Kara's door looked like a dozen other plain wooden doors in this plain public-servant hallway, windows spilling sunlight into the hallway at the end, a few feet away. It was a quiet area, a working area, with strong scents of lemon cleaner and sunlight permeating the space.

Behind her door, Mindspace buzzed with the conversation of several minds, strong minds with strong convictions.

I opened the door.

Two men stood there with Kara in the middle of the ten-foot office. She perched on the edge of her large wooden desk, looking—and feeling—unhappy. Blond and beautiful, a year younger than me at thirty-eight, Kara radiated frustration and indecision.

The others turned to look at me when the door opened. Silence fell.

"Hello," I said cautiously. Up until a few seconds ago, I'd been expecting Kara, only Kara. "Should I come back in a moment?"

"You're here now." The older man, Hawk Chenoa, didn't bother to hide his disapproval. He was one of Kara's extended family patriarchs—her father's eldest cousin, if I remembered correctly—and, unofficially, one of the most powerful men at the Guild. He had more gray in his dark hair and deeper wrinkles than the last time I'd met him but no less strength. He wore an American military uniform with a Guild mind-piercer's patch, another, smaller patch commemorating hundreds of years of Native struggle. As always, his mind felt focused and ready; I would not want to go up against him in a fight.

On paper, the power in the Guild rested in organizations: in the Council, in the heads of departments and the crushing money-based bureaucracy that moved it all along. But just as important were the old families, the clans that stretched back to Guild Founding, the groups that controlled the majority of the voting rights for both Council and legislative matters. The Chenoas in particular were an old, old family, grown large over the last sixty years, and Hawk was the one man the Chenoas would follow anywhere. More important, he'd forged alliances with several other families worldwide; when Hawk spoke, the Guild listened. Or, at least, it should.

The families were an important check on the power of the bureaucracy and had been for decades. The Guild founder, Cooper himself, had supported this system, as far as it went, and the Chenoa clan were staunch supporters of Cooper and his ethical system. Hawk would take his balancing role very seriously.

"Is this the man we've been talking about?" the second man asked, in his late fifties with a dark complexion and a hard face that seemed set in anger. "Joe Green," he introduced himself. In this case the voice-speech was definitely a distancing mechanism. "Guild First. If the Erickson-Meyers and the Chenoa clan are going to conspire, one of us needs to be here to keep them from doing something stupid. One man's life is not worth the entire Guild's. Much less when the man is already dead." His mind added subtext: the madness needed to be controlled at all cost, even if that meant evidence was destroyed. Meyers had killed himself anyway.

"I told you, Green, we're just talking." Kara said. "There's no need for dramatics."

"Green is welcome to stay," Hawk said. "There's very little I have to say that can't be known publically. There will be no cover-ups on my watch. Kara, I've told you that. Plus we have nothing to fear from the likes of *him*."

"What's Guild First?" I asked.

Contempt flashed across Green's face, though his Mindspace presence was controlled enough not to show it. Green's Ability rating was a heavy Seven at best, and the shields I had up past my "public mind" should hold just fine. Still, something about him made me defensive.

But he decided to tell me anyway. "Guild First does exactly that: it fights to protect Guild interests and Guild projects first. From funding pensions over charity to developing tools to help improve Ability and advance interests of the Guild nation, we put Guild first."

"Against the normals?" I asked.

"If need be. If they threaten us, we will be ready."

Kara spoke up then. "Is all this chest beating really necessary? We're here to talk about my uncle."

"Bringing in an outsider is going to raise questions," Hawk said.

"Adam's not an outsider, he's neutral," Kara said.

"I'm just here to talk," I corrected, firmly, but no one listened.

Hawk faced me. "This is an internal family matter. I'm sorry, but you're a criminal and no longer a Guild member."

"A criminal?" Green echoed, suspicion leaking into the air.

"Kara asked me to come and I'm not leaving until Kara asks me to leave. Kara?" *What's going on?* I asked her, mind-to-mind.

Hawk is angry over the death. He hides it well, but he's

livid. He wants people to jump and take orders like the military, and this isn't the military.

"Talk where we can all hear you equally," Hawk's voice cracked.

Kara said out loud, "This isn't the military. The best course of action isn't to take orders. It's to put our heads together and figure out a way out of this. Procedure isn't going to get Uncle Del's murderer found. It's going to erase every trace of him out of the air in the apartment and burn everything he ever touched."

"We can't afford to take a chance at Guild-wide contagion for one man," Green said. "Quarantine is the only way we move forward."

He might have a point, Kara, I said quietly.

If you're not going to help me, I don't know why you came.

Now, that's just out of line, I said. *I'm here, aren't I?*

"It's possible that he killed himself," Hawk said. "It's his right. But I agree, the method doesn't sound like Del. We hire our own people or import them from another location. We have plenty of experts in the family." *People who haven't been kicked out of the Guild as a criminal*, his mind added, broadly enough he had to know I'd hear it. "With someone in the family we have the control over the results."

"I want the truth, not control!" Kara said, too quickly, and then stifled her too-loud emotions.

I objected to the criminal label, and put that out there for anyone to see. I had been convicted, in both the normal and the Guild systems. I wasn't hiding that, but it didn't change my skills. Which I hadn't even volunteered to use.

"Kara, I said I'd show up and talk. Offer suggestions. What is it exactly that you're trying to get me to do?"

"Find Uncle Meyers's murderer." Her voice was firm, decided.

"If we get at the truth through an outsider, it will be my choice of outsider," Hawk said. "The telepath military teams have plenty of good men."

"None of whom can be trusted to keep their mouths shut like Adam has already proven he can," Kara returned.

"You should leave," Hawk said.

Oddly, this made me angry. "I didn't cut out of work early to get dismissed. I'm not leaving until—"

Kara cut me off. "Adam, just go."

Now I was angry at her. "What the hell! You call me in here? I'm not leaving until you—"

My mind was wrenched, grabbed, and flattened, before I could react. Pain. Disorientation. I couldn't move. I was frozen, in the middle of Kara's office, heart beating like a small animal's faced with a predator.

I forced myself to calm, to figure it out; Green had me by the public space, not an acceptable tactic in the Guild, but the reason I'd stopped doing the separated space concept years ago in the normal world, damn it. Left you too vulnerable. He had me pinned by a leverage hold on the front of my mind, incredibly strong, perfect leverage. I wasn't going anywhere. Well, not until he slipped up or got distracted.

"Let him go, Green," Hawk said.

Kara was very, very quiet, moving back to her desk, doubtlessly toward a panic switch. I thought about puppies and rainbows and the interview room and Paulsen screaming and whatever the hell I could fill up my head with that wouldn't give her away.

Green only moved closer to me, and tightened his hold. "The Guild won't tolerate interference from a *criminal*. You've been asked to leave. You'll leave."

He held my mind with crushing force. I breathed. One, and exhale, two.

Out of his pocket he pulled a small device, a sphere the size of a grapefruit, dull black with twists of wire on its surface and a small ring of lights along its equator. He hit a button and a light on top of the sphere blinked. Mindspace rippled, a disquieting sensation, the earth moving under your feet like you stood on a boat. The sphere was the exact center.

"Nice try, but you're not Jumping out of here with this on," he told Kara. "We handle this my way."

Hold up, why in hell do you have a Mindspace machine? I asked Green. *Those are banned by the Koshna Accords.* Not that the Guild wasn't experimenting with them anyway; I'd seen several in the last year when I investigated the Guild-related serial killer. *It's incredibly stupid to pull those out where anyone can see you. It could spark a conflict with the normals, one that would tear apart the whole building.*

The Koshna Accords are already being broken by the normals, Green said, the words hitting me with bruising force on top of an already intense pressure. *The Guild needs whatever tools it can build in return, and Guild First will build them.*

This guy was crazy! What had I gotten myself into? There were others who thought like him? If so, the Guild was in trouble.

"Turn off the device and give it to me," Hawk said then. "You're giving me a headache and this isn't solving anything."

Green shook his head. "Not until you tell me why you invited a criminal into the Guild to break our quarantine."

He tightened his grip, and I lost track of the conversation. My shields started to crack, Mindspace around fracturing like the world seen through a cracking pane of glass. This shouldn't be happening! I should be able to outmass him in Mindspace. My numbers were higher than his.

Slow down. I spackled up the holes in my shields. *Slow down.* He wasn't going to break me. It wasn't an option. And brute force, as my old mentor had taught me over and over again, was not always—nor usually—the best solution to a given problem.

His mind was right up against mine, holding that pressure. Right there.

Telepathy was a two-edged sword; you couldn't be this close to someone's mind without having your mind close as well. And I was a Structure guy. And he was clumsy, and all too focused on large scale and strength. All too distracted. If I could focus . . .

I seeped into his mind, following the shape of his grip around to the mind that controlled it, trickling in like water through a brick wall with no mortar.

He didn't even notice, amateur.

I moved through his surface mind, slowly, slowly, getting a feel for the space. In the back of my own mind, Kara's fear had relief added like a spice; she'd managed to hit the panic button, good for her.

And then I was in. Green's mind was consumed with a strong, self-satisfied position of control, me in his power, and visible strength in front of Hawk. He'd let me squirm, a little.

My anger spiked at that one, too quickly, and he knew I was there.

Why the overreaction? I asked. *And why be a bully about this? It doesn't even make sense.* As I'd done before in the interview room, I pushed at the core of the problem. Only here, now, I followed one thought trail back, and back, until I hit the source.

Oh. There.

Hawk was threatening him. The Cooperists were conspiring to take him off his Council seat in the upcoming election. And he'd make the Meyers issue—and the quarantine of the madness—the proof he was worthy to stay. They weren't going to meet up without him. They weren't going to have secrets. And they weren't going to endanger the Guild. He wouldn't let them.

In shock and surprise, he pulled back, dropping my mind.

He glowered at me. I stared back and picked the pieces of myself up, feeling bruised. Trying to figure out the next step if he attacked again.

"You . . ." He stared again.

Three minds burst into the room, the guard from the front of the building and two of her compatriots.

"This criminal committed a privacy violation," Green said with contempt. "Deep-thoughts, no invitation."

I frowned. "You attacked me first. I didn't even bruise you." More than I could say for him.

Turner moved forward, stickycord out and ready to restrain me. She was angry; that much was clear.

Kara took a breath and held up a hand for the guards. "Wait a second."

"Is this true?" Hawk asked, in a dangerously low tone.

"Is what true?" I asked.

"Did you go past his public mind? Without permission?" His mind was thunderous.

I stared at him. "He had me in a mental *headlock*. He was doing his best to turn me into tenderized steak!"

"I'll take that as a yes," Turner the guard said, next to me.

My own shields had slipped, damn it, out of practice, and she was quick. Got me.

I found myself on the floor, my body no longer under my

control, even my vocal cords paralyzed. *Damn it, damn it, damn it, damn it,* my mind echoed. The square of textured carpet in front of my nose smelled like oranges, fresh ones, not cheap cleaner. And my side and my cheek *hurt* from the impact.

Turner's grip on my mind, unlike Green's, was surgically precise. She was structurally trained; she'd done something to the movement center of my brain. I could picture getting up, blinking, turning my head, but I couldn't do it—literally couldn't. When I tried, I got an overwhelming impression of sticky bubble gum, strong smell of classic pink bubble gum. I'd be able to get out of this, with a few hours left alone, but not with her actively there. She was good.

Thank you, she said mind-to-mind, reacting to my surface thoughts. Then, out loud: "Tell me what happened, sir."

Green's voice solidified, and an odd sense of satisfaction and self-righteousness leaked out into the room, along with anger. "This . . . *criminal* charged into the office and threatened Ms. Chenoa. He attacked me when I tried to intervene. I immobilized him with *no permanent damage.* And then he stole into my private mind-files and ruffled around. He is not an Enforcer, and I am a Council member and not under suspicion. This is a clear privacy violation."

Kara made that quiet clicking-teeth sound again, and then a second guard's shoes came into my line of sight.

"Should I give him the ability to speak?" Turner asked, with absolutely no sense of humor.

"No," Hawk said. "Throw him in a cell and start procedures."

A long pause. "Do it," Kara finally said, in her very carefully political voice.

My heart sped up even faster, a bird in a glass jar. *Kara!*

"In the maximum shielding cells?" the other guard asked in a deeper voice, a male voice.

"Let him rot," Green said.

A strong telekinetic force lifted me up. Fury swept me. Then the world went black.

I heard screaming, high-pitched screaming, and sobbing, sobbing like someone's heart was breaking, and screaming like all that was evil about the world was locked in a small room with a small child. I staggered to my feet, feeling disoriented.

Across the way, a small woman with ragged hair and a torn dress huddled in a corner, looking at something I couldn't see while screaming, screaming so loudly it hurt my teeth. When she took a breath, the sound stopped for a second before resuming.

Her vocal cords had to give out eventually, I told myself. Eventually. No human could make that sound forever.

I was in a chilly concrete box that smelled of ancient urine, with a wire-inset glass-paneled wall in front of me emitting a low-level buzzing in Mindspace. Small metal dials were set into the glass wall about shoulder height, dials that spun and settled, spun and settled as the electric field on the wall ebbed and flowed. In case that wasn't enough, a small sign said DON'T TOUCH, SHOCK HAZARD.

The wire-inset glass door had moved along a track to shut with a *thud* I could feel in my soul. It must have been three inches thick, and nothing I could move or break without a lot of noise and even more time. Worse, the small metal commode in the back was probably the most disgusting thing I'd ever seen, clearly not cleaned in years. There was a sink beside it, just as dirty.

Seriously? I was in a holding cell for defending myself? I kicked the wall and cursed. Now my toe was screaming at me. *Kara, damn it!*

I stood up and paced, back and forth, back and forth,

anger pushing every one of my movements. I had come to *help* Kara. And she . . . she . . . she'd betrayed me.

Again.

You'd think I'd learn to stop trusting the traitor. But no. I was a damn stupid fool. A damn stupid fool.

I walked until the anger turned from hot flames to banked coals, I walked and turned and walked until the muscles in my sides hurt from the pivoting, until I could tell where the walls were without looking, until I could reach out a hand and touch the electrified front bars and not curse. I walked until my lungs complained and I wanted a cigarette so badly I couldn't think. They were gone from my pockets, of course. As was the lighter. And my shoes, damn it.

Thirst eventually drove me to the sink, where I wrinkled my nose before turning the grime-encrusted faucet. No water came through. So I lay down on the dirty floor and waited.

"Um, hello?" I called out eventually, more out of exhaustion than anything. I was starting to get cold again now that I wasn't moving.

"You're awake," a calm woman's voice said, a lovely contralto.

"Yes," I said cautiously.

"I'm two cells down from you. They brought you in unconscious. Sometimes people don't wake for days."

"Oh."

There was a long silence.

"Why do they let us talk to each other?" I asked.

"Best shielding in the building, right? The psychologists think if we get too isolated we'll go crazy. Well, the ones who aren't crazy already."

"The screaming ones," I said.

She sighed. "I don't know what she sees, but whenever

anybody walks by her cell she screams for hours like she's being attacked by a monster. Princess cries sometimes, but she doesn't talk and it doesn't last."

"And who are you?" I asked.

She was silent, even when I repeated the question.

I counted spots on the ceiling, my back getting cold. I tried to sleep, knowing this was the best response to conserve energy, but I couldn't. I just lay, with a mental stopwatch in my head, waiting for them to be done with this.

They had to be done with this soon. People would notice if I was gone. People would notice, eventually. Stone had said himself I wasn't a threat to the Guild. There was no point in keeping me locked up; this was to scare me, nothing more.

"Person two cells down?" I finally asked, to distract myself from the anger and despair that were doing their best to play tug-of-war with my insides. "Person? What happens next?"

"Next they forget about you. If the psychologists and mind-repairers can't fix you, or they think you're too dangerous to let out in the population, they forget about you here. Only place in the Guild you can't get past the shielding no matter how powerful you are. You'll break your mind trying, trust me. They put us here to isolate us. They put us here to forget."

"Who are you?" I asked.

"I killed my husband," the woman two cells down said. And again went silent.

I counted spots on the ceiling then. I knew this game. Make the suspect uncomfortable. Give him difficult conditions and leave him alone. Let him drive himself out of his mind in the waiting. But knowing didn't make it easier.

Hours passed, and the stopwatch in my head kept building, the stopwatch and the pressure and my thirst.

The girl started screaming, screaming again, high-pitched and panicked, in a tone that made my whole body tense.

I sat up. The world spun as my blood pressure changed too quickly.

A man stood on the other side of the glass front wall of the cell.

CHAPTER 4

Midforties, with dark carrot hair mixed with gray, the man was tall, with enough age and wrinkles to project authority without seeming old. His nose was a little more prominent than the average, almost hooked, and he had the posture of someone both highly educated and very used to being in charge. That, and the large Council patch on his jacket, told me I should pay very close attention. There were only twelve members of the Guild North American Ruling Council, and they made life-and-death decisions daily.

He moved to the side, his hand going up to press against the wall where I couldn't see him, and Turner was revealed behind him.

My heart leaped, and I forced calm as much as I could. I should have been able to feel her coming. Her, at least, I should have felt coming. The fog in Mindspace, like suffocating cotton, filled all my senses.

The screaming stopped, abruptly, and silence filled the cell. My ears rang with it. Behind them, the woman huddled in the corner, her sides shaking soundlessly.

The man hit a button. The door opened with a low screech. I noticed Turner was carrying a water bottle.

I pulled myself to my feet, to better face my jailer.

"Adam Ward," the man said, in an elderly statesman voice.

"Who are you?"

The man stood in the doorway, no farther, so that the field of the shielding still hid his mind from me. I couldn't tell how strong he was. I couldn't even tell what his Ability was.

Turner stood behind him, ready. We'd established she could handle me without backup, but this also seemed to establish that this man held her reins.

I forced myself to look away from the water bottle and back at the man in charge. "Who are you?" I asked again.

He took a breath, like a man preparing for a long speech. "My name is Thaddeus Rex, and I am the executive chair of the Council. I also lead the Guild First faction, which proposes to improve the lives of Guild members through better health, stronger safeguards, and innovative training and management techniques."

"Good for you," I said. "You realize that doesn't say anything at all, right?"

He frowned at me.

I wondered if I'd be harder or easier to interrogate than your average Guild suspect. I knew all the verbal tricks, what could and couldn't be said, and I'd spot the lies at ten paces, but I wasn't used to someone who could read my mind, not anymore, and I couldn't say for sure I could still lie mind-to-mind and not get caught. Still, if they left me in the shielding cell here, it might be a moot point. "I take it this is the part where you interrogate me?"

Rex shrugged, with a small smile. "You've been accused of a very serious privacy violation, and you owe the Guild Enforcement Division an astronomical debt. Technically, I don't have to interrogate you. I can leave you down here until you rot. Of course, I'd have to turn on the water eventually, but it's not very good water."

I stood my ground, swallowing. "I work with the police.

They will miss me eventually. They will send people look-ing for me."

"Likely they will—you're right. But I don't have to let them in the door; the Koshna Accords are very clear. You're still a telepath, Adam Ward. There's not much they can do except file a protest." He smiled that small smile again. "We receive a dozen protests a week on various topics."

I swallowed. "Won't Stone have something to say about that?" I'd mention Kara, but since she'd had them throw me in here, who knew her loyalties lay. With herself, probably—*the way it had always been*, I thought with a deep resentment.

"Stone reports to Tobias. Tobias reports, well, indirectly, to me," Rex said quietly.

My face must have fallen, because Rex smiled outright in satisfaction. He gestured to Turner, who moved forward cautiously to hand me the water bottle.

I took it, numbly. Thought about not drinking it, in case they'd put anything in it. I didn't need to be hooked on any-thing new. The Guild's damn drugs had done it last time quick enough, when I'd participated in a study of Satin's effects on the mind and gotten hooked on the second dose. Yeah, I wouldn't put it past the Guild to put something in the water here just to see what would happen.

"It's clean," Turner said quietly, and moved to the side of the cell, still watching me. Rex was still at the door.

I looked at her, trying to decide. Rex I didn't trust any farther than I could throw him, but Turner seemed like one of the pros I'd trained with and grown up around. She also had a small mallet-shaped pin, the Guild founder Cooper's personal symbol, the symbol for a system of ethics I ascribed to. Didn't mean she was trustworthy, though; the pins had been popular for years among the guards.

I held the water, deciding.

"I have a proposal for you," Rex said smoothly. "Green says you managed to get through his defenses with real skill." He held up a hand, waving away my protests. "Green isn't one to exaggerate, much. It takes quite a skill to manage such a breach while under attack and in the presence of several witnesses who saw nothing. Not to mention a great deal of moral flexibility to break one of the Guild's foremost ethical guidelines without so much as an accusation of wrongdoing."

"Foremost ethical guidelines? Really?" I said. "Since when is a basic probe anything but tactics?" I was uncomfortable with the compliment, and even more uncomfortable with the ideals behind it. "I did what I had to do."

"You did what you had to do," Rex repeated, like he was testing out the words. "A very interesting approach, to be certain. I can be appreciative of your skills, as long as you understand those kinds of ethical breaches can't be deployed on just anyone. Green, for example, was a very poor choice. He's a Councilman, after all, though not a particularly impressive one."

I barely repressed a snide comment about the Council and double standards. "No comment," I said. In the non-Abled world this would be the point at which I should call a lawyer, but the Guild system didn't work like that. And I hadn't paid Guild fees recently enough to justify an advocate being called for me, even if I could somehow argue I had a right to one. I wasn't a member, so technically I didn't have access to an advocate. But if they were trying to claim jurisdiction . . . honestly, the whole thing made my head hurt.

"Don't be modest. I have a use for someone with a high degree of skill and a weak sense of privacy. You're in great debt to the Guild, Adam Ward. I propose you work for me to pay some of it off now."

Great, the debt was coming back to bite me in the ass, just like I'd thought it would.

"Look, I showed up to talk to Kara. That's it. I'm not getting involved in Guild politics, and I'm not working for you. Thanks anyway. I have a job." But my doubt must have shown in my face, because he smiled.

"I can leave you in this cell on the debtor's system instead if you prefer. Let's give up the pretense. I have a highly political situation with a suspicious death. Kara's uncle, as you may recall. You have a debt to pay. There's no reason why we can't both get what we want. My people tell me it's very likely Meyers went mad and then concealed his illness from all of our watchdogs. I also can't afford to ignore the issue, or not to investigate. He's a fellow Council member, after all. We can't let a killer go, if indeed it was anything but suicide, which I am assured it was not. But neither can I expose my people to a potential contagion of this magnitude. If there's something there, it's already proven itself deadly."

I moved forward until Turner's gesture stopped me.

I did *not* want to expose myself to madness if it was going around. I tried one last-ditch effort. "This is *not* the first Guild death under suspicious circumstances. Hell, even if it's a suicide, it's not the first suicide in the history of the world. He's dead, and Enforcement is very capable. Why in hell bring me in?"

Rex's right index finger tapped against his leg. "I have my reasons. Let's just say, I'm better positioned to advance the causes of the Guild if you investigate. Plus I can argue we're saving Guild lives if something goes wrong."

"Let me get this straight. You want me to walk into a potential mental health death trap, to solve a case I'm not qualified to solve?"

"Exactly so, yes. You understand perfectly."

I shook my head. "There's no way in hell."

Rex stood at the doorway, unperturbed. "It's amusing to watch you protest. But you realize you don't have any choice."

"There's always a choice," I said.

He shrugged. "You can stay in the cell. The investigation into your privacy violation is already tending toward guilty. Between that and your debt, we'll call it ten years. Should pass quickly, I'm sure."

"I've agreed to work out the debt. And that's a huge overkill on a privacy violation!" I protested. "When I left it was a slap on the wrist. Two weeks, tops, and a memory deletion of the offense—and that was for stalkers. How in hell do you get ten years?" Even combining that offense with the debt would be four years, tops, even if they'd thrown the book at me in the old days.

"Don't be coy. We've changed a lot since you left the Guild, Ward."

"I guess so," I said with contempt.

He smiled, an almost obvious pride. "Privacy is sacred in the Guild now. Guild First has seen to that. We'll give you some reading material. You'll have plenty of time. Unless, of course, you take my offer."

I swallowed. After the Guild got me hooked on drugs and tossed me on the street, after I cleaned myself up, wiped out everyone who'd ever sold me drugs, them and their lieutenants, I'd told myself I'd never—*never*—be used again. I wasn't about to start now.

Rex smiled. "I'll leave you in the capable hands of Mrs. Turner. I'll expect a report every twenty-four hours."

My fists clenched as he walked away.

I looked at Turner and she looked at me; her facial expressions were as deadpan as could be, and her body language was merely prepared. I might be able to get past her in the holding cell, with the shielding removed, do something physical to knock her out—but physical was Cherabino's department. I smoked too much.

"How about I report you to the Council for using unethical tactics instead?" I said. "I've been away for years. What's your excuse?"

The sound of footsteps stopped, then resumed back in our direction. The screaming started again.

Rex held up a hand when he came back in sight. The mask dropped. I saw the man within, the utterly, utterly ruthless man within. "Don't threaten me, boy. I've been playing this game since before you took your Guild exams. You step out of line, I will discredit you and destroy you and then go after anyone who ever stood with you. That includes the lovely Kara Chenoa. You'll do what I say, and you'll do it with a good attitude. You report to Stone, for now. If he asks or anyone else asks, Enforcement as a whole has put their weight behind you. Naturally this will earn you enemies. That's not my problem. See that you toe the line—I wouldn't want to see a slip cost you everything."

He held up a Guild Enforcement badge, a red card, and a key. "You'll need these to do your job. I'll expect a full report in forty-eight hours."

He handed the items to Turner and then turned around.

"If I solve the case, I get my debt cleared," I called out after him. "I get my debt cleared and I don't get called up on any privacy violation."

"We'll see." Rex resumed walking.

I stared after him.

The water bottle in my hand felt suddenly very heavy.

"You sure this is clean?" I asked Turner.

"I didn't get it myself," she said, "but it came from the regular security refrigerator."

I looked at it, my thirst and my sense of self-preservation

warring, while in the background the woman screamed with a hoarse voice. "Give me the badge," I said. "The key is to the main doors, I take it? What's the card?"

She gave me the badge. "We're on lockdown, so if you want access to the major portion of the Guild you'll need clearance, which is the badge and the card together. They change the card every couple of days, so make sure you keep up to date. The key is for the elevators."

I took a breath. "What time is it?"

"Six a.m. Friday," she said.

I shook my head. I was due at work in less than two hours, and I'd gotten no actual sleep, just a few hours of forced unconsciousness from being knocked out. Plus I'd missed my regular meeting with my sponsor with no notice, which would trigger all sorts of worries.

Turner looked at me. "Restroom? I can get a male guard, but it takes a minute and I'd rather know now." Her tone wasn't exactly pleased.

I sighed. "I'll wait." I'd used the horrible little toilet once, and I'd rather have a clean washroom with a shower anyway, back at the department, even if she would let me take the trip. "I'd kill for a sink with running water and soap, though."

"I'll see what I can do," she said, and moved out of the cell to a point where she could watch me. "You first."

So I went first. The woman's screaming got even more irrational when we passed, and the crying one inched away. Two more cells went past, empty.

But in the last cell, we passed a man with a long, long beard, who sat in a cell the size of my previous one and stared at the wall. Even through the shielding in the cells was heavier than I'd felt anywhere in the complex, I still felt leakage through it—a disturbing feel, like worms burrowing into the edges of my mind. I moved faster.

"What did he do?" I asked.

Turner glanced over. *Poisoned five other members of his work group, one of which killed herself, before we shut him down. We tried to let him out, once. That will never happen again.* She sent a subtext of grave violence and chaos they'd barely shut down in time.

How long has he been here? I asked, disturbed. I'd never been this far in the basement before.

Seven years, Turner replied. *I was a rookie at the time. I'm told he's currently on a hunger strike. He may die. No one's willing to go in there to make him eat.*

We walked on.

Turner took me to a small break room two floors above where we'd been. Small paper cuts of turkeys and pilgrims were taped onto the cabinets. How . . . festive.

I washed my hands—getting clean an almost obscene pleasure—and drank five cups of tap water from a soy-paper disposable cup. I'd chosen a cup at random from the middle of the stack to be safe.

She stood well enough back to give herself room and watched me very carefully. She could watch me drink water; I'd had people watch me do far more personal things with far more interest. I had a sixth cup of water, balled the cup up, and threw it in the garbage. Then I pushed the Guild stuff into a pocket.

"Okay," I said. "Now you take me to the police station."

She shook her head. "Now you talk to Meyers's ex-wife. *Then* I take you to the police station. Assuming we get Rex's permission."

I sighed. "Look, I agreed to this. Sort of. I'll do my part." I didn't see any other practical way, and Meyers had been a good guy, at least I could tell myself that. "But I've got a real job that got me the expertise Rex wants in the first place. I need that job." I did, damn it. Routine and support kept you on the wagon, or so my sponsor said. That and getting plenty of sleep. I'd had no sleep at all and here I was already late to work. I was *not* falling off the wagon today. "You want me sane, you'll take me to that job."

Turner looked at me, no sense of humor.

"He didn't say I couldn't go back," I said. "It's Friday, right?"

She nodded.

"I'll come back tonight. You can park me in a cell for a nap and then we can get to work," I said.

"You still need to interview Cindy Ballon," she said. But I had her.

"Meyers's ex-wife?"

She nodded.

Time to give in on my end, cement this negotiation. "I'll talk to her. Fifteen minutes, okay? If I can't get the information from her in that amount of time, it's going to take a few hours anyway. How far is this away?"

"She's already waiting in the interrogation rooms down the hall," Turner said.

"Obviously the guards haven't slipped in expediency."

"We try."

I pinned on the badge. It felt weird, after all these years.

Cindy Ballon (formerly Meyers) was a square woman with a square jaw, plain with straw yellow hair and a body like a linebacker's. Then she looked up and smiled, and my whole impression changed; the jaw, the nose that had seemed so harsh now just seemed striking. Her personality filled her up, the strength of character she carried with her into Mindspace and the mannerisms she displayed making it all work somehow, so that you forgot your first impression completely.

She was also sad, almost unbearably sad, and not hiding it.

"Hello," I said, nodding the significant nod that was a greeting between telepaths. I introduced myself quickly mind-to-mind. *Have we met?* I asked, giving the contextual information about Kara's and my engagement and the years in question.

She thought. *No, I was stuck in D.C. with a government Minding job most of that time period. Del went on vacations by himself.* Regret tinged her mental voice. "Hello to you too," she said out loud, more out of habit than anything else I was betting. Minding—mental bodyguarding—usually required you to hold two conversations and/or two thoughts at once on a regular basis, so she'd be used to it.

I sat down at the plain table. Turner watched from a few feet behind me. If this was meant to intimidate me, she was out of luck.

"Let's do this out loud," I said, I glanced at the clock. Fourteen minutes would be . . . okay. I could do this.

"That's fine," she said. She took a breath, sadness leaking out. "Del and I divorced in August. It wasn't—he didn't want to end it. He begged me to stay. But . . . well, I'd met someone else." *In D.C.,* her mind echoed, along with a face and a subtle sexual overtone. "It didn't seem fair to anyone to prolong the pain."

"Do you think he killed himself?" *With an iron?* my own mental voice added. Might as well go straight to the heart of this.

Her public mind recoiled from the thought. "I . . ." She trailed off, looked at her hands, then back at me. "I honestly don't know. He seemed okay, after a couple of months. I checked on him occasionally. I had friends check on him. I still cared."

She should have thought of that before she cheated, my mind supplied.

Cindy winced like I'd slapped her.

I realized she'd read me, and rebuilt my shields. Amateur move. I had been interrogating normals far, far too long.

She pulled herself up, but some of that personality had dimmed. "I do know he was acting very strangely a few weeks before he died. One of my friends . . ." She trailed off again.

"What?" I asked.

"Well, mutual friends. He went over for dinner and they ate off paper plates with disposable silverware. He asked for a real knife when his broke in half trying to cut the meat—and Del said he didn't have any. That he'd thrown them all out. He gave some stupid excuse."

"He threw away the knives?" I asked.

Cindy looked away. "That's what he said. I looked up his trash allowance. . . . He'd thrown away three times the amount of nonrecyclables his plan allowed. They actually fined him. And Del paid the fine—the first time, with no arguing. Del would argue about anything, and he'd walk through fire to save a buck on what he considered a 'nonessential.' The Del I knew . . ." She paused here, swallowing back tears and disgust. "The Del I knew would spread out the extra trash over several weeks just to avoid the fine. Even then he'd argue about it." She looked at me. *I was a horrible man for the cheating comment,* her mind supplied.

I said nothing. In this case I agreed with her.

Behind me, Turner shifted. "He's the best hope you have of getting real answers to Meyers's death, Ms. Ballon. I'd answer his questions."

She looked at me, vulnerable and unhappy. "What do you need to know?"

I racked my brain. "Did he seem sad? Depressed?"

"Not particularly. He called me up, out of the blue, on

Sunday. He said he was tired of storing all of his stuff, and he wanted me to have his grandfather's old Shaker cabinet. That was one of his most cherished possessions; it's the master project from a carpenter in the nineteenth century, and it's been in the family for centuries." She took a breath. "I told him no, of course, but he wouldn't let it go. I finally said if it meant so much to him, I'd take it. It should have gone to our children, if we'd had any, he'd said." That had really hurt, her mind filled in. She'd thought that was maybe why he'd done it, knowing she wouldn't be able to throw it away or give it away, looking at it every day and thinking she'd cost Meyers his chance at children. A fitting punishment perhaps. And so she'd taken it. Penance.

"Do you think he was crazy, at the end?" I asked her as gently as I could, not that it would matter at this point. I'd probably already offended her as much as it was possible for one human being to offend another. But giving away prized possessions was classic suicide behavior, though that was not in itself what the Guild deemed crazy.

"Crazy?" she asked, and shook her head slightly. "He seemed perfectly sane at the time. A little too sane. Sad, you know? But together. I'm told that it's possible to carry madness for a long time without developing symptoms, though." She shivered. "The professionals are putting me under house arrest for another week just in case. At least I should be able to catch up on my reading." A slight twinge of fear entered the room.

That same fear, the fear of what I'd seen in that basement cell, what I'd felt trying to burrow into my brain, resonated with me. I was unlikely to develop madness from being in a room with her secondhand for fifteen minutes, I told myself. But the back of my head didn't believe.

The clock said fifteen minutes had gone by. "Thank you for answering my questions, Ms. Ballon."

I stood, but she didn't, her mind saying she was waiting for me to leave. Now.

I left, Turner walking a little behind me so I didn't attack passersby. Helpful of her.

A man was waiting for me in the hallway. He had a dark complexion, dark, short natural hair, and the overly smooth skin and too-bright eyes of expensive Guild age treatments, only really available to the political elite of the Council and its advisers. He had the movement of a long-distance runner, smooth and minimalist, but he watched his surroundings like a cop. Something about his mind and the way he shielded made me think he was older than Jamie, though how much I couldn't tell with the treatments.

He was wearing a plain black jumpsuit that reminded me of Turner's uniform without actually being a uniform. His Enforcement patch and rank insignia told me he was very highly ranked. And his stance when he saw me told me we were going to have trouble.

"Tobias Nelson, I presume," I said, making the first move in the confrontation. This was the man who'd threatened Meyers in open Council, the one Kara thought had killed him. And his job meant he could cover it up with impunity.

I did the intense nod the Guild did instead of a handshake.

He returned the greeting with a small, sharp nod. "You're interfering in my cases."

"I'm looking into the suspicious death of a man who deserves the truth," I said. As of the last half hour anyway. "You want me gone, I'd suggest you take it up with Rex." *I wasn't given much choice, and I'll try to stay out of your way,* I told him, privately.

"I'd rather turn you over to a mind-scanner."

I stared at him. Have someone ruffle haphazardly through my brain without my permission? For opposing his political position. Maybe he was corrupt as hell. "You're certainly welcome to try," I said. "But I will be missed, and I will object. Loudly, and often. Do you really want the scandal with the up-and-coming students?"

His eyes narrowed then, and an almost-respect leaked out into Mindspace. "I could kill you," he said. "I have the jurisdiction."

I sighed, and stepped forward. I was getting tired of people threatening me with death. I looked him straight in the eye. "You kill me without a reason and Rex will see to it that the Council takes your job," I said, with the intense belief of a self-lie made truth. Then another mostly truth: "Then you'll have the entire DeKalb County Police Department camped outside your headquarters. I am not that important to you. And I am not a threat. I just want to know what happened to Del Meyers. His family deserves the truth. Kara's family is not going to go away." I looked down briefly, then back at him, not an admission of weakness, but an acknowledgment of beta status. I hadn't survived as long as I had on the street by trying to be alpha male, head of the pack; I'd rather talk my way out of a fight than take a punch any day. But neither could I back down. The weak got dead in that world. Time to talk my way to the right balance and do exactly what I wanted in the first place.

The moment sat on the edge, him taking offense or letting it go, having felt he'd won.

"I am not a threat to you," I said again.

Someone cleared her throat. We turned to look at Turner.

In Mindspace, she was sending out vague waves of concern.

"What is it, Turner?" Nelson asked.

She was frowning. "Sir. It's on the radio. . . . There's . . ."

"Well, spit it out."

"Another sixteen people checked themselves into Mental Health in the last hour."

Impatience from Nelson, and the feeling that this wasn't a new trend.

She stood a little straighter. "John Spirale has been reported dead. Looks like suicide."

"Meyers's assistant?"

Mental confirmation from Turner.

Nelson winced, a visible thing. "How many people did he come into contact with yesterday after we let him out of house arrest?"

"Unknown, sir. Several dozen."

"What's going on?" I asked, looking back and forth, not sure I was following all of this.

Nelson turned to me. "We have a contagious madness situation that has now escalated into a second death. Rex is out of his mind if he wants you involved. You're no psychologist."

I swallowed. "There's still a chance this is a murder. Even in the normal world, you get copycat suicides. You get waves of the things. It hurts nothing to check it out." But I was still worried, and still waiting for an opportunity not to do what I was being forced to do.

Nelson frowned at me.

"You're a convicted felon," he said. "You could infect my people with more than whatever Meyers had."

I swallowed. Why did it always come down to that? "Trust me, it doesn't matter. If I know the Guild, you're cracking down on all nonessential movement right now. People are going to be largely locked in their rooms anyway. Who am I going to infect at this point? And anyway, I'd be exposed thirdhand. There's no way I'm contagious."

My brain caught up and I realized then that I was arguing

to do what I'd just been threatened into. Blackmailed into. What was I thinking?

But I could get rid of my debt, of the power the Guild had against me, by investigating the death of a man who deserved the truth. Maybe I did believe in this. Maybe enough to risk madness, if Nelson was standing in front of me covering it up.

"What do you have to lose, Nelson?" I asked.

He sighed, and told Turner, "Take him back to his police friends. I'll see you tonight," he told me then. "I expect you to stay out of my way and not cause trouble. Or I will cash in that chip, and you will end up dead."

"Understood," I said. Oh, joy, I was caught in a power struggle of epic Guild proportions. For a dangerous cause I had nothing to do with. And, worse, I was late to work.

CHAPTER 5

Turner dropped me off in the Guild transport vehicle two blocks from the department. She opened up the car door in the back, gridded-off section. I got out, cautiously, feeling like a criminal in a way I hadn't since my drug convictions.

"Now, remember, I will pick you up tonight at five thirty," she said. "I will have additional backup available. If you do not show on time, I will come and get you."

"I'll be in the police station," I said, huddling deeper in my coat against the wind. It seemed colder than usual today, colder than usual all month, actually.

"I will get a teleporter," she said. "I'm not playing. Pack an overnight bag. You may or may not end up back here for your job. Rex and Nelson were both very specific. Guild first."

"Yeah, that seems to be a theme these days," I said, and started the hike to the department, feeling like something the cat dragged in.

I knocked on my boss's doorframe, metaphorical hat in hand. Might as well head this off. Lieutenant Marla Paulsen didn't like being interrupted for anything short of an asteroid barreling toward the earth—but neither would she accept silence when I was this late to work.

"Have a minute?"

She waved me in, pulling together a set of papers and putting them on top of an already overflowing stack. There were deep circles under her dark eyes, and the lines on her face had deepened, seemingly overnight. She was a young sixty-mumble black woman with high standards and endless energy, but today, she seemed older and somehow smaller. Judging from that and the general feel of exhaustion coming off her in Mindspace, I'd be shocked if she'd gotten any sleep at all last night. That made two of us.

"We've got final budget arguments this afternoon, and so far it's not going well," she said. "I have ten minutes at most, and that only because of the stunt you pulled yesterday. You realize you were over an hour late to work today. After you left hours early yesterday, with no information."

"I left a message," I said. "I'm here now."

"And trust me, that's all that's keeping you in the job right now. Clark is angrier than I think I've ever seen him. He had to pull a double shift on no notice. What's going on?" She sat back in the chair, seemingly tired and kind, but I knew better. If I didn't have a good reason, she would roast me over the coals. Slowly. "You look like hell."

"Kara called. There's been a death in her family and she wanted me there," I said, which was true but not the whole truth.

"And Kara is . . . ?" Paulsen prompted.

"Remember the Guild attaché who came down to help us with the Bradley case last August? We were engaged a long time ago. She's helped the department more than once."

"Ah. Chenoa. I'm sorry to hear about that," Paulsen said. She sighed. "It's not family. You can't take unplanned leave if it's not family. Those are the rules. You owe Clark an apology and at least a couple of double shifts to make up for his time loss earlier. You also owe me some pay—I'll dock for the entire week."

"What?" I protested. It's not like I got to see the money—the department handled my finances for me—but a whole week? "That seems out of proportion." I knew I'd have to bring up the Guild at some point, especially if I couldn't do the double shifts, but I didn't know how to do it.

"Be glad that's all I'm doing," Paulsen said. "The department is under extreme surveillance by the powers that be, and I am out of rope with you." She paused. "Speaking of, the review board is less than two weeks away. Do you have your license?"

I swallowed. The PI license. Great, not another thing. "Not yet."

"I told you to have a license prepared by now. Your Guild inquiry didn't work out. What do you have?"

I took a breath. "I'm in final stages of appealing. There was no reason for them to slow down the process in the first place. Legally, I have passed all the requirements. I have all of the filing paperwork for you to show if you need to." It shouldn't be this hard.

"Appealing?" she said. "That means they denied you."

"I passed every test," I said defensively. "I've jumped through all the hoops for the Second Chance Act. I've done the rehab. You yourself have mandated the drug testing. We have, what, three and a half years of records?"

"Closer to four," she said flatly. "They're giving you issues about the felonies."

"Well, yes."

I could feel her pulling back a cloud of negative emotion, lassoing it, and setting it aside. Cops didn't like felonies. They didn't like felons. And me . . . well, mine were all drug related, and what I did made up for them. Mostly. On most days.

Finally she spoke. "I hope for your sake that you get your

approval. I warned you already, if you don't have some kind of license going forward, the odds are that the review board will terminate your contract. That review is in two weeks."

"You said you were going to stand up for my job," I said very, very quietly. I'd fought tooth and nail to get here this morning at all. I needed this job. I wanted this job. And she'd promised.

"I said I would do what I can," she returned, and looked down at another pile of folders on the side of her desk. Cutbacks, likely, again. The county was cutting back far too much from far too many directions lately. As she put it, "real cops" were losing their jobs. What right did I have as a felon to be here?

Obviously I couldn't tell her about the Guild issue right now, not and keep my job. It was Friday—I had the weekend to figure this out.

She was still waiting on me.

I sighed. "I'll get the certification. I will. I can't promise timing, though I'll do my best. I may need you to fill out a few forms."

She looked up as Captain Harris knocked and opened her door. "Yes?"

"We have a problem," Harris said, in an intense tone I only seemed to hear from cops when people were actually bleeding to death. "There's an arbitration situation that is about to turn violent."

Paulsen looked at me. "Emergency?"

"No," I said, and found myself ejected out to the hall-way before I could blink. The door closed with a *snick* as I looked at it.

The captain had been taking on arbitration gigs for years, and had been stepping up the high-profile ones lately (according to Paulsen) to help fund department paychecks. I wondered where the violence was coming from. Union situation? Gangs? Politicians with knives? Impossible to know. Whatever it was clearly was more important than me.

Instead of going downstairs to the interview rooms like I was supposed to, I locked myself in the coffee closet and took several deep breaths. I had debated going outside for a cigarette, as it had now been so many hours I couldn't count since the last one, but they'd taken my cigarettes at the Guild, and my sponsor, Swartz, said people before poison.

The coffee closet was dim today, one of the two lightbulbs burned out, the coffeepot still heating from last night; the smell of burned coffee and ozone filled the space. The two donuts left were so stale they clanked, and a small scout ant poked at the crumbs on the table.

I killed him, feeling bad about it, but knowing there would be two hundred more in an hour if I let it go. You didn't see many ants in the winter; I was betting they had an inside heated spot somewhere. Trouble.

Okay, now I was putting this off. I wiped off my hands, picked up the phone receiver, and dialed Swartz's number.

Ringing came on the other side of the line. He was still at home, resting up, with any luck having remembered to turn the ringer on again.

"Adam," came over the phone, in an out-of-breath voice. "Where the hell were you this morning? I called the station, but they said you weren't assigned anywhere. Do I need to come down there and kick your ass?"

I took a breath. That voice—that voice was the most comforting thing I'd heard in a long time. Swartz had been my Narcotics Anonymous sponsor for years, and he always knew the right thing to say. To do. To think about. He didn't let me get away with crap, and even since his heart attack, he was there when I needed him. When I didn't know what to do. "Yes. No. Maybe. I don't know, Swartz. No drugs—I haven't even had a cigarette this morning. The Guild—"

"What about the Guild, son?"

"Well . . ."

"I assume you're on break. Might as well spit it."

Something inside me loosened. "Yeah. The Guild locked me up and then decided to tell me I was going to solve a murder for them."

"A murder?"

"A guy I knew back in the day. Kara's uncle. He's, well, majorly important at the Guild now. On the Council."

"Intimidation? Really? What does Kara say about this?"

"She helped them throw me in that cell after I broke some stupid rule. Maybe I did, I don't know. But they're threatening me with a lot of crap, and I . . ." A pause over the phone, in which I saw another scout ant. I killed this one too. I hadn't told him about the debt. "I feel like I have to do this."

"How stupid a rule?" Swartz asked.

I poked at the crumbs. Of all the things for him to pick out of that . . . "Some privacy thing. It's a matter of interpretation. They've tightened up standards a lot since I left, and I don't think all in a good way." I thought about telling him about the mind-fight, about Green outmuscling me—it disturbed me still, confused me still—but I couldn't figure out how to say it quickly. "Either way it's do what they say or bad things happen."

"You need help getting out of town, kid?" Swartz finally asked, serious.

I laughed, long and hard. "Ah, no, thanks, though. The Guild are controlling bastards as usual, and I don't know what's going on with Kara. But madness is no joke, and neither is suicide, if that's what this is. Meyers was good to

me, and he deserves somebody who will find out the truth."
I sat back, blinking, realizing all of that was true. I'd made
up my mind, even if I hadn't realized it yet.

Swartz's voice softened. "Good for you. Good for you, kid."

I smiled then, a real smile. "Listen, about the service
project this weekend . . ."

"I'll give you a pass if you're working," Swartz said.
"But we're having a meet-up. I don't care what you have to
do to make it happen."

"I understand," I said, still smiling. We said our good-
byes, and I sat back.

I still wanted a cigarette. I was still exhausted within an
inch of my life. But for the first time, I thought maybe I
could do this. The weekend was coming up, two whole
days for investigation at the Guild. Two whole days, and
maybe I could do some good.

Maybe I could end up not dead and not imprisoned.
That would be fun.

When I showed up at Cherabino's cubicle, Michael had donuts.
Real donuts, fresh-baked today, with gooey fillings and sticky
yogurt frosting flavored with heavy spices I couldn't put
names to. He waved me over to the box and I helped myself
to three. And copious amounts of coffee. I'd already gotten
a cup from the break room of the burned stuff, and had
myself a cigarette.

"Everything okay from yesterday?" Michael asked.

Mouth full, I shrugged. *Don't really want to talk about
it, thanks.*

His eyes widened and he was suddenly on his feet.

Crap, amateur mistake. I must be way more tired than
I'd thought. Cherabino would have kicked my ass back
when I was new to this. Some cops still would.

Michael stood there, holding back his hostility.

Cherabino stood too, and patted his shoulder. "Takes you by surprise the first time, I know. Boy Wonder does back off if you tell him to."

"Okay . . ." He was taking her advice, and calming, without only the occasional look in my direction.

Cherabino shrugged. "Don't ask about the nickname. It's a long story."

Forcing myself to calm, I finished chewing the amazingness that was my new favorite donut and swallowed. Took another gulp of coffee. "I didn't mean to cross a line," I sighed. "I'll try not to do it again, but with the way my week has been going, I'm not making any promises. I've just been around telepaths a lot in the last twenty-four hours, over with Kara. It plays with your sense of personal space."

Michael was frowning, but he didn't say anything else, and it seemed hypocritical to read him at this point.

"These are really good donuts," I offered, to change the subject, then for good measure added, "Do we have any new information on the Wright case? Since I was down there for the murder scene, I want to help if I can." That's what I was getting paid for, right?

Cherabino gestured to an uncomfortable metal chair at the back of the cubicle. "We're about to leave for the Cardinal Laboratories. We could use your skills there, actually. I want to interview most of the staff, and I need to be back by two for the task force meeting." She had a sudden thought I could actually see crystallize.

I stopped walking with the chair halfway to the front of the cubicle next to the two more comfortable ones. "What?" I asked her.

"Clark was looking for you yesterday. He seemed pissed. Should you really be working on the case with us? I'll understand if you need to be in the interview rooms." She didn't sound happy about this; Cherabino had the highest close rate in Homicide because she got grabby and obsessive with cases. But I knew she would share resources if she had to. Bransen's department hadn't ever been willing to pick up my full-time salary and she had to be comfortable with that.

"I'll be here a little longer," I said, firmly squishing any internal guilt that might be leaking over the accidental Link with Cherabino. I was here, I needed to work, not feel sorry for myself. "What's going on with the task force?" I asked.

She looked at me.

I looked back at her. "Seriously, Why it is urgent all of a sudden? You've been working on the project for years now."

She sighed and pulled a huge stack of papers out of a drawer and plopped it on the desk, on top of an even taller pile. "This is this list of crimes Fiske is suspected of orchestrating."

"It's three inches thick. At least."

"Someone is observant today. Yes, it's three inches thick. Murder, extortion, human trafficking, drug trafficking, felony assault, illegal prostitution and gambling rings—sometimes in the same facility—car theft rings, oh, and I don't know, what's your favorite crime these days? He's got his guys doing all of it. Of course I can't prove any of it's tied to him. I can't prove he gave the orders, not in front of a jury anyway.

"The places shut down as soon as we find them. The evidence disappears—twice out of police lockup!—and the people involved leave town. When we can get something to stick, we have judges throwing things out left and right—he has a few of them on payroll—and we have witnesses disappearing. Those, by the way, are always the ones that can connect the crime to Fiske himself. The rest, he lets go."

She reached back in the drawer and pulled out another, much thinner file and set it on top of the first. "This. This is the new evidence. Ruffins—remember him, guy from the Tech Control Organization who hates you? Well, he's brought his network of informants in, and it turns out since Fiske is up to his ears in technology smuggling, Ruffins has stuff we can actually use. A lot of it. I don't care if the bastard goes away for taxes at this point, and nobody else on the task force cares either. We're going to take him down on technology smuggling and a couple of murders that happened along the way. Hell, taxes too if we can call the right guys. But we need to move in the next couple of weeks to be sure of getting the judge we know isn't bought."

"We need to go. We're going to be late," Michael said.

Cherabino sighed and put the paper back in the drawer with two hands. "It's always something, isn't it?"

She stood up and grabbed her suit jacket. "It's the lab now, isn't it?"

"That's right," Michael said. He led the way and I trotted to catch up.

"What do I need to know about this Cardinal Laboratories?" I asked as Cherabino followed, making notes to herself on a notebook with a pen.

Michael glanced back, slowing his pace a little to give Cherabino a chance to catch up. "It's the Wright case. Remember how he was fired from his official job?"

"I . . . think so," I said cautiously.

"It's the ax murder case," he prompted, which did it for me.

"Um, did you ever find the missing pieces?" I asked.

"No, actually," Michael said. "My trophy theory is all we've got, and it's not much other than conjecture. Based on the angles of the cuts and the focus on the head and arm, it's pretty clear the killer did the damage there on purpose, to take pieces with him."

"Are there similar cases in the database?" I asked.

"Nothing like this," he said. "There was the van Gogh murders with the ears missing five years ago, but the perp is still in jail."

"And we got him on DNA evidence," Cherabino put in, catching up. "That was one of mine. I'm sure it's the guy. Still, it doesn't hurt to cross-check." She said hello to a few detectives who were passing through the main walkway in front of the elevator where we were.

Michael pressed the elevator button.

"I assume you're already looking at perps who were recently released from jail?" I asked. "If there's a weird trophy thing going on, it could be someone who was doing the same thing a decade or more ago and got caught."

Cherabino sighed. "Unless you have time to go through all the files indiscriminately, we're going to have to keep moving. I'm not authorized for any more computer time this month, even for somebody else's database."

I blinked. I hadn't noticed that missing. "They took the computer back?"

I felt a small, suppressed twinge of hurt through the Link as the elevator *ding*ed its arrival.

We stepped on, and Michael pressed the button for the ground floor.

"I just let go of my last Electronic Crimes commitment, and the machine can be better used by somebody who's doing it full-time." Cherabino shook her head and put the notebook away. "My time's better spent on the Fiske task force anyway. If we can get the bastard, the whole city will be a better place."

"You still have the tablet?" I asked. She went through a deep background check every six months or so to let her have the technology, and I'd gotten a little used to its processing power, even if it wasn't linked up to anything else; I wasn't cleared for access to anything that hadn't already been Quarantined six ways 'til Sunday. Still, sixty years after the Tech Wars, with the public still scared of any computer technology more powerful than an oven timer, I was lucky to have access to even that much. Cherabino, of course, had access to far more.

"I'm sharing the tablet with another detective," Cherabino said. "He has it this week."

Michael prompted, "You wanted to know about the victim, Noah Wright, correct?"

"Probably," I said. "If I'm interviewing coworkers I need to know whatever's going to come up. And what we're not saying." The cops held back key details of the crime on purpose to weed out false confessions.

"The missing ear and arm section are being held back," Cherabino said flatly. The elevator door opened as we arrived and she pushed through, nervous energy making her move quickly.

Michael and I followed.

"Wright lost his job about six months ago. He was working on a government contract for technology applications and was fired 'for improper use of sensitive information.' There was a lawsuit filed from the state using the same language—it's odd, I had to look it up—but nothing's been done with it."

"You mean another lawyer filed an injunction or it got tossed out of court?" I dodged a few cops pulling suspects over from Booking, as Michael moved out of the way of one of the secretaries from the pool. Cherabino just cut through, and I ended up following in her wake. The main floor of the cop building was a madhouse, as usual.

Michael walked a little faster to keep up. "No, I mean literally nothing's been done with it. It's like the paperwork got lost somewhere. It hasn't been extended, it hasn't been dismissed, it hasn't had a court date assigned. It's like it literally got lost."

"That's strange," I said.

Cherabino pushed through the reception area toward the glass double doors, frosted with the cold outside. "Yeah, the information wasn't classified because it's a private company and it's not considered a national security issue. Still. We need to ask his coworkers about that. Sounds like something somebody would kill for."

"Information?" Michael asked.

"Sensitive information?" she replied. "Secrets? People kill for secrets all the time. *Especially* in the government."

Cardinal Laboratories was a low, industrial-boxy building in South DeKalb not far from the Georgia Bureau of Investigation offices. It had been constructed with a double-paned roof with a filtered drainage system; according to the sign out front, the rainfall and dust particles landing on the roof were monitored for fallout levels from the dirty bomb that had wiped out neighborhoods to the east years ago. According to the sign, government intervention and monitoring had led to a fifty percent decrease in the level of radioactive pollution in the last ten years. I didn't know which idea was more disturbing, the fact that there had been so much radioactive pollution they felt the need to monitor it, or that they were trumpeting its decrease. Could the government really impact pollution? And if so, did they have huge weather turbines or something? Should I be more nervous than I already was?

The parking lot was huge and cracking; employee aircars and flyers lined the rows along with the infrequent classic car and some too old or too broken to fly. The occasional tree planted in medians among the parking lot looked withered, a few steps from death. It wasn't a cheery place, despite the attempt at bioengineered flowers planted in pots by the front door. The flowers were mostly dead, shriveled with the winter cold, and frost covered the pots.

The main foyer was tiled in an echoing flat material that hit the bottom of your shoe with a texture I'd never felt before. Considering this was a science and materials research company, it could be some grand experiment or a new product in the early stages of testing, but I hated it. Not grippy enough on your feet and too grippy all at once.

Cherabino had a warrant, and split the list of interviews with me, her and Michael taking one room, me taking the other to make us get through the list faster.

I was set up in a room with two glass walls, soda machines, coffee carafes, a refrigerator, and a table and chairs. Break room. I seemed to spend my life in break rooms. Still, there was food if I got hungry.

CHAPTER 6

Wright's supervisor was Susan Cornell, a mousy woman with very messy hair, mismatched clothes, and a distressing tendency not to meet your eyes. Despite this, she had one of the most focused and interesting minds I'd come across in a long time. If science was a betting sport, with scientists lined up for a race to a breakthrough and money placed on all sides, I'd put my money on her, and that before she'd done no more than say hello. Her mind kept going off in odd directions not immediately called for.

"Hello," I said.

"Hello." Even after nearly a minute in the same room, she hadn't met my eyes.

"How old are you?" I asked point-blank, a question that normally offended any woman over twenty-five, which she'd passed a while ago.

"Forty-four years and seven months," she said, absolutely without emotional reaction. She was still looking at the table. After a moment: "How old are you?"

"I'm thirty-nine," I said.

"I am older than you."

"That's true," I said, still watching her mind. Huh. I was starting to think the avoidance of eye contact didn't necessarily mean she was hiding something. Her brain just seemed to process the "social" information differently than the norm. She did a good job of compensating, enough that she'd been promoted to management, but body language just wasn't there. She'd responded to my question with a repeating question out of socialization and habit, not interest.

That, plus the sideways thought patterns occasionally, made her a very interesting mind. Combined with the order I'd felt immediately, I was betting she was genius level or better in her field, and far more creative than the average in odd directions. I wished I had more time to watch that mind work in her element.

"I have a schedule today," she said, looking at the clock. "What do you need to know?"

Well, normally I'd ask if she liked Wright, but I had the feeling that wasn't the best question right now. "Why did Wright get fired?" I asked instead.

Now she glanced at me, then away. A few thoughts like fishes darted across her mind, some in odd directions. "Noah Wright, pay level four, was let go from his job for sharing sensitive information with noncleared sources."

"What does that mean?" I asked.

"I can't tell you the information."

"I didn't ask you to. What did he do with it?"

"He posted it on the WorldNet without password protection or quarantine allowances. He then posted several messages in forums to advertise the information. By the time he was discovered, the sensitive information was effectively worldwide. The government found the information. They are not happy."

"Is it still there?" I asked.

"I don't know," she said. "Several of our key employees worked to remove it. But once the information is out there, it is hard to erase completely."

"Several of your key employees?" I asked. "Let's talk to them first."

Over the course of the next hours, I talked to perhaps twenty people, most of whom had worked with Wright on a regular basis. A picture slowly emerged of a quiet man who treated his coworkers well, who made steady progress on his goals and steady contributions to his teammates, but was otherwise unexceptional.

The next person I talked to had a different story.

"Wright was a bastard," she said, a Nicole Sagara. She was a small, fragile-looking woman in a lab coat with a huge surge of anger going off in Mindspace.

"Why was Wright a bastard?" I asked calmly.

Sagara looked at Cornell, who was studying the file. Then she looked back at me. "It's no secret that I reported him for suggestive comments in the workplace. They weren't even at me. But I got tired of hearing dismissive terms for women. I got tired of him taking credit for my work—and Johanna's work—and Laila's work—without so much as an acknowledgment that we were on the team. I got tired of him being an asshole, and telling me to get him coffee. I requested a transfer. Three times. But I didn't get it."

Cornell's mind changed shape then, and she looked up. "Nicole. I told you that I knew about his exaggerations. He was not getting any extra credit for his falsehoods. Your work was good work. His work complemented your work. The final projects were stronger than any individual on the team could do alone. Teamwork is stressful. But good results happen."

"He threatened to take a laser pistol and stick it up my ass," Sagara said. "HR backed me up on the transfer. And the punch. They said it was justified, even if I did break his nose."

"He got a permanent mark on his record. He is fired now. Your work on both the Galen Project and the laser pistol technology is exemplary. I don't understand why we continue to have this conversation."

Traitor, Sagara thought so hard I could hear it despite her low numbers in Ability. Her anger was truly a thing to behold. "Just because he was a Free Data Campaigner doesn't mean he should get away with all of this!"

"The paperwork was submitted for prosecution. What causes Mr. Wright campaigned for on his free time are none of our business. When he released sensitive information without authorization, he was fired."

The third time, she thought. *And for all we know he was doing it all along.* "Can I go now?" Sagara asked resentfully.

"Don't forget your status report is due this afternoon," Cornell said. "You may go."

When Sagara left, I asked Cornell, "What's a Free Data Campaigner?"

She rearranged papers, then answered, "In the twentieth century in the early days of Internet networking, many scientists and engineers believed that sharing information freely would benefit humanity. The majority of information was scientific in nature. Some people still think research should be available to all. This lab appreciates the idea, but we have government contracts for various military applications. There are national security concerns we have that simple science operations do not." She recited this as if reading from a book.

"What do you think?" I asked.

Now she looked at me. "Wright did good work. But Wright should have followed the rules."

Then the next employee knocked on the door and I was off to the races again.

After it was all over, Cornell took me back down the carpeted hallway toward the lobby. I hadn't said I was a telepath, to her or to any of the interviewees. Perhaps this was a technical breach of privacy, but legally, I was okay. None of them had asked.

The dribs and drabs I'd gotten of the secret information they kept talking about had been sobering. This particular facility handled a lot of weapons, and a lot of Tech-level projects the government was moving forward with for one reason or another despite the bans. It sounded to me like the gun-control arguments they'd had before the Tech Wars: the government wanted the citizens to be gun free, even starting legislation to take away their rifles, while the government held stockpiles of automatic weapons all over the country.

It didn't strike me like the Tech laws were doing much better. Maybe the Guild was right to do their own research. Maybe not. Both sides were breaking treaties to do it, and it made me very, very sad. Cooper, my personal hero of all the Guild founders, was very much a fan of honesty and integrity in dealing with people and organizations. Hard choices meant hard answers, he'd said. That, and stand for what you stand for.

I think Swartz and Cooper would have gotten along okay.

When we arrived at the front lobby, the receptionist was gone somewhere and Cherabino was seated quietly in one of the comfortable chairs, Michael standing next to her.

"Thank you for showing me around," I told Cornell.

"I can't leave you unattended," she said.

"We're about to leave," I promised. There was a forthrightness about Cornell that I appreciated, though I still missed the occasional eye contact or social body-language mirroring; the lack was like a discordant note in a symphony. I'd been around normals too long, clearly, if physical cues were overriding my sense of Mindspace. Either that or the injury I'd had until recently had changed me.

She seemed hesitant but spoke anyway. "Noah Wright broke the rules, but he did not deserve to die. If there is something we can do to help you without breaking our promises to the government, it is the right thing to do so."

Cherabino moved us to the parking lot. "We're running late," she told me and Michael. "And when I called in, Paulsen was on the warpath."

"You asked me to remind you to stop for food," Michael said, once we were in the car.

"Yeah," she said. "You willing to be the one to go in and get it?"

"No problem."

"He's been in there ten minutes," I said.

"There's a line. You can see it through the door. And besides, you were the one who didn't want fried tofu again," Cherabino said. "It takes longer."

She sighed, and time passed.

"You're brooding again," Cherabino said.

"Am I?" I looked up, and noticed the shields between us had thinned. "I'll try to do it quieter."

"You can't let all of this stuff eat at you. It's not healthy. Plus I have to listen to it through that Link of yours. I'm not a telepath. Normal people shouldn't have to listen to people brooding. They shouldn't, damn it."

"It'll fade," I said, a quick, habitual protest.

"It's fading already, maybe," she said. "But it's not gone yet. Anyway, try to cheer up, okay?"

She sighed, moved some papers around, and pointed to the glove box. "Here, open that." A picture flashed between us, a picture of a nice pair of black men's gloves set in a box. She was nervous, somehow.

I had to force myself not to comment on the image or

the emotion; she hated it when I jumped ahead. So I pulled open the compartment she'd requested.

A wrapped package in garish paper sat self-consciously, just the size of the box of gloves I'd seen in her mind. I picked it up. What did she want me to do with it?

The thought must have leaked across the Link, because she said, "Open it." She swallowed the added "idiot." I felt it go by but said nothing. Apparently I was the only one here who wasn't allowed to jump ahead.

It was a truly hideous wrapping paper. Her niece's school sales project, her mind supplied. Twelve ROCs a roll. I opened the paper, pulling the bow off and ripping into the paper, which did not deserve reuse.

Inside was a linen-paper box, the expensive kind, with a pressed seal on its top outlined in ink. Some logo I didn't understand. I sat there for a minute trying to figure out what the lines were trying to represent.

She pulled the box out of my hands and lifted the lid, offering it to me. "They're gloves."

"I see that."

She pushed the box back into my hands. I took it, cautiously, in case she wanted it back.

"For you. They're for your birthday, Adam. I looked it up. Your birthday is tomorrow, right?"

I stared at the gloves, uncertain. I mean, they were just gloves, right? "Yeah, my birthday is tomorrow." She'd never given me anything before. Crap, I'd never given her anything either. I'd thought we weren't birthday people. To be honest, the only person in the world right now who cared about my birthday was Swartz, or that's what I'd thought.

She pulled one out of the box. "See, they're hydropolimat. They maintain body temperature better than wool, but they don't get too hot, and if you get blood on them at a crime scene, they'll wash clean. They also have a built-in protective layer, so as long as you don't leave the gloves in a puddle or anything they'll keep the blood and mud and ickies away from your hands. They're nice gloves." She paused then, glove in hand. "I'm hogging your present, aren't I?"

"Um, yes?"

She plopped the glove back in the box, and it settled half in, half out, on top of its brother. Then she settled back in the seat. "Sorry." Thoughts buzzed around her head like bees, none settling into permanency, and she'd remembered enough shielding that I didn't get them by accident.

The sun was falling into the car through her window, puddling on her face and behind her head like a halo. She looked away for a moment, and her profile was illuminated, as was the skin beneath the button on her shirt still unbuttoned near her neck. She had a beautiful neck, and those breasts—

I clamped down on my thoughts and looked away before I embarrassed myself. Back at the gloves. They were just gloves. But that almost made it worse. She cared, maybe. She cared. And what I felt, the deep things I felt and what I wanted, well, they were all about birthdays and Christmases, Thanksgivings, and New Year's and Valentine's Day, year after year, gifts and promises and—and things I couldn't have, I told myself sternly.

Swartz said I couldn't have a relationship until I could keep a plant alive, and I had twelve dead plants lined up in a row in my apartment.

"Aren't you going to say thank you?" she demanded.

"What?"

"Say thank you, damn it. It's customary when receiving a gift. You know what, never mind. Idiot."

I looked back over, and if anything she was more beautiful than ever. Her mind, open, if I would dare to touch it.

Michael tapped on the back window, and it was suddenly a flurry of dealing with food and napkins and paper.

I tucked the gloves away in my coat, carefully. Happy birthday, Adam. Happy birthday.

CHAPTER 7

We checked in with Andrew, one of the police forensic accountants, when we got back to the department. Or rather, Cherabino did and Michael and I tagged along. It was only the next cubicle over from hers and he had fantastic coffee.

"Have a minute?" Cherabino asked.

Andrew turned around in his chair. "Only about ten before the next meeting. What do you need?"

I gestured to the display of real gourmet coffee beans, grinder, and brewing machine.

"Go ahead," Andrew said, "I made a fresh pot a little while ago."

So of course I fixed myself a cup, humming happily under my breath. Blue Mountain coffee, real sugar, milk even. Andrew's cubicle was the Cadillac of cubicles.

"Have you had a chance to do discovery on Noah Wright's accounts yet?" Cherabino asked him.

Michael handed me a cup, and I made him coffee as well. Three sugars, no cream. Too much when he wasn't drinking department swill, that wasn't my problem. He took the cup with a polite nod.

Andrew poked around in some files, pulling one out. "Actually, yes." More shuffling papers. "Wright banked through our local New World branch. And his company was remarkably cooperative about sharing financial records on him and his 'retirement.' His pension was laughable. But he paid his mortgage and his bills on time, thousands of ROCs a month. He does not have the savings to support this."

"What are you saying, exactly?" Cherabino asked.

"The money doesn't work," Andrew told her. "I've looked under every rock and every tree, but no progress. He has cash deposits well under the amount that usually gets attention, and he's paying most of his bills with cash as well."

"Is there a rich relative that's supporting him?" I asked, knowing full well the evidence was pointing rather to a drug trade or something similarly illegal. Unemployed researchers didn't make large amounts of untraceable cash, not legally anyway.

"Not that I can tell, and I've looked." Andrew looked apologetic. "Perhaps it's a relationship with someone with extra cash, as in romantic relationship."

"Most likely, though, it's criminal," Cherabino said.

"Well, yes, it looks that way."

"Thanks, Andrew."

"No problem. Um . . . I do have the thing . . ."

"We'll leave now," I said cheerfully. Of course I was taking the cup with me.

We settled in Cherabino's space, across the narrow cubicle hall. I drank coffee. Michael held his cup. Cherabino wished she had coffee.

I handed her mine; she sipped and handed it back. Neither one of us commented.

"If he's up to something large-scale and criminal, why isn't he being tracked by the department already?" Michael asked.

"That's a good question," Cherabino said. "That's a very good question. If you get some extra time, go through the dispatch and case file records for the last year or so. I want to know if we just haven't put two and two together."

"Before or after I get an interview scheduled for the Pubbly case?"

"After. Oh, and see if you can find the car from the Kiershon case—it might be in a chop shop or something, but if we can find the bloodstain evidence, that'll prove our theory."

"How many cases do you have going right now?" I asked, amazed.

Cherabino sighed. "Too many. Far, far too many."

Later that afternoon, exhausted and unwilling to go back to the interview rooms, I did paperwork. Until I had an idea.

"Hi, Bob," I said. It was a little disturbing how good I was getting sneaking into the high-security area.

The balding overweight cop turned around in his chair. Bob was well over three hundred pounds, splotchy skin on his neck, and breathed hard when he got out of his chair. That didn't matter; Bob could run rings around the fittest cop on the floor in his domain, the Wild West of the small remaining Internet. He was a cowboy, a rebel, and one of the youngest people I'd ever met with a legal implant in his brain. Most people were too scared the viruses would turn their brain to Jell-O—Bob took the risks with both hands and helped to shut down the electronic criminals every day. That didn't mean he liked me.

"What?" he asked me. He'd been staring at a computer monitor—a much bigger, much nicer, much more restricted-level technology than anything Cherabino had ever used—and now was staring at me. "You're not supposed to be here."

"Hello," I said in return, by now used to this little song and dance of ours. "But I am prepared to offer you a dozen cream-filled chocolate donuts, delivered every week until Christmas."

He sat a little straighter. "With holiday sprinkles?"

"If you want sprinkles, you can have sprinkles," I said, feeling generous. "I'll even throw in a box of real coffee from the donut place you like. With holiday flavoring."

He wavered. "Zahir's cracking down on unauthorized projects, you know."

"This will only take a few minutes. No FBI files, I promise. Nothing behind a firewall."

He thought about it. I could almost see the numbers and probabilities going past him. Almost see, because I couldn't read him at all; Bob's computer implant created an electric field that effectively made his mind feel like gibberish to me. Electromagnetic fields interacted with Mindspace and Mindspace fields with electronics—anyone who's had a watch run down on their wrist from too much emotion knows this already.

Most people were too afraid of the computer viruses that had destroyed the world in the Tech Wars to want an implant, much less to work in the tiny remaining Internet, walled away from anything important. Most normals lived in a world walled away from anything breakable, with information routinely Quarantined before it even left. Bob couldn't be Quarantined; he was too deep, too often, swimming in the sea of information. That made him both dangerous and valuable, and for all his girth, he knew he was both.

"Make it half a dozen twice a week, and make sure they have sprinkles," Bob said firmly.

I suppressed a smile. "You got it."

He leaned his chair forward. "What's the puzzle?"

"I want you to find me the information that Noah Wright released on the Internet a few months ago. His boss says it's sensitive, and they've tried to erase it all. You told me once that nothing is ever really erased from the Internet."

"It isn't. Who is 'they'?"

"Cardinal Laboratories."

"Ah." He sat back. "This related to the soldier project?"

I blinked. "The what?"

"The government recently announced on secure channels that they're working with Cardinal Laboratories to design a biologically enhanced soldier. There's been a flurry of protest over it, but the military is emphasizing that the design is biologically based, and is on a different system from the hybrid Tech used before the war. The science groups are still up in arms. The laboratory has had protestors all over its New York office."

"Why haven't I heard about this?" I asked.

"It's all over the Net, but the government's suppressing the newspapers. There's free speech protests about that too, but it's starting to die down. Everybody with access already's had their say." He looked at me. "You really need to keep up with the news."

"Um, if you say so."

"What was the name of the guy again?" Bob asked me.

"Noah Wright."

"Think I know the guy. Goes by ArkFree?"

"I'd have no way of knowing. The lab's not giving anything away."

He turned around to look at the screen again, making a gesture with his hand, and a flurry of pictures ran over the screen. He must have had a haircut; for the first time, I could see the circular exterior of the implant, where one faint green light pulsed.

I forced myself to look away, disturbed, as I always was, by the thought of electronic technology actually fused to someone's brain. It was dangerous as hell—after all, that's how the computer viruses went blood-borne in the Tech Wars—but also a terrible idea. And I wasn't just saying that because I was a telepath and an implant would likely shred my brain through competing fields. It just was.

Now, a biology-based enhancement . . . maybe that might be worth looking into. The military project sounded legal, if extreme. But extreme was what the military did; half of my students back in the old days had been training for specialties in black ops and surveillance. Military paid very well for what it did.

Nearly three minutes passed while Bob searched. Three minutes was an eternity in his world, in which he could sort through data faster than I could think. Finally he made a small noise.

"What?" I asked.

Bob turned back around in the chair. Behind him on the screen was a picture of a paper document, with a red stamp printed on it and everything.

"They almost got it all," Bob said. "I had to raid a newsgroup's disaster recovery site."

"Um . . . thank you?"

"No big deal," he said. "It's printing now on the main printer."

Usually he was more helpful with summaries. "What is it?" I asked.

"A folder with several documents," Bob said. I could almost see the data swimming behind his eyes. Then: "ArkFree signed his handle to it and everything and kept the original lab marks there, if you know what you're looking for. The longest document seems to be an internal progress report on what they're calling the Galen Project. You'll have to read it for details; I'm getting an internal notification that there's a meeting in five."

"Thanks for doing this," I said.

"Make sure the first six donuts are here tomorrow," Bob said, and turned away. "Sprinkles. There'd better be sprinkles."

I fetched the thick set of papers from the printer without getting stopped, staring out the frost-rimmed window at the parking lot below. Then I walked out past the guard with the confident step of someone who had somewhere to be. He even waved.

Candy from a baby.

Now, onto the really hard part of the day: facing Clark. I had to do it, tired or no. I was here and the interview rooms were my real job. Even if I'd take a nap on nails.

Clark stopped in the middle of the basement hallway when he saw me.

"Hi, Clark," I said.

He didn't move. His anger bubbled up like a cloud of steam. "You—you—"

"Paulsen says I owe you an apology," I said. I was tired enough and stressed enough that the apology reference didn't hurt. Well, no more than eating glass.

Clark's face moved to a shade of burgundy, like the color change of a chameleon. "You left. With no notice. You haven't called in. In days. You can't do that." He spoke in a dangerously quiet voice.

"Well, I can—"

"You *can't*. Other people have lives. Other people have to pick up the *crap*—"

"Nobody asked you to be in charge!"

He took one, long, deep breath, and I felt the anger crystallize into something dangerous. "If it was up to me, you'd have been fired a year ago."

I didn't know what to say to that. I knew he didn't like

me, but what was I supposed to do? "What's the schedule like tonight? I'll take the shitty ones."

"I'm giving you the whole damn pile—with no explanation. It's better than what you did to me. I'm getting my coat. I'm on vacation next week. With any luck, you'll screw it up so bad you'll be fired by the time I get back. Here's to not seeing you."

Clark pushed past me, hard, bruising my shoulder, his contempt and disgust leaking through like acid.

Then he was gone.

CHAPTER 8

Halfway through the third hour, I was finally starting to get caught up. Or at least not lose my mind. The current suspect was being difficult, but as that suited my current mood, I wasn't complaining.

Someone rapped on the door. I needed a break anyway, and the suspect needed to stew.

"You just think about that," I told him. "You just think long and hard about that." Crap, I sounded like a bad Mafia movie. On a day when the director hadn't shown up. Even the suspect looked a little green from the telling—well, maybe it would end up working in my favor. Confess to get away from the bad Mafia movie impressions. I'd play it up later.

I closed the interview room door behind me. Frances, the file clerk, stood there with a small yellow square of paper. Or, more accurately, a pile of five identical yellow squares of paper.

"Sorry to interrupt, but you have a stalker," she said.

Now I felt a little green. "Male or female? How dangerous? Have they been taken into custody or questioned?"

She stared for a second, then laughed the hard-edged laugh of the startled and uneasy. "No, I'm sorry. It's a saying. You had a guy call for you on the main switchboard five times in two hours. He was plenty polite—no breathing into the phone or anything. Don't think he's an issue unless you know about him already, but you'll have to tell me." She held out the paper. "Says his name is Stone."

"Ah. Now it makes sense." I reached out to take the papers. "Frances?"

"What?" she asked, turning around, halfway to the elevator.

"Thanks."

"You're welcome."

I looked at the clock. I had twenty minutes before the Guild van was supposed to pick me up. I hated leaving a suspect but . . .

I ducked into one of the sound rooms that wasn't currently being used, and borrowed the phone, dialing the number on the message slip, labeled IMPORTANT, with a checked box next to it that said CALL RIGHT AWAY.

It rang twice before Stone's voice answered. I introduced myself.

"You're a hard man to get a hold of," Stone asked.

"Aren't you supposed to be watching me anyway?" I asked.

I felt a presence then, like a fist knocking politely on the outside of my mind. "That way was next, but it doesn't hurt to be polite. Plus you're surrounded by cops. I'm told they react badly if you freak out."

I strengthened my shields. "You took the tag off. I saw you take the tag off."

"I did," he said.

"So how do you find my mind so quickly?"

A pause. "Let's call it a trade secret. You listening or not?"

"I'm listening," I said.

"Turner came and found me to make sure I knew what was going on. Rex is out of his mind if he thinks I'm going to let you back in a high-stakes quarantine situation on no sleep. You're off for the evening. But—" And here his voice cracked like a whip. "If you are one minute late tomorrow, I will find you and Rex will be the least of your problems."

"Are threats really necessary? I do my job. Really."

"I'm still your Watcher," he said. "Don't push your luck. We need to meet up on neutral territory. If we're going to be working together, I need to lay out some ground rules first."

I sighed. "How do I know Turner isn't going to show up at the meeting point and cause trouble? Or Nelson? Thus far you Guild people haven't done a bang up job of communicating."

He sighed. "Just meet me tomorrow morning at Freedom Park, by the fountain memorial. Seven thirty a.m. sharp."

"You could just pick me up at my apartment instead," I said. "You've proven you know where it is."

"Seven thirty. Don't be late."

I looked at the receiver, now blaring a dial tone. If I wasn't so tired, I'd be more concerned about all the dramatics. There was something going on at the Guild. Half a dozen somethings.

But if I got to sleep in my own bed tonight, so much the better.

I paged through the rest of the slips, found one from Kara, and balled up the whole stack and threw it away.

Then I went back to the interview rooms to convince the suspect that yes, he really did want to talk to me. It took me half an hour. Then the next suspect was late, and I had a little time.

I pulled out the stack of paper I'd gotten from Bob and started to read. Without the active push-and-pull of a suspect, my exhaustion was starting to show. I had to read sentences two and three times.

Finally I got out two more pieces of paper from the bottom and flipped them over to show the white side. I used the paper to block off the one line I was dealing with, took a breath, and read. Slowly. This was not a game of speed. This was a game of comprehension. I'd learned some workarounds with my three-month-old brain injury, but it still wasn't clear sailing.

With the paper there, the words didn't float as much, and I read.

Ten minutes later, I sat back and rubbed my eyes. *Take this in small bites.*

Wright's controversial information was . . . well, less sensitive than expected, at least in the summary. That first section was a progress report on some kind of medical device, biologically based, that plugged into your nervous system to monitor your whole body's health. They were having trouble with some kind of molecular something designed to identify pathogens and chemicals in the blood; it kept misidentifying compounds in the lab, which was a problem.

One of the "desired features" was some kind of duct to release antibiotic, antiviral and/or pH-balancing chemicals when needed, but the report writer had doubts this could be accomplished anytime soon. "As long as the Galen continues to react to mutualist bacteria strains, any immune-booster response will be triggered near constantly. False positives are a large enough problem in monitoring without adding additional risks."

I had to read that sentence about ten times to understand. I opened my eyes and paged forward for pictures. No pictures. I had no idea what this device looked like.

Maybe this thing was related to the soldier project Bob had talked about? It didn't seem a big step to go from monitoring health and handling antibiotics to, say, releasing adrenaline and keeping someone awake and alert when that person felt like I did right now.

I sighed and looked at the clock. The suspect was very late. I tried to focus on the report, but I read slower and slower.

Finally my eyes closed, and I thought, *I'll just rest for a minute.*

"Adam!" Cherabino's voice woke me up from a sound sleep.

"Whaa?" I blinked. The world was having trouble focusing.

"You're drooling on your papers," she said. "Shift's over. I was supposed to drive you home, remember?"

I sat up, bleary.

She stood there, awkwardly. I could both feel her desire to ask a question and feel her reluctance.

"Just ask," I said, massaging my neck to try to get the crick out. "I'm not sure I can guess right now."

"Um."

I looked at her.

"It's weird." She paused. "You have weird dreams. You were throwing out all your cooking knives, and most of the silverware. Plus a hunting knife. I didn't think you owned knives. If you do, I should be there when you throw them out in case it comes up later."

"You saw my dream?" I asked, still fuzzy. I vaguely remembered something about knives, and being afraid. "You're right, I don't own anything like that."

She was uncomfortable. "I don't like seeing your dreams. You told me the Link was fading."

"It's fading!" I barked automatically. Then took a breath. "Listen, let's walk upstairs and to the car. I'm exhausted. And if you're getting the damn dreams, you're getting the exhaustion too." I stood. "Actually you should be. Why aren't you sleepy too?"

"Years and years of migraines teach you a lot about powering through." She opened the door and walked. I followed her, heavy stack of papers I still hadn't read in hand.

The hallway was dimmed, nighttime lights only, no suspects in sight, all rooms dimmed. I wondered if the night shift of interrogators (already light) had been cut completely during the latest budget round. I wondered why I didn't know already. I should know these things.

She pressed the button for the ancient elevator, then turned around. "Are you okay?" she demanded, but there was concern there too. "The knives thing wasn't . . . wasn't some Freudian thing, was it?"

That made me laugh. "Um, no. Even-odds it was just a dream." I didn't want to tell her about the Guild thing, not before I told Paulsen.

She was uncomfortable again. "How come I don't see the dreams at night?"

I turned, and realized all at once how very, very close we were. I had to take a step back and recite multiplication tables to prevent my body from reacting.

"What's wrong with you?" she asked.

The elevator arrived and I moved all the way to the back of it. I could still smell her perfume. I could still want . . .

"Nothing's wrong," I said. "I'm just tired. I'm just tired and stressed and not tracking well. Probably it was just a dream. If it's not . . ." Meyers had thrown out his knives, my brain reminded me.

"If it's not?" she asked.

"If it's not, it's either a bleed-over from Mindspace in the interrogation rooms, though I've never had that happen, or a vision, or my brain processing. It's a dream, damn it, Cherabino. They're not supposed to be analyzed."

"We need to avoid knives for a while?"

"I don't know," I said. "I don't know. I really don't." I changed the subject. "How's Jacob?" She liked it when I asked about her family, and since I'd helped her identify him as a telepath/teleporter and get him private training, I had an interest. He was a nice kid, even with the health issues that held him back.

"He's doing okay," Cherabino said. She pulled out a little billfold and handed me a picture, only slightly creased from wear. "She had new pictures made."

A boy about ten—though very small for his age—looked out at me with a gap-toothed smile that reminded me of Cherabino's sister. The dark, thick hair he had was all Cherabino, though. "He's gained a little weight," I said happily. His serious autoimmune digestive disorder made that difficult, and the last time I'd seen him he was practically skin and bones. Now the hollows in his cheeks were almost gone.

"My sister has him on a new diet from the doctor and he's actually getting most of it down. His body seems to crave the calories," Cherabino said. She was pleased; that was an unexpected result. *Thanks for arranging for that Irish teacher. He's made all the difference, and my sister is thrilled to have him home.*

Teleportation burns a lot of calories, I said. I hadn't heard of it improving digestion, but it wasn't like I'd met many kids like Jacob. *You still need to be vigilant,* I said. *We don't know how he's going to react long-term. The Guild will force him into the boarding school if they discover him.*

I know, she said, and the cheerful moment was over.

We walked through the main floor, the secretaries' desks empty, the cops' desks and Booking full. The reception area (mostly two chairs and a ring of plants) had an odd clump of teenagers splattered with something that looked disgusting . . . and oddly, as we passed, smelled like creamed corn. I was paying so much attention to them that I nearly missed it as a man I knew opened the door and walked in.

Cherabino stopped, moving away from the teenagers. "Special Agent George Ruffins," she said. "I thought you weren't coming to the office until tomorrow, for the task force meeting."

"Something's come up," Ruffins said, following her to the side. He was with the Tech Control Organization, the guy who'd brought all the new evidence against Fiske, and it was no secret that he disliked me. He was dressed in the white-shirt, black-suit getup of a federal officer, jacket over his hand, ID badge clipped to his shirt. On his left wrist was a tattoo like a thick multicolored striped bracelet. With his tattoo technology he could feel when I was reading him with telepathy, so I couldn't do it unless I wanted a lot of negative attention.

He held up a hand. "You're investigating the murder of one of my informants."

"Your informants? Which case?" Cherabino asked.

"Noah Wright. He was Informant Number 3041 in the task force file."

"Oh," Cherabino said. Her mind flashed a picture of a file. "That's a problem."

He looked at her, absolutely no sense of humor. His presence in Mindspace was twitchy, with a low-level buzzing I recognized, but that's all I could get without an active read. He scratched the tattoo on his wrist. "We're going to have to figure out how to coordinate the two cases. We can't let the task force falter over something like this." He looked at me. "Still no patch, I see."

"They still haven't made one up for the police telepaths," I said evenly. I'd been enjoying the anonymity of life without a patch identifying me as the enemy, thanks much. "Still carrying the divining rod, I see."

He felt stressed, though I couldn't tell about what.

"You're setting off the detector like you wouldn't believe. It's distracting. If you'd let the detective and I talk for a minute . . ."

I looked at Cherabino. *This okay?*

I'm afraid so, she said with a mental sigh. *If Wright is connected with the Fiske case, well . . . we're going to have to figure out how we want to handle things, and quickly.* She added: *I don't need to tell you to keep the Fiske timeline to yourself, do I?*

I can keep a secret. You know that.

"Give us a minute?" she said out loud.

"I was just leaving anyway," I said, a bit worried. "Good to see you again, Agent Ruffins." It wasn't, but it was the standard greeting.

Ruffins watched me all the way out the door, and I piggybacked on the Link with Cherabino long enough to make sure she was okay before I got out of easy range. I could "listen in" on her through the Link at any time, but it became more work as we were farther apart, the noise of the universe adding up between us. Cherabino liked this effect, as it gave her her much-lauded mental privacy. I hated it because trading too much on the Link despite the distance strengthened it, like pairing two particles in a quantum state. And I'd promised I'd let her go eventually.

The wind blew, cutting through all my layers of clothing, and I shivered again. At least my hands were warm.

Swartz met me at the coffee bar, already in our usual booth when I walked in. A cane leaned against the booth next to him, a dark, inlaid-wood antique I'd bought for him a few

weeks ago. I'd said it was to give him something interesting to lug around and whap people with, but the truth was,
I hadn't been able to stand the look of the geriatric five-
footed white formed-resin cane he'd been carrying before.
It made him look weak, and old.

Just a few weeks before, he'd been knocked to the ground
by a heart attack, and every time I saw him face-to-face, it
hit me again. He looked frail, like he'd aged ten years in a
few months. The doctors said he was lucky, lucky to be
alive, lucky to be recovering so quickly, lucky not to have
had the brain damage they'd been expecting. But he hadn't
been lucky. He hadn't been a candidate for an artificial
heart. He had been a hairbreadth from dying. And you
could still see it on his face.

So I'd traded everything I'd ever earned and more
besides—incurring a debt to the people I hated most, the
Guild, to arrange for him to be treated by a Guild medic
who could repair the heart with microkinesis. It wasn't perfect; he was frail, and would likely be frail forever now, but
he was alive. I'd do what they asked to pay that debt,
because I'd said so. Because they'd saved Swartz's life and
I owed them for it.

"You're late," Swartz said, just barely loud enough to be
heard.

"Three minutes," I said, and scanned the faces of the
other people there just in case. All the time with the cops
had rubbed off on me, sure, but what really made me check
a room before I entered was the months I'd spent with no
telepathy at all. I'd temporarily burned out my Ability and
I'd been a normal like everyone else, and even now it was
hard to break that instinctive feeling of wariness.

I stopped by the bar to pick up our drinks. The bartender,
a burly man with a faded navy tattoo and a beard, looked up
from an antique paperback labeled TOM SAWYER, to point

to a metal tray a few feet to his left. The thing was stained from years of use, but if you looked closely, you saw it was scrupulously clean. On top was an ugly ceramic pot and two uglier cups.

"Decaf?" I asked.

He nodded. "Licorice is a little stronger to make up."

"Thanks." I set my papers on one side of the tray, rearranging so everything else was on the other side. Sad part was, it balanced. The papers were that thick. I picked up the tray and bused it to our table.

Bartender was getting lazy, but what did I care? I set the tray down, its metal edges scraping the old wooden table, the scrapes adding to generations of others. Then I started pouring the dark licorice coffee.

"Three things," Swartz said. Every week for the last— well, forever—he'd asked me to come up with three things I was grateful for.

"The smell of late fall in the air. Peanut brittle soy-chocolate muffins. And gloves—Cherabino gave me gloves. Good gloves. Maybe too good gloves." My voice had gotten soft on the last. I straightened, and busied myself arranging things and finishing up the coffee.

Swartz looked at me. Just looked. "They're gloves. I'm a little out of touch with the current market, but I don't imagine they're worth much of your particular brand of poison."

I shrugged, pretending it didn't matter.

"Why did she give you gloves?" Swartz asked me as I scooted into the old leather booth, its surface cracking audibly. A homey sound.

I sipped the coffee. Hot, and the fragrant licorice stung my sinuses and filled up my head. I coughed, a little. Too much would be unmanly. "Ahem. For my birthday."

"Ah," he said. "That is about now, isn't it?"

I looked up, expecting him to have a little package wrapped in recycled paper waiting for me. Instead he just looked embarrassed.

He'd forgotten. He'd forgotten? Swartz had forgotten my birthday?

He rubbed at his chest absently. The coffee sat untouched in front of him. He looked pale and tired. His thoughts were slow, limping along without any force behind them.

In an effort gargantuan in its selflessness, I forced myself to think about him. It hadn't been that long ago he'd had major heart surgery. He probably didn't even remember what week it was, or what month. He was in pain. There were reasons he'd forgotten my birthday. Real reasons. And he'd shown up late at night for me anyway. There was no need to be an ass.

"Adam, I'm sorry—"

"It's fine. Really. I was going to ask, how's the breathing?"

He blinked, thought, concern floating over his brain, and finally settled. He took the out. "Better. Doctor says it's a good thing I quit smoking. Saved my life. Still can't make it up the stairs without a rest break." He made a face. "But at least it's only one now."

"I'm glad you're feeling better." The smoking hadn't had a lot to do with it, of course, but I hadn't told him, and his wife likely didn't have the words. "Any news as to when you can go back to teaching?"

"I've got to manage to stay awake the whole day first," Swartz said. "It's not going to be this semester." He looked down at the coffee, still untouched.

I caught the edge of the information-thought: doctor said he couldn't have caffeine. He wanted the licorice, but his chest still hurt too much to be stupid about something like that.

"It's decaf," I said.

"I still can't—"

"It's fine. I'll get you an herbal tea." I stood up and went over to the bar, angry with myself. I should have remembered. I should have! But nothing was normal anymore. Nothing. Damn it.

I returned with a stupid cinnamon apple thing in a tall floral china cup, and set it gently in front of his side of the table. Thing would break if I looked at it wrong.

"I'm not an invalid!" he barked at me, and coughed.

"And I'm not usually an idiot. Drink the tea."

He stared me down and finally took a sip.

"Time for us to do our reading yet?" I asked, twitchy, not sure what to do. Usually he was a lot more in charge. Usually he would be making me feel better.

He swallowed and set the china cup down gingerly. "She gave you gloves, you said? Does she usually give you a birthday present?"

"Well, no." I frowned at him. I wanted to talk about missing the meeting earlier in the week. I wanted him to pull the situation with the Guild out of me. Instead he was harping about gloves? I was trying not to think about the gloves. Or overthink the gloves.

"What do you think the change in behavior means?" he asked carefully.

"I don't know," I said quickly.

"Ah," he said.

"No, really, I don't know, not for sure. And anyway, you were the one who told me I couldn't have a relationship until I could keep a plant alive." I had another four bioluminescent plants on my windowsill at the apartment this week, two of which were clearly dying. I had high hopes for the fourth one, which was only a little droopy.

"Maybe I was wrong about that," Swartz said.

And the world tilted on its axis. "Wh-wh-what?"

He looked at the stupid china cup pensively. "I've been thinking a lot about life, since I almost lost mine. I don't know what I would have done without Selah. Not just because she was there, all the time, in the hospital, at home. But when it was me on that floor with doom barreling in on me, when it all went to hell, I thought I had to get through this for Selah. I couldn't leave her alone. I'm not afraid of death, you know that. God and I are on good terms. But I fought—and fought hard—to stay with her. I'm still fighting."

He looked up. "You need a reason to fight, kid."

"I have reasons to fight. A lot of them. We go through this every year." I squashed down the unrealistic hope. He'd been through a lot. It was completely understandable he wanted to talk about it. "Cherabino's great, she is, but—"

"You're in love with her," Swartz said flatly.

I stared. He'd never . . . "So what if I am? I'm a work in progress. 'Adding another person to that mix is just making it harder to put the pieces together and might do more harm than good.' That's a direct quote from you."

"Ask her out," Swartz said. "This isn't some random person off the street—it's your partner. You've worked with her for years. She's seen you at your worst."

A huge black hole of possibility settled into my soul at that moment, me bracing myself against the gravitational pull of this idea . . . this thing. I wouldn't be able to resist it forever, and I already had the Guild and Clark to deal with. "Swartz, if this is a test . . ."

"It's not," he said flatly. "Worse comes to worst, she says no, and you end up right back here where you are. Best case, she says yes. You get a chance to answer some questions you've had for a long time."

"What if it . . ." I trailed off. He didn't have to tell me. We'd talked about the thing with Kara enough. Despite her betrayal, the pang of seeing her married and all the anger I still carried about it sometimes, I wouldn't go back and undo the time we'd spent together. I couldn't see me feeling any different about Cherabino.

"There's no sense staring at the problem," Swartz said. "Your brain's an enemy in this case. Ask her. This week. I'll expect a full report at our next meeting." He rubbed his chest, absently, and leaned forward with the help of a hand on the table. "Now, let's do the reading before Selah comes back to fuss at me for being out too long."

With everything in the whole world different in the space of a few minutes, I nodded like a puppet and pulled out the Big Book without question. Reading about other people's experiences with alcohol and drug recovery might help. It might not, not today. But it was something we did.

Swartz dropped me off at the apartment, and I climbed the stairs, exhausted. I still checked Mindspace and my own senses before I opened the door; I'd had too many unexpected visitors in the last few months.

Seemed clean, although I had a message light on the answering machine. I pressed the button.

"Hi, Adam, it's Kara," it began. "I'm so glad you got out okay. I didn't mean to—"

I hit ERASE.

CHAPTER 9

Feeling like an idiot, I put on a hat and sunglasses and a coat against the weather and found my way to Freedom Park via the MARTA station nearby. This time of year, in mid-November, the bone-deep chill had settled into the wind, and even the tree line, trunks twisted waist-high from the Tech Wars, couldn't shield me from it completely. Seemed awfully early to be out in this kind of cold, especially on a Saturday.

I settled down into a park bench designed to look like a smoothly curving shell of some kind; it was surprisingly comfortable, if a little cold and covered in graffiti. The arch fit my back nicely.

Around me, flat grass was dotted by the occasional line of trees and stones, some landscaper's idea of "natural" surroundings. A running path led out to the left, a bank to the right separating the park from the edges of Freedom Parkway, a mammoth concrete-set road that rivaled the nearby Interstate 75/85 for sheer weight. Flyers darted in their lanes above the parkway, but the area in grass and stone around me was empty. Completely empty; it was too cold for casual park-going.

In front of me, the Tech Wars Memorial stood, a large twisting sculpture made out of ceramic and metal, with water flowing in smooth arcs around a flat panel, the water manipulated via antigravity fields into impossible shapes. That central panel, cradled in the curves of the water, the ceramic, and the metal, held all the names of those in metro Atlanta who'd died during the initial days of the Tech Wars, as a direct result of the actions of a madman. The ones who'd crashed when their automatic cars failed. The ones who'd starved to death or suffocated in their smart homes. The ones whose brains were eaten by viruses gone blood-borne. And the ones killed in bombs set off from military computers without their owners' knowledge or okay.

There were similar memorials in every major city left in North America, with lists of names as long as this one.

The names were just barely large enough to read from a few feet. There were four columns on the display on both sides, four columns more than five feet tall. It sobered you, to see such a list. Made you think your own problems were small, even if you didn't have anyone you could talk to about them.

I settled back and watched the spiraling waterfalls as they moved through the sculpture. Time passed. I put my rapidly chilling hands in my coat pockets—and they hit the gloves. I smiled without meaning to and pulled them on.

A mind neared, focused on me in particular and I looked up. The human mind was hardwired to detect that kind of focus, which was why even normals noticed you staring at them. A survival mechanism. In the case of telepaths, survival was not a theoretical concept.

I stood. "Edgar Stone."

He stood, gruffly, hands in the pockets of his antique leather jacket, a faux-fur hat covering most of his head. "Adam Ward."

"Please, sit," I said, gesturing at the park bench.

He shook his head. "I'll stand, thanks." Too cold, his

mind leaked. Didn't want a chilled seat on top of chilled fingers.

"I'm getting quite a few stray thoughts from you," I said politely.

His face went blank, and I suddenly couldn't see anything in Mindspace but a heavy, shiny mirror. "I am not a student. Watch yourself."

Crap, offending him was not my intention.

"What was it you invited me here for in the first place?" I asked.

"Apparently you pulled quite a privacy violation the other day."

"That was exaggerated," I said.

"Maybe."

Was I leaking? I checked my shields again. No, still locked up tight, without even the Guild-standard public space.

"I expect you to conform to the highest standards of ethics during our investigation," Stone said. "I'd be a lot happier with your police partner, to be honest."

"I appreciate the vote of confidence."

"Unfortunately I was overruled. It's felt that if you step out of line, the Guild still has the right to kill you. This is very comforting to some."

"Nelson, I take it." I added in subtext that Kara suspected him.

Stone shrugged. "Be that as it may, you were expelled for improper behavior and massive betrayal of the Guild's ideals. There are some who would rather not see you back."

"I've never liked the way they put that. It was a drug habit, not sexual misconduct."

"Doesn't matter."

"It matters to me!" I took a breath. He was deliberately being difficult. "Listen, I just—"

"You've been assigned to go into the middle of an Enforcement investigation, with a full madness lockdown, and screw with vital evidence—including people's memories and mental states, directly or indirectly—in the middle of a Guild you now have no part of. Having just proven your ethics have slipped in the last few years. I am concerned."

"Sure, my ethics have slipped when it comes to self-defense," I said. "I fight dirty. I do what it takes to survive. If that's going to bother your high-and-mighty ethics, then—"

"You saw it as self-defense?" he interrupted. "The privacy violation."

"He was manhandling me at the time," I said.

"That's not how he tells it, and Kara's testimony has been declared invalid."

"Why the hell? Kara's a levelheaded bureaucrat. Wait. Did she speak for me?"

"She's also the grieving survivor of a controversial death that's being quarantined as a public health issue," Stone said. "And she hasn't been the most levelheaded lady lately. Calling you is a perfect example. It's believed she may have been contaminated. She's under house arrest. And yeah, she spoke up for you loud and clear. Almost obsessively so."

I was surprised, and oddly pleased, that she'd spoken for me. Even so, I said, "Did you call me out here in the cold to insult me? A hell of a way to start a working relationship."

A pause, during which I watched the gravity-assisted water float around its tracks.

"Here's the thing," Stone said. "The Guild is a political tangle right now. We have major factions fighting for control of the future course of the organization, and none of them are playing nice."

"I'm listening."

"Rex is trying to use you as a pawn," Stone said flatly. "And the ethical violation . . . I need to know you're not some kind of hired spy working for Guild First or one of the families. Especially with the kind of madness potentially in play."

"What kind of madness? What kinds are there?"

"I need to know you're not some hired spy."

I laughed. "A spy? Really? That's ridiculous. I'm here ultimately because Kara called me. Yeah, I have a debt to pay, and yeah, half the world is threatening me to get me here, but so what? I do, actually, believe in innocent until proven guilty. Let's find out what happened."

He looked at me for a long moment, and then nodded. "And the ethics?"

"I've been working in the interview rooms long enough to believe that people will tell you what they're thinking eventually with words and body language without you doing a thing. Will I go rummaging around in heads willy-nilly? I'm not planning to. Why, will you?"

"Now you're insulting me."

I shivered as a particularly cold gust of wind blew some of the fountain water at me. "Let's call it even. What kind of madness are we talking about here? I need to know what I'm getting into." And how likely it was I was going to end up in Mental Health, or down in that cell again.

You really believe in innocent until proven guilty? Subtext he sent along with the words implied a provincial point of view. A naive lie the normals told themselves, not how the world worked.

I do, actually, I sent back, along with the overtones you only got with a deep-held truth. *Evidence and innocent until proven guilty.*

You've worked for the normals too long, he sent, with a slight overtone of dark amusement, *but that does, actually, make you neutral. I can work with that.*

"The madness," I prompted.

"Fine," he said. "They're thinking it's another North Rim."

I waited.

He said nothing.

"What's North Rim?" I asked.

"You don't know about North Rim? North Rim, Arizona. Twenty-five years after the end of the Tech Wars. The Guild researcher enclave."

I racked my brain for ancient school lessons. "You mean the people who researched Ability? The second generation? Went off into the desert and figured out training and mind structure and such."

"That's the one."

"Could we move this along?" I asked. "I'm freezing my balls off out here. And I need to know."

"There's no reason to teach schoolchildren about how North Rim ended. At least there wasn't."

"Okay?"

"For the first few years, they were effective. Their disciplines kept getting results and showing us how to better train, how to improve, how to do practically everything with the mind that we know today. Individuals came and went from that commune over a decade, out there in the desert. But then they found a new technique that destroyed the mind's natural barrier to madness, or they ran into something that amplified their deepest fears and used it against them, or they uncovered a deep mental flaw in the new recruits in the worst way possible. Nobody knows. Whatever happened, someone came down with the first recorded case of madness, a new kind of madness. And then it started spreading. Out of a commune of twenty-eight people, all but three died. One of those was the park ranger at the canyon visitor center. She holed herself up in the station and didn't leave. But the other two made it halfway to Vegas and infected over a hundred fifty other people before they shut it down."

I processed that. "How did they shut it down?"

"They killed anyone infected. Dead. And quarantined anyone who'd come in contact with them until they showed symptoms. The St. George town sheriff remembered the Tech Wars, was a stubborn old bastard, and he pulled the trigger nearly every single time himself. He stopped it, with brute force. After five rounds of contagion."

"Five?" I asked, and laughed. "Ludicrous. The odds of anyone infecting another telepath, much less a normal, at more than one remove are tiny. Tiny. It's the foundation of all the mental health procedures at the Guild."

"With everything except this. The madness spread from person to person in a chain. Quick. It didn't take repeated exposure, and some of the normals were affected too, mind-to-mind, though they couldn't spread it. Violence came with the illness, homicide and suicide both. Nobody knows what it was. We've never seen anything like it. They still wonder what would have happened if that sheriff hadn't stopped it at the end of a gun."

Suddenly it seemed a lot colder out here. "No cure, then?"

"None that we know of."

"Okay. Why—why do you think it's not a regular kind of mental health transmission right now?" I asked. "Normal person-to-person influence and power of suggestion? The Guild's notorious for spreading power of suggestion throughout the population. Isn't that more likely?"

"We don't know anything yet. And no matter what the politicians say, Nelson isn't going to let executions start until we're sure. If it wasn't for the outbreak in Antarctica eight years ago, we wouldn't even be—"

"What?" I asked. "When was this?"

He looked at me. "That's right, you weren't with the Guild then. They managed to keep it quiet from the normals. Fifty-seven deaths, the last fourteen from a ship docked on the last day. There was only one survivor, a low-level telepath, and he killed all fourteen before killing himself. They say it's spread by deep mind-to-mind, anything past the public space."

"Oh," I said. "Oh. That's why the hullabaloo about the 'privacy violation.'"

"Yes. It's a Guild First policy, but there's a reason for it. Most of the Guild has adopted it wholeheartedly." He looked around, then sent me a picture of the official Guild aircar, over the ridge. "We should get back."

"Are they really calling for executions?" I asked suddenly.

"It's not innocent until proven guilty at the Guild," Stone said quietly. "It's truth, and whatever is good for the majority."

"As defined by those in power," I said.

"As defined by Enforcement, largely, me and my fellows," Stone said. "There's a reason we're separate from the rest of the Guild power structure."

He started walking, and I followed.

I was cynical about the Guild's system, all too cynical. It bothered me that Stone—a decent guy, from what I could see—could buy in to it so easily. Innocent until proven guilty and evidence really did matter. The Guild's way assigned blame quickly, then mind-scanned to determine if they were correct. Some of those reads were so clumsy that the suspects were lucky to get off with a two-day migraine. Sometimes they'd been known to lose memories, or have a personality shift for weeks or months or permanently. Damage was routinely done by Enforcement, if needed to find out a truth you were hiding from them or from yourself. I liked trials, I liked innocent until proven guilty, even if the result was less certain. But I also liked walking around without someone else's madness in my head.

"You realize that we expect excellent work in exchange for a payment on your debt," Stone said conversationally.

In other words, he reminded me who held my leash. "I do good work," I said.

Stone parked in the member-only garage on the back side of the Guild's main skyscraper. Two other buildings towered to our left, with the lower garden area jutting out of the tallest one halfway up. The garage, which should have been half-empty and buzzing with people going to and fro (in the present and in Mindspace), was strangely empty of all emotion.

The member entrance was a double set of doors down the hall, in sight of the atrium but not within in. There had always been a camera there, to track who came in and out of the Guild. The camera was still there, with two new ones I assumed recorded at different frequencies. The Guild had never had the hang-ups about recording the normals did, but this seemed excessive.

Ahead were four security guards, extended rope barriers funneling us straight ahead to them, and to the large machine behind them. It was a long, multiple-textured arch in shape, with flashing lights and strange matte panels above a low chair with a headrest and what looked like automatic restraints, currently deactivated. The dark-colored chair was inset with shiny metal circles along the back and in the headrest, circles that looked similar to the monitoring devices the Guild used to screen schoolchildren for Ability.

"What is this?" I asked, wary.

The first guard said, in a low, bored voice, "It's for your own protection."

Sure. And being locked up or destroyed—according to Stone, the only recourses—was for the Guild's protection, not mine.

"No, thanks," I said. "How about I keep my mind to myself and we'll call it even?"

Stone held up his Enforcement badge. "We don't have time for this. Give me the form and we'll move through."

"It's for everyone now. New rules, new lockdown. Sorry." He didn't look very sorry.

"Fine," Stone said gruffly. He sat in the chair.

A low buzzing came from the machine as one of the guards powered it up. Then a sense of wrenching pressure and an Escher-like impossible bubbling and twisting of space—and then it was over. The red lights on the arch turned to green. Stone let out a small pain sound.

Now with sweat dripping down his face, he stood, wobbly. He rebuilt his former stoicism, then walked to the wall to wait for me.

I thought about leaving then, about turning all the way around and getting out of Dodge. Kara could fend for herself. I didn't need extra trouble in my life; I had plenty with the police. I needed to stay on the wagon and stay healthy.

"If you want to test the Guild's threats concerning failure, turn right around," Stone said. "Otherwise move."

"Just so you know I'm not happy about it." I walked up to the Throne of Frightening Lights and sat.

A guard hit a few buttons on the side of the arch, then that sound as it powered up.

Pain—unimaginable pain—as someone put my mind through an invisible blender. Razor blades pulled apart every shred of me from every other—

And then it was over. Utterly, completely over. My entire being rang with the sudden silence.

The guard in front of the arch pulled his eyebrows

together in a worrisome look. "No madness, but you're not exactly a—"

"Does he pass or not?" Stone asked.

"He passes."

I staggered to my feet, unwilling to be in this horrible chair any longer than necessary. I pushed off and duck-stepped away, to the far wall. I stood against it, breathing, trying to recover.

One guard laughed to the other. I suppressed the urge to throw that pain at them. I had things to do today. I couldn't be in that cell again, not now.

Obviously it had been far, far too long since I'd been through pain desensitization at the Guild. But even when I'd done that, even when I'd been there, it wasn't like this. We hadn't had our minds shredded for no more than a test. We'd been treated with respect, not like cattle in a line. Even if the threat was imminent, there was something about the whole thing that left a bitter taste in my mouth.

I didn't feel like holding out my mind for the cattle prod again, and if the rank-and-file Guild members were used to it, well, that didn't make it right.

The guards gave us a yellow flag to pin to our badges, a flag that said we'd been cleared this day, and we moved on.

"You seem out of sorts," Stone told me as I trotted after him. Enforcement had their own floors set into the basements of the professional building—far more basements than I'd known about previously. We were traveling to the third-level underground, something that required a special elevator and a flat rectangular key that fluoresced in the light. Tech, I was betting, even if only the lightest possible touch of living circuits and bioluminescence.

"I don't like all the security," I said. "I don't like having my mind shredded when I haven't even been exposed yet."

He turned around. "It's necessary. If we have another North Rim on our hands, it will get worse before it gets better."

"Even so, all you have so far is a suicide and a madness report, I assume in the usual fashion. It doesn't add up to anything this frightening yet." Did it? Was I just lying to myself to avoid facing the real danger I was under?

"Over a hundred people have checked themselves into Mental Health, some with third-degree exposure. It's a problem, Ward. A much bigger problem than you realize."

The elevator *ding*ed and the doors opened. The hallway was dimly lit, long, with a tiled floor and doors on both sides spaced widely apart. Straight ahead was a set of double doors with small windows that leaked light onto the patterned tile.

"We need to go. I don't know how much longer we can hold the body, so that's our first step." He strode toward the doors.

I followed, pulling myself in a little in Mindspace. The surroundings were rather grim, but I smelled a faint lemon scented cleaner, which helped. "Where to after that?" I said. "I'll need to talk to whoever reported Meyers as mad in the first place, and the last person to see him alive."

"The last person to see him alive was Enforcement leader Tobias Nelson," Stone said. "He, of course, is above reproach, and has interviewed with me to my satisfaction." His mind added a full stop to that thought, and an unwillingness to discuss this truth any further. Stone pushed through a double set of doorways at the end of the hallway, and they swung, loudly.

On the other side was a plain room with rows of metal tables and easy-to-clean tile on both the floor and the walls. It looked like the morgue in DeKalb County except for the charts (Guild reading charts in blues and yellows) and the lack of buzzing in Mindspace. In the morgue, they used quantum status drawers to keep the corpses from deteriorating; here, of course, the way they affected Mindspace would be a constant low buzzing, which might change a measurement significantly.

The room was smaller than I was used to, and cold. Very cold.

There were two minds in the room, a bright, cheerful skittery-kinetic mind belonging to a short plain woman near the far table, and a deeper mind like a French horn playing into the darkness, stronger and subtler and more tinged with pain than the woman's mind. He was closer to the doorway, and looked up when we entered.

He was a large man, late forties, muscled like someone who expected to fight on the front lines, with a haircut just as short. His eyes were odd, red with white striations, a central black pupil staring at us as he blinked too often. A network of fine scars encompassed his eye sockets, cutting through one of his eyebrows and halfway down a cheek; whatever had happened to him to require the artificial eyes had clearly been traumatic.

Stone had already moved forward to greet the man, and they were engaged in a conversation.

"This is Adam Ward," he said.

"Nice to meet you," I replied, making sure my mind reflected that and only that. I did the strong nod of greeting. "I'm sorry. I didn't catch your name."

"Ruthgar," the man said, in a voice like an ancient smoker's. "I'm the necrokinetic on duty today. Sandra over there is my assistant. She's micro, but remarkably talented."

She waved hi from across the room, where she was currently pulling out one of the drawers to release a body onto the stretcher.

"Nice to meet you," I said.

Not here to be social, Stone's mental voice told me again.

"Necrokinetics?" I asked.

Ruthgar smiled, a disturbing sight, although the mind behind it was genuinely pleased. "It's a quiet specialty," he said. "Not common, and we don't get a lot of press. Necrokinetics specialize in dead tissue. We determine cause of death, as the MEs do in the civilian world, but we also deal with necrotic tissue or near-death patients. I was particularly good with isolating the effects of chemical weapons in soldiers; our unit had half the death rate as the average in Brazil during that period, although of course the injury rate was similar."

"Of course," I said, for lack of any other clue what to say.

"Well, you didn't come here to listen to war stories. Shall we talk about what I found?" he asked.

I frowned, uncomfortable.

"Let's see what there is to see," Stone said.

With the help of a small antigravity plate in the bottom of the stretcher, Sandra had moved the body to the table. Well, it was "the body" until I moved closer; Meyers had always had a large birthmark, a red-purple splotch down the side of his neck, and seeing that now was like a calling card. Like a distinctive tattoo or a signed letter reminding me of who I was looking at. Seeing his face screwed up in what was obviously horrible pain was disturbing.

He'd deserved better than this, even if he had been crazy. He'd deserved care and help, not this ridiculous panic reaction from those around him.

Cherabino's words about looking at the floor if it got too much, words that she'd said the first time she took me to the morgue in DeKalb, came back to me then. I fought through it, sitting on the emotion hard. It had been a long, long time, and it could as easily have been me on that slab.

"You knew him," Ruthgar said to me, quietly.

I stared him in the eye. "It was a long time ago."

"I hadn't realized." He went over to the front of the table, by Meyers's head, and placed his hands on his face. A dull crawling sensation moved through Mindspace like a half-heard song.

"You don't—" Stone started.

"It's done," Ruthgar said, still blinking too often. He stepped away.

The seized look of intense pain had disappeared from Meyers's face, to be replaced by a look of peace, of sleep.

"Thank you," I said, amazed. Even the best micro guy I'd ever met would have taken a lot longer to accomplish anything like that. And the skill with which he'd done it . . . Necros apparently were in a league of their own.

He blinked five or six times in a row. "It would have been done eventually anyway, for the funeral. Most investigators prefer to see the original circumstances first, and the Chenoa family has been very insistent that investigators be given full access." He blinked again and moved away.

I noticed then that Meyers didn't have a Y-cut; whatever they had done to determine cause of death hadn't used knives. He was naked, of course, but that was the same in the police system.

Sometimes I wished that emotion and thoughts clung to a person's body after death, not just the scene around him or her. But times like this, I didn't. The emptiness of the room was comforting. There were no surprises here, just the sad waste of a good man whose life was over.

Sandra lifted up Meyers's right hand in her gloved ones, angling it so we could see the palm. "You'll notice the entry point for the electrical arc was here." A dark burn pattern covered most of the hand, moving up partially toward the wrist. Even two feet away, days after the fact, I could smell the burning flesh. My stomach roiled.

Ruthgar moved around me toward the feet. "Exit burn on the right heel, as the electricity left the body along the metal ironing board feet. Enough amps moved through the tissue to cook it, ensuring death in at least four ways, but the heart stopped likely in the first few seconds of contact. That's what I'm calling the mechanism of death in this case, for the sake of simplicity. It wasn't pretty, but it was quick.

"My sympathies for your loss," he told me.

"I didn't know him that well," I said, looking at the burns again, overwhelmed with a sense of senseless waste. But now I was thinking too. Something Cherabino had said once about a case nagged at me. "Doesn't household electricity not usually leave a mark? Or a really small one? I remember the police having trouble identifying cause of death in one of these cases. This looks obvious—maybe too obvious?"

Ruthgar blinked twice.

Sandra said, "This was household power?"

"The electricity was being pulled from the shielding system, not the household outlet," Stone said.

"Is that normal?" I asked.

"No."

"Shall I leave you two to discuss the case?" Ruthgar asked.

"We're leaving now," Stone said.

Sandra pulled a sheet up to cover Meyers's face. It wrenched me then, all over again. Of the two of us, the one who should be on that slab was me; I'd done the risky drug behavior, lived on the street, dealt with the dangerous people. He'd worked his way up to Council. Been a decent guy. Done the right things.

He'd even thrown out his knives. Who died after throwing

out their knives? Even if he was crazy, that told me he was actively avoiding violence. Considering what had happened at North Rim, it made me respect him more. He'd been avoiding violence, not embracing it.

And now he was dead.

Outside the morgue, I asked Stone, "Why was the electricity being pulled from the shielding system? I mean, it's an iron."

"I've already set up an interview with the woman who reported Meyers as disturbed," Stone said. "We can go talk about the electricity and the expert's findings afterward."

"I'd like to do that now."

"We're doing it afterward."

I paused, in the low light of the hallway. "Fine."

"Fine."

CHAPTER 10

"You realize it's not efficient to have the interview rooms in a separate building from the Enforcement offices," I told Stone once we'd crossed the chilly covered walkway back to the main spine of the Guild's living quarters.

"The Sinclair Building has better shielding throughout because of anyonide fields in the living quarters stacked together," Stone said. "The fields are built into the building, so it's cheaper and easier to extend that system into its basements than to build a completely different system at twice the energy cost. Efficiency of time is not the only consideration."

"And the shielding takes a considerable amount of power, I take it?" I was still thinking about the too-visible, severe burns on Meyers's body. "How much power?"

"I have no idea. Orders of magnitude more than the household electrical system. The Guild has to contract with the city for special power grants. It adds up. That's why most of the shielding is in this building. Easier to circulate the power than separate it."

I waited, but he said nothing else. "How do you keep the electrical systems separate?" I finally prompted.

"I'm not an electrical engineer, Adam. It's a custom design. They inspect twice a quarter."

"When was the last inspection of Meyers's apartment?"

"About three weeks ago." He'd looked it up, his mind supplied. They had given the apartment a clean bill of health.

I waited. "Well, isn't that a short amount of time for a short or whatever to develop?"

Stone nodded, reluctant for some reason. "That was the first reason I classified this one as nonaccidental. The second . . ."

"What?"

"The second was the madness report. We're going to see the woman who made it now."

"Okay." I noticed all over again how empty the halls were. Even the main elevator shaft, the open air extending into the endless levels circled above, felt empty. I didn't see a single person outside his room, even in the far-high floors. "They've really got the Guild shut down, don't they?"

"Essential personnel and prescheduled events only," Stone said. "If it weren't for the Eleventh Hour testing today, the school would be on total lockdown as well." Final testing for advanced Guild students took weeks to schedule and prepare for, and wouldn't be easily moved. It was a good sign that they were continuing with it for now.

"Let's say I believe we're dealing with a full-blown madness situation. Are all these steps even enough?" I asked. "I mean, you don't even know how it spread in the first place. Seems dumb to scare people if you can't do anything about it."

"Assuming the team is right, and it spreads only via repeated deep-mind contact, this should be more than sufficient to prevent an outbreak," Stone said. His mind, usually so disciplined, let leak a thin trail of worry. They didn't understand what this was. They didn't understand how it transmitted. And waterborne or airborne illness was a trouble of an entirely different level. The Guild wasn't set up to process either. Everything they were doing was just a hope, just a prayer, against this fear.

"I hope you're right," I said, but my mind was still dubious and I didn't work too hard to hide the fact.

"It has to be enough," he said, and I got that leak of fear and a picture of a boy's face, a kid about ten years old, and a woman behind him.

Your family? I asked.

He started. But he had let the thought slip into public space. *Yes,* he said finally. *My family. They live here too. Anything that effects the Guild, that brings the contagion to the Guild as a whole, will affect them as well. With respect to Meyers, he made his choice. This should all have been shut down from the beginning, for the sake of the Guild.* For the sake of his family, his mind added.

His fear bothered me. He was like Paulsen, like Cherabino; I'd seen him face real danger with no more than healthy respect. But when a cop—or an Enforcer—got truly afraid, it was time to run.

And I, like a fool, had agreed to go deeper into the belly of the beast.

I followed Stone through the basement elevators and back onto the floor with the basement-level interview rooms where I'd seen Meyers's ex-wife. Oddly, I felt comforted; the industrially cold small hallway with two empty rooms and a monitoring station reminded me so strongly of the department basement where I spent most of my time. Plus everything was clean, something not true of the department.

"Johanna Wendell is waiting in the first interview room," Stone said. "I'll be monitoring over the video system."

"I'm used to a babysitter by now, Stone. If you want to be in the room, be in the room."

His presence in Mindspace was hardly there, he was shielding so hard. "That would be my preference, yes."

"Fine. Any rules I need to know about?"

"Don't kill her. And try not to rummage around in her mind if you don't have to—Enforcement prefers to have that done by official readers anyway."

I didn't respond. "You have a file on her?"

"Not really," he said. "At least nothing outside official Guild records. You and I don't qualify. Reports go up, not down."

"Fantastic."

I opened the door, and went in, smiling. Stone followed, taking up a seat at the back of the room.

A pretty late-twenties brunette sat at the table, Johanna Wendell. She was thin, with an angular face and an elegance of carriage and the kind of professional office clothes that made me want to take her seriously. Her body language reflected impatience, and disgust, briefly.

Then she brought it under control; her presence in Mindspace flattened out immediately, and she smiled. The smile was perhaps a little fake, but I'd been there.

"Hello," I said.

"Hello," she responded, in a smooth voice. "I was told Enforcement wanted to speak with me?"

"This is about the madness report you submitted last week on Del Meyers," Stone said.

"We want to ask you a few questions," I put in, setting the folders I'd borrowed down on the table. "Would that be all right with you?"

"Of course," Johanna said, and clasped her hands in front of her on the table. "How can I help?" She studied me.

I explained myself as an independent investigator consultant who'd been brought in by Enforcement yesterday.

"Please feel like you can talk to me," I said. "I'm here to find the truth through good old-fashioned evidence, not deep-reads."

"I assume you want to know why I reported Meyers to Mental Health."

I sat. "That would be a great start, yes."

"He was acting very strangely, to begin with." In Mindspace, there was an odd effect when she said that, something I couldn't put my finger on. Her body language changed to more "open" and she seemed sincere. Then: "He had volunteered to help me study for my precognition recurrents, so I saw him rather more frequently than normal these last weeks."

"You're a precog?" I asked.

"Yes. I also have a low-level Four telepathy rating." Just enough to speak with other telepaths if they "spoke" loudly, but not enough to read normals or anyone else weaker.

Something about her felt off . . . felt *wrong*. But I didn't know what.

"Meyers was also a precognitive," she said. "His frequency was rather less than mine, but his visions typically foretold large-scale natural disasters. He'd started in Disaster Response. Originally, I'd thought he could help me turn my gift into something more . . . significant."

"You wanted to increase your accuracy?" I guessed. "Oh, you wanted to be one of the Preferred Futurists. Do they still pay them so much better?"

She nodded. Then she looked down at the table. There was that odd fluctuation in Mindspace again.

"What do you mean by acting strangely? Was he having odd visions?"

"No, nothing like that," she said very quickly and firmly. "No. It was . . . strange. He kept talking about chickens. He paced the hallway over and over. Then he canceled our meetings with no explanation." She moved her head to one side and her body language changed subtly, to a more wistful, closed-off place. "I was concerned. When I asked him about it, he pretended nothing was wrong. When I dropped by, I caught him talking to thin air and he threw a heavy stapler at me. I still have the wound." She touched the side of her head, under the hair, and I got a faint impression of pain, though I could see nothing.

"He threw a stapler at you?" I asked. "Why would he have a stapler at his desk? Isn't that his assistant's job?"

"It was on loan," she said quickly. Then, slower: "He was putting together stacks of paper that didn't make sense. Stapling them four times in the right corner. I didn't understand. But what really worried me . . . ," she went on, and I started to miss things.

I realized then that something about the way she talked, the way she held her head, reminded me strongly of someone I'd known a lifetime ago, on the street. She'd been a sometime drug pusher who turned the occasional trick for money until she'd found out she could convince charities to pay for her room and board with a good sob story. She'd been younger, rounder, and infinitely more cynical than Johanna was here, but there was a definite physical resemblance, especially in the way they moved. The resemblance was jangling at my instincts like a dinner bell pulled by a child, making me see things that might not otherwise be there, making me distrust Johanna.

"Are you listening?" Johanna asked me.

I checked—yes, I'd been shielding hard. The mix-up with Meyers's ex-wife had taught me at least that much. I shielded a little harder and adjusted my body language to project sadness. "Yes," I said. "Go on."

"He complained of being manipulated. He sounded like one of those paranoid people on television. He told me he couldn't trust anybody but me. And then he got angry with me—for absolutely no reason—and wouldn't see me anymore. John—his assistant—was told not to let me come around anymore. It was very hurtful." She paused, looking at me.

Something felt off. But I had to speak anyway. I told myself the lie first, told myself to believe it, then did, as much as possible. "How sad it is that a man in his position would treat you so badly," I said. "He must have indeed been going crazy."

A little anger flashed across Mindspace then, but she pulled it in. "I'm only sorry I didn't report him sooner. Maybe John would still be alive if I had." She put her hands over her face, and breathed. "I can't believe John killed himself. Or Meyers. This is all my fault."

"This is not your fault," I said habitually. If I had a nickel every time I'd said that in the interview rooms, I could be retired in Bora-Bora by now. "Can you tell me anything else about Meyers?"

She pulled her hands down and stared at them. "I'm sorry he's dead," she said. "He was a good guy."

"Were you sleeping with him?" I asked.

"No," she said. "No, nothing like that."

But there was no surprise either in Mindspace or on her face at the question. She was a good liar, but she was hiding something.

Stone glanced over at me, saw that I had nothing, and told her, "You did a good thing by reporting him to Mental Health. It escalated the situation to the proper authorities and it's likely saving lives right now. We may be in and out asking a lot of questions of a lot of people in the next few days. Don't let that stop you from coming forward if you think of anything else."

"I understand," she said. But she looked at me carefully. Probably she wanted to know if I'd guessed about the affair. None of my business either way, I supposed. Made me think less of Meyers, though. I forced a smile and some joviality. "I appreciate you spending the time answering the questions. I have one more."

"Yes?"

"What do you know about the Guild's electrical shielding system?" I asked.

A note of surprise and worry entered the air. "It works by creating a moving electromagnetic field at the right frequency to resonate with Mindspace and prevent mental waves from being propagated across the intersection line of the field because of a modified fractional quantum Hall effect."

It was nearly a word-for-word quote of the Guild's physics and Ability textbook. I was impressed. More impressive was the concepts folding out in her mind as she quoted the words. No dummy, this one.

"Did you kill Del Meyers?" I asked.

"No," she said firmly. I believed her. Just the affair, then, huh?

"That's it?" she asked, after a moment.

"That's it. You have a nice day," Stone said, and held the door until I followed him out. "What was that about?" he asked me in the hall when the doorway shut.

"Collecting information," I said. "Is there a phone here where I can check in with the police?"

"I'll be listening," he said cautiously.

I paused, thought about what I intended to say. "Just don't record, okay?"

He nodded.

Stone showed me a small alcove with a phone in one of the adjoining rooms. He left the door open and settled outside, to give me the illusion but not the actual presence of privacy. I'd have to be careful what I said. I was planning to anyway, seeing as this was the Guild, and the Guild's thoughts about privacy were loose enough to allow random monitoring. But even so.

I dialed Cherabino's office phone. With her working—what, five? six? eight?—cases right now, I had absolutely no doubt she'd be there on a Saturday catching up. Unless there was another murder to have her out in the field.

I wondered what Swartz was thinking when he'd asked me to ask her out. Would that really—

"This is Detective Cherabino," her voice came over the phone.

"It's me," I said.

"If you have the time, I need help on updating murder books," she said. "I'll buy you Mexican. Michael's got a family thing."

"I'm tempted," I said. "Unfortunately I've got a commitment this weekend. But I found some information you might find useful."

"Oh?"

"I got a copy of the information Wright disseminated. Don't ask how I got it."

"I have no intention of asking," Cherabino said. "What is it?"

I caught her up on what little I'd understood from the document I'd partially read, and what Bob had said about the soldier project, only without using his name and while trying to keep all references as vague and unhelpful to the Guild as possible. "I'm thinking the two are linked, but I don't have a lot of information about either to make a decision with. You might talk to somebody over at Electronic Crimes," I said. Oh, what the hell. "Specifically, Bob, if you can."

She sighed. "I've got meetings most of the afternoon for

the task force. We're close, Adam. We're so close to getting that bastard for good, him and half of his whole damn crime organization. The DA just has to sign off on it and we can move, and Ruffins says the TCO can bring in some extra firepower."

"Congrats!" I said. "You've been working on that case for years. It'll be great when it's over."

"How important do you think the file is to the Wright case?" she finally asked.

"Considering they wouldn't let us into the research portion of the lab, pretty critical."

She sighed. "Fine. Is there a copy of the report somewhere I can look at tonight?"

"There's one in my apartment," I said. "I have a spare key in the junk drawer in your office. It's labeled Cat."

"I'd wondered about that. I haven't had a cat in years."

I had needed a backup, and considering her mess, it had seemed the safest storage. "Yeah, well. I probably won't be back there tonight, but you're welcome to grab the file. When are you going to move on Fiske again?" I asked, without meaning to. Crap, I should not have asked that over a phone line at the Guild. Damn it.

"There's no need to rush," she said, but she said it in her Official Answer voice. She wasn't offended—good. "Why aren't you going to be at your apartment tonight?"

"I *may* not," I said, trying to decide what to tell her. Finally I settled on "I'm taking care of something for Kara. It's on the up-and-up, just not something I'm comfortable talking about yet."

"Oh. Okay." She paused. "Does Swartz know?"

"Not yet, but he's got doctors' appointments today with Selah. I will tell him, I promise." I was a little resentful about all the checking up on me, but I understood it. "Listen, what's Ruffins doing with the murder victim? What kind of information was he feeding him?"

"Ah," Cherabino said obliquely. "That's an excellent point. We'll have to look into that more later."

"He's sitting nearby, isn't he? Waiting around for the task force meeting. That's why you needed help with the murder books. He's taking up your time."

"That's correct."

"And you're not going to discuss details in front of him?"

"That's correct," she said, and nothing else.

I sighed. "I'll call you later, okay?"

"You do that," she said, and hung up.

I went back out of the tiny room. "Satisfied?" I asked Stone, who was carefully not paying attention two feet from the door.

"Perfectly," he said.

"You should know something," Stone said as we waited for the elevator again.

"More revelations?" I asked, tired. "Fine, tell me what's going on."

"Well, two things. The first is that Ms. Chenoa is under house arrest and will not be allowed to have visitors. That includes you. They didn't disconnect her phone, which in retrospect was a mistake; she's been talking nonstop to her family and hindering our efforts."

"Okay."

But there was madness in the Guild and, knowing what I knew, panic too. "They're taking her actions as evidence she's been exposed to the madness as well, right? Where is the major cluster of cases, by the way? You know, so we can be somewhere else."

"The major cases are in the luxury section of the apartments, and we'll have to go there to look at the scene," Stone said. "As for judgments, I have no idea what 'they' are doing, but Nelson says not to let her out of house arrest. Ironically, she and Hawk Chenoa have demanded that I appear—with you, I assume—for a progress report tonight. The notification just came through. I may or may not go."

"Why would you need to answer to them? Isn't it better to be impartial, especially if they think she's contagious?"

He sighed. "I'm new to the case; I think I was perhaps the eighth person suggested to the family, and the only one they would accept. Well, after they'd made a stink about the original investigator. Hawk Chenoa liked my work in the Barksdale AFB scandals. To be honest, I think it's the only reason they put me in here. I'm not qualified, not like the others. But I also can't be seen to be partial."

"That's right. You're not an investigator?"

"I'm a Watcher," he said, too firmly, and with more than a little heat. "I watch. I determine the truth. I get inside people's heads and follow them back to the truth. It's my job. I haven't done this kind of investigation work—where the main witnesses were dead—since my practicum."

"Oh," I said. Seeing Stone out of his depth was at once terrifying and liberating. No wonder he'd browbeat me before letting me over here into the Guild. He'd wanted to know he could trust me to be the expert. Not that that wasn't a scary thought.

I looked at him. "Nelson, the Chenoas, Rex, and I bet Health and Human Services are all breathing down your neck right now, aren't they? You're between a rock and a hard place."

His jaw set and he was silent. Finally his mind supplied *What must be done must be done. We process the suicide, you back me up with the family so they'll allow public health measures, Nelson gets the information he needs, and everybody lets us do what needs to be done to stop the outbreak. There is no other way. There is no other possible way.* Not for the Guild as a whole to survive without fracturing. Not for the Guild as a whole to survive the madness.

Not for his family to survive.

"I know you want a quick answer," I said. "And I can see how a quick answer can benefit the Guild. But quick doesn't mean true. Quick doesn't mean right."

"I understand what you're saying," Stone said, grieved a little by the implication. "A quick answer may still save all of us."

"What's the other thing you think I should know?"

"They found a suicide note from Meyers in some of his office papers a few hours ago," Stone said. "Well, sort of."

"What do you mean, sort of?"

"He was a precognitive, and the note records a series of visions he has in which he takes his own life. A notable one was with knives."

"Which he then threw out," I said. Suddenly it made sense, but what a horrible thing to see. I'd come face-to-face with danger in a vision, but never anything like that.

"And then a vision of hanging, after which he threw out sheets, towels, belts, and ties."

"He didn't want to kill himself," I said. "Or he wouldn't have gone to such extreme measures."

"According to the note, he thought he was losing the battle."

I digested that. "What a horrible feeling."

Stone nodded, then sighed. "Let's move on. I'm going to have to report in before too long."

"Okay," I said, still wondering what it would be like to have a vision of your own suicide.

The Guild's Sinclair Building, their residential and meeting skyscraper, had a hollow central elevator, floors opening around it like the ribs from a spine of some great animal. You looked up and up, a hundred floors or more, all the way to the great skylight all the way at the top of the building. It was a beautiful sight, and the extra open space worked with the strong-shielding fields to ensure total privacy inside the living quarters.

"Why are we waiting for the elevators up to the living quarters?" I asked, trying for calm but not really succeeding. "I thought we were going to talk to the man who processed the iron."

The woman who processed the iron works for a mechanical subsection of Research, Stone replied. *Working on a project for Guild First, a project you would be better off not knowing about. And the iron is at the scene, where it was being processed when the family kicked us out. We're going to see the scene now. It's easier.*

They kicked you out of the scene? I asked. I rechecked my shields. This was the building with all the madness contagion, correct? Even so, it seemed strange to lock Stone out of the scene. "New quarantine measures?" I asked.

After a pause, Stone said out loud, "The family, actually. They haven't wanted anyone official near the scene. Or the body, for that matter, but there's a limit to what she can do with him already in the morgue. I'm hoping your connection to her will get you past the door."

The elevator arrived with a *ding* and we entered. The car was clear glass all the way around except for a handrail; I swallowed against vertigo as it started going up at a very fast rate, the main floor shrinking below us at a fast clip as I fought my stomach and my fear of what I might be exposed to in the next few minutes.

"Meyers was in the penthouse, I assume?" I asked, to distract myself. The elite of the Guild stayed in the top two floors, well above the peons I used to be one of.

He shrugged.

I waited, but he let nothing seep into his public mind, and I wasn't willing to look any deeper. That's how I ended up in a cell to begin with, and I'd been lucky—and more than lucky—not to end up mad from it. Finally I asked, in the most public way possible in Mindspace, *Well, what did the expert say? About the iron?*

"It's an iron," he said out loud. "And the electrical system was jimmied; the thermostat should have shut the electrical flow down when it got too high, but it didn't. Our expert didn't get a good look, because she was fixing the wall wiring. She had us shut down the electricity to the whole section. I was there holding the flashlight while she cursed at the wires. Apparently someone cross-connected the shielding system into the outlets, which pulled in a great deal of power that was never designed to go in those circuits. She says it's a miracle all the breakers tripped in time to prevent a larger issue with the whole apartment block. She fixed it, but she said there was no way it was an accident. Perhaps Meyers set it up before the suicide to make sure it wouldn't harm anyone else. He had the knowledge."

I thought about that. "But it wasn't on the note. No fingerprints anywhere?"

"We weren't there long enough to tell. But with the heat it's unlikely anything biologic survived on the wires, which is all we care about. And no, it wasn't on the note, but the note seemed a week old at least."

CHAPTER 11

Stone guided me through the maze of hallways. We ended up in the luxury block, where the elite leadership and the highest earners of the Guild lived. Even the carpet was lush and quiet underfoot, and both the soundproofing and the Mindspace shielding were exceptional; all I heard, all I felt, as I walked down that hallway was a quiet sense of preparedness. Well, that and the beating of my heart. Was I really going to do this? Walk into possibly the worst contagion zone?

Apparently I was.

One of Kara's cousins stood in front of a door along the hallway. Specifically, one of her large Swedish cousins I'd met maybe three or four times during family reunions. He was tan with very blond hair that might have been dyed, and had the physique of someone who spent a lot of time at a gym. This was a very unusual physique for Guild members outside of military service, even more so for strong telepaths, as the time and energy involved in mental training tended to make you unphysical, thin in terms of calories burned and muscles not used. I blinked at him one more time on meeting. Yep, he was at least six feet tall, well trained, and . . . still into extreme sports, clearly.

He was a very good choice to slow down the bureaucrats. I racked my brain and still couldn't come up with his name.

"Adam! Long time!" the man said warmly. He was genuinely pleased to see me and wasn't ashamed to say so in Mindspace, which only made it worse.

"How's the snowboarding coming?" I asked, keeping the conversation out loud. "You still into tournaments?"

"I placed third in the All-Swede Finals this year," he said, his accent very light. His English was fluent, but Swedish was still the first language. What was this guy's name? Cousin on Kara's mother's side maybe?

It's Gustolf, he sent through Mindspace. *My name.*

"Congratulations," I said, as warmly as I could manage back, trying not to be twitchy about the mind-to-mind. I'd either get exposed to the bug or I wouldn't. *Thanks, Gustolf. It's been a while.* "Do you mind if we take a look at the room?"

"Hawk would rather you didn't," he said. Nobody in or out without Hawk there was what the man had said, his mind supplied.

I paused. "Is Hawk dictating to the Erickson-Meyers clan now?" I asked.

Gustolf smiled. I'd asked the right question. "No. Kara has been elected to speak for us, even with the house arrest. She says the fastest way to find out the truth is to let you do your thing."

"Good for her," I said, and meant it. "Is she giving out a lot of orders?"

"Yes, but they all make sense."

Even better; from the look of him, she'd won their respect, no small thing. Kara had just become a major player in the Guild, at least until the Erickson-Meyers family sent somebody over from Europe, which they might decide not to do.

"You want him in or out?" Gustolf asked, referring to Stone.

Now I smiled. Choices. And, surprisingly, a Kara I recognized was working for me behind the scenes. Maybe she hadn't betrayed me after all. They had said she'd spoken for me.

"I'd rather take a look without him the first time," I said. "It's an easier read."

"Go ahead." He moved out of the way.

Stone sent him some kind of private message over telepathy, and Gustolf crossed his arms.

"Kara says Adam's the expert," Gustolf said, out loud, making a point. "What he wants goes until Kara says differently. I've told you before. What Johanna has to say is her business. She has the right. But we're not letting this go. Nobody's getting in without permission."

Stone sent something else; I got the edge of its passage through Mindspace but no real content.

"Enforcement has already made its position clear," Gustolf said. "If you go through me, the rest of the family would be glad to show up in response."

Stone looked frustrated. "We're on the same side," he said. "I am not the one trying to eliminate evidence. That's not me."

A disturbance in Mindspace—

And a one-foot flame appeared in Gustolf's hand. His humor was gone. "You try to influence me again and I will burn you alive."

The air nearly crackled in front of Stone as his mind settled for battle. Enforcement training was brutal. He'd probably been burned before and wouldn't blink at doing it again. With Guild medics on standby, your opinion of serious damage changed radically.

"Stop," I said.

Both glanced at me. Heat poured from the flame in

Gustolf's hand. Mindspace rippled from the force Stone was holding in potentiality.

"We all want the same thing," I said carefully. "Guild First would love you fighting among yourselves. Gustolf, Kara trusts Stone's judgment. Stone, Gustolf is protecting his family against people who are trying to destroy evidence. Both of you want the same thing. All I need is ten minutes to check out this crime scene. Can you wait ten minutes?" I asked, hitting the number deliberately hard.

Gustolf turned off the flame.

Stone slowly let the energy dissipate.

"We'll wait," Gustolf said.

Stone thought about that with a cop's cold calculation. Finally: "He doesn't touch anything."

"Agreed," I said. While I'd originally asked for time alone for convenience, now it was an actual necessity. This much roiling emotion in a crime scene was asking for trouble, and would likely obscure anything I'd find. "Ten minutes," I repeated. "I'd suggest you spend the time calming down. Whatever is going on here won't be helped by anger."

Then I went in, praying they wouldn't kill each other. Praying that whatever madness looked like, it wasn't what I'd just seen.

I closed the door behind me and took a few steps forward to let space (and the Inverse-Square Law) insulate me some from the minds behind me. They still made waves I could feel, of course, but the farther away, the fainter those waves felt. I took another step, and the Guild anyonide shielding took effect; it was like the rest of the world didn't exist.

I closed my eyes against the bland entryway and just enjoyed the sound of nothing. The feeling of Mindspace calm like a lake at rest, with no bleed-over from any other minds.

Something in me relaxed, something that hadn't fully relaxed in years. Nothing would get through those shields to surprise me, but my mind was unchanged.

In my apartment, in the machine I'd rigged based on the design of a friend, the shape of the electromagnetic fields were the opposite of my brain waves in Mindspace, like those headphones you wore to hear nothing. The two sets of waves canceled out, but my brain always felt fuzzy and disconnected. Here, the world was still there, my mind still there in perfect clarity, but I didn't have to hear the sound of others thinking.

I enjoyed it, just enjoyed it for a second, and reached for calm. What I'd told them was true. Three days later, the traces of a murder would almost certainly be here, but fading. Any strong present emotion might obscure potential clues, even fear, even justifiable fear. The crime scene wouldn't care.

So I took a breath, opened my eyes, and focused on my surroundings as a way to lose the fear. It was the nicest Guild apartment I'd ever seen, decorated in pale blues and golds and browns with navy striping, clearly done by a professional decorator. No man I knew would have chosen the sprig of pale purple fake flowers over the mantelpiece on the right, for example, but it suited the space and seemed restful, if a little feminine. The knickknacks out and about and the oddly shaped blobby coffee table were all a little too casual, a little too planned. But they—and the blues and browns—added up to something a lot better than your average Guild apartment, which normally was a white-painted box with a brick gas fireplace and a white-cabinet kitchen. To be honest, they worked you too hard most of the time to think too much about living quarters; most Guild members moved every few months to few years, going where the work was.

Clearly, in the last few years Meyers had had money and power both, as well as good taste. He'd planned to be in this city for enough time to worry about the apartment, and he'd gone to the trouble to get a designer and crew into the building past security. Or maybe the elite luxury apartments had that done for them; it's not like I was in a position to know.

The living room area and open kitchen areas were relatively neat, a few dishes in the sink now with small spots of mold starting to grow, untouched for days. I wondered how long the cousins had been standing there, to keep people out.

A jacket lay on a chair at the light wooden table, linens around it untouched except for a single stain on one side, like something spilled from a glass that hadn't been cleaned up. A pair of shoes sat next to the large couch. Small things; he'd been a neat man, but he'd lived here. I could almost smell the scent of his mind, a fragrance sunk into the space. His baseline emotion seemed a mix of concentration and worry, but he had a high-level political job. Perhaps that was normal.

For that matter, I could also smell something odd in the physical world. I went back into the bedroom, through a hallway to the left, past a laundry space with waterless washer machines that looked no more than five years old. Also an upgrade from typical Guild digs.

The smell, a kind of scorched tacky thing like burned popcorn mixed with some kind of oily material and left to rot, got stronger as I moved down the hallway. When I opened the door, Mindspace exploded.

The very air screamed. Energy and death—I squinted past the incredible sensations. Stinging crazy energy too hot, too hot, too hot. Madness?

I closed it out with determination, with grit, with a strong shield that wouldn't budge. Mindspace remembered here. It remembered all too well what couldn't seep away through the apartment shields. But, shielded, I didn't feel any different. Just another crime scene.

The real world came into focus, and the first thing I saw was a long black mark up the wall on top of an electrical outlet. An ironing board, tipped over, on the floor. A man's dress shirt wadded between it and the floor, also scorched, places burned away—or was that the ironing board cover? And next to both, still plugged in, an iron.

A stain covered the carpet for a few inches next to the iron—a brown, oily, textured something—and the face of the iron had the same stuff coated on it, a long piece of it extending past its edge. Someone had been burned, and burned badly.

But that scorch mark up the wall, the sensation of Mindspace . . . that was an electrical death. That smell—that horrible smell—was the smell of that burn, that death, that horror. The hole cut in the drywall had to be where they'd accessed the electrical system, two feet to the left of the burn mark.

There was no body on the floor here, though a few other stains could make out its shape if you looked hard enough. Two dark stains and scorch marks that once might have been shoes. Lighter stains where he must have fallen.

Suddenly what I'd agreed to hit me like a ton of bricks. It was my job—and mine alone, without Cherabino—to decide what had happened in this room full of screaming Mindspace.

I went to sit in the bathroom, away from this smell, for just a minute, and talk myself into lowering my shields. Either I'd come down with madness or I wouldn't. They could treat it—probably—and I'd agreed to this. They'd saved Swartz's life.

It was the strongest and the worst thing I'd done in a long time to force myself back into that room. A break was fine, Swartz had said once. A break was totally fine, but you couldn't run from something this bad. You had to face it.

So I screwed my courage to the sticking place and opened the door again.

Again, the smell hit me in the face like a hammer. And again, Mindspace screamed unimaginable pain. Meyers's Ability had been strong, and the scene reflected it. But just a scene, just a scene, I told myself.

I breathed through it this time, and started to pay attention, to sink down into the midst of it and examine it from the inside. I let it wash through me, let the pain run where it would. No worse than the second rehab, where they wouldn't give me drugs for withdraw symptoms. No worse than the Guild locking me in a box to dry out, screaming over and over and over again for someone to make it stop.

The pain settled, and I emerged "under" it. I could see again. I was deep into Mindspace now, deeper than was strictly safe without an anchor back to the real world. Deep, with some terrible, terrible pain above me. If I wasn't very careful, I'd get lost here, like a deep-sea diver unable to tell which way was up. I'd suffocate, eventually, swimming forever deeper, until the very space crushed me.

I missed Cherabino. I missed her being there as an anchor, and I missed her. I swam around the room, slowly. Odd. The death-spot, the hole in the fabric of Mindspace that should have come and filled in and settled, was gone completely, nothing there. He had died here; I could feel it. But there was no evidence in the field.

Did that have to do with the electricity? Had it obliterated the usual signs of death? I'd never dealt with something

like this before, not in Mindspace. This was the kind of
death the department usually trusted the medical examiner
for.

I moved, carefully, carefully, around to see if there was
anything else I could pick up.

I sorted through traces, strong ones, faint ones, nothing
notable. A disturbing dream in the bed to my left. A calm
sexual moment. Worry about work. Pages and pages of fic-
tion read here, few making enough emotion to leave anything behind. And there—there!

Mindspace was rippled, like the ocean floor after wave
after wave had passed through the water above. I'd never
seen anything like it. And the ripples went deep, like they'd
been here for weeks.

I moved slowly, tracing the ripples back . . . to one, exact . . .
yes, there they joined into one spot and got wider as they
moved out. This was not a natural phenomenon, I thought. No
way this was natural.

I rose out of Mindspace slowly, very slowly, ever so
careful to follow the path I'd left behind. It was fading,
almost gone, and without it I might lose track of up and
down, and wander forever. Slow steps forward, forward,
up, ever up, as I scratched against the pain of the deep and
prayed for direction.

I was drenched in sweat by the time I surfaced, my hands
shaking from excessive adrenaline. I felt lightheaded and
strange.

But I'd done it. I'd surfaced, with the shape of the space
in my mind.

Years of practice among the normals let me map the
real space to the mind space; I walked over to the one spot
the ripples had emanated from. The headboard. There was
a painting over the headboard.

The back of the painting over the bed had a discolored

place about the size of a golf ball, square, with a tear in the paper backing at the top and a notch in the upper frame, like something had been attached with wire and glue and then ripped away too quickly.

I checked. The mirror and the paintings along the right wall all had a layer of dust on top of them. The print over the bed, not so much. Nowhere else did a frame have a tear in the back of the paper.

"Gotcha," I said.

Someone had planted some kind of device, and I was betting it was an influencer, something that had made Meyers's mind continue to see visions even after he took such extreme steps to end their possibility. I'd seen plenty over the last year, plenty enough to make me believe the Guild had this kind of technology.

And the same someone who knew the Guild well enough to sabotage the shielding system without burning down the building—well, that someone probably also knew the Guild well enough to get to the hidden technology.

When I opened the door Stone and Gustolf were laughing about a rugby game, laughing a little too hard with suppressed tension.

I waited until the laughter died down. "Let me show you both what I found."

Stone closed the clamshell-shaped case. It held various small compartments, the largest containing the usual latex gloves I'd seen everywhere in the cop world, others with tweezers, spray-bandage, and other assorted things too folded to see clearly. At the top of the clamshell were three flat things with inlaid designs, each no bigger than a pack of gum, two of which had flashing lights. He'd pulled out one and taken readings of the area around the painting. Now, he folded everything up and put it away.

"That's it?" Gustolf asked.

"That's it. This was good work," Stone added.

"Chain of evidence rules—"

"Oh." Stone cut me off. "No, we don't have those. You take a photo, you take a reading, and that's usually plenty. Investigators have to explain conclusions to Nelson, not a jury. Nelson's pretty quick on the uptake."

That was assuming he wasn't covering anything up. "What's a reading?"

Stone pointed to the upper section of the clamshell. "Fingerprint fluorescer and imager, camera with multiple light frequencies, Mindspace field reader. Not that the last doesn't act up in cases like these, with so much noise. Research is still working on it. To be honest, I've never had a reading be all that useful in the field. The mind's a lot more useful tool. But Nelson likes documentation."

He was toting around probably the most complex—and likely illegal—computer-based technology I'd seen since pictures of pre–Tech War life in history class. "Those are very sophisticated devices there," I observed.

"Don't worry. We have a secure storage facility for when the normals send their inspector. We're careful," Stone said.

Wow. I took a moment and absorbed the ethics of that, especially as Gustolf didn't seem to blink an eye.

"Well." I explained what I suspected about the device. "I'd like you both to put out feelers. We need to know who makes these things and who would have access to them."

"I'll make some inquiries, but it will take a while," Stone said. "Getting access to Research takes Nelson and a hell of a lot of paperwork."

"Oh," I said, now worried. If Nelson was behind it . . .

"I'll ask," Gustolf said. "We have cousins in the lab in

Chicago who might be able to find out. I will contact you if they know anything."

"Thanks," I said.

I looked around again, at the physical location, the unmade bed, the stain on the floor, the burn marks, the smell. Trying to figure out if I'd missed anything.

My stomach rumbled, loudly. I was used to skipping meals under Cherabino's driving pace, but it was maybe three in the afternoon and I hadn't eaten since early this morning. "Food?" I asked. Was it odd that the smell wasn't damping my appetite?

"If you want," Stone said. "We were just leaving anyway."

I pushed the elevator button for Level Five, the skybridge. The doors closed.

"Good work in there," Stone repeated.

"Thanks." Unable to help myself, I added, "Seems like way too much trouble for a regular suicide, don't you think? Especially from a guy who'd throw out half his apartment to keep a suicide from happening?"

"Yeah," he said, not happy.

The elevator stopped on Level Four, someone pushing through into the elevator. Stone was already off, too late.

I followed. A long line of people stretched around the side wall, some standing, some sitting on the floor with their backs against the wall. One guy near the end scratched at his face too hard, over and over, and the people standing near him were pulled away as scratches spread through the whole line, one person after another scratching face, hands, arms absently.

An overwhelming fear feeling came from the man at the end of the line, and I shielded up to my gills. Suicide or homicide, the Guild still had the Madness contagion to worry about. And me—well, I had that to worry about too.

Stone studied the line, and the sign that said MENTAL HEALTH, not twenty feet away to our left. The line was on the way to there.

It was all I could do to force myself to stay there, in the middle of it, as the door closed with a *ding* behind me. Telepaths were suggestible, I told myself, as the itchy feeling started to settle on me too. Telepaths were highly suggestible, and the best thing I could do for myself was simply not to believe any of it. Not believing would help the crowd too; the more discordant notes in the symphony, the weaker its global effects.

Then why did I feel so damn itchy all of a sudden?

Johanna moved out of the double doors marked MENTAL HEALTH, a stack of forms in hand. That's right, she worked for the health division, and they'd likely need all hands on deck for something like this. Two guard types came behind her, their entire arms covered by thick long gloves.

She raised her voice, mental and physical, and boomed, "Attention please!"

The entire line quieted. A scratch here. A scratch there.

"You did the right thing by coming here, and we will get you checked out as soon as possible. In the meantime, please fill out these detailed questionnaires. I've included a form at the back of the packet for you to write down everyone you've been in contact with for the last thirty-six hours. Please be precise. The Guild's future depends on your honesty."

The man scratching at his face was now bleeding, the skin abrading under his fingernails. But still he scratched. *Bugs, get them off me, get them off me,* came from him across the space. The people around him gave him another few feet.

"Sir," Johanna said, only out loud, but specifically in his direction. "Sir, I'll need you to come with us!"

The guards advanced, and I pushed past Stone.

"Let's take the stairs," I said, and rushed out of there as quickly as my legs would take me.

Stone followed, his concern emanating like strong cologne.

I took careful stock when I left—I didn't *feel* itchy. I didn't feel mad. Did that mean anything?

CHAPTER 12

At the bottom of the stairwell I ran into someone—literally.

I corrected, and apologized. It was Green, the guy who'd accused me of violating his privacy and gotten me thrown in the cell.

"You have *got* to be kidding me," I said.

He pulled back. "You! Why is a criminal still walking around like free people? You should be in a cell."

"And the case was dismissed," I said rudely, which might be true. Maybe.

Green looked at Stone. "You're coming with me while I file a protest. You can explain to Diaz why you're letting a criminal free in the building."

"Your boss hired me," I said, petty anger floating to the surface. "Check with Rex. It's already done." I had no idea who Diaz was, but Rex seemed like the kind of guy who was senior to everyone else.

Green stood there while his shields leaked disapproval and contempt. "Be sure I'll check that."

"Go on, Adam, I'll handle this," Stone said.

"Fine." I added silently, *Weren't you going to follow up with Kara, or Hawk?*

I'll do that after I take Green to Nelson. It's his department and he's signed off on it. He can deal with the fallout.

I didn't envy Nelson all of a sudden.

"Are you coming with me or should I go to your boss?" Green said. "I can pull your voting privileges if you irritate me, you know."

I wasn't sure if that was a real threat or not. When I was here last, voting wasn't something you lost once you'd gained it. Guild membership might have been compulsory, but voting privileges for Council positions and the occasional policy legislation were not. You got them if you were both born with Guild parents and had a certain Ability rating, or if you hit certain high-level marks in your career. Practically no one still in school—even advanced schooling—would be able to hit those marks if they didn't have a vote by inheritance. In practice, only about forty percent of the Guild had the right to vote, and only a third of those hadn't been born into the privilege. Once you'd gotten votes, you had them forever.

"Can he really do that?" I asked.

"Let's ask Nelson," Stone said. Then, to Green: "After you?"

Green turned on his heel and walked out through the stairwell door. His mind muttered behind him about political power and biased charges.

You know your way? Stone asked as he hustled to catch up.

Yes, I said, but he was already gone.

The rest of the Guild felt deserted, hollow, with Mindspace and reality curiously empty of minds. The main atrium, which was nearly always full of people, had one student on an errand and a guard. That was it. It was eerie.

I wondered how Cherabino was doing right now. I worried at the thought, trying to figure out if I would really ask her out as Swartz said. It would change everything, but maybe for the better. Or maybe he'd been right the first time.

Now I walked along the skybridge between the living quarters building (luxury apartments at the top, of course) and the "work" building, which housed pretty much any work the Guild did on-site with the exception of the school and research. I'd worked in the school, so while I'd seen the admin building through Kara's eyes—in the smallest, least important areas—I hadn't had much cause to go into the high-security bigwigs area.

Fortunately I had just the excuse to do that today.

The skybridge was beautiful and warm, light and airy with frost-tinged glass on every side, a pleasant cross breeze of plant-scented air, while below the small formal winter garden beckoned. All pollution-resistant plants, and most taller and more deeply colored as a result. Insect-eating flowers shared space with more normal bushes and trees. It was an oasis even in November.

A student sat in the middle of the bridge, on one of the low seats on the side built for that purpose. He was fourteen, maybe, and awkward, tall and thin with zits all over his face and misery written on his mind. A Seven, maybe, in telepathy, by the feel of his mind, though it could be another similar Ability. He was upset, and afraid of something, hiding out from the rest of the Guild in this relatively isolated spot.

I thought of stopping; I'd been a professor once, and this kind of thing happened more often than you'd expect. You took kids out of their family homes and lumped them in together with little training, and hurts happened. Hurts happened a lot; I'd found out the last year I was here that some of those hurts were encouraged, so as better to toughen people up.

"You lost, mister?" the kid asked me. I'd hesitated too long.

"I used to work here," I said, to cover whatever I might have projected into Mindspace. "It's hard to know sometimes what to do when you come back after a long time away. Are you okay?"

I saw a series of lies flit across his brain, then a decision. "No," he said, "but I don't want to talk about it." His mind leaked a roommate who was yelling about Guild First, a girlfriend who wouldn't stop talking about everyone going mad, and a teacher who did nothing to stop the chatter. And his classmates, his hallmates, who were convinced he was a carrier of the madness even though he'd passed the screening. They wouldn't talk to him anymore. They ran when they saw him coming. And now his girlfriend was starting to believe them. He wanted time to sit, and be, and pretend things were normal again, pretend the shame of it didn't matter. He hadn't done anything. But the shame still burned.

"Fair enough," I said, keeping my mind calm, responding only to the verbal thoughts. I didn't think he realized he'd spilled, and I wasn't the person to offer comfort, not now. Helpless, I asked, "Can you tell me how to get to the employment administrative offices?"

He straightened. "Yeah. Sure." He told me detailed directions twice and then forced a smile. "Hope you find your way."

"Me too," I said, and left. The memory of my own hurts from my school days echoed too, made that much worse by this idea of contagion. His fellows might never let him back. Never. Over some imagined idea that spread like wildfire. There were downsides to a life among telepaths. There were downsides to a life among humans.

As I entered the cafeteria, I felt a familiar mind emerge close by. I followed the mental sense around the corner and all the way across the room, to the section where you emptied your trays.

"Jamie!" I called, genuinely pleased. One of the strongest minds at the Guild and impossible to miss, but I was glad to see her. Her presence made all the madness seem far away. If anyone in the building was least likely to get infected, it was her. She had the willpower—and the numbers—to disbelieve anyone around her, to be the influencer and not the influenced.

She looked around, confused, before spotting me. Jamie was one of a handful of Level Ten telepaths in the world, her mind impacting Mindspace like a stone dropped in a pond even when she was controlling it. She was a sixty-something woman now, with graying hair pulled into a chignon (she insisted on the term) and a silk skirt suit at the moment. She had two older-teenager students behind her, a Latina with very long hair and a dress at maybe sixteen years old, and a short Indian-looking male student in slacks and a button-up shirt at maybe seventeen.

Why are you guys out despite the lockdown? I asked, still ten feet away.

Adam, her thought hit me in return. *Meet Marta and Rohan.* She pulled my mind into an open rapport with their minds, easily and smoothly. There were reasons why Jamie was one of the best mentors in the Guild.

I stopped about three feet from them, a comfortable distance. *Hello, Marta. Hello, Rohan.* I sent a small packet of the me-sense to both, a greeting among close friends or colleagues. I received their return greetings and mental signatures with formality. They both seemed nervous in body language and mental signature. I sent a quiet calm in return.

They're about to take their Eleventh Hour testing, Jamie explained.

"Ah," I said out loud. "Good luck. I know you'll do very

well. Jamie's one of the best telepathy mentors in the Guild. She mentored me back in the day, you know."

"Did you pass the first time?" Marta asked in a high, hesitant voice.

"Top marks in every category but one," I said.

"You always did struggle with distraction." Jamie smiled. *Is there a reason you pulled back from the connection?* She sent on a private channel to me.

I blinked. I hadn't realized I'd done that. *Around normals too long,* I said. And then added subtext that I was worried about something.

You work with normals? Rohan's mental voice put in. *You don't seem like a Minder.*

I blinked at him, shocked. That had been a private sending, laser-targeted to Jamie's mind and hers alone.

Oh. Forgot to warn you, Jamie said, a trace of amusement in her voice. *Rohan is . . . well, we call it 'seeing around corners.' There's not much he can't interpret in Mindspace. My hope is that we'll get him involved in some heavy-monitoring situations.*

Military? I asked. Then, to Rohan: *Sorry I startled. No, I'm not a Minder. Once upon a time, I worked Structure.* I leaked in all the layers of what I was: professor, etc. *I've been . . . away from the Guild for a while and work for the police now. How do you 'see around corners'?*

The kid looked at me. *How do you see in Mindspace?*

Um . . . I thought about it. *Good point. You just do.* That was the one thing you couldn't quite teach somebody; I'd tried. Either you could "see" the space between the minds, like me, or you couldn't, like Stone. You could be a good telepath either way, but the difference could not be taught.

Yeah. I just kinda do. Jamie saw me doing it and pulled me out of the regular class. I was getting into trouble anyways.

I could imagine people would be very bent out of shape to have their private conversations public. *Maybe sometime you'll let me 'piggyback' and see what you do,* I offered. *Sometimes I can learn techniques that way so we could teach others.* It startled me that I'd used the "we," but it felt natural here.

Maybe, he said, but I felt a reluctance, partly because he liked being unique, and partly because I was betting he didn't feel quite comfortable around me. Good call, kid, I thought quietly behind a shield. Stranger danger and all that.

We need to go, Jamie said on a wide band. Even controlled, she was loud enough in Mindspace that people sitting at tables ten feet away looked up. Or, well, about sixty-five percent of them, the usual percentage of listening-telepaths in the crowd.

Good luck, I told them both. *Don't let the proctors intimidate you.*

They took their leave then and headed off. I wondered if I should have kept my distance.

Jamie sent a small, quiet laser-tight sending to me after they'd already turned away: *Let me drop off the kids. Then I'll meet you back here?* She sent a quiet welcome and a request to catch up.

Sure, I said, but I'd had to put way too much power behind the sending, enough power to make my head hurt. They were only a hundred feet away down the hall now. *I'll be here.*

Seeing her brought it all back, those days when I was on top of the world, a part of something greater than myself. When I was happy with Kara, and happy teaching, and happy following in Jamie's footsteps. The world seemed so clear then. The memory cut me now, like a blade.

I would never be what I was, never again. And now, I
had to work all too hard to send a decent distance-message.
It was afternoon, when my brain was tired, and I was still
recovering from a mind injury. I'd probably overstrained
finding my way back from Mindspace in Meyers's apartment. That's all it was, just a little overstrain. But deep
inside, I doubted. It was just one more thing that made me
different, made me less, than what I had been.

At nearly four o'clock on a Saturday, you took what you
could get from the Guild cafeteria. In this case, it was a
three-bean chili they'd set out with corn bread and some
greens in the entryway; the main food line was, of course,
closed at this hour. I was hungry enough not to care about
content, and ladled plenty of everything.

When Jamie showed up, I was in the long, brightly lit
seating area, in a booth toward the back under a picture of
Gabriela Gee, the original firestarter back at the founding
of the Guild. I'd always mistrusted something about her
eyes in pictures, but the booth was clean and quiet, with
privacy awnings set up with enough low-level electrical
fields to prevent accidental thought spillage into other
booths. Now that I'd had some time to think about it, I
regretted talking to the kids mind-to-mind; I felt fine, but
if I'd been exposed to madness, I had no business spreading it. I was out of my league here, and unsure. What risk
was there, if any?

I'd warn Jamie to look out for signs, I decided.

I'd finished about half the bowl of chili, enjoying the
spice, and most of the greens and corn bread, when I saw her.

Jamie smiled and slid into the booth, a sense of tired-
ness and apprehension for the students coming through.
She had a cup of tea in her hands, the strong smell of

chamomile flavoring the air. The feel of her mind, like sunshine and ozone over baked grass on a summer's day, complemented the smell of the tea and reminded me of days long past. Even the ebb and flow of Mindspace around her impossibly strong mind felt comforting, familiar.

Every time I looked at her these days, I blinked. It was like she'd aged ten years in a day. She hadn't, of course; I'd aged the ten years too. But I'd been there for that part. For her—well, it was new.

I swallowed the food. "Yes?"

She held the mug with both hands on the table. "You work with Justin, right? How is he these days?"

I requested context silently. "Oh, Captain Harris. He's fine, as far as I can tell. Doing a lot more arbitration work with the recent budget cuts. The chief of police is thrilled with him if you believe the rumors."

She looked down at the mug, and a tinge of wistful might-have-beens and complex mixed emotions leaked out. "Good to hear," she said quietly. She and Captain Harris were married once upon a time, well before I'd known either, and apparently the parting hadn't been all that straightforward. As usual, though, she brought her emotions under painful control after only a few seconds.

After an appropriate pause, I said, "It's good to see you again."

Now she looked back up. "It's good to see you too. I've heard you're looking into the death of Del Meyers."

"That's right," I said.

She sighed. "Del was a good man. He wouldn't want his death to start this powder keg."

I leaned forward. "What do you mean?"

"Health is screaming about quarantine, Guild First is taking the excuse to reach for more power and more votes, and the Cooperist clans are screaming for blood and truth and a lot of things nobody thinks they're going to get. And the more they posture, the more concerned I get. It's the ordinary people who are going to get the short end of the stick, I fear."

I smiled. "You including yourself in the 'ordinary people' category?"

She laughed. "In this case, perhaps so. What a change."

"Listen, can Council members really take away voting privileges?" I asked, and explained the context. Without meaning to, I let my concern about the madness spill out as well.

Sorry, I added, and pulled back in.

Jamie blinked. *You've got a lot on your mind right now, don't you?*

I nodded and took a bite of the now-cold chili.

She leaned forward a bit, her hands cradling the mug a little closer. "I won't clutter you up with a lot of telepathy, then. Green is a lot of bluff—he's very concerned with his personal power and the position of the Guild for his faction—but he has, actually, taken away voting privileges from four people. It took the assent of the entire Council, but he did it."

"That's . . . disturbing," I said.

"It's a new world," she replied. Then: "If you're worried about madness contagion, I'd go by the screening machine before you leave. You don't have to, but it's there as much for your peace of mind as it is for the health of the Guild as a whole." *Her idea,* she put in mentally. A real answer did a lot to address the panic and prevent the more susceptible minds from "catching" the illness. She'd have the students do it too, when they got out of testing.

I didn't know how I felt about that. But it would probably

work, at least for me. "Thanks. I'll go by there," I said. "If it stops me worrying, a little pain is worth it."

Changing the subject, I asked her some more questions about the politics going on with the upcoming election, and she answered at length.

Finally she said, "It's a blessing that so much of the senior staff and Council is away at the health care conference. At least for now the politicizing has died down. You can't walk down the hall anymore without getting a student projecting some party line."

"Didn't they rule mind-to-mind advertisement disallowed?" I asked.

"Not in the last five years, and they've got students earning money that way. I feel for the students, but I'd like a little peace and quiet. At least, what little they'll give me." She sighed. "Like I said, the Guild isn't what it was."

"Change happens," I said, one of her sayings.

She laughed. "I suppose it does. It sure isn't like it was back in your day!"

From there the conversation turned to the old days, to when I'd first been one of her students, and then a professor. We talked for maybe an hour, and for that hour, I forgot I was in the middle of strangers with agendas. I forgot I was years away, and worlds apart. I forgot I didn't belong, not anymore.

And I remembered, finally, what Jamie had been saying for so many years about living by example, about doing the right thing because it was the right thing.

As I walked out, I realized I hadn't told Paulsen or Cherabino about the Guild. I'd been avoiding it, for no other reason than that I didn't want to tell them. The old me wouldn't have liked that. The old me would be in her office, trying to live by example.

So I decided to take the bus to the department and hope

Paulsen was still working overtime. I needed to tell her, and I needed to tell her before I chickened out.

So I left, dropping by the scanning machine at the door as Jamie had suggested. I passed the test, and even the pain of it didn't detract from the knowledge that I wasn't mad. Maybe there was something to that after all.

CHAPTER 13

Paulsen held up a finger. One ear was cradled against a phone at her shoulder, her hand was scribbling notes, and the other hand held that finger up before returning to the phone. "No, I understand, sir. It's a difficult budget situation for everyone. If I could get your support for a two percent . . . Absolutely, no, that's not what I'm saying." She paused. "Two percent is— Don't interrupt me. Two percent is . . ." She listened, nearly huffing, for a long moment. "Fine. You have a nice day too." She hung up the phone with a little more force than strictly necessary. "Asshole."

She looked up and waved me in. "Close the door, please. What are you doing here so late on a Saturday? Your hours were cut."

I closed the door and walked in a step or two. "I'm not filing for overtime. I have a bit of a situation."

"If you don't get a license, there's not much I can—"

"That's not it," I said. "Can I sit down?"

She took a breath. "Yes, go ahead."

Her office, normally messy, looked like a hurricane of paper had run to shore against her desk. Drifts of colored paper notes littered the floors in front of the walls, as more notes stood three deep on the walls themselves. She even had a small pile of files sitting on the guest chair, something normally too sacred to touch.

"Can I move these?" I asked.

She sighed, got up, and took the files out of my hands, placing them on top of a leaning tower of law books next to her desk. "You're over your hours this week already, for the third week in a row. I know you work with Cherabino, but she's salaried, and you're not." She straightened and held up a hand. "Even if you don't ask for reimbursement, it's a problem. If we get audited—which looks likely if I get this two percent increase we're asking for—someone will go through and compare hours worked and paid, and a discrepancy on either side could land us in legal trouble. You need to go home when I tell you, Adam."

I sat, gently. "Well, in that case I have good news for you."

"Do you, now?" She sat as well, leaning a little forward.

"I need to take the next two days off, maybe a third."

She sat back. "Well, that would seem to solve our hours problem neatly. I've got most of the part-timers in this week, so the rooms will get covered. Still, you left without warning last week. What's the reason you need to be out?"

"Here's where it becomes a situation." I took a breath. Yes, I was really going to do this.

"I'm listening."

"Remember Kara? Tall blonde, wears suits? She's come here a couple of times as the Guild's liaison. She's helped solve a number of cases for us."

"You realize you introduce her every single time she comes up? Where is this going?"

"Her uncle recently died, and she thinks it was a murder."

Paulsen got very, very still. "We don't have jurisdiction on Guild personnel. Koshna is very clear."

"You don't," I said. "The law is considerably fuzzier if they invite an ex-Guild consultant in for opinions."

She didn't say anything for a moment, then put forth very carefully: "It sounds to me like a conflict of interest."

Paulsen was so very, very still. Her mind was trying desperately to withhold judgment until full information was had, but the Guild was potentially the most dangerous enemy her department could have—whether the Guild meant to be or not. Normals didn't like the Guild, didn't trust the Guild, and having the appearance of being in bed with said Guild could shut down her job and the jobs of most of the department. Neutral was the only thing here that could work. Strictly, strictly neutral.

She met my eyes. "I'm giving you an opportunity here to explain to me why it's not a conflict of interest."

Other than the fact that Kara's word might have a beneficial effect on my PI appeal? "She's my ex-fiancée," I said. "And she's asked for my help. Confidentially? Her uncle is one of the leaders of the Guild. They want a neutral investigator. It's important to them that I'm unaffiliated in this context. If we take that to its logical conclusion, the department can play the same card. It's very important to you guys that I am also unaffiliated. We saw in the Bradley case that my contacts at the Guild could play very useful to the department."

"And in the Hamilton case your ties to the Guild cost a good man his life," she returned. Her mind was still open, decision unmade, but she was squirrelly about this, and about trusting me. Her worst fear was me doing something stupid behind her back again.

"You're talking about Bellury," I said. "Bellury and my last fall off the wagon." It hurt, because she was right. I pulled back into myself a little. "Bellury was my fault, for being stupid." I hadn't called for backup when I should have done so. It would haunt me—well, it wouldn't let me go, and that was, as Cherabino put it, as it should be. It should hurt. It should. "But," I said, "it's important to note that you were investigating Emily Hamilton's death as a normal murder, not a Guild case. Her connections to the Guild were even more recent than mine. I'm not saying that what happened was anyone's fault but mine, but I am saying that the Guild's politics is affecting cases with normals. You still need someone who can bridge that gap. Someone neutral. And I've passed every drug test you've put in front of me. That shouldn't be an issue, not anymore."

She settled back in her chair, her mind going hard and calculating and a little sad. "Neutrality will have a heavy price tag for you," she said. "I can't put you in the interview rooms as a department representative if you don't represent the interests of the department."

I hadn't expected this. I felt like I stood at the edge of a cliff. A big, wide, deep cliff, where one step would take me over the edge.

But I owed the Guild a debt for Swartz's life. And Kara had come through for me many, many times, and Meyers had been a good guy. "You've said yourself it's very likely that my job will be cut because of politics on this side anyway. And nobody's to say you can't continue to employ a neutral third party for casework and suspects you need insight into. You call in Piccanonni for profiling. She's not with the department."

"Piccanonni is Georgia Bureau of Investigation, statewide law enforcement. It's not the same thing. I'd caution you, Adam, to think this through all the way. You'd go from likely to lose your job to almost a guaranteed loss. You may get hired back part-time as basically an assistant to Bransen's team. If—and only if—Bransen decides you're worth the political fallout. Either way you're out of the interview room and out of my department."

"You're saying if I help Kara out you'll fire me?" I asked

carefully. The cliff was right there. Right. There! "They're not exactly asking nicely. There have been threats."

She sighed, looking more tired than I'd ever seen her. "I'm sorry. I really am. You need to make your best choices, but as far as this department goes, I don't have any other choice but protecting our interests. We can work out details on finishing up whatever case you're working with Cherabino— you deserve that much, at least—but barring a miracle I think there's no other way this can go. Is this really what you want, Adam?"

I considered lying to her. She didn't monitor the interview rooms much anymore, and Clark and the others for good or ill were more than used to me bailing on my usual schedule for the sake of one case or the other. Usually I came back and took all of their interviews for cases later, so they went home early, but not always. I could tell Cherabino I was in the interview room; if she was really working as many cases as all that, she wouldn't have time to think about it. Everyone else would assume I was working a case with her. I might very well get away with time away with a few good lies.

But Swartz—Swartz said you had to face up to your decisions like a man. You had to stand up and *do* something, and deal with what you'd done honestly. Lying about your actions was the mark of a child.

So then, the question became, was this thing for the Guild worth my job? Threats or no, was it worth my job?

"Adam?" Paulsen prompted.

"I need the next two days off, possibly a third," I heard myself saying. "You do what you need to do when I get back."

Her face fell in genuine disappointment. "Clear out your desk and locker tonight. I'll have an officer escort you off-site."

"That's it?" Really? How could that be it?

"I'm sorry, Adam. You've made your choice." She picked up a stack of folders from the floor and opened the first one. "See yourself out."

I felt like she'd slapped me. "You said I could work with Cherabino . . . ?"

She looked up. Her face was like stone now. "We're done, Adam. You need to talk to Bransen now."

She looked back down at her notes and picked up her pen, a clear dismissal.

I pulled my heart out of my boots, streaming pain, and limped out of the door. I staggered down the hall and stopped, leaning against the wall dumbly until some cop asked what was going on. He had to say it three times before it registered.

"What?" I said, my bereft tone leaking pain like the rest of me.

"I've been assigned to escort you to clean out your things and clear the building," he said. A big guy, with a scar on his neck almost covered by a geometric black-and-white tattoo.

I blinked, and made myself actually be present. Actually care, though it seemed painful and pointless. I knew this guy; he was one of the special tactics bruisers who'd invaded the warehouse in the Bradley case. Though I couldn't remember his name for the life of me. He'd been nice to me back then. He looked stern now.

"Where are we going first?" he asked.

His contempt made me angry, oddly, and I stood up. "The locker room. I have a bag there that should hold everything else. Then the cubicle upstairs. I hope you're prepared to wait. I'm taking everything." I swallowed, then tossed out the ultimatum: "And you're driving me home when we're done."

He wasn't happy with that one. I didn't care.

The cruiser dropped me off in the front of my apartment building, my breath visible in the light of the streetlight above. The building was a faded former office block converted to apartments—and converted badly—in the aftermath of the Tech Wars. It had a few surprises left in the walls, surprises I'd used to my advantage, but it was, essentially, a dump. Or at least it seemed now, with my world in free fall.

For all of the lower-income families that lived here and my single neighbors, there was no drug problem in this building. I'd looked, more than once, in the early days. The lack made part of me happy, very happy; I'd have to make the trek out all the way to Fulton County to ruin my sobriety. That part had turned in anyone who'd ever sold to me in DeKalb, which was why they wouldn't sell to me anymore. But the rest, the suspicious and cynical pack rat that still wanted the drug, that still wanted to fall off the world and get high, that part was sitting up today.

It had been a while since we saw each other last, and I waved hello tiredly as I climbed up the long flights of stairs to my apartment, every step a triumph. I was paying attention, enough attention to see if anyone was waiting for me in my apartment again, but not much else.

The rest of me was working out how to get to South Fulton, or maybe East Ponce de Leon Street, and take my chances on the yuppie blocks not far from the public housing. It was pretty late, though, and my telepathy was better but not a hundred percent at this hour. I couldn't rely on changing the seller's mind to see that I was okay and not a cop. I might get shot. And the buses to Fulton County could very well stop running by the time I got down there and leave me stranded.

I argued with myself, back and forth, back and forth, but it was an old, well-worn argument and one already won. I had to be down at the Guild building at eight tomorrow morning, which meant I had to leave at six thirty.

And more important, I'd have to be in the midst of countless telepaths all day. Once I'd been a liar, mind-to-mind, when I'd had to be. Once I'd kept secrets from the brethren, and largely succeeded. I was not that guy anymore, and my telepathy was not that reliable anymore. I couldn't rely on hiding anything.

So the decision was simple: if I had any chance at all at showing up and doing what I'd promised, of not ruining all of my credibility within the first half hour, I couldn't use tonight. I'd just told Paulsen, the best boss I'd ever had, to jump off the cliff so I could show up and actually have a chance at being the good guy for once. What was the damn point if I couldn't follow through?

So I unlocked my door—after checking the mat was empty—and let myself in. The same empty room awaited me, a barely there kitchen with an antique microwave taking up most of the counter space. A ratty old couch and coffee table. The infinitesimal bathroom through the door on the back wall, and the depressingly empty bedroom through the door on the back right. The grand total of my kingly castle, currently dirtier than I'd meant it to get.

I made myself a cup of rehydrated dehydrated soup, continued the worn argument in my head for another hour, more out of habit than anything else, and then went back to the bedroom to lie down.

As the machine turned on, canceling out my brain waves, I pretended it canceled out the argument too. I dreamed of pack rats clawing me, and I woke up tired and far too early.

I got breakfast, scrubbed the apartment more for something to do than anything else.

Regret rode me for not falling off the wagon last night, but the decision had been clear, and regret was an old friend. He didn't scare me anymore.

The phone at my apartment rang with a piercing shriek just before I left the door. I sighed and went back for it.

"Hello? Who is this?"

"Hi, this is Rachel Muñez," a woman's voice said crisply. "Is this Adam Ward?"

"Yes," I said, and sat down on my cot. "What is it?" Rachel had been one of the department accountants handling my money for years; she wasn't warm, but she wasn't cold either. The numbers were just the numbers to her.

"I realize it's Sunday, but we've got audits all week and I wanted to make sure that I talked to you. It's going to be the weekend before I finish up the paperwork and get the final books update done. Honestly, maybe next week. These political guys are driving me nuts. Anyway, I don't want to hold up your accounts. If you're willing to work with the paperwork I have right now, I can transfer ownership this morning. You'll have one more paycheck coming, but we can—"

"Hold on. What?" I asked. I felt like I was tracking everything. It was still pretty darn early.

"I'm sorry. Was I unclear?" her voice asked, very tired. "Which part?"

"You're transferring which accounts?" I asked.

A pause came over the phone. "Um, I was told you were leaving the department."

I swallowed. "Well, yes. Paulsen's department anyway."

"Do you anticipate other arrangements?" Rachel asked. "I'm not trying to push you into anything. But with your relationship with the department ending, the money relationship does as well. You have a right to your accounts if you want them."

I looked up at the ceiling. *Years* of other people having to approve every purchase. Like I was a child. "I do want them," I said, a crazy, bright sense of relief popping up in the back of my head. "If we can get this done this morning, let's do it. How much do I have?"

"Well, with the recent transfers to the Guild Medical Fund and the—"

"How much?" I asked.

"Oh. Just a second." The sound of shuffling papers came over the line. "You have about seven thousand ROCs in cash, and another thirty in investments, plus the usual retirement funds. I've withheld tax for the rest of the year already, so that's not a concern." She paused. "Do you have a preferred bank?"

I blinked. Holy crap, that was more money than I'd had at once since my Guild days. Way more than I thought I'd had. "I thought we cleaned out the accounts for the medical stuff," I said.

"Not quite. And you've been spending considerably less than you've been making for years. We talked about investing several times, Adam. You said to go ahead." Her voice was annoyed. "Did I do wrong?"

"No," I said. "No." I racked my brain, and finally came up with the name of a credit union who'd been particularly difficult to get information from in the last case. "Let's put the money there," I said.

"I'll get it done today."

"Thanks," I said, and hung up.

"Well, I have good news and bad news for you," Cherabino's voice said over the phone. I'd called her presumably to ask about the Wright case, but actually to hear her voice. With everything else . . . well, I just needed to hear her voice right now.

"Give me the good news first," I said. I needed good news.

"Well, I read your mysterious file and did some research on the soldier project. Then I called Cornell to ask her about them. You know, Wright's supervisor at the lab? It turns out Wright was upset when the project turned from a medical monitoring and stabilization device to an enhancement project for the military. He objected to the secretization of what they were doing—supervisor said he literally screamed at her at one point, something about the good of all mankind."

"She didn't strike me as the kind of woman who'd be all that offended by that. Socially awkward and all, but she seemed to be satisfied that justice was done when he got fired."

"That wasn't my read of the situation at all," Cherabino said, thinking it through. "She seemed satisfied all right, but her employees all seemed a little afraid of her. One said she had a way of lashing out at him when he did something wrong. She could say really cutting things, he said, and when he tried to defend himself he thought she was going to throw something."

"Are you sure we're talking about the same woman?" I asked. "She seemed so harmless to me."

"Let's be honest, Adam, you were hanging on her every word. Of course she seemed harmless to you. I didn't like her."

"I spent a lot more time with her than you did, and there's always that one guy who complains," I said. Cornell'd had such an interesting mind it was hard to believe she was a bad guy, but maybe I had been distracted. "Did she set off your cop instinct?"

"She didn't seem normal," she said cautiously.

"Really, Cherabino. Do you think she could have swung the ax that much? She's not a big woman."

"She runs marathons, according to her file. She has the fitness level. And the ax was at the most five pounds."

I was disturbed at the thought that I had met someone who potentially could have killed someone that violently. Especially someone with that cool new kind of mind. "She just . . ."

"Doesn't seem the type? Maybe. I don't believe in types anymore. I've seen too many people do too many bad things."

I took a breath. "What was the good news again?"

"Ah. The ME found a tendril of some kind of foreign biologic matter in what's left of the back of Wright's head. She's been running every test known to man on it, and coming up blank. I sent her a copy of the report—and she thinks it's a piece of this thing they were testing."

"Contamination?" I asked.

"No, she thinks it was installed—I don't know with or without the lab's permission—and Wright was using himself as a test subject. And get this, Adam, the report references a section in this creature-thing designed to go down the skin on the top of the arm, you know, to control it or something. I don't really understand the science."

"And we had that missing piece of the arm."

"And the back of the head," she said almost gleefully. "Yes, exactly. That gives us motive. I say the supervisor killed him in retaliation for spilling company secrets, take it a step further, say stealing company property. She takes it back—and the rest of the ax wounds are there to cover up her primary purpose."

"That's . . . diabolical," I said.

"You said whoever killed him got really focused there at the end. That it was about control. That would fit."

I tried to remember the scene in detail. "Yeah . . . but that mind . . . I didn't think it was a female."

A pause. "Is that something you could get wrong? Or do I need to keep looking?"

I looped through the footage of the scene in my mind, the feel of that mind, the violence. Then back to my interactions with the supervisor. "She doesn't have a typical female mind. And that kind of violence would skew any kind of read I'd have of someone. Most people don't get that violent in everyday life." I took a breath. As much as I didn't want to think it . . . "Yeah, it's as good a theory as any. It explains the missing pieces. If you can bring her in and get a confession, that will get one more case off your desk."

"I'd rather you interrogate her, given the choice. She likes you already. When are you going to be here? I have some leeway in scheduling, though I'd like to get her here in the next few days."

"Um, the thing is . . ."

"What?"

Might as well just jump in. "Paulsen said I can't work in the interview rooms anymore, because of the Guild thing. Apparently I've lost my credibility." I didn't understand it even now. I mean, what credibility did I have to lose? I was a felon, and the cops never let me forget that anyway.

"You got yourself fired *again?* Wait. What Guild thing? I swear I'd like to jump through this phone and strangle you. You have to tell me this shit if I'm supposed to get you hired back!" She made a low, frustrated sound. "How bad is it? What exactly did Paulsen say?"

I sighed, and caught her up with what had happened,

and about the case I'd taken on for the Guild, partially for Kara, and partially because I didn't have any choice. I left out the debt but included the threats. "I mean, the only thing she said was that I definitely couldn't do interview room work again right now. She said what Bransen wants to do with his team is up to him."

She made an airy growling sound. "So I have to clear this with Bransen now. *Why* didn't you tell me before we started talking casework?"

"I already have all the pieces. It's not an information concern. Look, I know you're overwhelmed. I figured I'll see this Wright case through, give you as much help as I can, maybe use the results to talk to Bransen about coming on full-time. If not, there's always the FBI."

"I thought that was stalled."

I sighed. "Who knows?" I paused. Worse comes to worst, if I was out on the street again . . . "Want to open a private detective agency, just you and me?" I asked, half joking.

"Don't tempt me," she said, a little too quickly. "They gave me another two cases yesterday. I don't know where they think I'm getting the time for this." Knowing her, she was already sleeping at the office to try to catch up.

"Like I said, I'd like to help."

She sighed. "I appreciate it. Let me arrest this woman and see if we can get a confession. If we can, I'll bring you in on a couple more cases if Bransen says it's okay. Um, I have no idea if you'll get paid for it."

"If it helps get me rehired with his department, I can do without the money for a while. Besides, it helps you out."

She huffed. "Thanks. Really. I'll feed you at least."

"Mexican?" I asked. She hated Mexican food, my favorite in the world.

"Not all the time."

"Okay."

No matter what I told Cherabino, I knew it wasn't all that likely Bransen would hire me on at the end of all of this—for one thing, I'd have the exact same problems justifying my job that I'd had with Paulsen. I really did have to call the FBI, and see if they'd meant that job offer a few weeks ago. But here, now, I didn't have anything else to lose, and Swartz's words just wouldn't leave me.

"Cherabino?" I asked.

"What?"

I jumped in, no prep, rip the bandage off. "I wondered if you'd like to accompany me to a restaurant tonight."

There was a pause, and I knew her well enough to know what she was thinking. We'd been to restaurants plenty of times; why was I asking? "Like a date?" she asked.

That didn't seem promising. Normally I was better at this, damn it. "I—"

"Okay. But you're taking me somewhere nice, right?"

I closed my mouth so as to avoid the appearance of a dead fish. "Um, well—"

"Yeah, your payment thing. I'll bring my wallet and you can get the accountants to reimburse. We can go Dutch. I can play the feminist card. Whatever. That's not really the point, is it?"

"No, not at all." I blinked. Really? That was a yes? I thought on my feet. "How about the French place on the square?" They had candles on the tables and everything; you could see them through the window.

"I've never been there."

"Want to walk over after work?" I asked. Cherabino was one of those health nuts; she'd rather walk anywhere than drive, and I was getting so I didn't mind. "Let's say seven? I can meet you at the station."

There was a long pause on the phone.

"If tonight's not a good—"

"No, that'll work," she said. "Seven sounds good."

A minute or so later, I hung up the phone. Part of me had relaxed. The rest was twisted up in knots. What in the world had I gotten myself into? I was going on a date. A date. With Cherabino.

Was there time for me to buy a new shirt?

CHAPTER 14

Selah answered the phone. "Hello?"

"It's me. Is Swartz around?"

Her voice seemed bleary. "Adam, it's eight thirty on a Sunday."

"Don't you have church at eleven?" I asked.

She took a deep breath. "Not today. He's sleeping. It's been a hard week for him. He already came out to meet you Friday."

"Can I come by later?"

A pause. "I don't think it's a good idea. The doctor says he needs to rest. His heart is still struggling to adjust. Adam?"

"Yes?"

"If you need something, maybe you should go to a meeting."

I thought about that. "Is there one on a Sunday morning?"

She sighed. "I guess I can look it up for you." I heard footsteps, a cabinet door opening, then the rustling of papers. "Here it is. Higher-Power-based meeting, heroin focus, ten a.m. Sunday in the East Atlanta Community Center." She read me an address, which I wrote down. "Or there's one at noon in Tucker. That one's faith-based."

"Thanks, Selah. I really appreciate it."

"You're welcome," she said. "If you can, send a card or something this week. He's feeling pretty isolated."

"You got it," I said. "If you decide I can visit—just to say hello—let me know."

"Okay."

We said our good-byes and hung up. And I was left with the address of a meeting in East Atlanta. Assuming the buses ran on time, I should be able to make it a little early, even.

The East Atlanta meeting was held in a brick building that smelled of old sewers, with industrial carpet that hadn't been changed in decades if not before. But the feeling in Mindspace was like a well-loved sweater, worn over and over until it sat like a hug. Children's art projects were displayed proudly in the lobby. Even a little dirt couldn't take away from that.

A printed sign pointed down a hallway to the right, and I followed the smell of coffee. People greeted me warmly, but when I didn't want to shake hands, didn't push. Looked like it was a men's-only group, and the overall feel of the group was like the feel of the building, well-worn and comfortable. This room had framed leaves up on the walls, somehow still green, and of course the ubiquitous display of program leaflets. Maybe I should poke through those to look for survival techniques while juggling two jobs—the program probably had a brochure with the topic. They had a brochure on everything.

I settled in with a cup of coffee to my preferred place about halfway back, where I could see everything but not be the center of attention. The leader, an older black man with a calm personality and nearly white hair, opened us up with the usual readings for the month, words that washed over me like a balm.

Selah was right. I was feeling better already.

Men told stories, funny stories, tragic stories, everyday

stories, around their recovery and their struggles. Like Selah had said, they were mostly heroin addicts here, but some of my best friends on the street had been in that category, so it felt as familiar as anything else. My drug was an odd designer one anyway.

I listened to a guy get up, raw and new, and start talking about his first weeks without his drug. I started turning over things I could say—until he caught my attention.

"I thought it would be easier, you know, since I switched to Satin from Blue the year before. I mean, even together they didn't hit you with the same wallop. But I still want Blue, and when I don't want Blue, I want Satin. It hurts. I still walk by the same block and I wonder if Jimmy still has the stuff."

One of the older guys spoke up then. "Sometimes you gotta take another bus."

"Walk a different street," someone else put in.

"It's easier to stay a long way away than say no up close," a younger guy said. "You're making it tougher than it has to be."

I took the effort to read the new guy then, and found, unexpectedly, that he had a significant precog Ability. Those kinds of future flashes could be as much a curse as a blessing, and I could understand wanting to get away from them. Satin would have hooked him hard and fast, just like it had me; the chemical affected the part of the brain that hosted Ability, so that the stronger you were, the stronger it hooked you.

While I was in his head, insidiously, I stole the information about which block he was talking about, a place at Little Five Points where he got most of what he wanted, what Jimmy looked like, and what you said to get him to sell to you. He was thinking about the topic anyway, so the breach wasn't too terribly deep, I told myself.

I hated myself for it, but I stored the information away carefully, in case of future need. The drug, as they said in the program, was a wily foe.

If Swartz had been there, I would have stepped up and talked about that, maybe, a little. Here, in a group where I was a stranger, another older guy spoke and the moment was over.

I went to the bank and got real money, just to hold, just to have, and bought myself lunch—an excellent deli sandwich and a cup of hot soup to ward off the cold. Then I went back to the apartment. It was still hours before I was supposed to meet Cherabino.

I picked up the phone and dialed, expecting to leave a message at the FBI switchboard.

Instead a man's voice picked up. "Special Agent Louis Jarred."

I sat back on my small couch and told him who I was. "I hadn't expected you to be there on a Sunday."

"Paperwork waits for no man. What can I do for you, Ward?"

I shifted. Might as well rip the bandage off and just ask. "Listen, we talked a while ago about a possible job consulting with you guys on cases. Is that offer still on the table?" I winced, waiting. That could have been smoother. That could have been a lot smoother.

He cleared his throat. "Ward, I'll be completely honest with you. The bureau has managed to hire a part-time consultant telepath. We've been very happy with her work."

"Oh." My heart fell into my stomach. No job? I'd just lost the thing at the police station, and now no possibility of FBI work?

"I'm sorry, Ward. I don't see us looking again for a while."

I swallowed my pride. "Well, if you have a heavy work-load of cases or something local, you can call me anytime."

"I'll keep that in mind," Jarred said.

"Please do."

There was a pause over the line. I tried to think of a good small-talk question. I was terrible at that sort of thing.

"There may be an opportunity for a contract job, a week or two at the most, occasionally. But it would be on no notice."

I paused exactly two seconds, so as not to appear desperate. "Subject to the approval of my boss here, that should be no issue. And they can approve quickly."

"Good to hear."

A minute or so of small talk—which he ran—and it was over.

Maybe, just maybe, there was a glimmer of hope on the horizon.

A fresh shave later, my apartment was excessively clean, and I was debating the merits of the new shirt I'd bought versus the older, more-broken-in one. Which would make me feel less awkward? I went back and forth before deciding I was expecting too much out of a shirt. I sat down, gut churning, and reminded myself of what Swartz had said. She'd already seen me at my worst. I'd already basically lost my job. What was I really nervous about?

That didn't help at all.

So I called Swartz, and he was actually awake and willing to come to the phone. He calmed me down and gave me homework. Swartz was useful like that.

A woman in a tight blue dress stood at the bottom of the police department steps, a dark coat set over one arm. Her breath fogged in the light of the streetlight behind her.

My thoughts trailed off as the woman turned.

It was Cherabino, her hair down and set in some kind of new curl. It stretched halfway down her back and framed her face to perfection; a new cut perhaps. I hadn't seen it down in months. The dress was modestly cut, but it clung to all the right places; it was a little too tight across her significant breasts, which I appreciated.

I drew my attention back to her face, which had subtle makeup on, the most makeup I'd seen her wear outside a funeral. I pulled my brain out of my shorts and said, "You look beautiful." I added a pulse of sincerity through the Link so she would see sincerity, admiration, and a pleasant surprise. "You didn't have to dress up," I said.

She smiled, and was suddenly Cherabino again through all the layers of beauty. "I don't get to wear a dress very often anymore. Don't worry. I still have a gun."

"Where?" I asked before I could censor myself. The dress was tight.

"Don't ask," she said, but she was smiling.

"Shall we?" I asked, gesturing in as gentlemanly a way as possible toward the square.

"Sure, why not," she said. "Here, help me with my coat."

I took the coat and folded it out. She put one arm in, and I helped her find the other, bending over slightly to her level. We were close; my breath warmed the back of her neck.

She shivered and pulled the coat around her carefully, turning around.

I waited for the rebuke, but none came. She was soft, and beautiful under the streetlight. The moment seemed to stretch forever.

Cherabino glanced back up at the well-lit glass windows of the police station; a siren sounded, likely someone coming in with a suspect. "Let's get out of here," she said.

So we did.

I vowed to myself that at no time during this miracle of an evening would I talk about the police department or my recent firing. Knowing myself—and knowing her—I had done what Swartz nagged me to do, and planned ahead. Taken most of the afternoon, but there it was. I had a list of not-work topics carefully handwritten in my pocket in case I got stuck.

Who knew if the evening would ever happen again?

We walked along Church Street, the flyer dealership to the right closing down for the night, the small local-owned nightclub to the left already forming a line in front. The high notes of Irish electric fiddle spilled out through the door as someone entered. An old homeless man had found an out-of-the-way corner near the heater vent at the side of the club; Cherabino noted him but let him be.

"How is your sister doing?" I asked, first on my list of topics. "With Jacob and the new teacher?"

She looked up and smiled. "Jacob's doing very well, like I said. My sister is at her wits' end with his stunts, but to be honest she's thrilled he has the energy."

"A good teacher can make all the difference," I said, out of rote, and then caught myself. It had been a long time since I was a professor. Some shred of pride in it still remained, obviously; maybe there was a reason I connected so well with Swartz.

"I just wanted to say thank you again," Cherabino said quietly. "I would have had no idea how to handle the situation. I'd do anything for Nicole, especially with Jacob. It's been a hard road for him, and he's . . . he's a special kid. I'd do anything for him as well."

"You're welcome," I said. Our conversation was constrained, of course; probably no one in the crowd was Guild or had Guild interests, but we couldn't take the chance. Until

Jacob was old enough to join the Irish Telepath Corps in his own right, the Guild discovering him would be a disaster. It was unlikely he'd survive the harsh world of the Guild.

But I'd let the conversation lag too long. Now she was thinking about my firing, and her conversation with Bransen, which hadn't gone as well as she'd hoped. I told myself I wasn't supposed to be snooping in her thoughts, and put some distance and a wall between us.

I searched for a topic, any topic. Finally: "Jacob has brothers and sisters, right?"

"That's right?"

"How are they handling all the extra attention for him?" I asked.

"Oh, the usual kid stuff." Cherabino moved into a funny story about a failed water balloon fight in the backyard, and the awkwardness was put aside, at least for now.

We passed the Decatur MARTA subway station and several small luxury goods shops: a handmade woodcraft shop, a jewelry store, even a toy depot and a paperback bookstore, along with a small specialty deli on the corner. The conversation went pretty well, my list coming in handy.

Then we found the restaurant, and the maitre d' seated us, doing that fancy thing where he pulled out the chair for Cherabino and settled the napkin on her lap. I could *feel* her tension at a stranger getting that close without warning, but she held on and I held on to her earlier laughter.

Then the waiter was filling water glasses and the moment was very quiet, and very romantic. A real flower graced the table. A candle burned, a spot of light in a dim room. And soft music echoed throughout the small space; we were away from the window, as Cherabino had requested, all the way back in a corner with her facing the room. I felt comfortable enough that I'd feel a mind approach before it got close not to mind facing away.

"This is a pretty place," Cherabino said quietly, and looked anywhere but at me. It wasn't about the firing, but I couldn't tell what it was.

The menus arrived, and I looked through them, more for something to do than out of any real hunger. I paged through a few times, and realized absently that after ten years away, I could still puzzle out the French terms. My French was borrowed, not properly learned, from Kara. Her mother's side was European, based out of Brussels and Sweden but living all over Europe, and multilingual all. I had a couple of languages in my head that way, but French and German weren't at all common in the cases we worked; more Spanish and Japanese than anything.

The waiter came, and Cherabino ordered a few items in badly accented French; that made me close the menu and stare. I knew for a fact that she did not speak anything but halting Spanish; apparently she had access to my skills through the Link. I ordered in English, worrying the whole time. Had I done something? I'd promised her that the Link would be temporary. Was I breaking my promise?

Meanwhile, another waiter showed up with a wine bottle, and I wasn't fast enough to stop him from pouring. Red wine, the thick stuff, the stuff that smelled like great meals and great people, the stuff I associated so strongly with Guild training staff dinners, senior folks only. Alcohol and telepathy didn't mix well unless everyone involved had great control; otherwise thoughts spread and rippled like a game of telephone, impossible to turn off. I wasn't allowed to have alcohol now either, but for an entirely different reason. A reason that had everything to do with Swartz and nothing to do with staff dinners.

A spark of startlement came over the Link and Cherabino, wineglass in hand, set it down. "I didn't think, I'm sorry." She waved for the waiter. "Take these away and bring us tea, okay?"

The waiter did, but then the manager arrived in a snooty suit. "There is something wrong with the wine, madam?"

"We'll pay for it," I said. "Just don't bring us any more."

Cherabino smiled too brightly. "My new meds interact with the alcohol. I'm sorry. I forgot."

Relief washed over me. I didn't have to be the one at fault.

When the manager left, Cherabino leaned forward. "Look, I'm sorry. I forget."

"It's fine," I said, but the shiny had worn off the evening. I was reminded again of everything I wasn't anymore. Everything I wouldn't be again.

We sat in silence for a long moment, me trying to pull it together. I shifted, and the paper list in my pocket crunched. I should pull that out and come up with something else to talk about. I'd prepared.

"You know what, this was a terrible idea," Cherabino said.

Panic hit me. "What are you—?"

The food came, and she said, "Put it in a box, okay? We're going to take it with us. And bring the check."

"It's my fault—I picked the place," I said, too quickly. "I'll pay."

The evening was over before I'd even gotten a chance to kiss her! Crap, I was acting like a fifteen-year-old. I sat on my disappointment and my panic, sat hard and put it in a box to be dealt with later. I could be gracious. I had known this was a bad idea, Swartz or no Swartz. "Let me take you back to the station," I said carefully. I would handle this. I would. "You don't have to drive me home. I'll get the bus. It will be fine."

She leaned forward again and said very quietly, "Don't

be an idiot. We're going to have a picnic at the deli, and you're going to walk me back and kiss me. Like a proper first date." She looked very small for a second. "That is, if you still want to."

"Oh," I said eloquently. "Yes, yes, of course." The boxes arrived and the details of the check were taken care of—by me, the one spot of pride in the evening. Getting fired at least had one perk.

Walking out, though, Cherabino pulled her hair up in a clip. A sense of relief crashed over me like a tidal wave as we left the restaurant.

The deli, on the other hand, was run-down and the owner was cranky until we bought something from him too. This made me feel much better.

"I'll take potato chips," I said.

"And two teas," Cherabino said, amused.

The owner came back, grumbling, and overcharged us for disposable paper-stock forks. His demeanor settled me down, though. Made things go back to clear, to real. And when he cozied up behind the counter with a crossword, we were alone in the place. Potato chips went surprisingly well with escargot.

We ate, and I went back to my list. I got Cherabino to laugh, the forthright belly laugh I loved about her, the one that hit my brain like fizzy flecks of gold. I sat there and enjoyed it. Perhaps inevitably, as we were most of the way through the food, a uniformed officer poked his head in the door. "Oh, good, I found you," he said. "The last homicide detective on duty is throwing up from food poisoning. Captain wants to know if Cherabino can come in and take care of a murder on Mimosa Drive."

"Do they need me?" I asked.

"No," the officer said. "Seems like a straightforward

shooting. Witnesses got a clear look at the guy. But it needs processing."

Cherabino glanced at me.

"Go on," I said, doing my best to hide my disappointment. There wasn't any way I could go too, not now.

She looked back over at the officer and just stood up, no hug, no anything. I could feel her mind settle back into hard-shelled Cop Mode.

"See you," she said, a generic sound. Nothing about doing this again.

I forced a smile. It had been inevitable, after all. "See you."

I threw out the rest of the food as soon as she left, and went to find the bus stop. At least I'd get to tell Swartz he was wrong. This new leaf of his after his heart issues was clearly making him soft.

I had an impulse to go down to Fulton County to score a few hits of my drug, even got so far as to check the bus routes at the closest stop, but I knew I wouldn't go. Nothing had changed, after all, and if Swartz had pushed me, well, I'd let him. Nothing had changed, I told myself again. This was a crappy reason to fall off the wagon after nearly four years clean.

Didn't mean I was happy, though.

The next morning I was staring at my microwave, churning away to cook my last frozen-biscuit breakfast, feeling sorry for myself, when it hit. A sudden premonition crawled up my spine. Someone was about to charge the front door.

Before I could react, a loud *bang* from the apartment door four feet away. I stood up, took two steps. I was going to have to move if all these damn people could—

My adrenaline spiked. Three guards in Guild uniforms were in my living room.

"I negotiated for time—" I started.

Turner was at the back. "You need to be at the Guild. Now."

Then I was on the floor, looking at their shoes again. *You can't do this,* I thought. *I work for the police. You can't just push me around like—*

You don't work for the police anymore, Turner said. *And you're overdue to check in with Rex.*

And then the world went black.

CHAPTER 15

I **woke up** in the empty interrogation room where I'd talked to Meyers's ex-wife and the woman who'd brought in the original madness report. I didn't see a camera, but I was certain one was there.

I blinked, hard. My head hurt, a pounding pain that settled in my teeth, and my vision wouldn't quite focus. "Damn it, I would have come here voluntarily," I told the air. "There was no need to knock me out."

I shook my head, trying to clear my vision, but it only made the headache worse. I poked around in my head, to assess the damage. Near as I could tell, no one had done anything but knock me out, which was both comforting and yet not boding well for the future.

"You know, I'm getting tired of being pushed around. Whoever's watching me might as well come in."

So I waited. And waited.

After a while, I stood up and tried the door. Locked. I shook it. Not a flimsy lock, and by the looks of it something complicated. Even assuming I could find something in here to work as a lock pick, I wasn't sure I could manage this particular setup. Plus there was the camera I was sure was there, and the Guild didn't know I could pick locks yet. All in all, not worth it now.

I sat back down, grumbling. I'd wait a little while.

After what felt like seven years, there was a knock on the door.

"That's awfully polite," I said. I'd been rethinking the lock concept again, so this was a welcome distraction.

"Can I come in?" Kara's voice came through.

You sent the guards? I sent to her, along with a sense of shock and mounting betrayal.

A scraping sound, and then she opened the door. "No. No, nothing like that," she said out loud. Stone was behind her.

Kara came in. I looked at her. She looked at me. There were deep, deep circles under her eyes, which were puffy like she'd been crying. Her hair was dull, pulled back in a messy ponytail I hadn't seen on her since exams. Finally she gestured for Stone to leave the room and close the door.

"Rex sent the guards. He's getting nervous, or so Turner said. She's giving me fifteen minutes, so I have to talk fast," she said.

"How do I know you're telling the truth?" I asked her. "You're playing your family's game. You always have been."

She flinched like I'd hit her. Then set her jaw. "Listen or don't listen, but like I said, we don't have much time. We found a device in the assistant's room, the one who killed himself. Stone found it. It's a mind manipulator, similar to the one you found connected to Tamika weeks ago. Someone was influencing them both."

I blinked. She'd gotten my attention. "What are you talking about?"

"As near as we can tell, it's been used on both Meyers and his assistant. This is a device I was told would never, never be developed for use, even if there was another war. I was assured her plans were burned—and our family expert tells me this version is worse."

"Is this a trap?" I asked her point-blank, and looked

back up at the ceiling where I assumed the camera was. "You knock me out, you come back in here and start spouting conspiracy theories? You're trying to get me on tape as conspiring against the Guild so you can lock me up, is that what this is?"

Kara's Mindspace presence wavered again. I ignored the hurt feeling coming off her. She'd been hurt far too much while manipulating me. She could probably manufacture the feeling by now.

"Stone has disabled any listening devices," Kara said. "You don't understand. These devices are a problem. Someone manipulated Uncle Meyers and Spirale into committing suicide and blamed it on madness. Someone started all of this hell on purpose!" She breathed hard. "The device matches the hole behind the painting you found in Uncle Meyers's apartment. We shut down the scene fast enough to keep them from removing the device from Spirale's place, apparently."

She barreled on: "The killer used Guild official resources. Official ones. There are tracked parts, official parts with official serial numbers in this device. We've looked it up. There's enough parts out of the inventory for three devices. At least. Requisitioned by an official lab. Who knows what else they're building, what damage they'll cause? And someone official approved this crap!" She set her shoulders, took a minute to get back under control.

"You and your family will destroy the Guild," I said, chilled.

"I didn't say that," she said, quickly, but she didn't look at the camera. She truly didn't believe she was being recorded. And that fast—that fast—my whole attitude changed.

"I don't have a lot of time, Adam. I'll do whatever it takes to shut this down. The Council and Guild First and all the Tech in the world aren't going to stop me. And Hawk will back me up. I will do whatever I have to do—*whatever I have to do to protect my family and what is right.*" She was breathing hard now, and angry too.

"What do you want from me?" I asked. I was going to get caught in the wheels of this, wasn't I? We were well beyond a single murder investigation now. "Kara, you need to be sure it's official before you do anything rash. Experiments are one thing. Anybody could break into the vault— we saw that with Bradley. It doesn't mean—"

"These things should not exist!" she yelled at me. "Guild First is destroying everything! You can't build a bomb and then not use it. You'll be tempted every single day!"

A scraping sound, and then the door opened again. Stone stood there. "This isn't a good place to have a screaming match," Stone said quietly. "They have to be on their way by now." He looked at me. "You want process. You want a chance to prove innocence. It's the time. Help us bring Meyers's murderer to light. Help us do it the right way," he added, looking at Kara with suspicion.

I didn't know how much he'd heard, but clearly they weren't easy allies.

I took a breath, forcibly damping down the anger and the pain until I could think. Then: "Show me the device. This thing you found that fits the tear I found in the room."

Stone produced it. The thing was a cube with blinking lights, on the surface very much like the horrible thing that had made me suggestible the day Bellury died a few weeks ago. I wanted to throw it to the floor and jump on it until it was little pathetic pieces. I wanted to fillet it with knives and crush it with rollers and then let Gustolf burn the pieces. Twice.

That's about how I feel, Stone told me. *Some things should never, never be used on our own people.*

They should not exist, Kara added, with heat.

On second, closer look, I saw the circular inset used to control the thing, a more highly engineered, more professionally produced piece. Small resonators, little square wires, covered the thing. Dane's research into mind-waves perverted.

I turned and deliberately said out loud, "Kara's right. Some things should not exist."

Stone moved farther into the room. "The only way to shut this down is to find the people behind it. We've got resources but you've got more. And honestly, it has to be someone high up in the Council to pull this off. No one else has the power. I'm asking you to help us figure out who before this escalates so we can bring them to justice before things get worse." He looked at Kara again.

"I trust you to tell me the truth," Kara said reluctantly. "But we won't hold off forever."

"I'm stuck between a rock and a hard place, aren't I? Seems to be what you specialize in, Kara. Just so we're clear: this is a Koshna violation. This kind of technology is illegal in all fifty states for normals, and so illegal for the Guild that war will start over it if someone is caught out. This country needs another war like I need a lobotomy. I'm doing this for that reason, Kara."

"I don't care why you do it. This stuff needs to end," she said. "Find me Uncle Meyers's murderer and I will make it end."

"I told you I would find the guy," I said. "I told you that. Just promise me you're not going to start a war over the information."

She was silent.

"We need to go," Stone said.

How in hell was I going to solve this in time to keep

things from blowing up? There was far, far more at stake now than just one guy's murder, no matter how good a guy he'd been.

There was the Guild as a whole, and more than one kind of war at stake. Who was I to stand in the way of all this?

But it had been my Guild once too. I had to try. I had to figure this out, and soon.

Turner and another three guard types brought me to a small room on the top level of the professional building. The clear glass windows had a fantastic view of the Buckhead business district, the towering buildings already starting to show their evening light schemes, office workers moving around, sitting at desks, working late.

At the end of the room staring out at the office buildings was one Thaddeus Rex, who even at rest had the carefully cultured successful-politician stance. I could almost see the photo in an editorial spread in the newspaper. Waiting in the opposite corner was head of Enforcement Tobias Nelson, who looked less regal but more dangerous.

"Adam Ward and Edgar Stone to see you," Johanna said. "I assume you'd like someone to take notes on the proceedings?"

Rex looked up. "Thank you, Johanna, but no. Not this time. You're welcome to go home."

I thought I felt a flash of anger from her direction, but when I looked closer she seemed perfectly composed. "Mrs. Martinez will be back tomorrow and I won't have nearly the free time I do now. Are you sure there's nothing else I can do for you?"

"No, I believe that's all for now. Kind of you to fill in when my assistant fell ill. I'll make sure to note your helpfulness on your file."

She nodded. "Thank you, Mr. Rex."

"Close the door on your way out?"

That almost-there flash of anger again, something I could have sworn I'd seen. But maybe it was me. Maybe it was my distrust of her because of who she reminded me of. Either could easily result in seeing things, not to mention the suggestion of madness in the place.

She closed the door behind her, and I found myself alone in a room with major Guild power players— and Stone, who'd proven over and over again he had his own agenda.

"You wanted to see us?" Stone asked. "We are in the middle of an investigation and time is short."

Rex turned and picked up a paper from the large desk in front of him.

Nelson waited, but while his presence in Mindspace was cold and hard, his body language was uncomfortable and impatient. He was watching Rex too much.

"You're here to rake me over the coals, aren't you?" I asked. "Either that or mind-wipe me. Why else would you send goons to my apartment to drag me here while I'm out doing what you asked me to do in the first place?" I lowered my shields, a risk, but I'd rather see what was coming, especially in this kind of room.

Rex's head came up then, and he looked like someone who had scraped something off his shoe. Tobias just looked angry.

"I've been told you have no viable suspects in the death of Del Meyers," Rex said. "It's been several days since I recruited you, and I told you then I expect results. What results do you have?"

"None whatsoever," Nelson said.

"I can't discuss ongoing investigations," I said, because I didn't want to discuss anything with Nelson there, just as a matter of principle. "We are making progress and expect to have an answer for you soon." I monitored Mindspace, even the slightest change. There was a mind, maybe, outside the door. Johanna listening in?

"What about you, Stone?"

Beside me, the man adjusted his stance. I could almost see the conflict of loyalty. I honestly didn't know if he was going to stay quiet.

I put up a light shield, enough to keep my thoughts from spilling. I knew that Kara wanted him—wanted me—to stay quiet. That she had some kind of epic family scheme going on to deal with the Tech. Though of course she hadn't told me what it was. In fact, she'd left at the first possible opportunity.

And I also knew that if you really wanted to know the truth about something, confronting someone with information could be the best way to go. It had worked for me time and time again in the interview rooms. And it was, just barely, possible to lie to a telepath. In fact, if one did it out loud, and one was used to lying out loud, it might be very possible indeed.

And if they were really, truly going to lock me up or mind-wipe me anyway, I might as well go all in.

I dropped the shield again and let my decision crystallize where they could see it. Then I read Mindspace ever so carefully, down to the slightest wave. Down to the slightest change of a mind in front of me.

"We've found a Tech device that influences mind-waves left in both apartments," I said freely, letting my words be a skipping stone along a pond, always moving. "We have evidence to show that you, Rex, planted them there."

Rex did a double take. Then he turned to Nelson. "What in the hell have you done! I gave you latitude with that stuff—but it was never to be used against the Guild!"

"But—I didn't—" Nelson sputtered.

Bingo. I used the moment of distraction to seep into Nelson's mind.

And there it was: Nelson had been receiving security devices from Research in exchange for getting them certain parts. Certain illegal Tech parts obtained from . . . I saw a shadowy face, and an exchange.

Tobias had met with Fiske. Personally. Had been meeting with him for years.

Stone's mind was suddenly right there with me, as he'd grabbed my arm or some such. I shared what I knew. He, in shock, moved away.

Tobias's attention went to us then, and he moved all of his defenses against me—

Too slow. Too distracted.

I activated the sleep center of the brain and pulled back.

Rex was saying, "—so-called evidence is clearly a plant to cast doubt on the Guild First party. To be honest, I didn't think the Cooperists had it in them."

He looked to the side, reacted to Nelson's collapse.

"What did you do?" he said to me in a dangerous voice.

I said, "I found your killer."

Rex pushed a button on his desk, and the air *popped* as teleporters displaced the air. I found myself staring into the barrels of two guns.

Stone grabbed my arm. I could suddenly *feel* his anger and shock and concern. *You knocked out the head of Enforcement. The head of Enforcement! They'll execute us. They'll do worse.* He added layer upon layer of his own conflicting loyalties and what I'd told Kara.

I wrenched my arm away.

"You just made a very serious accusation," Rex said, in a cold voice. "Nelson appears to be breathing, so I'll give you the opportunity to explain yourself. Choose your next words carefully. They may be your last."

I looked into the barrel of those guns and reality hit. I blinked, and talked for my life. "You're looking for the person who manipulated two leading people in the Guild into starting a madness epidemic, or at least the suggestion of one. With illegal Tech, a device with parts supplied by a man named Garrett Fiske. Fiske is arguably the most important man in the Southeast organized crime world, and he and Nelson have met. Repeatedly. Over the last several years."

Rex took a step forward. "How do you know this?"

"I read it from his mind," I said, turning my attention to him, though the back of my head screamed to look at the gun. He was the danger. He. Even if I could somehow disable both guards here and get away, he had promised to track me down, and I believed he would. "You hired me because I can get into and out of the deepest part of people's minds quickly and without them knowing. You recruited me because you wanted me to do this for you."

"He's telling the truth," Stone said.

I glanced over. He was pale, adrenaline moving all too quickly. He'd set his gun on the floor and had his hands in the air.

Rex regarded us. "You saw Nelson using the device you referenced to kill Meyers? Or, I suppose, force him to kill himself?"

"No," Stone said, and stepped into my mind to take the information he wanted. I let him. "Adam saw him meeting with a man he knows as Fiske."

I had to step in then. "Fiske is a very dangerous man, and he's had his hand in the underground Tech trade for a while. Furthermore, he's had a hand in Bradley's and in Tamika's criminal enterprises, which threatened to publically embarrass the Guild—maybe worse. Is it such a big leap to think he's involved here? An unstable Guild only benefits him. If the government and the Guild fight on a large scale, that only benefits him. It wouldn't surprise me if he's behind all of this."

"And how does that benefit him?" Rex asked.

"Cherabino says he wants power. Instability gives him a vacuum to step into." I took a breath. I'd been talking out of my ass . . . but I actually believed it. Now that I'd said it I thought maybe it was true Fiske was doing all of this for some bigger reason. "There's no way that Nelson could be helping the Guild by cooperating with Fiske," I said. Then added, mind to mind on a private channel, *Unless those illegal shipments of yours that were getting hijacked are no longer in play.*

Rex was very unhappy with having me in his mind, and shored up the beach that separated his public from his private thoughts. *The Guild deserves every advantage in the cold war with the normals. I will not apologize for seeing to those advantages. But no. Those parts were purchased from a custom-order depot in Canada and smuggled across the border. Most are experimental. All are numbered and tracked internally in high-security locations with official labs. Most of the technology is there simply to give us additional information and resources. None—I repeat, none—were purchased as a result of high-level deals with criminals. And while the majority of the Council would rather not know details, they know it is going on. The Council chair has approved all dealings.*

He took yet another step forward, now only feet from me, barely out of the line of fire of the guns.

Stone took a step back.

I looked, again, at the barrels of the guns. The guards seemed positively unhuman in their stillness.

"You have made a very serious accusation, and it will be

dealt with appropriately," Rex said. "Moby—that is your name, is it not?"

"Yes," the man on the right said, pointing his gun at the floor but continuing to watch me carefully. The other one, on the left, a short-shaved guy with a scar over his ear, continued to point the gun.

"Moby, I ask you to take Tobias Nelson into custody. Put him in the secure cells, and don't let any of his immediate reports see him. Assuming the remainder of the Council agrees, he will have a deep mind-scan beginning tonight. Under no circumstances are you to allow him to escape, do you understand? No one else in the cell, no access unless and until I authorize personally."

Moby looked over. "Nelson, sir?"

"That's what I said. Please be quick. Your job will be much harder if he wakes up."

"Understood, sir."

He went over, picked Nelson up with some difficulty, and teleported out.

"And as for you," Rex told me, "as I said, you have leveled a very serious accusation against a respected senior member of the Guild with voting status. If—and I mean if—your claims have some validity to them, you will be rewarded. I will consider this a significant step toward paying off your debt and fulfilling your charge. The truth is welcome at the Council. However, if, as I believe is more likely, your claims are spurious, I will personally see to it that your Ability is wiped and you are released on the street with the last ten years of your life erased and no resources whatsoever to put it back together. Have I made myself clear?"

I stood only from force of habit. He was talking about undoing all of my recovery, all of my learning, everything I was, to put me back in the horrible place I'd been right when they kicked me out the first time, no resources, no knowledge of the outside world. And to do it with no Ability . . .

"That's far worse than killing me," I said, and immediately regretted saying it.

Rex smiled then, a cruel smile. "Davidson, take him into custody. Same rules as with Nelson. And be careful—this one's tricky, and he has no problem rummaging around in your mind without permission."

"We going to do this the hard way or the easy way?" Davidson asked me.

Which was how I found myself in sticky cuffs in a bear hug from a sweaty male person who was about to teleport me God knows where.

"And now for you, Stone," I heard Rex's voice say. "Don't think you're going to—"

And then the world scrambled into a kaleidoscope.

CHAPTER 16

I was in the same damn chilly cell for three hours, three echoing hours in which I had no one and nothing except my own thoughts. At least there was water this time. The floor, of course, was just as sticky and cold and uncomfortable. The sound to the other cells was turned off, though, so I didn't have to listen to the screaming.

So instead I listened to my own thoughts telling me I was going to die—or much worse, that I was going to be unmade, made something not me. I pulled out Swartz's voice over and over again to tell me not to overreact, to calm down. Sometimes it worked. Sometimes the panic seeped into my bones and took over.

Footsteps came down the hall, and I sat up like a startled rabbit. I went as close to the door as I could get without being shocked and looked down the hallway.

"Hello, Adam," Jamie mouthed when she saw me. I couldn't hear anything, but I saw the words. She had a man in uniform with a gun with her, but his body language was more wary of the surroundings than hers. I was betting she'd called in a favor with a former student.

She stepped up to the cell and pushed something in that control panel on the side of the cell. A small beep came over the cell. She said, "It's good to see you."

"What are you doing here?" I asked her.

"What are you?" she returned. "The student I trained would never have misstepped this badly."

"I didn't . . ." I trailed off.

Her eyes focused on me, and I realized all at once how much deeper the wrinkles around those eyes were. She was older—I was older—than when she'd trained me. So much older.

"Things have changed. The whole world has changed, the Guild notwithstanding, and I'm supposed to keep up with everything all at once? I don't have a rabbit for you, Jamie. I don't have a rabbit for anyone, it seems. My hat's empty."

Jamie looked at the man, who nodded and walked back to the end of the row, keeping an eye on the surroundings but giving her some privacy.

Her mind was strong enough that even through the insane shielding between us, I could feel an echo of it.

"I just finished giving my testimony to a roomful of Council members. They wanted to know if you were reliable." She held up a hand to stave off my automatic objections. "They wanted to know if you were a reliable Cooperist all those years ago. I told them that you, like Cooper, believed in unbreakable ethics. That you believed the ethics and the rules mattered more than the cost you had to pay to keep them. And even your drug habit was induced by an experiment that you did not fully understand the consequences of. I told them you were reliable, once, and that if your experience with the normal police should prove anything, it's that you've learned to be reliable again." She paused. "Did I tell them the truth?"

I stood, inches from a door that warped reality with an electrical field that might kill me if I touched it. I stood, an unthinkable distance from Jamie, in ways that had everything and nothing to do with that electrical field.

"Are you still a good person?" Jamie asked, her old wise eyes demanding me to tell her the truth.

"Yes," I said, in a rush. "Yes, I'm a good person—I am now. I want to be. I want to stand up for something that matters. I want to do something that matters, again. The Guild is getting too arrogant, Jamie. They're doing things that could break the world. And what's worse is, I don't think all of you believe in those things. Do you realize what Guild First will cost you if some of their tactics come out into the world?"

"Do you realize what it will cost us if they don't?" Jamie asked sadly.

I was floored. Jamie was . . . she was a Cooperist. She'd always been. She'd taught me!

"I'm sorry, Adam. I can't stand for idealism anymore. The normals are arming themselves against us. Not just detection devices built into their very skin, as if that wasn't worrisome enough. No, their military is arming themselves with what they're calling bats, small devices they believe will immobilize anyone with Ability through repeated bursts of Mindspace waves, like a bat's call paralyzes its insect prey."

I took a breath. That was terrifying. "Does it work?" I asked. I had no reason to doubt her; Jamie's family, like Kara's family, was an old Guild family heavily involved in the normal military under contract. If anyone in the Guild would have military information that was supposed to be secure, it would be one of these two old families.

She smiled, but it wasn't a happy smile. "It works somewhat. But not on all Abilities, and not nearly as well as they think. There's too much bleed-off into electromagnetic waves, and not enough into Mindspace directly. This will change, Adam. They will get better."

"You're Guild First?" I asked, still in shock with all

of this. "You're in favor of arming yourself against the normals?"

"I'm a pragmatist, not a proponent of podium-slapping and propaganda," Jamie said. "You know me well enough to know I believe in discourse and freedom. I'd like to try every other conceivable tactic before we use anything irrevocable. But if you're asking whether I'll side with the Guild in a war against the normals . . ." She smiled that not-smile again. "Isn't the choice obvious? There's still a place for you here, Adam. There's always been a place for you here."

"There hasn't been a place for me here since I got kicked out!" I spat. "And now you come here to gloat while they decide to do it again, only worse? That's nothing at all like the Jamie I used to know."

"That's really what you think? That I'm here to gloat?"

"Isn't it?"

"I'm here to show you support. To visit you in your dark hour. The deep-scan has already begun. If you're certain of your course, you have nothing left to fear." She took a breath. "Tobias Nelson is an incredibly powerful man. If he has done things to hurt the Guild, someone had to speak up against it. I'm proud of you for being that person. Whatever else you have become, you've become brave. And that much I recognize." She turned, as if to walk away.

"Jamie?" I asked, more quietly.

"Yes?"

"The Council sided with me for the deep-scan?"

"They recognize your training"—and there was a real smile—"and the expertise you've built the last years. The vote was overwhelmingly in your favor."

"They'll still wipe me if I'm wrong, though," I said.

"I don't know. If they do, I'll sit with you while it happens," she said, that gentle, grandmother's voice.

"You won't stand up for me?" I asked.

She took a step toward the door. "Adam, if you're lying, you're putting one of the most powerful men in the Guild through an incredible amount of pain and suffering because you were too lazy to do the job you were set to. Or, I suppose, too incompetent. I'll sit with you. I'll make your transition as easy as I can make it. You were my student. But at that point you will have earned your fate."

"That's a hell of a vote of confidence," I said.

"I'm reasonably certain you're telling the truth as you understand it," Jamie returned gently. "I must go."

"Wait. Don't—"

But she'd pushed the button already and couldn't hear me. I watched her walk away, and wondered all over again in the silence: Had I done the right thing? Fiske had to be behind this, but apparently the Guild First persons were far more concerned about their maneuvering against the normals than they were about the letter of the Koshna Accords. Would it even matter that Nelson had been making deals with the devil? Would the Council even care if people had to die as collateral damage? I realized all over again that the mind-scanners all worked directly for Nelson. They would have every reason to cover this up.

And then even Jamie wouldn't speak for me.

I was dragged out into the elevator again, then across the walkway to the main elevator for the professional building. Johanna was there when I was marched out, in cuffs.

"You're everywhere," I said. "Why are you everywhere?"

She smiled a smile that felt a little empty. "This is a Health and Human Services crisis, which is demanding the full Council vote. My boss is out of town at the conference and has empowered me at this point to take her role on the

Council. Plus there is a great deal to be done and I have the expertise to do it. Here, I'll show you where you're to go."

Back to the top floor, where a central open area had plenty of flowering plants that set off my allergies immediately. I sneezed. The guard pulled me along anyway.

"How do we tell they're ready?" the guard asked her.

"There's a light. We'll go ahead and get queued up."

We passed through two hallways, me sneezing like mad, finally settling in front of a closed double wooden door. No benches or anything stood in front of it, just the door and some empty carpet, no windows.

We waited there for maybe five minutes while we looked at the red light above the door. My tension kept ratcheting higher, and it was everything I could do to remain standing and not broadcast in Mindspace.

Johanna looked bored. It struck me as odd.

"Aren't you going to wish me good luck?" I finally asked her, more to keep my focus off what was to happen than anything else.

She glanced at me. "Luck has nothing to do with it." She was certain, then, even in Mindspace, certain about something I didn't understand. The job promotion had been good for her, maybe. Or she was pretty sure I'd get exonerated. Only she didn't feel pretty sure. She felt certain.

"Do you know what the deep-scan found?" I asked her.

A green light turned on, and she smiled.

My first time in the Guild Council room opened as the doors did.

"I'll walk under my own power, thanks," I told the guard, and did.

The room was a massive thing, raised desks in a row curving around a central open space while behind, ten-foot-high frost-free windows looked out over the city. Talk about perspective.

The raised desks meant the Council members looked down on me, literally. I was too worried about what was to come to feel anything but impatience.

Behind me, a line of chairs rimmed the outside of the wall nearest the door. Several of the chairs were filled, and it bothered me that I couldn't watch both them and the Council at once.

A woman beside me announced loudly in Mindspace, *Adam Ward, no status, removed from Guild for improper conduct, provisionally reacquired, under judgment for accusation against Tobias Nelson, Guild member First Class, voting rights, all privileges.*

Don't you think that's prejudicing the room? I broadcast back to her.

The prisoner will be silent until spoken to, Rex's voice said with hard condemnation.

A feeling of movement, of mass discussions in Mindspace, then private thoughts flying back and forth, causing waves I could feel. I couldn't intercept the thoughts without a lot more time and the willingness to be terrifically obvious. So I started cataloging my surroundings instead.

Nelson sat in a small chair near the tall desks, almost literally overshadowed by them. He looked like he'd been awake for days. His presence in Mindspace flickered like a bad lightbulb. Next to him was a man in clothes so plain they were almost a uniform. He had the quiet intensity I associated with a bodyguard or a Minder.

"Can I speak?" Nelson asked the court, in a voice that sounded . . . pained.

If you must, Diaz said. *Try to keep it to a minimum. Did you have something to say?*

"No, just the question." He looked at me, and it wasn't a pleasant look. It wouldn't be the first time someone had blamed me for the consequences of their own actions, but making an enemy so high up in the Guild was not something pleasant.

Is the scanner here? the man sitting highest, in the middle, broadcast. The chatter in Mindspace eased off.

I assumed this was Julio Diaz, head of the Council, and by all accounts, neutral between the various factions. He looked ancient, wrinkles upon wrinkles, balding, gray, and possessed of a brittle strength in Mindspace, but he did not look familiar.

She's on her way, the woman next to me said. An officer of the court, there to keep things moving. I returned my attention to the raised seats in front.

Of the ten seats, only six were currently filled, Thaddeus Rex, whom I recognized next to Diaz, a pale woman with a blue badge of an acting member next to him at Financial and Budgets, a woman I vaguely recognized from Research— was her name Chin, or was I making that up?—and Chris Tubbs, Kara's ultimate boss, behind Guild-World Relations. Charlie Walker, whom I'd gone to school with, was currently sitting behind Military. Had it been that long that one of my classmates had risen so high?

The Employment Guild chair was noticeably empty; with Meyers and his assistant both dead, and others at this conference I'd heard so much about, there was likely no one to fill it.

Johanna Wendell climbed the steps to take her seat at the second-to-smallest chair, her own blue badge clearly displayed. Where she'd gotten it in the last few minutes, I had no idea. She sat, of course, behind Health and Human Services, where her boss worked.

The last permanent Council member was Joe Green, my accuser of deep-thought theft from earlier. He sat behind Academics and Training, a decision bad enough to make me cringe internally; that man had no business leading teachers and students.

Ethics, the chair specifically set aside by Cooper to question the Council's actions, was noticeably empty. I hoped the member was at the conference. I hoped.

The door behind me opened, and I turned. A tired woman in scrubs entered. She reminded me of a younger Paulsen in looks, the shape of their faces and the way they held themselves similar, though this woman's complexion was a shade or two darker. She was also far more ordered, more precise in her presence in Mindspace, but then again she'd have to be, living among telepaths, working as a scanner. She'd had to learn to get along, not to lead, and her mind reflected that.

Latisha Jones, reporting as requested, she said in a way that broadcast both her mental exhaustion and her high-level control. She "spoke" just loud enough to be heard by all, and not a fraction louder.

Thank you for agreeing to speak so soon after a scan, Diaz said, with overtones of great respect and appreciation. She'd just labored at one of the most demanding jobs at the Guild, his mind put in, on very little notice and with no rest. Going through a person's entire life with a fine-tooth comb while the person tried to stop you . . . well, it was exhausting to say the least, and required a great deal of pain and suffering on all sides. If it was not an emergency, they would gladly have provided rest time. *We appreciate your sacrifice.*

She nodded. The whole room was strangely silent.

The woman beside me, the officer of the court, then broadcast as though reading from a script, *Adam Ward, no*

status, formerly of the Guild, has accused Tobias Nelson,
Guild member first class, voting rights, all honor, of two
serious crimes: one, the consorting with a known normal
criminal whose interests lie in opposition to the Guild's,
without the knowledge of his superiors and for the clear det-
riment of Guild interests, and two, the knowing and planned
manipulation of Council member Del Meyers and his senior
assistant to the Council, John Spirale, for the purposes of
their death and the creation of a contagious madness crisis
in the Guild, for unknown reasons. Latisha Jones, senior
deep-scanner first class, voting rights, all honor, has been
asked to determine the truth or falsehood of these claims
beyond argument through the application of a total scan of
Tobias Nelson. She paused, a clear sense of waiting coming
from her mind next to me.

Rex shifted, but Diaz held up a hand before more than a
sense of thought could come from him.

Tell us what you found.

The court officer nodded. *Ms. Jones, your testimony is*
beyond reproach. Have you examined Tobias Nelson?

I have.

And what is your judgment of the charges laid against him?

Ms. Jones shifted her weight, and I got a careful sense
of not looking at me. *There is both truth and falsehood to*
the charges.

Explain, Rex said, leaning forward.

Referencing the first charge, it is true that Tobias Nelson
has met and bargained with a man named Garrett Fiske
several times. He believes Fiske is both fully mind-deaf, as
charged, and working for criminal interests, as charged.
These criminal interests and power were referenced sev-
eral times with full knowledge. Whether the criminal inter-
ests are in opposition to the Guild is undetermined.

Diaz looked at me. *Explain your knowledge of Fiske.*

The context was that I should transmit as much information as possible, in images and memories rather than simply words.

I hesitated. *Fiske is part of an ongoing police investigation. I am not to discuss the details of the investigation. Officers' lives could be at stake. Most of what I know is the details of the investigation.* I put my certainty of that fact into the words, and my mixed regret and determination.

Rex leaned forward. *You are no longer employed by the police. The results of this inquiry could result in your death or mind-wipe. We expect the full truth from you.*

I swallowed. I knew what I faced. But Cherabino was on that task force, along with other officers I knew and liked. Bellury had worked on that task force, to provide additional information. Could I let his work go to waste? Could I endanger Cherabino by talking with the Guild about her most difficult case, the one she'd spent years on the fringes of?

I realized I'd thought those thoughts in my public space, and likely with enough emotion that they'd broadcast to the room.

I spoke out loud, for the illusion of control. "If you kill me or you don't kill me, if you wipe me or not, I'm not going to endanger people who are just doing their jobs. Whoever wipes me is going to have to swear to keep the secrets until all of it is over, or I won't cooperate."

Protecting your criminal friends will get you nowhere with the Guild, Green said then.

You no longer work for the normals, the woman from Finance put in, after a glance at Green. *There is no benefit to protecting them.*

Don't they treat you badly? Tubbs, Kara's boss asked.

Most of the room was filled with a sense of seeking understanding, not anger.

*They took me in when I was nothing, and they gave me
a chance to be useful. To make a difference. How they
treat me doesn't have anything to do with those essential
facts,* I said to the room, just realizing it.

A long pause while people looked at Diaz and Diaz
looked at me.

For the first time, he spoke out loud, in a quavering bari-
tone that sounded nothing like his sure mind-speech. "You
may pick and choose what you say, out loud if needed, to
tell us what we need to know about Fiske."

I was surprised, really, genuinely, surprised. "You don't
know this stuff already?"

Would we ask if we did? the woman from Research
asked me. *Why do you believe he is dangerous to the Guild?*

"Fiske is dangerous to everyone," I said. "He seeks power.
He's risen in the ranks dramatically in the last three years.
And he's already reached out to corrupt politicians and
attempted to infiltrate the police. He's . . . well, he's getting
involved in things I can't talk about, in crimes I can't talk
about, and as near as the police can tell, there's some kind of
master plan they can't see." I realized I knew a lot more than
I should as a direct result of my mind-Link with Cherabino
these last months. What to choose? Stick to the question. "I
believe he's dangerous to the Guild because he's tried so
hard to get in here. He's dealt with several people—including
Nelson here. He's meddling, and from what I know about
him, his involvement is never for *your* benefit. It's for his. He
was the one who was working with Bradley and buying his
technology, something that clearly was bad for the Guild. I
know you paid attention to the Bradley case. You assigned
me a Watcher, for crying out loud. You realize how dangerous these things were."

A blank moment, and finally Diaz nodded. *That was my
doing,* he said, and the feelings around it in Mindspace

were simply determined. *You have made yourself infamous, and possibly dangerous.*

"And then you hired me," I said. "And then you let me inside the Guild, at least some of you—" I looked at Rex. "And wanted me to solve this murder for you."

He killed himself, the pale woman said.

Madness, madness, and *fear,* the room echoed dimly.

"No, he didn't," I said, in as clear and certain a voice as I could get. "Do you know how I know?"

A burst of concern from the podium, maybe from Green? He wasn't looking at me. Huh.

How? Diaz asked.

Because we found a device influencing him through Mindspace, a device we also found in his assistant John Spirale's apartment. Meyers also threw out his knives and even his sheets and towels to avoid any possibility of the death he kept seeing in visions. He left a note telling us that those visions had happened. My mind added all of the details of the case I'd found to support my belief in homicide. *The electrical system was tampered with. Kara Chenoa, a smart woman, thinks Del Meyers would never, ever have killed himself in that way. I believe her.* My complex feelings for Kara and my anger about her leaked out; I couldn't help it. *Kara may not be for me personally, but she loves the Guild. She loves the truth. And there's a reason you're letting her family get involved in what should be a Council matter. There's huge benefit to dialogue. To discussion. To truth.*

Then, quietly, in Mindspace, with overtones of exhaustion: *Can I please finish my testimony?* Ms. Jones, the deep-scanner, asked.

We all looked at her.

Of course, Diaz sent, with great overtones of apology.

The court officer had a moment in which she collected herself in Mindspace. Then she stabilized. *Ms. Jones, what about the second charge? The proposed manipulation and madness causing.*

She again concentrated on not looking at me. *The second charge is categorically untrue. Tobias has neither caused nor participated in any action contributing to either the deaths noted or to the current crisis in the Guild.*

Loud discussion in Mindspace swamped the room. I shielded, hard, to block out the huge noise.

And then I turned, and stared at her.

"How can that be true?" I asked.

The prisoner will be silent until spoken to, Rex's mental voice cut through Mindspace with outright tones of anger. *Ms. Jones deserves rest!*

Order in the room, Diaz put in. *Thank you, Ms. Jones. You may go.*

She nodded gravely and turned to leave, never once having looked at me.

It hit me then: I was wrong. I had been wrong. I had assumed . . . but assumptions were for idiots and fools. What he'd done, to meet with Fiske, was bad enough. But to leap to conclusions when my life—

Quiet your thoughts! Diaz told me, on a private channel, the tone blistering in its ferocity.

I looked up at the old man, strong in his position, wrinkled and old, and quieted my thoughts.

Then he spoke out loud, in that quavering voice that did not match the mind behind it. "Tobias Nelson, do you have anything to say in your own defense?"

"What I did I did for the good of the Guild. What was done with the parts that I obtained is not my doing."

Rex looked over at the Research chair. "Ms. Chin—"

Aha! I had remembered her name correctly.

"—what are the results of your inquiry into your department?"

Patience, Rex. There will be plenty of time for that, Diaz said.

Chin sat very straight, and I got a faint feeling of embarrassment and shame from her.

Nelson, finish.

Nelson pulled himself up. He still looked awful, like he'd been run over by a truck and then had the flesh wounds healed. You still got the impression of unimaginable pain and exhaustion. But there was strength there too, and anger. "A member of this Council told me to obtain certain parts. Parts that the Guild could not get any other way. I did as I was told. No one asked where they had come from. No one wanted to know. Any deals I made with Garrett Fiske in addition to those parts were intended to keep the Guild safe."

Diaz turned an eye to Rex. *What did you—?*

It was me, Chin said, and the room grew totally, completely silent. *Or rather, it was my department. I am ashamed that we have brought embarrassment to the Guild.*

And why did you require specialized parts we could only get from a criminal? Diaz's mental voice was very, very dangerous.

I—

Sir, do we really want to have this conversation in front of an outsider? Green said, in the most reasonable voice I've heard so far. Of course, in Mindspace, "outsider" had entire layers of negative connotations that wouldn't translate into language, and specifically referred to me. There was a clear overtone of "criminal" as well. Thoughts were such a rich medium, well beyond words, and for the first time I had cause to hate that fact.

I'm not in any hurry to leave, I said.

Diaz looked at his son, then me. *Let's wrap up the matter at hand, then, and then turn to the why and where-fore.*

The Council officer beside me straightened. *Adam Ward, no status, has been informed of the severe consequences of a false accusation against someone of the first class.*

And I held my breath, waiting for the ax to drop.

The officer went on. *Tobias Nelson has admitted to con-sorting with a known criminal whose interests do not lie aligned with the Guild's.*

She paused for effect, making a silence as clear in Mindspace as a drumroll. *It is traditional for the accused to be sentenced first. What say you, Council?*

My heart beat faster.

Diaz sat, his mind releasing grave determination as his robes settled around him. *Further investigation into Nelson's transgressions is required.*

I agree, Chris Tubbs said, *but Green's point is valid. We must sentence him now, at least provisionally. I propose Nelson is removed from his current post pending that investigation and reduced to the rank of base Enforcer until and unless such a time as he is cleared or earns his status back. Additional penalties to be assessed in the result of future findings. What say you?*

I am ineligible to vote. Chin's mind-sending was weak, quiet.

You are, Diaz agreed. *I vote aye.*

My old classmate Charlie voted aye along with Tubbs, and nays came from the pale woman from Finance and from Rex. Then, quickly, two ayes from Johanna and Green.

So mote it be, the officer of the Council said.

I couldn't breathe. Obviously Nelson had had the sup-port of some on the Council, and now he was being stripped

of his rank for being caught carrying out Council orders.
No other reason. It seemed harsh.

*On the matter of the accusation of Adam Ward against
Tobias Nelson, what say you, Council?*

"May I speak on my behalf?" Nelson asked, true hatred
now in his voice.

You may, Diaz said.

"This man falsely accused me of murder and worse. He
has done damage to my reputation and to the reputation of
the Guild as a whole. By removing me from duty, he has
damaged the ability of Enforcement to respond to the current mental health crisis. And he has conspired with
many—including Kara Chenoa—to discredit me and other
members of the Guild. He was removed from the Guild
once and he has returned to wreak more damage. He has
been convicted of felonies in the normal system and he
does not learn. I argue he should be killed."

Was this how it was going to end? Because of the
enemies I'd made and the mistakes I'd put through? I'd gotten Bellury killed. I'd screwed up, over and over again. I'd
screwed up here.

Do you have anything to say for yourself, Adam Ward?
the official asked.

We have a great deal to do this afternoon, Tubbs put in
immediately, with a censuring thought. *This is not a cut-
and-dry case, and it is not the most important thing on the
Council's docket. I say we delay the matter until a better
time.*

You want to keep him here during a madness crisis? Charlie asked, unbelieving. *It's stupid to waste good resources on
watching him.*

That hurt. We'd been in school together, and he was
treating me like a stranger.

We could throw him in a cell, Tubbs said. *Worked last time.*

And Kara's boss, just as heartless. I felt my heart sinking.

Throw him out on the street, the pale woman said, without any compassion.

Won't he run? asked Chin.

Give him a mind-tag, Johanna said, the first time she'd said anything. The implication was that they could find me anywhere if I did run. She, like the pale woman, seemed utterly without compassion.

I was going to die.

We could just kill him now, Rex observed.

I braced.

Release him, Diaz said, as if coming to a decision. *In two days, we'll meet again. And, Adam?*

"Yes?" I said, feeling like I was in shock. Divorced from all of my surroundings. Confused.

You will receive that mind-tag, from a member of Enforcement. If you do not report back here on time . . . well, there are worse things than death. And far worse than a removal of your Abilities. Think about that.

I backed out of the room, numb, numb, so numb. I backed out and, when the door shut behind me, collapsed on the floor.

"What did they decide?" Stone's voice asked me.

I struggled to breathe, the pressure so great. The only thing worse than dying today was not knowing if you were going to die in two days. I let go of the information, letting it *whoosh* out in Mindspace in an uncontrolled, amateur blast.

He took a step back.

I stared at the floor. "You're still a member of Enforcement?"

———

After it was over, Stone had Turner drive me home. I kept poking at the tag in my head, the little piece of Stone's mind stuck onto mine, temporary in theory, but this was the second time we'd done this. Every time I poked at it, I had pain, pain like poking at the empty place where a tooth used to be.

The city lights passed over us as the aircar settled into a ground lane and Turner took a turn.

"You know when to show up?" she asked, flatly.

"Yes."

"Do you need me to pick you up?"

"I think I'll find my own way, thanks." Even if I had to take the bus, it was better than them ferrying me around, especially if it was going to be . . . I shied away. I shouldn't think about that. It wasn't helpful. It wouldn't do any good.

She didn't say anything else, and after a while the aircar came to a stop.

"It's time to get out now," she said.

"Yeah," I said, and looked up, walling off my thoughts as strictly as I'd walled off the rest of the world, as strictly as I'd walled my mind against Mindspace.

We were sitting in front of my apartment building, an old converted office building with lovely architecture . . . and stains and cracks so deep you could hardly see one without the other. It looked . . . sad today. It looked defeated.

I got out and closed the car door; the car started moving right then, without waiting. Ignoring the cold, I trudged up the cracking stairs and into the lobby, where some home-less guy was settling on our couches. I didn't know where the security guard was. I didn't care. The key got me into the stairs, and the stairs got me onto my floor.

I paused outside my door. Too many people had been in

my apartment over the last months for me to ever go in without checking. A mind sat in the middle of my living room, a mind I recognized.

I turned the key and opened the door.

"Hello, Cherabino," I said.

CHAPTER 17

"How did you—?" She stood. "Stupid question. The Link, right?"

"That's right," I said, closing the door behind me. I wanted to collapse. I wanted to shake. I wanted to do anything and everything except stand here being brave, being normal in front of her.

Maybe some of that leaked out onto my face.

She came over and leaned into me, putting her arms around me. "Stupid Link. It will be gone eventually. It will. You promised."

I stood stock-still.

She gripped harder. *What's wrong?* she sent over the Link, getting through even my tightest, most tightly clenched shield. *What's . . . wrong, Adam?*

Her kindness and concern melted the hard shell I'd put over my emotions and I started to shake. My knees softened.

She pulled me over to the couch. I barely made it, staggering like I was drunk.

"What's wrong, damn it?" she yelled.

I was shaking. They'd let me go. They'd let me go and now I had to go do it all again. I—they'd kill me. They'd do worse.

Cherabino climbed into my lap and held my head in her hands. "Talk to me, please." Her voice was hard, desperate.

"I . . ." I shook my head. "I can't . . ."

And then she kissed me, slow and quiet and comforting. I kissed her back, and I gathered her in my arms, and I just shook.

Sometime later, with me stretched out on the couch and her stretched out on my chest, rubbing her hand up and down on my arm, I thought I could try.

"Can I ask you a favor?" My voice was low, hesitant.

She looked up, concern in her eyes. "Anything."

"Would you drive me to the Guild day after tomorrow?"

She nodded, slowly. When I didn't say anything else, she asked cautiously, "Why?"

I let go enough to tell her, mind to mind, quietly.

"Ooof," I hissed as she hit my stomach trying to stand.

Now she was standing and screaming, in a rush of words that didn't make any sense, mostly curses.

"Who do they think they are?" she finally said, making sense, eyes alit with some dangerous fire. "We'll fight this. We'll fight this!" And more in that vein.

I sat up, and sighed. When she quieted down enough that I could be heard, I said, "They own me, Cherabino. Legally. For all I've done to get away from them. And all they've done to push me away. That's what Koshna means. I'm a telepath, and you can't touch me legally. And you can't touch the Guild. They can kill me in broad daylight in front of witnesses, and other than some bad press, there's nothing anybody can do. They can find me anywhere now."

She came close, bending down to look me in the eye. "You can't give up. We will fight this!"

I blew out a breath. "Please. Help me stay distracted. Help me— I don't know, Cherabino." I ran my hands through my hair. I'd never done this before, this facing inevitability. Well, that wasn't true. I'd done it once, and I'd checked myself into rehab. But there was no rehab here, not for me, not for this. "Drive me there and stay with me, okay?"

She knelt on the floor and looked up. "You want me to take you to these bastards? Give in?"

I nodded. "Yeah. If I don't go it'll be worse."

Cherabino shook her head violently and got back to her feet. "I don't know if I can do that," she said.

"Can you at least stay the night?" I asked. "Not—not for sex," I added, before I could think better of it. I'd promised her I wouldn't make the Link any stronger than it was. And if they were going to turn my mind inside out or torture me, I didn't want to draw her into it. I didn't want her to be tortured too, or die when I was killed. As much as I wanted to lose myself in sex right now.

"You want me to sleep with you? Just sleep?" she asked.

I looked down. "If you need to leave—"

"You're loaning me a shirt to sleep in," she said, in a brittle voice.

I went over there and put my arms around her. She went stiff, and then relaxed a little into me. This was all new, all too—but I didn't want her to leave. If I didn't want her to die, I also didn't want her to leave.

I was too much of a coward to want to face this alone.

Neither one of us slept all that well.

"We should have gone to my place," she grumbled more than once. My cot was not even the size of a twin bed, and not intended for the weight of two people; you could feel the support bars beneath you. We were so close together, with not an inch to spare, that I got several good handfuls of pleasant parts without really trying.

And she didn't push my hands away, I realized with a pang. If I was really going to be wiped, or worse . . . I adjusted my position to curl around her. I wanted more and my body agreed, but neither she nor I commented.

She stole the only pillow, got comfy, and started to snore. I sighed.

As the minutes rolled by in the dark, I found my attention going back to the hidden compartment over our heads.

Up until just a few months ago, I had had a stash of my drug sitting there, waiting for me. I knew where to get another one now.

I wondered if I'd done the wrong thing by having her stay over.

Six thirty a.m. Cherabino rolled out of bed, hitting the floor with a curse. She sat up, looked for her gun, and blinked, bleary-eyed, at the offending morning.

"Coffee," she barked at me.

I got up and limped over to the tiny kitchen counter I had in the main room of the apartment. It was clean. That was about all you could say for it. But the five-foot counter was large enough for a small coffeemaker, a sink, and a microwave, and a fridge beside it that suited most of my needs.

I set the coffee brewing and opened the cabinet. I was out of cereal. I hadn't slept very well for a hundred reasons, but I'd missed my apartment mind-canceller the most. I had no idea how it would interact with someone else's mind-waves, so I'd left it off. My mind felt beat up, without a chance to recover, even though I felt better emotionally after sitting in the edges of Cherabino's mind all night. So it took me a moment to process.

That's right, the weekly delivery of groceries hadn't come. I had money now, but no job and no grocery service. If they killed me it wouldn't matter.

I caught myself halfway down a really intense pity moment and replayed one of Swartz's pep talks in my head while I visited the bathroom. It helped. Some.

Standing in the middle of my living room in my pajama pants, watching a grumpy Cherabino complaining loudly about the state of my kitchen, helped a lot more.

She'd found a toaster I didn't know I'd had, and bread from somewhere, and was coaxing the microwave to cook some kind of egg-and-cheese thing I didn't know I'd had the ingredients for. All of this apparently required an ongoing litany of abuse against the tools and complaints about the early-morning hour. She was really cute.

I smiled. None of that was out loud, was it? I should have backed out of her head a little then, but why?

Ding went the microwave, interrupting both our trains of thought.

She fished out the bowl, cursing at the heat, and plopped it on the counter. Triangles of toast were added to the edge, and then she found a towel to carry it to the coffee table in front of the couch; I didn't have a regular table.

"What are you doing? Get us some juice," she demanded.

I complied, smiling.

Cherabino practically inhaled her food, which I didn't mind, since she was wearing one of my shirts and not much else. The view was nice. The haste, perhaps, was not.

"You're going into work today, I take it," I said.

She nodded, still chewing. *Cases to solve and people to see.* I didn't think she realized she'd said this over the Link. *Have to leave in twenty minutes, tops, and I still need a shower.* She looked at me critically, like she thought I was going to be an obstacle to said shower, an obstacle she was going to overcome.

"Shower's all yours," I said, hoping I might get a glimpse of a less-clad Cherabino at some point in that process.

She got the edge of that thought. *Down, boy. We don't have time. Don't you . . . ?*

I could almost feel the knowledge of what I'd told her last night hit her.

She nodded, to herself. Then looked back up. "We'll find a way to fight this. The Guild isn't everything. Bransen— well, we'll go ask him what he thinks we can do. He's sneaky with the law stuff, more than Peter ever was. We'll figure this out," she said again, with real heat behind her words. If she was mentioning her dead husband, this was serious.

"Who are you trying to convince, you or me?" I asked.

"We're going to fight," she said, meeting my eyes. "You're going to fight." Then she looked at the clock behind me again. "We have fourteen minutes. We'd better hustle." She pushed the dishes at my hands, and I took them as she darted back toward the bathroom.

Her breasts bounced in a delightful way during the whole process. Perhaps the dishes waited a little longer than they should have.

Sergeant Bransen was the quintessential man in a suit, a fortysomething white man with overstyled hair and an air of perpetual confidence I found off-putting. In previous meetings, he'd made it all too clear he found me off-putting as well, so I wasn't looking forward to this meeting.

It was early, almost too early, before the main press of day-shift cops started coming in to demand things from Bransen, but he still looked tired. I wondered how much of Paulsen's crusade against the budget he was playing the knight for. Looked like no one was getting sleep these days.

Bransen's office was smaller than Paulsen's, with a very battered desk and single desk chair. His door was open, and Cherabino's knock on its frame made him look up.

"Isabella," he said, with a genuine smile, which dampened when he saw me. "Ward."

Cherabino pushed me toward the chair.

I stood too, since Bransen was standing. "Sir—"

"I told you, I wasn't going to give you an answer for a few days. I needed to think about it," he said to Cherabino and only Cherabino.

Her lips pursed. "That's not exactly—"

"What is it, then?" This was as impatient as I'd ever seen Bransen in person, his habitual smile completely gone. "Paulsen has already told me what happened, and if you think working for the Guild is going to make me—"

"Sir," Cherabino interrupted. "That's what we're here to talk about." She looked at me significantly.

I coughed. "Yes. I—"

"The Guild is threatening him with execution tomorrow," Cherabino interrupted again.

Now I had Bransen's attention.

That's not the way I would have said that, I complained to her.

She didn't react.

I sighed.

"Are you two sleeping together?" Bransen asked.

"No," I said at the same time she said, "Yes."

I glanced at her; she shrugged.

Bransen sat down then, shaking his head. He looked at me, and this was the moment with Paulsen that would have saved me or damned me, based on the words I said next. I didn't know Bransen as well, but the damning was likely forthcoming.

I did what Swartz would have told me to do. I faced the problem square-on. "The Guild had a murder investigation they wanted an outsider to investigate. I was the only outsider with the right experience who they thought they could intimidate into staying quiet about whatever I saw. I made a bad call, and now they're following through on the threats. With Koshna, they have full rights to do it. I'm not sure why Cherabino is so determined to get you involved."

Bransen blinked, and I could practically hear the wheels turning. "Don't do anything halfway, do you, Isabella?" He laced his fingers and set them on the desk. We all waited.

And waited.

The decision crystallized just as I was starting to get nervous.

"It's okay," I said. "I wasn't expecting anyone to help me anyway."

"Damn it, don't interrupt me!" Bransen said. His mind echoed that I hadn't earned the right or the respect to do half that.

I was quiet. And confused. Very confused.

"Humph. Well. First, before all of this I was planning to allow you to work with Cherabino under provisional unpaid status as a test. We'll go ahead and do that, though God help me, you'd better realize I don't do a tenth of the hand-holding Paulsen does. If you need my attention more than once a month, twice in an emergency—maybe—you're fired. I don't have time for that crap—I don't care what your close rate is. You play by my rules. You cause trouble, you're out. You fail to impress me with results, you're out. You sneeze one too many times and annoy me more than you're worth, you're out."

"Understood," I said, still confused. If they were going to kill me anyway, what difference—

"What—" Cherabino started.

He held up a hand.

She subsided.

"I don't have jack-shit jurisdiction over the Guild or anything the Guild decides it wants to do if it doesn't affect citizens. You, Boy Wonder, are not a citizen." He held up a hand again to forestall any additional objections from the peanut gallery in the person of Cherabino. "How*ever*, despite this jurisdiction issue, I don't have a problem telling said Guild it's awfully unfriendly to go threatening my provisional employees. I will make that phone call today. I may ask a politician to do the same *if* I have the time and *if* they are free to take the phone call."

He leaned forward. "I wish you luck and the kind of golden talking that keeps getting you rehired in this damn place in the middle of layoff season. If you make it back alive, I expect a report. Promptly, understand? Even from the hospital. If you don't, I will promise you several phone calls to prominent reporters to set them on your case. We'll make a stink such as the Guild hasn't seen in decades." He paused. "Plus give you a decent funeral, if they'll let go of the body. Seems decent."

Cherabino was gearing up for a righteous lecture. "Sir, you can't possibly—"

He waved that hand again, and she shut up. Cold.

I stared. Even in the middle of my storm of emotions, I'd never seen her stopped from a full anger lecture before.

"That is *all* I can or will do in this situation, and you'd better be grateful for that, Isabella. It's your word—and yours alone—that's making me do half of it. I'm already late for a meeting with the captain. You'll see yourself out."

"Yes, sir," she said, turned, and left, suppressed anger vibrating every fiber of her body. I stood and left too, numb and afraid.

Hearing him tell me what they'd do if I died made it that much more real. No one—no one—could help me now.

Except, well, except maybe me. There was always a way out, always. I just had to figure it out.

CHAPTER 18

I smoked half a pack, one cigarette after the other, on the cold gray wet smoking porch, looking out on the half-dead yellow grass stubs in the courtyard, the back of my mind telling me that I shouldn't be here. A suspect had gotten killed here in front of me by a sniper, and no matter how many times I reminded myself the killer was locked up, it still felt dangerous.

Today, dangerous was okay. Dangerous was good. Meant I was alive. And the wind wasn't even that bad today.

I felt the mind approach before I heard the door open.

"Hi, Michael," I said without turning around.

"Cherabino says you're working with us on the Wright case again?" He stopped then, half-formed questions about the rumors of my firing swirling in his head. He decided not to ask about any of them. Decided he wouldn't have liked someone asking.

It was a painful effort not to respond to the thoughts. The Guild would have considered them public space, as clear and obvious as yelling into an empty room, and just as fair to hear.

"Wright case?" Michael prompted.

"Yeah," I said, and stubbed out the cigarette. Might as well do something useful while I waited for the back of my head to deliver the miracle. I'd already called Swartz's

house and heard from Selah why he couldn't be disturbed. I
didn't have time for a meeting, nor did I think it was advis-
able to go back to my apartment. I needed to keep moving
while I figured this out.

"Isn't the Wright case closed? That supervisor woman,
with the odd mind?"

He looked at me, wondering if I was all right. Of course,
he was a cop and cops couldn't ask that.

I adjusted my coat down to cover my cold hand. I hadn't
wanted to get ash on the gloves. "I'm fine. Did the interview not confirm her as the killer?"

"The interview cleared her of all wrongdoing. She was
with a boyfriend during the entire window of the murder."

"Wait. She didn't . . ." I trailed off. "Then who would
have killed that guy with an ax? And the parts missing?
Were they under a couch or something?"

Michael shook his head. "Cherabino and Ruffins are
talking about it in one of the conference rooms. I thought
you'd want to be there."

"Thanks," I said.

It was surreal walking in on a meeting, in a conference
room, at a place I almost didn't work, on possibly my last
day on earth. But the program said keep yourself distracted, keep yourself moving, keep doing something useful, and this was that. If nothing else, this was that.

I'd figure this out. Or I'd run, far and fast and wide, and
roll the dice and pretend I could stay free for a week or two.
Until they caught me.

I wondered if they'd have Stone torture me, as punishment for him and me both. More likely, send one of the
students as a final project, with a mentor trailing, of course,
to ensure that it was done correctly. It's what I would have
done, if I'd been a professor in Enforcement training.

I wondered if it would hurt more or less with a student. Probably more. The mentor would correct, over and over, until they got it right.

"Adam?" Cherabino asked. I couldn't quite feel her emotions without reaching out, which bothered me.

"You didn't say he was coming," Ruffins said. The Tech Control Org agent didn't seem happy to see me.

"You'll just have to put up with your detection tattoo screaming at you for a while," I said, with no sympathy. "I'm a member of the team today, and you should have thought of that before you had the damn thing installed."

Ruffins scowled. "Left our manners at home, did we?"

I sat. "It's been a hell of a day. A hell of a week, really."

"Play nicely or I'll kick you both out," Cherabino said. Then, to me: "Ruffins is here because Wright was one of his informants for . . . well, another case. There are some legalities to the investigation, so it's easier to just keep him in on."

I noticed then that Andrew, forensic accountant and Cherabino's cube neighbor, was seated at the end of the table. He waved, a small half wave.

I nodded back, and Michael sat.

"Like I was saying, it doesn't add up," Andrew said.

"Which part?" Cherabino asked.

"Wright's accounts have been supported by payments from the TCO for a while now, for informing. There's been payments from Fiske's organization, like Ruffins told me to look for."

Wait. Wright had been working for Fiske? And Ruffins had been the one to point this out? What had I missed?

But Andrew continued without pausing. "The payments just stopped, the day of the murder. Both sets. One or the other organization should have had some delay, but there's none. But a third set of payments—from another account—started appearing a week before the murder and hasn't stopped. They've been increasing, actually."

"That's ridiculous," Ruffins said. "A mysterious third set of payments? Doesn't it seem more plausible that the bank made some mistake?"

"Who all was Wright working for?" I asked, finally tracking the conversation.

Heads turned in my direction.

"Well, he was working for Fiske, or at least selling him secrets. I assume largely because you asked him to?" I asked Ruffins.

He looked uncomfortable, a little too uncomfortable for a man who was usually combative. If anybody else, I would have read him to find out why, but with his wrist tattoo, he'd know immediately.

"Yes," Cherabino said. "He was bait. Him no longer being living, testifying bait is a problem that we are currently working to solve."

Ruffins objected, "You shouldn't be sharing task force information with this guy."

"This one's not going to make any difference to anyone," she replied. Then back to me: "Finish your thought."

"He was working for Fiske, he was working for the TCO, but all over that house I saw hobbies. Stuff that takes a lot of money. And he wasn't just paying his bills. He was feeding those experiments, or projects, or what have you. Some of it looked recent. Obviously he was selling stuff—I'm betting some kind of invention that crossed the line into Tech territory, though who knows—but I'm also wondering if he had some kind of deal going with the company."

"The lab?" Michael asked. "We didn't find any evidence of that at all, and we dug deep enough that we should have if it was going on."

Ruffins said with an odd tone, "Maybe they were paying him off the books, you know, on the higher levels."

"After firing Wright so forcefully?" Cherabino shook her head. "Besides, we talked to nearly everyone. And who is the higher levels? There's always a person. Or several. But concrete, real people, and we talked to everyone there, I thought."

"Not the senior executives," I said.

Michael shifted. "Maybe he extorted them for money and threatened to take that thing in his head public if they didn't pay up. Then they went over with an ax to remove the danger."

"But he'd already put so much up on data channels," Andrew said. "How much more could there really be to leak?"

I glanced at him.

Andrew shrugged. "I'm curious. And you guys talk loudly one cubicle away. If it's a case you've brought me in on, it seems fair game to listen. It's also a slow week."

"You listened in on confidential case information?" Ruffins asked. He looked appalled.

"Next time just come on over if you've got the time," Cherabino told him, her mind very intentional. "I can always use another set of eyes on things."

"Thanks. When it's slow, I'd appreciate something to do."

And I realized then why Cherabino had the highest close rate in the department. It wasn't just that she obsessed over her cases' details until she could quote them to you six months later with accuracy. It wasn't just that she worked so many more hours than everybody else. It was this: that she asked for help in odd places and never, ever, turned down a second opinion.

You got interesting things with help sometimes, it seemed. An idea started to pick up its head from the back of my mind, but when I reached for it, it spooked and ran away. It would be back.

"The extortion tactic seems much more like Fiske anyway," Ruffins said, with a suspicious glance to me. "As I said in the task force meeting, it seems easiest to lump this case in with the rest of his crimes and sort them out when we have him in custody." He kept looking at me.

Cherabino sighed. "And as I said in the meeting, I'm happy for you to be here if it makes you more comfortable, but I'm going to follow the evidence. We're not going to have a killer go free because we just assume it was him. Fiske is not all powerful, and this one seems too sudden to be coordinated."

"Look, I have an appointment with a CI I need to get to," Ruffins said. "Task force is at three, right?"

"It is," Cherabino agreed. She was frustrated with him; I could feel it. But he was important to the Fiske case somehow.

As they walked out, the idea in the back of my head snuck back in and looked at me with wide eyes.

The idea coalesced.

Captain Harris had barged into Paulsen's office earlier about the arbitration emergency. He was trained as a go-between and was good at getting agreements.

Second fact: the Guild had a long and distinguished history of using third-party arbitrators. The Koshna Accords were only the most famous example. If I'd paid my Guild dues long enough, I might have had access to one from inside the Guild. Unlike a lawyer, whose job it was to block as many runs from the other party as possible, a Guild arbitrator was assigned to find the best solution for the accused that the Council or accuser could live with. There was a lot more negotiation, and a lot less questioning of facts, since truth or falsehood was already established with a deep-read. A good arbitrator could get your sentence commuted, or paid slowly over time, or taken out of your salary and your community service and your creativity rather than your hide. Then he or she followed up to be certain both parties kept up their ends.

Third fact: Harris had once been married to Jamie; they had been divorced long before I'd had her as my mentor, but as a senior student I knew who she was. According to the rumors of the day, he had stayed over at the Guild for some of that time, in addition to his residence off-site. While the Guild might not accept just any police captain as a neutral party, Harris had been cleared as a former spouse of a Guild member, and a sometime resident.

So, unlike Bransen, Harris could actually walk in the doors of the Guild and speak for me. Furthermore, he was qualified to do it reasonably well.

That is, if he would.

I bought sandwiches from Swartz's favorite deli, fresh homemade bread like clouds cradling a bounty of beautiful soy-pepper loaf and vegetables, real roast beef, and fresh-made stone-ground mustard, with slices of fancy cheddar cheese cut so thin you could see the shadow of your finger through them. Best part? I bought them myself, with real money, in the regular line, without having to talk to a manager. The department had been handling my money for years, and now I had it myself. There was temptation there, sure, but here, now, it was freedom. Bittersweet to taste that freedom today. Today of all days.

I took a taxi—a real, honest-to-goodness taxi with a grumpy taxi driver who wanted to talk sports—and paid him with real money.

And then I was climbing Swartz's front steps.

Selah answered the door in a ridiculously flowered dress and wool socks, a scarf around her neck. She smiled when she saw me—and the deli sack I carried in my hands. "He's awake," she said. "And he'd love a visit."

"Thanks," I said.

She stopped me. "It's not that high-sodium thing, is it?"

"No, ma'am." I smiled. I'd remembered. Low-sodium and healthy, all the way. I felt virtuous.

She let me through.

Swartz was seated on his faded old couch, fiddling with some kind of wire hook. Fishing gear, maybe. Clear line and oddly colored feathers littered the TV table in front of him like the leftover bits of a bird left by a messy cat's lunch. He frowned at it through thick reading glasses. The frown turned into a smile when he saw me.

"Come in, come in." He pulled a pocketed envelope from the couch beside him and started tucking things away into it.

"What are the feathers for?" I asked.

"Ah, even pollution-resistant bioengineered fish like a fly with some shine to it. Makes them bite better. I don't go much, anymore, but I like the flies. Plenty of call for them, and keeps me busy." Subtext in Mindspace was that a little extra money was welcome while he was on teacher's disability, and his doctor liked the activity. "Sit down. Tell me all about things. Did you ask her to dinner?"

I looked for Selah.

"Let's get the food on the kitchen table, dear," she said kindly. For all Swartz lived here, the house was hers.

I unpacked my offering on the old wooden kitchen table while Selah got out the good plates.

"So, did you?" he asked.

I looked up. "You're a meddler, you know that?"

He sat, setting the cane against the wall next to him. "So

what if I am?" He was breathing heavy, even from that little move across the room. I wondered if he was getting worse, somehow. "So, did you or not?"

"I did," I said, almost sheepish. For once in my life I didn't really want to talk to him about it. Too new, too fragile, too uncertain. Too . . . improbable now, with what today meant. "Well, she said yes. It was, well, it was awkward. But okay. Really okay. I think she likes me."

He pulled the deli bag toward him. "I could have told you that years ago."

"Then why didn't you tell me to ask her out years ago?" I asked, a little forcefully.

"You weren't ready, kid."

I digested that for a moment. Still, regret burned at my stomach. Deep, full regret, of what might have been.

He regarded me. "You had to learn to believe in the program. In God. In yourself. You're not there yet, but you're on your way now. That is, if you keep up praying."

I blinked. He thought I was on my way. Even with the qualifier, it was one of the best compliments I'd gotten in a long time. And from Swartz. Today of all days.

Selah arrived, found the little red pepper salad I'd gotten for her, and pecked me on the cheek. She moved it to the dining room table, where she had some papers laid out for a project she was working on. So it was just me and Swartz. We ate, companionably, together.

Swartz finished about half the sandwich, blotted at his mouth with a napkin, and pushed the plate away. He looked tired, but his mind was still razor-sharp. "You're not here in the middle of the day to talk about Cherabino, are you?"

I took another bite of sandwich, which was suddenly ash in my mouth.

"What are you here to talk about?"

I looked at my plate.

Swartz sighed. "I have a cane now, you know." A reference to how many times I'd told him to whap anyone who got in his way.

"I . . ." I trailed off. Took a breath. "The Guild's been making threats. Credible threats. They wanted me to investigate this thing for them."

"You told me. It was Kara who asked, right?"

"She's not in the picture anymore." I forced myself to move on, no matter what it cost me. The words came out slowly, at first: "Now it's the politicians. And I've stepped out of line, to their thinking, and gotten too ambitious, and gone after somebody too high up. I've caught somebody in wrongdoing, but it's the wrong guy for the murder and they're . . . well, they're threatening to mind-wipe me, Swartz."

Surprise and concern came from him across Mindspace. "What . . . what exactly does that mean?"

"In this case, they say they'll erase the last ten years of my life."

He sat, grave. After a moment: "Can they?"

"They can. Maybe they won't. Cherabino has ideas. I have ideas. I am going to fight. But reality—"

"The Koshna Accords," Swartz said.

"Yeah."

A long pause, in which he thought and I tried not to feel.

"I'd . . . I'd rather they killed me, you know. Leaving me back there after they kicked me out of the Guild, without any of *this*." I waved my hand around the kitchen, to him. "Without any of *me*."

"Ten years ago you were sliding toward the street. Addicted."

"Yeah."

"The habits are still in your brain."

"I know."

Odds were, I'd wake up in the middle of the worst Satin

addiction I'd had, and if I wasn't physically addicted at first, those desperate habits and cravings would send me right back into the throes of it. I didn't know if I could get myself out a second time. Not without Cherabino and Swartz, and what were the odds of finding them again?

"They might kill me anyway," I said.

Swartz leaned on the table and thought. And thought. I could see the thoughts, like a master cardplayer shuffling through cards, dealing and collecting and fanning them out one after the other.

And I waited, an idea—and this hope—the only thing left.

Finally he nodded. Then he looked up at me, and the pain in his eyes hurt me. Physically hurt me. "We can't stop it?" he asked.

"I'll try, but . . . I can't run. I'm marked. I'll show up at the Guild or they will make me."

"That's it?"

I nodded.

"I'll go with you," he said, and grabbed the cane, half standing.

"I don't think you can," I said. With all the Tech and various Mindspace devices at the Guild, even if they'd let him in the door, there could be issues. I didn't know how stable his heart was right now, and the heart was controlled by tiny neurons linked into the rest of the body's neural net. One of the scariest lessons in Deconstruction was learning how to manipulate that net in someone with a weak heart to cause worsening of symptoms and possibly death. Not that I think anyone would do anything deliberately . . . Well, maybe I did. They'd used his condition against me before. I took the plunge and lied: "They wouldn't let you in anyway. It's tomorrow. I'm getting Cherabino to take me."

Swartz nodded. "Isabella will know what to do." He settled back in the chair, leaning on the cane. "What do you need?"

"Not to think for a while. Cigarettes aren't doing it, and I'm wanting the drug way, way too much."

He nodded. "Stay here today. Selah needs some help in the garden, and there's plenty of flies to be made. You can talk if you need, and we can put our heads together." But the feeling I got from him, for the very first time, was uncertainty. Huge, gaping uncertainty and worry. And sadness, over and through it all.

And that scared me worse than anything so far. If Swartz didn't have an answer . . . Maybe there wasn't one.

I was covered in sweat and dirt in a borrowed oversized sweatshirt of Swartz's, digging holes for fence posts in the semifrozen ground, when Cherabino's police car pulled up, sirens flashing, in the front yard.

Selah stood up, taking off her gardening gloves.

I felt Cherabino before I saw her, strong emotions hitting me like a blow, layer after layer of panic and worry and anger and everything else, layer after layer poured out. Raw strength with no control—my strength, perhaps, and her lack of control, if the Link had anything to do with it. Maybe I was just attuned.

She trotted to Selah, emotions so painfully loud, so painfully out of control. "I'm sorry. I need Boy Wonder."

"Will he be back?" Selah asked, eyebrows down. "My husband—"

"I'll call Swartz later." Cherabino moved next to me. "Let's go."

I set down the shovel. "What's wrong?"

"Nothing's wrong, I'm just running in a hurry. You were hard to find, and my informant gets twitchy if I'm too late."

She'd closed two cases the last time he contacted her, and she didn't want to miss the guy.

"Okay . . ." I pulled off Swartz's gardening gloves and dropped them on the ground. "You realize I'm covered in dirt. It will get in your cruiser."

"You realize I said out of time? We'll clean up the dirt later." She grabbed my arm and pulled.

Selah watched us go.

The siren sound turned on as we entered the car.

CHAPTER 19

"**That was a stoplight,**" I said. "Stop sign! Stop sign!"

Cherabino brought the car to a screeching halt as a handicapped man cursed at us from the sidewalk, hands on his anti-grav scooter, which had barely stopped in time.

She imagined slapping me; then I got a flash of her sensei's face. Too violent, his face said. Nonviolence is the only way. Nonviolence and control. He'd made her run twenty miles the last time she hit me, and he'd been right to do it, even with her bad knees. She breathed out through her teeth. "I'm driving," she said, in her "Take Charge, I'm a Cop" voice. Inside she was brittle, and irritated, and worried about being late.

Besides, I was right. "Sorry," she muttered, almost too low to hear. "I can be a little pushy when I'm in a hurry."

"No kidding," I said. I hadn't realized she'd talked to her sensei about me. But it made sense. Her sensei was her Swartz, her guy to help her figure out life.

"I'll work on it," Cherabino said, not sure if she meant it.

The man's scooter made its ponderous way across the intersection at approximately five feet a minute as we waited, Cherabino impatiently. The car behind us honked, echoing that impatience.

And then it happened. My precognition, my stubborn future sense, decided to work.

The universe dissolved out from under me all at once, no warning. I was in an old barn, the smell of moldy hay and ancient horse droppings overwhelming. The world was fuzzy, the clouds of sunlight and dust making watercolor streaks in my vision so I couldn't see clearly.

I turned, trying to get a fix on my position, trying to understand where and when I was. The air was cold, the sunlight thin; midwinter, maybe? Soon? Not a year from now, not two.

There: in the center of the barn in a cleared space, two figures. One in a chair, moving in a strange way that made me think, *Tied up*. I squinted. A boy? A boy about nine perhaps? I knew that boy.

I was suddenly, unreasonably, afraid for that boy.

The other figure looked up, and I knew without a shadow of a doubt despite the fuzziness of my vision that it was Sibley. The strangler for hire I'd put in jail just a few weeks ago. The man I knew worked for Fiske, doing his dirty work.

I held a phone in my hand, the round receiver a weight I didn't like. A voice sounded in my ear—a voice my future self knew was Garrett Fiske.

"Sibley will kill him," Fiske's voice said slowly, with promise built into the words. "He will kill him and you will watch. You deserve to be put in your place."

"Kill me instead," my future self said, voice shaking. "You can't do this! He's just a boy. Kill me instead. I won't fight you." I tried to move but couldn't. "You can't do this," I said again.

"No, you don't get to be self-sacrificing today," Fiske's voice said. He was behind the paralysis, I knew, like he was behind all of this. "You deserve to suffer through the results of your actions."

Sibley pulled out a rope and the boy started screaming,

high-pitched hysterical screaming. I screamed too, feeling his panic, feeling death approaching.

I felt Cherabino in my head then, piggybacking on the vision. *Jacob*, she said. *It's Jacob. Fiske has got Jacob!*

Her panic combined with me ripped the vision apart, and we were back in the car. The man in the scooter ponderously moved onto the sidewalk.

Cherabino gripped the steering wheel with white-knuckled hands while the car behind her honked again. The emotions bubbled up again, panic the strongest one, panic and anger and determination and a sense of *wrongness*, emotions so strong and roiling they were like two overly strong colognes stuck in the confines of the car with us.

"That was one of your visions," Cherabino said.

"Yeah," I coughed out, just now starting to breathe.

"Fiske getting Sibley to kill Jacob. My sister's kid."

"I—"

"Over my dead body," Cherabino spat out, and pulled the flyer away with a screech.

I coughed again. "We don't know—"

"I know what I saw," she said.

The anti-grav engines *whined* as she took the car airborne in a highly illegal vertical lane change in the middle of a city street. When honks came all around, she turned the lights and sirens on. She had a goal, and a purpose, and no citizens were going to stand in her angry way.

"We don't know it's going to happen," I protested, but I didn't believe it. The vision had been too inevitable, too real.

Cherabino looked over at me, narrowly missing a floating lane marker. "Tell me your accuracy rate isn't more than seventy-five percent. Tell me this one's a fluke. Tell me, Adam!"

"Look at the road," I said instead. I was certain. Of all the visions in the world, this one had the weighty quality of certainty.

The vision had happened in winter, in a time not far from now. And Cherabino was about to move on Fiske with her task force.

"Tell me I'm wrong," she spat.

"I can't," I said, the bottom dropping out of my world.

She screeched down onto old asphalt and accelerated. We were in the richest section of the Atlanta, near the governor's mansion, on one of the smallest streets in between trees, and she was treating it like a four-lane highway.

Too fast, too fast, my brain yelled, still trying to process, still trying to catch up with her emotion, with my emotion, with the vision.

"Fiske does not take Jacob," she said, and threw the car into a sudden turn.

She screeched into the open gate of an Italian-style mansion, white stone lions on either side. She swept around the circular drive and threw the car into park too fast, too fast. My heart pounded like a drum played by a teenager.

She reached over me into the glove compartment, then grabbed the rifle from the rack behind us, pushing in a bright green electrically charged stun clip, her anger making her hands move faster than I could see. She'd more likely survive if she used nonlethal methods, her mind informed me.

"His men will be here any second." The words flew out of her mouth. "Now's the time to do your disable-their-brain thing."

She was out of the car before I finished processing that tidbit. Fiske's house? Fiske's? This was happening too fast—

The first two guards arrived, in full combat gear, one with a napkin still tucked into the front of his tactical vest. They both had rifles with long sights, swiveling around to point at Cherabino.

"DeKalb PD," Cherabino yelled with her gun up.

No hesitation; the front guard was aiming. Cherabino was in danger.

My old battle training kicked in. I reached into his brain, found the right spot, and had him out cold before he let out his breath.

Now the second rifle was swiveling toward me.

A second mind, this one with poorer valence, our minds meshing less well in the fabric of Mindspace; his finger was squeezing the trigger before I finished.

I dodged, and came back to his mind, hitting the right spot one more time with greater force. The asphalt where I had been standing exploded in a shower of debris. A piece hit my leg. Pain.

Two sleeping bodies in tactical gear slumped to the ground.

I cursed. "There's more coming," I said. I could see the minds. "We shouldn't be here."

"How many?" Cherabino cut me off, her hands out in front of her, aiming the gun, sweeping the area in front of her. An intense focus came from her mind. She was moving, absolute commitment to the project going forward.

"Three!" I limped after her, "Damn it, damn it, damn it," repeating like a litany.

"DeKalb PD," her voice came again, and the sound of a shot.

I was around the corner. Another guard was on the ground, jerking from the electrical shock. The green stun bullet stuck out from his shoulder. Cherabino kicked his gun away.

A large residential door stood open behind him, a metal-grate mesh security door latched behind it. Three bushes to the left, and a long gravel pathway moving behind the house.

Two more guards came from behind the house.

"Left!" Cherabino screamed, and was aiming.

I disabled the guy on the right, his body slumping down, into the nearest bush, strings cut like a marionette.

Burst of pain in Mindspace from the guy on the left she'd stunned. I winced, feeling his pain as my own. I was years out of practice in battle training. Years. I didn't have the pain tolerance or the focus I'd once had. This was a suicide mission.

I pulled myself out of Mindspace by sheer will, tired already.

But I couldn't let her go in alone.

She was in the middle of a side kick. Her back foot slammed into the mesh door, right by the lock, and it was open.

A person on the other side; I got a grip on his mind, disabled. Stars swam across my vision lightly as I limped after Cherabino, who wasn't slowing down.

Tile entryway, looked like, with a curved open doorway beyond, warm compared to the weather outside. A woman slumped on the floor, unconscious. A small trail of blood came from her forehead where she'd hit it on the way down. Crap. My fault.

Cherabino was through the doorway, moving quickly, and I followed, cursing. I was out of mental juice, without recharging for a few minutes. And it looked like she wasn't nearly out of stupidity yet. I had no choice; I followed her.

We were in a room with full-length glass display cases on three walls out of four, while heavy curtains covered the windows on the fourth. Bright lighting came from inside the cases, illuminating hundreds of objects each in turn, some large, some small. All had small tags beside them explaining what they were; the cases closest to me were dominated by smashed bricks, pieces of computers, and small, shriveled biologicals.

A late-forties man with graying blond hair and a small scar under his left eye looked up. An assistant type behind him, skinny guy with office wear, brought out a gun.

"Put the gun down, Detective Cherabino," the late-forties man said. He had a quiet assurance about him, and a light trace of an educated Boston accent. I recognized the voice from the vision—this was Fiske. He was outfitted in a golf shirt and khakis by a rich man's designer, hundreds of ROCs for just the shirt, and a small chain around his right wrist that looked like platinum.

"Or what?" Cherabino said. For the first time, she had a twinge of doubt.

I felt the mind only seconds before he moved, and I couldn't get a grip on it fast enough to do anything.

A large bruiser came up behind her, a large-bore handgun hitting her temple lightly. "Or I shoot you." He was angry at the damage to his fellows, with a strong enough untapped Ability that I could read him like a book in Mindspace without trying. He'd also be harder to knock out, dangerous on more than one level, and not someone I'd be willing to tackle without another ten minutes to reset. He'd be a hell of an enemy to piss off.

I felt Cherabino consider some judo move to flip him, and I got ready, rest or no rest. Then I sighed, backing down as she discarded the judo move as too risky with the gun in play and so close. On her mental query, I confirmed it was a gun and not another object of the same weight.

Cherabino lowered her own firearm, and the assistant type came forward to take it from her.

"You do *not* touch my family. My family's off-limits, and if you cross that line I will cross lines you've never heard of," she said, her voice like a whip. "Back off," she said, gun to her head, and yet, in that moment, she was dangerous.

Fiske frowned in displeasure. "I don't normally target the families of police, Detective Cherabino. I certainly can, I suppose, if you're going to invade my home. Mantel?"

The bruiser behind her said, "Yes, boss?"

Cherabino pulled away. "I have it on good authority you're planning to kidnap my nephew. I'm here to give you fair warning. If you touch him, I will kill you." A burst of anger and determination. "Don't think I won't."

The bruiser grabbed her arm again, forcing the gun uncomfortably into her temple. She was undeterred.

Fiske looked thoughtful. "You know, I actually believe you. Your information is bad, Detective. I don't have anything of the sort planned." He waved vaguely at the door. "Take her outside, Mantel. Let her call her family to assure herself they're fine, but monitor the conversation. Don't hurt her unless she gives you trouble, but don't let her go. If she shows any sign of trouble or she talks out of turn, kill her."

"Happy to, sir. What do you call trouble?" he asked, his brain thinking violence on many levels.

Fiske smiled the self-satisfied smile again. "See that she throws the first punch. Oh, and send Peterson in while you're out there."

Cherabino swallowed. "Adam . . ."

Two more guards arrived and they took her away like a captive sheep, Mantel angry and scared of his boss, a combination that I thought made him all the more dangerous. I turned to follow, thinking I could calm him down. Maybe. Given enough time.

"Stop," Fiske said, the command of a well-practiced

leader with the power of life and death. "Adam Ward. You stay with me, for now. Your police detective doesn't have to stay intact."

A guard came behind me, just far enough away to use his gun, making his presence very clear.

Cherabino was broadcasting low-level fear and anger and very intense attention. She thought she could probably overcome the one guy if she had to.

You okay? I asked her.

Think so, she said, trying to figure out if she believed Fiske. Trying to figure out if her warning had registered, and how she was going to get out of this.

Do I need to fight? I asked, adding the fact that I probably couldn't knock anyone out for a few minutes yet.

Keep him talking, she said. *We'll figure it out. I can handle myself.*

Okay, I said. I turned back to Fiske as Cherabino was pulled out of the room, angry. She was at least twenty feet away and moving even farther, judging by the noise between us on the Link. I was worried.

Another guard type, this one dark and short with whip-tight muscles and a vest only half-fastened, moved up to the room from the foyer.

"Peterson," Fiske said.

"Yes, sir." The guard was worried, intensely worried enough I could feel it in Mindspace.

"You are the head of my security team."

"Yes, sir."

"You let two cops stroll into my home." Fiske pulled a gun out of the back of his khakis and shot the man twice, once in the gap of the vest, and once in the throat.

My ears rang with the gunshots. Peterson slumped to his knees, his throat making a horrible gurgling sound.

Shock and pain moved through Mindspace, and the

guard behind me tightened the grip on the barrel of his gun so hard I felt it.

I stared, the reality of our situation suddenly all too clear.

Fiske looked to the other guard. "Congratulations, Rodriguez. You are now the head of my security team. I expect you to find how they got in and eliminate the issue when this is over."

"Understood, sir," Rodriguez said, mixed fear and determination coming off him. He kept looking at his buddy on the floor. This didn't do good things for his control of the gun, and I moved away a little.

In Mindspace, a huge hole opened up where Peterson's mind had been. He Fell In, dying in despair and agony I couldn't completely shield from. His body jerked with a last nerve pulse, and then I smelled the scent of urine being voided.

Fiske looked at me. "I should thank you for revealing a hole in my security. So I'll be generous. This time."

Why kill him in front of me? Oh. Fiske knew about my felony drug charges. He knew I couldn't testify in court; I was a guaranteed unreliable witness. So he could do whatever the hell he wanted, and I could do nothing. Even if I told Cherabino, it would be a secondhand account.

Fiske accepted a handkerchief from his assistant, wiped off the gun, and put it back in the holster in the back of his khakis. "Now, now, Mr. Ward. You'll see your partner again in a moment. Come over here." I took a few steps toward Fiske, mindful of the guard. According to the clock on the wall, I had maybe ten minutes before I was up for another round of sleep-baby-sleep. Give it fifteen just to be safe, what with the work I'd just done and my recent brain injury. Time to talk my way out of this—if I could.

Well, today I didn't have anything to lose. I could ask anything, do anything, and be in no worse danger than I would have been tomorrow. The Guild's sentencing hung over my head like an anvil, so that there was no more room for fear.

I tried to remember how I had handled this kind of thing with Marge back in the day, back when I'd bought drugs from her organization and before I'd shut her down with the cops.

Finally I settled on "I'm sorry we intruded on your afternoon, Mr. Fiske." I walked over farther in his direction, his assistant standing by with the gun on top of his notepad, sideways, ready at a moment's notice. "Honestly, I'm just here to talk a little and get your perspective." I pitched my voice and my body language as slightly submissive; not enough to be a victim, but enough to be a beta, not an alpha, in the room. I would get nowhere through a battle for dominance anyway; I was better off talking and then disabling.

Besides, it had been a long time since I'd been anybody's alpha anything. You get out of practice.

Fiske settled a bit, reacting to my, to him, appropriate body language. He nodded at the assistant, who put a small syringe back in a box.

My heart skipped a beat, adrenaline hitting my system all over again. Needles carried by bad guys were never a good idea.

"Under what circumstances would you threaten a child? Given the information we have, it seems to be the logical question." I asked, mind open enough to smell a lie if he told one.

"I like an intelligent opponent," Fiske said, "and, as I said, I will be generous. This time. But don't push your luck.

You have barged into my home and caused damage to my guards. Impertinent questions are hardly the way to walk away from this."

"I understand," I said, my standard answer to suspects for whom I had no answer. The conversation was getting away from me. I felt a distant sense of relief, relief flavored with Cherabino's mind through the Link. She had a connection with her sister, then.

"Do you know what this is?" Fiske asked. He was looking at one of the display cases. I was thinking about the needle.

I hadn't lived this long by being stupid around dangerous people. If he wanted to play games, I'd play games. You lived longer that way. "No, I'm afraid I don't know what that is. What is it?" I pitched my voice interested, casual. I didn't feel casual, not at all, but Nelson had been sure he was mind-deaf.

He smiled, and I knew he was. "This, Mr. Ward, is a pre–Tech Wars fully functional mental implant, in full working order. I've had it serviced. Its owner died from the Kappa virus during the third round of the Tech Wars. Very rare piece. The virus is still active, of course."

I swallowed, and finally looked. It was a small cylinder, the size of your thumb, covered in withered biological circuits like octopus tentacles out of the water. But the core— the core was a round thing with layered quantum chips and a glowing red pulse.

"Still active?" I asked, nervous, trying to remember which virus the Kappa had been. The Guild hadn't been all that concerned with the details of the Tech Wars' tactics in its secondary education classes, because the virus had only affected normals with implants, not telepaths.

"Of course." Fiske smiled again, the smile of a shark

inspecting its prey. Delighted to find such a lovely morsel in front of him. "It overwrote the victim's brain with nonsense, with unreality, over and over again until the mind lost cohesion. Then it sent the body out to infect others. Any kind of biological interface to the body—a pacemaker, a Tech-controlled organ, an artificial limb—was fair game."

"Modern limbs and such have virus protection," I said. But I took a step back from the case.

"A convenient lie the manufacturers tell," Fiske said.

There was a short pause, during which I absorbed this, and he walked farther along the row of cases. Weapons sat, some jury-rigged out of car-body aluminum and steel bars, some forged in happier times, all with blood still on them. Round donut-shaped magnets, connected to plastic tubing and copper wires, set in worn harnesses, for the day the normals figured out how to fight back against the machines. Not that it had done more than stem the tide. They'd still needed the telepaths to end it.

Small rare-earth magnets, exchanged as tokens among the resistance, now changing the shape of Mindspace in quiet ways, like a rock in a stream. Maps. Pieces of bombs. Pieces of what might have been.

I looked back at the clock. Maybe another six minutes. My interrogators' instincts said if I didn't take charge now, there were even odds that I would end up as cannon fodder or "victim" status in this guy's head. What to ask?

Well, if I was risking death anyway . . .

"I was admiring your work the other day," I said. "The researcher. Noah Wright. The ax was telling. It almost kept us from finding the prototype in his head. Removing the arm for the control section was particularly genius."

He blinked at me, unreadable. "You're not going to ask me about how much of my collection is still dangerous?"

"I think it's obvious that it's all dangerous," I said. "That's why you collect it, isn't it?"

The corner of his mouth crooked, and a small, quiet burst of satisfaction came from him. "Excellent, Mr. Ward. You impress me."

"The question in my mind is whether or not you've inoculated yourself against the Kappa virus, or whether you leave it there as a test."

"Why can't it be both?" Fiske asked me. For the first time, I got a clear picture of the wily mind that had been part and parcel of every bad thing that had happened to me in the last months. He'd been behind Bradley, and Tamika, ultimately, hijackings and deaths and a specific threat against me. And he was honestly, truly, a no-holds-barred genius.

"What are you doing?" he asked.

"Just admiring your mind," I said. "Observing. It's not often I get to meet someone who works on so many levels at once."

"Flattery, Mr. Ward?" But he was disturbed.

"Truth," I said, in the same sincere lying tone I used with suspects. "I did wonder, however, why you were working with Tobias Nelson. You know, from Guild Enforcement. He bought parts from you, personally. I thought you didn't handle parts sales personally."

"Impertinent questions." He retrieved a small device from the shelf, put it around his neck.

"An opportunity to show your genius," I said. "What's that?"

He pushed a button.

An unthinkable pressure in Mindspace pushed at me. I held—and held—and held. I could stand upright. I could think, barely. Maybe. But there was not a chance in hell I'd be able to read or disable anyone with that thing on.

Fiske smiled and looked at his assistant.

The man spoke. "It is an infinity wave generator, the only prototype ever made. It was created the year after the Tech Wars by the US government and during the time of the signing of the Koshna Accords. The lab it was produced in was burned to the ground a week before signing. Everyone there was killed."

Fiske took a step toward me while I struggled to pay attention. "The device resurfaced decades later in a private auction. Only one man in the world could get it back to working order. I killed him as well. This is the one defense no one can stand against, because no one's seen or dealt with it before.

"You see, Mr. Ward, I'm an old-fashioned man. I believe telepaths should be kept away from normal people, locked up in their little towers, and not allowed to influence the works of real men."

"You sympathize with Guild First," I said, overwhelmed but thinking. Thinking.

Fiske took another step toward me. "You're not paying attention."

My head was starting to pulse pain. I guessed. "You're trying to get into Guild politics to get access to an army of telepaths to enforce your decisions. Or to have the Guild give you concessions. That's why you worked with Tobias. That's why you worked with Bradley."

"Independent telepaths are an affront to society and a dangerous sign of our degenerate times," Fiske said, looking straight at me. "They threaten the greater order. The Guild is bad enough, but systems can be dealt with. Independents— well, they are dealt with differently."

"You said you would be generous this time," the assistant said cautiously. "Do we kill them anyway?"

Fiske turned, to look at the assistant. "No, I did say that. Mr. Ward, I am giving you an opportunity. Either you remove yourself from my affairs—permanently—and control your police friend, or I will do it for you. I have three witnesses, and you have only the word of a drug addict." He glanced at the assistant. "See that he leaves."

"It will be done," the assistant said.

"What about Noah Wright?" I asked. "The researcher killed with the ax? Why him?"

Fiske turned, with a cruel, cruel smile. He hit the button, and the pain stopped. "I'm told you can tell whether a man is lying or not."

I nodded, suddenly afraid. There was something about his mind at that moment that was the most dangerous thing I'd looked into my whole life. Like walking from your tent into the darkness to take a leak only to find yourself face-to-face with a jackal.

"Then you'll know I'm telling the truth. Noah Wright isn't mine," Fiske said.

"What?" It took me a moment to catch up with the sudden shift in conversation. "I thought he was selling you something."

"The blueprints and project notes were useful, of course. Under other circumstances, I might have tried to recruit him. But he was so obviously double-crossing that TCO agent of his."

"What? Who killed him?" I asked.

"Now, now, I'm not doing your work for you." He paused. "Now, while you're paying attention—I do not now nor do I plan to take or in any way harm a member of your partner's family." He was telling the truth.

"You didn't include her in that list," I said.

"Very good, Mr. Ward. You'll notice I also did not include

you. It's time for you to leave, or we'll find out how many bullets I have left in my gun today. You come back to my home, and I'll do worse."

His mind leaked the knowledge that killing me, or Cherabino, would likely be more trouble than it was worth considering the little damage. He would do it if provoked, though; he did not tolerate disrespect, and he'd swallowed enough of it already to tolerate the trouble to kill us if needed.

And Fiske turned, as if I'd sunk beneath his notice.

I left quickly.

The assistant escorted me out into the cold, him with a gun, me with my mind ready to disable him before he could pull the trigger.

Cherabino had a black eye and a foul mood, but was both relieved and pissy enough despite large amounts of duct tape that I was certain nothing serious had happened. She did judo sparring all the time; a few bruises weren't going to do anything but piss her off.

She was surrounded by not one, not two, but four hulking guards in a niche in the garden surrounded by brick. None looked happy. The closest was weighing Fiske's exact wording on the Do Not Harm policy, whether broken bones would count as harm or not. If not, he had favorites.

"We're releasing them," the assistant said in a carrying voice to the group.

"Mmmph!" Cherabino yelled at the closest guard.

He sighed, and ripped off the duct tape over her mouth all at once.

"—of a *bitch!*" she screamed. "That hurt, damn it."

"Really? Glad to hear it. Stop squirming and I'll cut you free." He pulled out a knife and cut at the duct tape, not very carefully. Cherabino stood absolutely still.

The assistant took a breath, ready to deliver a speech, but I cut him off.

"Yes, yes, we know. Come back and you'll kill us. Very dead. We get it. Can we go now?"

The assistant stared.

I tilted my head, implying "bring it on." My mind had recharged, and there were five people here total. None of whom had license to kill me. "After the fourth death threat in a week, it's getting old. I believe you, don't get me wrong, but I'd like to skip the speech if it's all the same to you. She's going to be hell to get home."

One of the guards went for his gun—

And I had him out cold on the ground. Everyone else's guns came out, pointed at the ground, the guards nervous as hell.

"Anybody else want to try me?" I asked.

A twitch—and the guy on the right dropped his gun. Outright. It hit the concrete with a *clatter*.

"That's right," Cherabino said, hands free, and stalked over to me.

"You're going to be impossible, aren't you?" I asked.

"Maybe."

"Keys."

"No way."

"Keys or I leave you here."

She handed me the keys. "You seem . . . pissed off."

I slid into the driver's side of the police car and opened the door for her from the inside. Kept an eye on the guards lined up behind us. Everybody still looked wary, but that could change soon.

She was in and seat-belted, and I was driving. Away. Quickly.

"Is Jacob okay?" I asked.

"Yeah. He's been at home all day with the tutor." She felt like an idiot for jumping in so quickly, but on the other hand, if her message was received . . . "The future can be changed, right?"

"Usually," I said.

"Then he won't mess with Jacob." That made it worth it, even if she lost her job for this.

I kicked the engine into higher gear and got on the right on-lane for Northside Parkway's skylanes. "We don't know that. All we know is that we've pissed off a very dangerous man."

"You're not going to Decatur," she said.

"No, I'm not." I moved up into the skylanes, feeling okay about driving despite the fact that it had been a while. I was tracking all the other cars, hyperaware of even the birds coming through above me. I was pissed off, and the adrenaline was flowing.

"You're not going to tell me where you are going?"

I debated what to say. "Fiske said Wright wasn't one of his kills. I believed him. And then he said Wright was double-crossing Ruffins. There's . . . We need to check to see where Ruffins was during the murder. And we need to do it now."

She processed that for a second, with conflicting emotions. I must have leaked information over the Link, because she finally settled on "You're still going to the Guild tomorrow. You're showing up for your own funeral on time and with a smile?"

"I'm going to fight," I said. "And I have an idea."

It took me a moment to identify the emotion coming off her—it felt faint and far away. Pride. It was pride.

"Stop that," I said. "Seriously, stop."

"What?"

I went through a dozen scenarios and couldn't find an explanation that made sense. "Nothing."

She closed her eyes. "You're going to the Midtown TCO office, aren't you? For Ruffins."

CHAPTER 20

"Look, Adam, I appreciate the fact that you had a heart-to-heart with a charming guy who happened to—"

"Are you calling me an idiot?" I asked.

"No." She changed tactics. "Fiske has every reason to lie to us, and his charm isn't—"

"Stop. I've interviewed how many thousand suspects at this point? I can tell the difference between the charm and the truth, Cherabino. Plus he wasn't all that charming."

"It's very likely he himself ordered the—"

"Seriously, Cherabino, don't treat me like an idiot. You think I'm falling for honeyed words? From somebody on that level? Which, by the way, he didn't bother with and I wouldn't fall for. I know better than that. You may not have been there, but I can do interviews. He was telling the truth as he understood it. I just want to check."

That sat in the car between us for a good while as I navigated the skylanes with the other, homicidal drivers around me. In Atlanta, turn signals were information, not a request, and you were advised to react accordingly. I reacted, decelerating to allow the ugly green flyer to pull in front of me. He kept going across four lanes of traffic, of course.

"You've never ever been wrong about the lying thing? Nobody's ever lied to you and gotten away with it? Ever?"

I made a low sound of frustration in the back of my throat. "I strongly doubt this guy's good enough to lie to a telepath convincingly."

"Even so. We check and we double-check before we accuse some officer who's only doing his job. Especially if you're operating out of some stupid theory. We can't go to the TCO office. It won't turn out well."

"What? Why not?" I swerved to avoid a driver with engine trouble who was losing altitude into my flight space. Fortunately he had his screamers on and everyone else was swerving too. I pulled us back in an even flight space and remembered why I hadn't driven in Midtown even when I could drive. "What did you say?"

"You show up at this guy's work with accusations, and either they're not going to respond well or they're going to take you all too serious. Either you stall the inquiry or you tip him off or they take over, and none is good for us. I'm not implicating somebody who's just doing his job."

I made another frustrated sound while I thought it over. "Cops are touchy bastards."

"I know."

But I took the next exit, to look for a pay phone, like her mind was suggesting quietly.

"You know that stunt at Fiske's house was stupid," I said. "We could have both gotten killed."

"Maybe. But it's Jacob. He was screwing with my family. You can't screw with a cop's family and get away with it. He knows now that I'm paying attention. He knows there's a line. He knows I know where he lives and how he works."

"He got the better end of that deal."

"Him spending all that time with you? And then you handling the guards at the end? Yeah, he got his bit, but he's going to remember today. That's all I wanted. He needs to hesitate before he does anything like that again. Bransen will back me up. Maybe." But inside, she wondered, and regretted.

"We probably changed the future, right?" she asked me finally. "Kept him from hurting Jacob, for sure?"

"I don't know. There's no way to know yet."

She made another frustrated sound. "Well, at least this won't impact the task force. None of the critical evidence is a direct tie to me. Fiske will go down either way." Even if she got fired, her brain said. And she was alive. "We had to have changed the future. Jacob's safe. That's what matters."

I finally agreed, because she expected me to. I still wasn't sure why she'd charged in like that. But what was done, was done.

Cherabino hung up the pay phone and trudged back to the car. In front of us, the back of the Fox Theatre rose, ancient and soot-stained, its lights still cheerful after so many years.

The car door opened, and she slid into the seat.

"So?" I asked.

She sighed. "His supervisor took my credentials. Ruffins was supposed to be in Montgomery that day. They pulled his tracking records and he was actually in the area of the victim's house."

"Tracking records?" I asked.

"You really think the government gives him all those shiny toys to play with and doesn't keep track? There's still satellites up there, for all people don't want to talk about it. There's still a big independent space station with full technology. And he's got more than a few things tattooed on that arm of his."

"There wasn't a flag on it immediately if he wasn't doing what he was supposed to?"

She shifted in her seat. "There's professional courtesy. There's trust. There's a guy doing his job who doesn't need his arm joggled every time he makes an independent decision. I don't like this, Adam. It doesn't prove anything, and that's all they know."

"Fine," I said, "but we're going back over the evidence with a fine-tooth comb. There's something there. I can feel it."

Cherabino sighed. "I already called Michael to have him pull the files. I hope you're expecting to work late tonight."

We'd taken over one of the empty conference rooms, and I was going through every piece of paperwork in the room and driving Cherabino and Michael to do the same. There was something we were missing.

Hours passed, until Cherabino sent Michael out for food.

My hands landed on the fingerprint reports from the crime scene again. Ruffins, again, but he'd admitted to being there several times. Wright had been his informant.

I paged through them, eyes blurry, frustrated and feeling like Cherabino had won. It probably was Fiske. I'd probably been lied to.

I stopped, and went back. There. One of Ruffins's prints. On the inside of the front door, like he'd hit it on his way out. The lab tech had grouped this print with all the others identified as Ruffins's—but this one was in blood. The victim's blood, in all likelihood.

It had been grouped in with all the others.

"I found the smoking gun," I said.

Cherabino came over. "Oh," she said, when she saw it. "Well, crap." She sighed. "Let me talk to Bransen."

———————

An hour and a half later we were in Bransen's office, and Paulsen was sitting in a guest chair on his side of the table.

"The evidence is damning if you know where to look," Cherabino said, and with gravity laid out what we had, including Fiske's assertion that Wright had double-crossed Ruffins, and the sudden appearance of the extra money in Wright's account about the same time.

"Why were you there talking to our primary suspect in a major transagency case this morning?" Paulsen asked in her quietest, most dangerous voice. She was looking straight at me.

"If I don't work for you anymore, you don't get to yell at me anymore," I heard myself say, and then looked down.

"Point taken," she said.

Cherabino's spine straightened. "As I told Sergeant Bransen, I received a credible threat against a member of my family and responded accordingly. We have discussed how the department would be better served through the use of normal channels and backup."

"As well as sufficient patience and the use of protective duty personnel and case-building rather than stupidity," Bransen added wryly.

Cherabino added, "Whether or not my information was sufficient to justify my actions is a question for the inquiry hearing. Right now we need to talk about Ruffins. What are we going to do?"

Paulsen thought. "This isn't a good situation. Are you certain the prints aren't cross-contaminated?"

"Certain, ma'am," Cherabino said.

"We're on dangerous ground accusing any member of another agency," Bransen said.

"That's why I came to both of you," she said. But Paulsen was already on another line of thinking. She asked me, "You were there at the scene. Does Ruffins fit the profile of what you saw and felt?"

I went back over that crime scene in my mind, in detail. "The anger, the need for control, the carefulness at the end—it could be Ruffins. The mind wasn't inconsistent with what I know about him. But he's . . . he has a device that lets him tell when I'm around, and more so, when I'm reading him. I can't get any information from him without a big red mental flag pointed right at me. So I haven't read him much. I don't have . . ." How to explain this to a normal? "I don't have familiarity with his mind. You put him in a lineup with similars, his mind could be any one of them."

"So the only thing we have definitive is this fingerprint in blood," Paulsen said.

"All the circumstantials support it," Cherabino said.

"Ruffins's testimony and informants are a major portion of the case against Garrett Fiske," Bransen said quietly. "It's the result of countless man-hours and expense by this department and other agencies. Furthermore, his testimony and connections are key to prosecuting several of the hijackers we arrested a few weeks ago. The first of their trials starts in three weeks. We need to take a moment here and look at what we're doing."

"It's a murder, sir. With an ax," Cherabino said. "As near as I can tell, to cover up evidence and keep this man's life work from being shared the way he felt it should be. Are we really comfortable letting a fed—with all the powers of a fed—wandering around with this kind of crime and violence on the table? Even if we're only ninety percent certain?"

Paulsen shook her head. "Let's think this through. We move on this, we don't move on this, either way there's injustice to somebody. The question is, which set of injustices serves the people better?"

"It's murder, sir."

"There's no statute of limitations on murder, Isabella."

"You can't seriously intend to wait on this one," I said.

"It would let us move forward on the Fiske trial. Revisit the rest of this later."

"Think about that, sir. Garrett Fiske has the kinds of lawyers who are more than willing to drag all of us through the dirt on the slightest excuse. Cherabino and I just talked to him. I think it's likely he knows that Ruffins committed this crime. Cherabino says all of the critical evidence for the task force was obtained through him."

"The case is dead in the water either way," Bransen said. He seemed composed outwardly, but internally he was burning angry at having Fiske slip out of his hands.

Paulsen looked at Bransen. Bransen looked at Paulsen.

"Fiske will wait," Paulsen said, but her mind felt heavy all of a sudden, like she stood up under impossible pressure.

A spike of mixed emotions from Cherabino, quickly controlled.

"He's waited this long already. He'll wait a little longer until we get our house in order," Paulsen said. "I'll find the budget somehow."

Bransen stood.

Paulsen followed suit, as did the rest of us. She looked at me, specifically. "Adam, good luck tomorrow. We're . . . Well, good luck."

I read her then, mentally, even though most of the time I didn't feel comfortable doing so. I read her and found determination, and regret. The largest regret was that, even if there had been something she could have done for me now, she wouldn't. She liked me, and regretted, but I had made other choices.

I turned and left.

The vision . . . in the little downtime I'd had, I kept thinking about that vision, that boy. Was it Jacob? I didn't know. I couldn't see him.

It might not matter anyway, not if the Guild took me out tomorrow despite my best efforts.

I did Cherabino's paperwork with Michael while I waited for the arrest to go through. An hour into it, her phone rang.

I picked up the phone.

The dispatcher's voice came through: "Adam Ward?"

"That's me."

A clicking sound, and one, droning line of the public service announcement that was the hold music.

Then: "Don't hang up, Adam." It was Kara, sounding torn up.

"I'm in the middle of something. Can I call you back?"

"The flyer crashed. The private long-distance flyer—the one carrying the Council members back from the international conference. There's some evidence against . . . They're saying Charlie did the sabotage, Adam."

My old classmate turned Councilman. "That's impossible. Charlie's the straightest shooter I've ever met." I looked at the clock. "Does this mean my hearing is rescheduled?" I had a moment of corrected priorities. "I assume everyone got out?" With teleportation the norm, it seemed unlikely that—

"They all died, Adam. Every last one." She took a shuddery breath. "We haven't had this many Council members die at the same time in the entire history of the Guild. We'll have to promote people, find people, do an emergency election, and even then I don't know—"

I had a sudden, horrible thought. "What political group were they in?" I looked at Michael, who had looked up and was now, carefully, studying paperwork.

"Oh, look, I need coffee," he said, and left. I let him go. Kara was still saying nothing.

"What political group were they in?" I asked. "Guild Firsters? Cooperists? Family groups? Independents? Who, Kara?"

"They were all Cooperists but one. And she was no fan of Guild First."

I took a breath. "So, in one fell swoop, the entirety of the Council is favorable to Thaddeus Rex."

"Diaz isn't."

"What is his health like?" I asked.

She was silent.

"The only other one standing up is who, Charlie?" I looked into the face of the abyss that was Guild politics. "Doesn't it seem coincidental that he's accused now?"

Again, a long silence.

Finally Kara spoke. "This isn't a secure line. I wasn't—"

"Give my regards to Gustolf," I said, to make sure I understood what she was going to do.

"Oh, I will," she said in the low, quiet voice that meant danger. "I will." Good. Her family would get involved, and her family was a significant force to be reckoned with. With her at the helm, they might make all the difference.

I tried to figure out how to ask if I should run, get out of the country, show up in Dublin or Moscow and trade information for protection from the local Guild. Hope the chaos here kept them from coming after me. "The hearing?" I finally settled for.

Kara paused long enough that I knew she understood what I was asking. "It's still being held tomorrow morning, early. Gustolf and I will be there."

I asked the critical question. "Will you support me?"

A long pause. Then she said, "No one is dying on my watch for asking a reasonable question. Martin Cooper wouldn't have let that happen. Besides, you've shown up for me plenty of times."

A small sense of relief—and comfort. But Kara was playing her own game now, a game I was no longer sure had anything at all to do with her uncle.

I looked at my options—all of which involved me leaving everything I'd built for myself and all my systems of sobriety—and threw the dice in one critical direction.

Someone had to accuse Rex, right?

And I was the only one who really could. If anything, my idea would only strengthen that power. Rex, the man who'd twisted me into knots for stupid reasons, who'd threatened me over and over and over again, would face his peers over the truth.

"I'll be there," I said. "But, Kara?"

"What?"

"No matter how this turns out, you owe Isabella Cherabino a favor. A big favor. Anything she asks."

"Agreed."

I went to find the television in the break room and turned it on to the news station. News of corruption in county politics, a murder on the subway train system, illegal Tech smuggling, the usual. I was just about to leave when the screen changed.

"In breaking news," the news announcer said gravely. Her face, frozen with age treatments, hardly moved. "Our station has recently heard of a major flyer crash near the Chattahoochee River. Nine passengers on board, all dead including the pilot. Three homes destroyed. We bring you live coverage of the scene."

I turned the sound off as the footage began. A long, long furrow from the edge of the river, trees scattered in every direction, raw red dirt exposed like flesh. At the end of it, the reporter stood a hundred feet away from a twisted mass of wreckage and metal slammed into a wooden house, now splintered boards. Darker splotches fell into the furrow, what might have been seats or people or plastic, impossible to tell at this distance. The silence made the wreckage cold, and unfeeling.

I turned it off. Nobody could have survived that.

The powder keg that was the Guild's political system was about to erupt, and this was the match.

But I had a job to do here at the police station.

Ten minutes later, I was sitting at an interview table by special permission from Bransen, ash and gall all I could taste. Outside, Cherabino read Special Agent Ruffins his rights while inside, a babysitter sat there, ready to report back to Bransen.

The door opened. A look of abject hatred came at me from across the room. The emotion in Mindspace was more of the same.

Ruffins shook his head. "I'm not going to be interviewed by a teep."

Today, as in so many other days in this interview room, I swallowed the insult and—barely—forced a smile. "I'm all you have available today."

Ruffins turned, but Cherabino stood in his way, very unfriendly. Behind her, some of the special tactics guys waited for an excuse. Nobody liked a dirty cop.

"Sit down," Cherabino said.

"I want my phone call," Ruffins said.

"You'll have it after you talk to Adam. But don't think about calling your supervisor. He's been fully briefed. You've been read your rights."

After a long, hate-filled moment, Ruffins sat.

Cherabino went to the corner—Bellury's corner—and

sat in the babysitter's chair. That was different. That—well, it threw me off. I stared at her.

Don't screw this up, I heard in my brain over the Link.

I turned back to Ruffins. He was holding his hand over his tattoo, nervous. Below that, the soft subtle smell of . . . fear. I felt fear in Mindspace, real fear, the kind of fear a recovering arachnophobe felt when seeing a tarantula through glass. Strict control, strict thought, but underlying terror, fear much bigger than any average normal felt when faced with a telepath.

And suddenly I knew how to handle this.

"Special Agent Ruffins," I said.

He just looked at me. Silence was his best bet, and he knew it.

"I'll make you a deal," I said. "That meter on your arm—you can feel it when I read you, is that right?"

He looked down at the multicolored band of his tattoo. Likely so, his brain supplied.

"We can test the theory if you—"

"No!" He took a breath, and returned to silent waiting punctuated by angry fear. It wasn't illegal for me to read his surface thoughts if I told him I was a telepath, and he likely knew it.

I sat back in the chair, a slightly less threatening posture. "We can do this the easy way if you like. You tell me the truth and I won't do an active read."

I had his attention.

"I'm sure you're wondering what that means. I'll tell you. I'll still be sitting here and I'll still monitor Mindspace around you. That means if you have a strong emotion, I'll get a whiff of it, like cologne. If you lie to me I'll spot it. But I won't get thoughts. I won't get a view of the inside of your head at all. I stay over here, and you stay over there."

"Why would you do that?" he asked, wary, still rubbing his arm.

"I don't have a dog in this pony fight. Cherabino, over there, cares. She wins something if you're guilty, but she wins something if you're not. She has a preference for which it is. Me, on the other hand, I get the same pay either way. I only care about the truth. You give me the truth, the real truth, with no fudging or corrections or half lies, and I don't have any need to read you."

"You'd do that?" Ruffins asked, a feeling of contempt, anger and a note of relief coming off him.

"Ask Cherabino over there if I keep my promises."

We looked. She, reluctantly, nodded.

In Mindspace: *Not about the drug,* her mind echoed.

I never made you a single promise about Satin, I left in her mind. *And there's a reason for that.*

She shifted uncomfortably in the chair, but I was already onto Ruffins.

"Do we have a deal? The truth in exchange for keeping my mind to myself?"

"If I lie?"

"You know the answer to that," I said, injecting as much certainty and doom into the statement as possible. His imagination would be far, far worse than anything I could say to him.

He considered it and then nodded, cautiously.

Line on a hook, I had him. The way I had primed him, any half-truth or fudging would now carry a burst of that same fear.

"Let's begin," I said, with a smile. I asked him where he was the day of the murder, the usual softening-up question.

"I killed him," Ruffins said quickly. "It wasn't intentional, or, well, it wasn't planned. It just . . ." He trailed off.

"Start from the beginning of the conversation with Wright

and tell me what happened," I said, in my most neutral inter-viewer voice. Wow, that had been easier than expected.

He nodded and sat a little taller, his voice taking on that official confidence I'd seen in him already so many times. "Noah Wright was a valuable asset into the workings of Fiske's crime organization. He'd already sold information to the man through an intermediary and was poised to meet some of the organization directly. When he lost his job, I applied subsequent financial pressure to get him to agree to infiltrate the higher-up portions of Fiske's enter-prises on my behalf. I gave him information, a good mix of accurate and false approved by my superiors, and set him loose. He was doing well." He took a breath.

"And then what?" I prompted.

"He started getting cold feet. Saying that this wasn't going anywhere. He wanted to sell some of his inventions. Or, really, with that insane Free Data mantra of his, he wanted to release them as widely as possible. He started talking about giving away that medical device he was so obsessed with. I thought I talked him down. I thought . . . " Ruffins was look-ing at the back wall of the interview room, no longer at me, no longer at anything. Telling the story. "The day before, I'd checked his accounts to make sure he'd been reporting all of Fiske's payments correctly. And I found the other payments. Payments even my superiors had trouble tracing."

No fear anymore, not any. His emotions had the even keel of someone telling a true story from recent events.

"Go on," I said.

"Well, I went over there and confronted him about the payments. He told me it was the Chinese. He'd sold them the Galen device! Like it didn't even matter! The US mili-tary was already under contract. I pushed him, why would he do that? National security trumps freedom. We could all die in a slip. And then—"

"And then what?"

"And then he said he hadn't sent all the data yet. I lost it. The ax was just sitting there, just sitting there." Disgust filled the air. "I swung it and I swung it until he couldn't get up. Until he'd never sell anything again. He'd never destroy anything again. And then I took out the prototype in his head." He looked up, meeting my eyes. "I took it and all its parts to the shed in my backyard and I burned it. Once with wood and once with a blowtorch and once with lighter fluid. No one's going to use that DNA now. Not the Chinese, not anybody."

"You burned it?" I prompted, when he was silent for a minute.

"I protected the American people. You would have done the same." He paused. "You really haven't read me, have you?"

"No, I haven't."

He nodded. "Respect. Respect was all I was really looking for."

And there was the truth. He could have turned the man into the authorities, arrested him, locked him up, allowed his information to be used to benefit everyone. But instead the disrespect of his own informant turning against him had made him turn violent, ax murder violent. It had made him act to control Wright at any cost. This was not a heroic man, for all he protested otherwise. This was not a heroic act.

I tidied up the last few lingering details gently and then ended the interview.

Cherabino and I stood in the hall, totally silent, as the special tactics bruisers escorted him downstairs to the holding cells. He never struggled.

And I wondered. Had we done the right thing? He'd done wrong, very, very wrong, but so had Fiske. It didn't seem fair that his wrongdoing should buy Fiske freedom—but I didn't know what else we could have done.

And maybe that—that—was why Fiske was in charge of one of the largest criminal organizations in the Southeast. He was a puppet master, and I couldn't help feeling like I'd had my strings pulled.

But Ruffins had killed a man.

I'd caught a killer. But this was not a happy day for me, not at all.

CHAPTER 21

When the dim hallway was empty, interview rooms lit on each side, I sighed. "You realize we've been played, right?"

Cherabino nodded. "Fiske? Yeah. We were. But Ruffins should not have done what he did. One bad apple and all that. What else could we do?"

We stood there for a moment. She was right. She was.

"Then why do I feel . . . so . . . ?"

"Unsettled?" Cherabino said. "Sometimes it's like that. We do this for the justice, and to bring resolution to the families. We're doing that here. It's the right thing to do, no matter what the consequences are."

Then I added, "Fiske didn't have a reason to keep track of Wright, did he? Not more than usual."

She turned to look at me. "Unless he knew he was working for the feds. Yeah, I know. I'm betting somebody put the ax there, even. Doesn't make it right. You don't go axing your informants. You just don't."

"He did kill Wright," I said.

"Yeah, he did." She waited, to see if I was going to need to talk this through more.

I said nothing.

"Like I said, Adam, sometimes it's like this. Sometimes

not everything gets resolved the way we want it to. We do the job anyway."

And in that moment, I believed. I believed we'd done what we could. I believed . . . well, mostly I believed in Cherabino.

We did the job anyway.

The moment passed, and I saw the time. "Listen, I have one more stop to make before we leave. Meet you up front in half an hour?"

She frowned at me, but giving Cherabino a chance for more work was like giving me access to my poison. "Sure."

I knocked on Captain Harris's door.

"Come in," came a gruff voice.

I opened the door cautiously and closed it just as cautiously behind me. "Thank you for agreeing to see me," I said. I was only ten minutes late.

Harris nodded and set down his pen, gesturing me forward to the desk chair. I went.

He was a gray man with gray hair and a perpetually tired look, several pounds overweight, and he had enough power and creative problem-solving to manage most of the DeKalb County Police Force and get funding from half a dozen additional sources. In addition to arbitration outside the department.

He had very little patience with me in particular, and I'd only sat down with him three times: once when I was hired, once when I was rehired after my fall off the wagon, and once when I'd had the vision that had ultimately saved Cherabino's life. He could still ruin any chance I had of employment with a single word to one of his friends. But he also used to be married to Jamie, decades ago.

"I'm not getting any younger, boy," he prompted.

"I don't know if you knew this, but I'm one of Jamie Skelton's old students."

"Does this have a point?"

"Do you still have your Guild pass?" I asked.

And now I had his attention. He leaned forward. "As it happens, I do. It's current. Jamie and I still talk, sometimes."

Relief washed over me. The first part, the hard part, of my idea was done.

I started talking.

I left, half an hour later, having been chewed out to within an inch of my life for allowing Cherabino to go to Fiske's without a hell of a lot more backup than just me. For repeating the same stupid mistake in backup that had gotten Bellury killed, he said.

I walked out black and blue, chastened on every level, but I walked out with a promise.

He'd speak for me.

I asked Cherabino to drive me to her house. "I'd like to stay with you tonight," I said. I kept flashing back to the vision, and to the case, and to tomorrow's sentencing. I didn't want to be alone.

She glanced around to make sure no one was watching and kissed me on the mouth, just long enough to be a real kiss. Then she led the way to her car.

Cherabino drove back to her apartment, making steady conversation to distract me. "They've set up an inquiry into the visit to Fiske's house. I have an appointment with the union lawyer; supposedly it's a split opinion on whether your vision is sufficient cause."

"I'm sorry," I said. It hurt, but I said it.

"I was the one who charged in there. I'll take my lumps. If it saves Jacob, it's worth doing. It's worth doing a hundred times over." I didn't correct her. I couldn't bear to put yet more worry into the air.

Cherabino kept up a steady stream of conversation, determinedly cheerful, the entire trip, while she plotted something. Hopefully something that involved a nice dinner; she was a hell of a cook, and I'd appreciate a good meal.

Finally we pulled up to her house and got out, me pulling the bag I'd brought from the back in the hopes this might happen.

The door clicked behind her, and I felt her decision.

She jumped me. Her lips were on mine, her body forcing mine back against the wall. I kissed her back, like she was oxygen and I was suffocating. Our minds merged and her hands were everywhere.

A nagging thought pushed at me as I had my hands in her hair, on her back, on her body. A nagging thought that wouldn't let me go, even as she sucked on my collarbone in the most delightful way. . . .

She knew where this was going, and my body was right there with her, standing at attention and eager to please. But.

I grabbed her hands, gently; she pulled them away, suddenly, shutting down an automatic defense reaction only by sheer will. She stepped back, chest heaving, three buttons down the front of her blouse undone, showing the lace of her bra. Had I undone the buttons? Had she?

"Too fast?" she said, uncertain. "I can slow down."

I struggled to breathe, to think. Only a promise, only a promise and knowledge of unavoidable consequences kept me those two feet apart; I wanted to close the distance with everything I had in me. "Do you have tea?" I asked. "Hot tea, maybe?"

"Um, sure," she said, straightening her hair. "You want tea, I'll make tea." She was confused, a little taken aback, a little offended. But the Link was on full-bore, and she couldn't help feeling the conflict, the "stop" within me. "Hold on, I'll make you the damn tea."

When she brought two steaming coffee cups out of the kitchen, I was settled on her too-small couch. I'd finally gotten myself under control, though the memory of the last time we'd been here was still strong; she jumped me then too, and I'd turned her down then too, for reasons that had seemed good at the time.

I bricked up my mind, little by little. I reminded myself of my promise. Of the very real risk to her life if I was killed tomorrow. And then I took the tea from her. It was warm, and the warmth seeped into my hands.

She sat down on the far end of the coffee table, not far, but not very close either. "What's going on, Adam? I thought this was what you wanted. Considering."

I took a breath, and met her eyes. "You made me promise that this Link between us would fade. You've made me repeat that over and over and over again until we both hear it all too often. Sex is the opposite of that."

Now she was wary. "What are you talking about?"

I found a coaster and set the hot cup down on the far side of the table from her, untouched. "Sex with telepaths doesn't work like sex with normals, Cherabino. It's . . . it's a bigger deal. It's a much bigger deal." I struggled to say out loud what I'd grown up with. To explain why that promise changed everything. "If two telepaths are very careful, they can have a one-night stand. But only one; and only between total strangers."

She frowned. "What does—?"

"Let me explain this!" my voice cracked out like a whip. Her face fell.

"I'm sorry," I said, and I was. As much as every apology hurt, as much as I hated every one, this time I said it. This time I was sorry. "It's not that I don't want to. Trust me, Cherabino, I want to. But we're not strangers. And worse, we're Linked."

Now she looked away, but I could feel slow understanding seeping in.

"You made me promise you—I promised you, Cherabino—that the Link would be temporary. I promised. And I meant it. If we have sex tonight, that promise will be broken. The Link becomes permanent. And tonight, tonight that could kill you."

She backed away, toward her gun in the other room, slow, slow. "What do you mean kill me? How dangerous are you, exactly?"

"In the wrong context, I'm a loaded bomb. If they kill me tomorrow . . ." I took a breath. Regrouped. "In the right context, I'm a puppy dog. You can ask Kara. It's not—"

"Why in *hell* are you always talking about Kara!"

I stood up, defensive. "Why in *hell* do you keep pushing me? I'm only a man, Cherabino. Eventually I will tell you yes and you won't be able to deal with the consequences."

She took a breath, and another. I felt her, slowly, clumsily, feeling for the Link. She wanted to read me. She wanted to know what I was really thinking.

I opened every door I had and let her walk right in. She could see whatever she wanted.

She went two steps in, poked around, and then ran.

She turned, sat on the bench near the door, heart beating far, far too fast.

She'd seen my feelings for her.

"Should I leave?" I asked, damning the pride, the anger, all the rest. I was doing the right thing, damn it. Why did the right thing always end up with me caught up in thorns, bleeding for the thing I couldn't have? "Do you want me to leave?" I repeated. The buses would have stopped for the night by the time I got to the stop, but a taxicab should come out this far. I had money. I could leave.

It would hurt like a second-degree burn on my soul, but I could leave.

"I thought you wanted sex," she said very quietly.

"I wanted to sleep. Like we did before. Just that. Just—"

"Could you really kill me?" she asked.

"Maybe. Yes. But I wouldn't. Not on purpose. But if we have a deep Link . . . if they kill me, if they do worse than kill me . . . you'll get the backlash. You could die too. You'll get the pain too. They could torture me, maybe. It's a risk. And I won't, I *won't* risk—"

Then she turned away. "I think you should go now."

I took a step toward her. Reached out to touch her shoulder. "This doesn't mean—"

"Stop it." She pulled away.

"I—"

"Stop it. If you say one more word, we are through."

Anger and relief and rejection mixed like oil and water inside my soul. I swallowed them down and added shields until I could breathe. "I'll get my coat, then."

As I waited outside in the cold night, I wondered if Swartz hadn't been right the first time. Maybe I didn't deserve a relationship, not yet. I looked back at the house, at all I'd said no to, and wondered. If I could say no to that, maybe I didn't deserve anything at all.

Maybe tomorrow was just as well.

"Little Five Points," I told the cabbie, by impulse.

"Where, buddy?" he pushed. He was a rough-looking impatient guy who'd have been perfectly at home in the London cabdrivers' world of a hundred years ago. He even had the grayish hat, worn from years of use.

I squelched the impulse to drop the information in his head, instead giving directions out loud. Then I sat back and sat on my conscience. I needed that boy's screams out of my head. I needed Cherabino's rejection out of my head.

The section I wanted was nowhere near Joey's territory. It was in a more upscale club area, surprisingly well lit, with a steady stream of foot traffic, most on the way to clubs or on their way back from them. Heavy brick buildings dominated the area, but there were wide sidewalks, cheerful art on every corner, and playhouses and salons and every other kind of business. Drugs were a large part of the minds around here, especially those headed down to the end of the street. In another mood, that would have bothered me. Now it just meant I was in the right place.

The cabbie let me out on a corner with a brick building lit up with flashing lights. I tipped him just enough for him to forget me and looked up the dark street.

The guy from the meeting had had very specific information about where to get Satin, and it started about a block from here, at the back of a closed antiques store.

All I had to do was knock and tell them the password—hero—and they'd let me in.

Maybe it was an old password, not good anymore, the decent part of me put in, hoping.

The rest of me—the dark, angry, fatalistic me—knew the password was much too current.

It was a matter of fifteen minutes to get what I needed, or as much as the cash on me would buy. Two doses and a medically wrapped needle that should be safe. A beginning, at least.

I should have shot up in the alleyway behind the place, or the one next door, with the rats climbing over the Dumpster behind the burger joint. I should have locked myself in a bathroom somewhere in one of the clubs and ignored the sticky floor and done it there. But instead I got another taxi and headed home.

That was my first mistake.

Paying attention to the cabdriver, who was talking about his kid, was my second mistake. Despite all odds, the kid went to the same school that Swartz taught at. He was off his usual route. He had just dropped somebody off. But he kept going on about the school, and the teachers who'd actually woken up his kid and got him liking school.

The kid was a troublemaker, apparently, walking with the wrong crowd. Until this one coach intervened. Sent him home with a note. And then started teaching him base-ball.

"He still can't hit worth a damn. But he goes to practice most every day and takes care of the balls. He's learning how to pitch, he says. He's home at a decent hour, and when I go to school to pick him up, he'll introduce me to his friends. It's the damnedest thing."

He dropped me off at my apartment building, taking the one twenty-ROC note I'd saved for the trip without com-plaint. It was at least three dollars short, never mind the tip, but he'd said he appreciated me listening.

And now the tall building sat under the streetlight, the cracked and worn steps mocking me.

I climbed them, slowly, and then the stairs up to my floor, the minds all around quiet and sleepy. Every step had an axiom from the program. Most all of them held Swartz's voice, line after line of wisdom and censure mixed together.

When I reached my apartment, I put the bag with the drug on the coffee table. I sat, in front of it, telling myself tomorrow might be it. They might kill me, if my idea, if my plan didn't go well. Rex might kill me, for accusing him.

But all of that, no matter how it happened, all of that

would still make Swartz proud if I stood up like a man. If I did what I thought was right and changed what I could and accepted what I couldn't.

If . . . if I didn't take the poison in front of me. Hangovers destroyed lives, Swartz said, but the highs were worse, because they seduced the very life from you.

I threw away the damn drug.

And then I sat, in the middle of my bedroom's wave generator, and called Swartz.

Selah picked up, bleary, but that was okay. She still let Swartz tell me he was proud of me before I had to hang up.

CHAPTER 22

The next morning dawned bright and early. Too early. Far, far too early.

Captain Harris drove me there in total silence, my own nerves threatening to get the best of me.

Cherabino probably wouldn't have driven me anyway, not after our last fight.

The captain's Guild pass was yellow, a bright, cheery canary color with lettering on both sides and a picture of him as a much younger man. I had never seen a yellow Guild pass. White, green, red, pink, silver, and many other colors, but never yellow. Perhaps it was only that the pass was so old, from a time when I'd still been in early Guild schooling. Perhaps not.

Even under full lockdown, that pass got Captain Harris admitted to the Guild immediately, the guard in the atrium giving him a smile and a greeting. I, on the other hand, got only censure.

The tension was building in me with every beat of my heart. *Boom. Boom.*

Would this work?

Boom. Boom.

Would I . . . as me . . . leave the Guild intact? I had a fistful of dice, no more.

Boom.

Finally we stood outside the Guild Council chamber, once again with no seats to wait on. The most annoying company run by normals had seats to wait on. Not this one. Not the Guild.

Jamie was waiting for us. She was surprised—and happy, and sad—to see Harris.

"Justin." Her voice was even.

"Jamie." So was his. Unimaginable currents lay between them, in a dimension much deeper than Mindspace. One I couldn't touch and feel.

And then the moment was over.

"What are you doing here?" I asked Jamie quietly.

"I'm here to stand with you. I've already spoken my piece." She looked away then, and I could feel her sorrow, her grief, starting to creep out of the bounds she'd placed around them. She held her arms together, one thumb running over her wrist, back and forth, back and forth, the physical sensation designed to calm her, to override her emotions. It was working, slowly; most of what she projected without meaning to was that calm movement. At a Level Ten, Jamie had all sorts of coping mechanisms no one else had to have, like a giant who had to be careful where he placed his feet. I felt the deep grief leaking out again.

You knew the people in the flyer that crashed? I asked quietly.

All of them. Some were students. Some . . . some I knew in school myself. She sent layer upon layer of faces and memories and emotions. Then she stopped, pulling it in.

There was nothing to say in the face of such facts. *I'm sorry,* I said, the words hurting me as the situation hurt me.

Before she pulled away, I saw one, small thought: she had missed me too, mourned my loss with so many others.

Del Meyers too. Too much death, too much loss. At least I'd come back. The others . . .

Without any real Ability beyond whatever Link they'd once had, Harris pulled the taller Jamie into an embrace, rubbing her back. She was stiff, but collapsed into it finally, crying.

I was disconcerted. I'd seen Jamie cry perhaps twice, ever. If she was crying, the world had fallen apart.

The door opened and the court officer said quietly, "They will see you now."

I trudged in and faced the court that could be my death. Jamie and Harris followed, quietly, her wiping tears.

Diaz, the head of the Council, looked like he hadn't slept since the last time I'd seen him, like he'd aged ten years in two days. Even Rex had his polish scraped off, and the others—what there were of them—haggard. Except for Johanna, but her makeup was piled on deeper than I'd seen before. The Research chair, who'd had the questions asked about her department earlier, was noticeably absent, as was Charlie, my old classmate. Green was angry, fighting stupid angry, but the rest of the Council was full of sadness and shock. All of Mindspace rang with it, until it shattered your soul.

Diaz's hand shook.

After the court officer introduced me and Jamie, she introduced Harris by name and the rank "neutral person." Diaz paid a lot of attention then.

"I've heard of the flyer crash," I told the Council. "You have my sincerest sorrow with you. If there is any aid I can give, I will give it."

"Thank you," Kim Lee said, the woman in charge of Finance, and the only woman at the table by appointment. The others had died or been replaced all too recently. "The

Guild calls on all its members in need." *You are not a member,* her mind implied.

Adam Ward, Rex said, with a dark satisfaction. "You are accused of conspiring against Guild interests and providing false accusations leading to unnecessary harm of a high-ranking Guild citizen, accusations that may or may not have led to a decrease in security that contributed to the death of leading Council members. Is there anything you have to say before you are sentenced?"

Harris held up his yellow badge. "I am here as mediator for the matter of Adam Ward, a man who belongs to both the Abled and Normal worlds. What proof exists that Ward is conspiring against anyone? Who are his conspirators? What is the nature of the lapse in security?"

Whispering went across the chamber.

The evidence has been . . . Diaz trailed off, and switched to spoken word. "The evidence has been presented to the Council over the last two days."

"By who?"

"Many Council members have worked tirelessly to bring detailed information to our attention. Most of this information is not available to anyone outside the Guild."

I noticed that Edgar Stone stood, quietly, at the right, near enough to the Council to be called on but not so near that anyone would think he had real power. He was that heavily shielded mirror I'd seen from him before, almost not-there in Mindspace. But his physical body language, the thing that always gave him away, told me he was uncomfortable with the collection of evidence they were talking about. I went a little cold at that.

I'd better start my play, or I'd risk being caught in someone else's.

Green sent a private message that I caught the edge of.

The message had gone to Johanna, I thought, or the Council member past her. And suddenly I noticed something I hadn't before.

I had had a complicated plan worked out, one that accused Rex and took him down with me for conspiring with Guild First and not the Guild as a whole. One that had counted on Kara's family here. One that gave me half a chance or better to walk out of this, I'd thought.

But Kara's family was nowhere to be seen. And as Harris asked more questions and the Council answered them, my attention had been caught by Johanna.

Her mind, like all the others in the chamber, projected a leashed distress and sorrow and sadness. In fact, the emotions were exactly—exactly—the mix currently in the mind of Kim Lee right now. That was not what had caught my attention.

When people were truly sad, truly overcontrolling their grief and emotions, they looked down. They hunched. Or they sat too straight, too controlled. When people had the emotions I was feeling out of Johanna, there were certain ways their hands folded, their bodies sat, their eyes grew red.

But not Johanna. Her face was scrunched, like an exaggerated bad-actor portrayal of grief. And her hand, her hand stroked her wrist over and over again.

That was Jamie's strong-emotions habit. I'd never seen anyone else use it. And more important, I wasn't getting any projection of the physical sensation over Mindspace. It was like Johanna had seen Jamie and was copying her blindly, the gesture like the mental copying of Lee's emotions, aping of the people around her without any true feeling.

If you weren't looking too closely, if you depended on Mindspace as your primary sense, overriding all others,

Johanna seemed just like everyone else in the room. But if you looked at her like a normal, only from the outside—

She was very charming, very helpful, wasn't she? Hadn't she reflected every single thing she'd thought I'd wanted to hear?

And she was sitting in a row with some of the most powerful and influential people in the Guild. She'd gone from an assistant who fetched coffee to a woman of real power in the space of a couple of weeks.

What had Kara said? With the Council so decimated, they'd promote anyone with experience, do whatever it took, call for elections?

And who would win those elections? The woman who'd already dealt with a mental health crisis as Health and Human Services acting chair? What did I want to bet that the "madness scare" would flare up over the next week, only to die when she implemented a new policy?

The puzzle pieces moved together. I'd thought it was Rex who'd benefitted most. I'd thought it was Rex who'd done this. But his people would be watched like hawks during the next year. They were suspected of killing opponents now. His days of subtle maneuvering would be over.

But Johanna—there was a reason she'd put my back up in the beginning. She was one of Those People, one of the sociopaths I'd met in the interview rooms. One of the people who truly felt no empathy for other people, no fellow feeling. That's why her body language didn't match her Mindspace signature; in a world of telepaths she'd had to learn to fake the one flawlessly but not necessarily the other. Telepaths trusted the evidence of their own minds.

And the evidence of their senses. She'd planted the mind control devices, hadn't she? I'd seen her talking to the old Research chair. She'd started all of this moving, and then had the gall to accuse a good man of madness to make it seem more real.

How many had died? How many more had their careers destroyed to have her sitting there?

"Ward was in the presence of multiple police officers during that time period," Harris said. "Even he can't be two places at once. Unless you think some of that was done in advance . . . ?"

Edgar Stone shook his head, projecting his words loudly. "There was a full inspection the day before. The technicians have been mind-probed. The vehicle checked out. Whatever happened was during that time period."

"Wait," I said.

They ignored me.

Tubbs, Kara's ultimate boss, said, "Ward has plenty of criminal contacts. It was him that told us about Fiske to start with. Who's to say he didn't have one of his contacts— perhaps Fiske himself—do the honors? A mind-probe here seems justified."

Faintly, on the level of a faint normal mind, I felt anger enter the air from Harris next to me. "We've repeatedly screened Ward. These past months, we've been monitoring him heavier than ever. He's purchased his drug this last week, but that was a low-level criminal who wouldn't be capable of what you're suggesting. He hasn't seen or talked to anyone else."

"You know about that?" I stared.

He turned, mouth down. "Paulsen was geared up to defend your job to the political powers that be before you quit. And then you go and do this. I'm very disappointed. You'll be taking a drug test when this is all over."

"Ah," I said, numb. How did they . . . ?

Stone was looking at me, waiting for me to meet his eyes. One small nod.

I swallowed. "Seriously, wait. I have something to say."

And I felt Jamie's presence in the public part of my mind. I hadn't hidden anything. She saw the unused drugs—and she saw my conclusions about Johanna. She started moving toward that part of the room.

"Silence," Rex said. "The prisoner will not speak."

Green's contempt projected across the room. *You've proven your character or lack thereof many times. This sabotage happened only when you reentered the Guild. The timing cannot be coincidence.*

I took a deep breath, and projected as loud as I could. *We've all been manipulated! We've all been led to believe—*

A force like a sledgehammer hit my mind. I staggered, pain and pressure knocking me sideways.

Tubbs, Kara's ultimate boss, held the other end. "You cannot respect protocol even in the hour of your sentencing."

He had locked down on my mind, literally locked down, until I could do nothing, say nothing. I was a prisoner in my body. I beat against the restraint like a bird whose foot was caught in a trap, wings beating as hard as muscle and bone would support—hurting only myself.

I was a Level Eight telepath! I would be free!

The restraint held.

Level Eight no longer, Tubbs said to me, quietly. *Stay still or I will make you.*

I tried to send him my suspicions about Johanna, but he cut me off, like a wet blanket.

Pay attention. My mind was forced to the front, to the outside.

Rex smiled, a small cruel smile. "For your crimes, the Guild will sentence you—"

Diaz put a hand out, in front of him, where the man couldn't help but see it.

And then the double doors crashed open, and Kara's

family, thirty strong, arrived in a wind of teleporters and firestarters and unthinkably strong Ability.

Hawk Chenoa, one of the strongest and most politically powerful men in the Guild, the Guild's primary liaison with the United States Military Services, stepped forward. "Council of the Guild, we bring challenge. Under the bylaws of the Guild, if you repeatedly endanger high-ranking full members, we have the right."

Tubbs's grip slipped, and I had my Mindspace senses back. My senses, but not my freedom.

Concern and shock radiated from every person on the Council. Every person, that was, except Johanna.

My attention returned to her in time to catch one, small smile.

Diaz threw a bolt of energy into the center of Mindspace.

The world turned over, and I fell. Jamie still stood, Harris on his knees. Half of Kara's family behind me remained upright; the others shattered. But my mind was free, was clear. If I could just stand, just think . . .

I am still the Council, Diaz said. *Mutiny is punishable by mind-wipe. Be very, very careful of what you say.*

Rex leaned forward on the table. *We will destroy you if you challenge us.*

They were one front.

Hawk Chenoa nodded grimly. *You will hear what we have to say. No matter what it costs.*

And Tubbs let go of my mind completely, his concentration broken by fear. *A full war,* I felt from him, *a full war to shake the foundations of the Guild.*

I tried to stand—and fell. My mind still gummed up by whatever Tubbs had done. I tried again—and made it to my knees, then upright.

Diaz sent out a loud—and forceful—demand, and Hawk responded with freezing resistance, his people behind him settling back into Mindspace in a stable front.

Harris spoke up loudly. "Peace. Peace for two minutes, while noncombatants leave."

Rex looked down. "This is not a fight we need to have in front of an outsider."

Diaz held an amazing amount of force in his hands, force coiled like a spring compressed, ready to move in Mindspace. Hawk held a series of tight intentions, like sharp arrows, close. Gustolf's hands cradled fire, waiting to move. The Council and its supporters stood at one end, ready. Hawk and his supporters waited in a semicircle opposite.

Two breaths passed.

"Leave," Hawk finally said.

Harris grabbed my arm, forceful. "Time to go."

The physical pain finally cleared the fog. I pushed his mind away, pulled my arm away. And stood. I projected loudly, out loud and in Mindspace to back myself up, so that no one within forty feet in any direction could possibly avoid hearing me.

"You have all been manipulated," I said.

By you? Green's mental voice rang out.

Manipulated, manipulated, echoed through the room.

It's too late. Men are dead, Hawk's voice said.

Too late, from Rex. *Council members dead.*

"Listen!" I yelled. "Listen. Before it all falls apart and you bring Cooper's worst nightmare to life, listen. You have all been manipulated by one brilliant mind. She planted devices to influence good men to madness. She used her position to target specific people. She is sitting here in this room."

I glanced at her. She sat, all masks stripped away, calculating. Jamie had been moving, moving in the confusion, and was now only a few feet away. Good job, I thought. Jamie will disable her if no one else can. She's a Level Ten.

Tubbs teleported to a few feet away from me. The air *popped* as it displaced with new mass. "You're spinning more lies to save your life. You've probably provoked the Chenoas and Eriksons to violence yourself."

I refused to be intimidated. "And when did I have time?" I asked. "You yourself charged me with shirking the responsibilities you gave me." I raised my voice to the crowd. "Yes, he hired me to find Del Meyers's killer. It took me longer than it should have, and I accused one man for the wrong reasons. But now—"

"Who are you accusing exactly?" Kara asked, anger and betrayal on her face. "I had nothing—"

"I accuse Johanna Wendell," I asked. "She's—"

"That's ridiculous. Johanna's been very helpful," Hawk said, at the same time Diaz said, "She's been a vital part of—"

Both men looked at each other.

"Look at her," I said. "Just look. Her body language— her real-space presence—doesn't match her Mindspace one. She's been faking it all, mirroring what we wanted to hear."

And then it was too late. In the space between one heartbeat and the next, Johanna was on the main floor, with a vibroblade to Jamie's neck. "Anyone moves, anyone touches my mind, she dies. That includes you, Jamie. You squirm, you might end up filleted. Now, we're going to back up, slowly. I'd suggest you all clear the way."

An odd humming came through Mindspace at the same time the teeth-jarring humming had started from the vibroblade.

Stone moved forward, but Johanna's grip tightened,

and he stopped, unsure. He looked for Nelson, who was never here because of the demotion. No one was in charge, not now.

Next to me Tubbs flickered, like a bad movie effect, air making a strange sound. He came back to reality with an overwhelming sense of nausea and almost fell.

Johanna's pretty features were twisted into a look of disgust, her lips pulled up. "The antiteleportation device being tested by Research? I should mention I have one. Don't think to follow us. I will kill her." She backed up, one step at a time, one of her hands steering Jamie by gripping her shoulder, the other holding the knife.

Jamie looked terrified.

All around, shock and dismay poured out on both sides. They acted like they'd never seen a hostage situation before.

Maybe they hadn't. They'd locked up Charlie, the only black-ops-experienced guy in the room. Even Hawk was more used to defined battle than hostage situations.

Next to me, Harris's mind had gone to the dark, calculating place that Cherabino went, the all-hell cop place. "Jamie is not involved in these politics," he said, enunciating too clearly. "You cannot let her die because of your stupidity."

Johanna shook her head, stepping back one step, then another. "Sorry, Grandpa. Politics don't really matter to me. You should have let me be," she said to me, and then took another step. "I didn't do anything against you."

A flicker in Mindspace that felt like Jamie.

Then blood, blood pain, as Jamie's arm was sliced bone deep. Mindspace was suddenly, completely cold. Still. No one moved.

Johanna was breathing hard. "You do that again and you'll start losing body parts." She looked over at Rex. "That's it. All of you let go of your weapons. You hurt me, you threaten me, and body parts are going. You need her intact, and you know I don't. Do it. Do it now."

Diaz's huge-force spring slowly let out, and Hawk's intention arrows started to disappear, the others following suit.

"Nobody follows me," Johanna said.

CHAPTER 23

We all waited, a long, tense moment.

"You ready?" Captain Harris asked me.

"Give it another second," I said. "She's not as strong a telepath as some here, and Jamie's presence will cloud things, but she'll still be able to feel us coming more clearly than the suspects you're used to."

"You can't go after them," Tubbs said. "She'll kill her. One of the strongest telepaths in the Guild, and she'll kill her."

I looked at him. "She'll kill her anyway if we don't move."

Harris looked around. "We need physical backup here. People who won't escalate the situation, somebody I can count on in a fight."

I looked around. "Gustolf. Stone. You're with us. Tubbs, you call Enforcement."

"I need all entrances and exits to the building cut off. Anything I should look for with this lady? Can she fly or something stupid?"

"She can see the future reliably, medium-term. An hour or two is preferred."

Harris shook his head, working that out.

I thought about that. "Okay. We get the exits blocked off. She'll see that."

"We plan to send Ward in alone," Harris said.

A burst of muttering moved through the crowd, but Gustolf and Stone had already stepped up.

"I can get more physical backup," Stone said.

"If we can get Turner here quickly, do it," I said. "But too big a group she'll see it coming. I'd like you to plan in your mind to hold back when we get there and not start any violence. I'd like you to make that decision now, and stick to it in your mind unless and until something happens."

Gustolf smiled, seeing where I was going. "You got it."

"Let's go," Harris said.

"What right do you have to make decisions for all of us?" Diaz asked.

We paused halfway to the door. "Obviously no one else here is doing it. We've both seen hostage situations before. Plus you and Hawk have a lot of talking to do before I get back. It would be a disgrace to the Guild founders if you let one woman manipulate you all into destroying the Guild." I put heat behind the last and made myself believe it.

And so we turned and walked out, Gustolf and Stone following without further questions.

Outside in the hall, Mindspace was disturbed, too disturbed; after Diaz's force-bomb, it wasn't holding on to signatures the way I expected.

Harris had kept walking. He looked back. "This way."

"How do you know? Mindspace is empty," Stone said.

"I was married to the woman for years. Mumbo jumbo or not, I can find her in a snowstorm. She's used this against me more than once."

A Link. And we turned back.

Diaz and Hawk had entered the hallway.

"Don't be underfoot," Harris said, and walked.

Right turn, left turn, a long walk straight before another turn while Harris stood and tried to decide where to go.

"I feel the telepath stronger to the right," Stone said, then frowned, a tight stream hitting him in Mindspace, then over. "Wait. The building's entrances are now blocked off."

"She's changed directions," Harris said. "There's something wrong."

"We'll wait while you figure it out," Gustolf said.

Diaz limped up closer to me. He was slower than the rest of us, but sheer stubbornness kept him moving. And we'd established he could do some loud and crazy things with Mindspace. I didn't trust him.

"You're not as strong as half of our Enforcers," Diaz said. "You should back down and let the professionals handle it."

"What, your professionals?" Hawk said. "You want another chance to manipulate the situation, don't you? Take away more of the Guild's rights. Well, it's not going to happen on my watch."

"Shut up, both of you!" Stone hissed.

Gustolf nodded. "Every moment you delay us, every moment you change the future by being here, is one more chance for her to take it badly and kill Jamie. You need to back off."

"I'm the head of the Guild Council," Diaz said, affronted. "And this man is an outsider, and hardly a Seven. Why should I trust him at all?"

A Seven? I felt like he'd struck me across the face. But I hadn't managed to stand up to Green. . . . Maybe it was true. I'd had a brain injury. Sometimes you didn't get it all back. But: "I spotted Johanna when no one else did," I said. "Strength had nothing to do with that. I'm . . . I'm good at people. I'm good at spotting lies, and body language, and outthinking people. I understand desperate people. That's more than any of you do anymore. You've gotten lazy in your ivory towers, both of you." I spat the last, angry. "You figure this out. We have work to do."

Hawk waited, and Diaz shifted, the first hint of danger in his mind.

Harris was there then. "Ward can talk his way into and out of anything with enough time to think about it. I've seen his tapes. He's seen sociopaths before. Hell, I've seen sociopaths before. You want your telepath back in one piece, you bet on Ward. But you do it right. You leave him the hell in peace to think."

I looked at one of the most powerful men in law enforcement, someone who clearly believed in me. Someone who thought I could do this.

He waited, total attention on two of the most powerful men in the Guild. "Work out your differences. We'll see you in a few hours."

Then he turned around and trotted. I followed, and Diaz and Hawk stayed behind. I heard a small, quiet, Mindspace sending, then another, then another, the edges bleeding into Mindspace without giving away their content. They were talking.

Stone and Gustolf waited a moment, behind.

"Do you really think I can talk my way out of this?" I asked.

"Shut up, Ward. I need to find my ex-wife and kill the bitch who took her." He paused. "You screw this up, you'll never work in this town again."

"Thanks," I said, finally feeling back on solid ground again.

We passed through a thick door alone on a long wall—on the other side was sunlight, bright, blinding sunlight. Two large lights on posts curved overhead, unlit.

Don't come any closer, Johanna sent to me.

Pain came from Jamie, sharp pain from her arm, and fear. I felt her rubbing her wrist again, the steady attempt at calming not doing enough right now.

I stopped walking, Captain Harris next to me. I grabbed his sleeve to stop him too; there were downsides to having a normal in a high-risk telepathy situation. He stopped, though.

If you need us, we're ready, Stone told me through the tag he had in my head, the smallest, quietest kind of transmission there was, short of a Link. Nearly guaranteed to be undetectable. He and Gustolf stood on the other side of the door.

Be calm, I told Johanna.

My eyes finally cleared and I saw we had exited onto a . . . kind of an oval-shaped open deck. We were still twenty stories up, give or take, and the thin railing was all that separated us from open air on every side. The main bulk of the skyscraper still continued behind us. Other Guild buildings continued to the right, while a main road with skylanes sat on our left. Straight ahead was the reception building for the Guild, its glass atrium dome many stories below us.

Here, on the deck, vegetable beds, bushes, and trees filled pots in evenly spaced geometric forms, like a formal garden on a roof. A main aisleway continued in front of us, perhaps twenty feet out, plants on either side. At the end of the aisleway Johanna stood on top of a wooden bench, Jamie there next to her, terror emanating from her.

You come any closer and she dies, Johanna told us, in a carrying voice in Mindspace. The vibroblade in her hand still buzzed dully.

They were less than a foot from the low balcony—and in plenty of room and space to throw them both over that balcony. She'd thought this through. Anything we did to take the knife from her would make Jamie that much more vulnerable to the heights. My heart sped up.

Harris poked me, with a finger in my ribs like I was a child. "Talk," he hissed.

I took one step forward and stopped. Johanna's grip on Jamie tightened, and it all was far, far too real. Jamie, the woman who'd mentored me, who'd taught me right from wrong in telepath circles, who'd been there for me for years. She had her own agenda, own life now. But once . . .

I was terrified for her, and it didn't matter. Nothing mattered but Harris's charge to talk.

Let's talk about this, I said. *How can we help you get where you need to be? What will it take to get Jamie her freedom?*

Johanna thought about that. And my interrogator's brain started moving ahead, making connections, guessing what she wanted, getting inside her head without ever bridging the gap in Mindspace.

I was a good interrogator. Today, for Jamie, for me, I'd be a great one.

There's a way out of this, I said. *You let her go, your odds of getting away clean are better. The Guild is less likely to pursue. You find a place in one of the nonaffiliated Guilds. Russia or India would appreciate someone of your talents and skill. Who knows, you might end up with more influence and position there. Your training will be unusual there. You can bend things to your advantage.*

I don't speak Russian, Johanna said.

You'll pick it up quickly with a telepath-assist, I said. *Plus, you'll have new problems, and I'm told Russia appreciates a certain ruthlessness in one of its operatives. You could do very well in that kind of culture.*

What do you mean? she asked.

You're good at hiding what you're really thinking. You're good at lying mind-to-mind and you don't mind taking people out along the way. If what I've heard about Russia is true, they will appreciate those things. You can be you, without having to hide so much. You might find you like it better than even a Council position here.

A decision crystallized. I took a step forward, then stopped, again.

She returned, *Fine, you want the strong-telepath back in one piece? You get me a way out. We can negotiate. I'd like a fueled flyer capable of transatlantic flight. A million ROCs. An escort to international waters. A parachute and a life vest. You get me there, I drop her where you can retrieve her.*

I took a moment to process that. *She's bleeding. If the sharks get involved, I don't think they'll just let you go.* I took another step forward.

If you can't give me what I want, there's not much point in me staying around, is there? She gave me a stare. *Stay right there. You talk to the Guild. You get me what I want.*

I'll get you what you want, I told her, allowing the concern for Jamie to slip through. Then: *Stone, did you hear that?* I asked, in that same, quiet sound he'd used for me earlier.

Loud and clear.

Any chance of at least the flyer?

Guild's not going to let her escape. I can get you something to make the right noise, but give it another five or ten minutes and we'll have snipers on the next building. There's no walking away from this kind of threat to the Guild. I've been monitoring the private Enforcement channels. They're furious, and the entire Council and most of the family is screaming for blood. Enforcement will act accordingly.

What about Jamie? She was one of two Tens in the world, and vitally important, I thought.

Silence answered my question.

Well, crap. Score another one for Guild ruthlessness. I swallowed. At the angle they were at, any sniper fire was very likely to kill Jamie too, even if they didn't aim for her. Between the fall and the blade, she was in a death zone. The blade particularly. Those vibroblades were dangerous; I'd seen one slice through concrete—and almost my hand.

I want assurances now. Johanna tightened her grip on Jamie, and a burst of fear ran through Mindspace at a strength only Jamie could manage. I felt the fear hit me like a hurricane. And then I decided.

Whatever the Guild was going to do, they were going to do. All the fast talking in the world wouldn't stop them from responding to what they thought was a threat to their entire system. And with the break between the Council and the family, a common enemy was getting everyone incensed. Good for the Guild long-term, but fatal for Jamie now, perhaps.

If she could just fight back . . . I looked into her eyes and saw only fear. Telepaths weren't trained to fight physical danger. Not even in battle training. And she was bleeding, a small puddle of blood now on the concrete under her arm, her hand covered in red. Blood loss would make her weak.

Whereas I was used to getting hurt now. I was used to physical. And I'd woken up this morning knowing I could die today.

There wasn't any real choice now, was there?

Stone, get the flyer. That sending I put real volume into so that Johanna would be sure to hear me.

"Tell you what," I deliberately said out loud, where Harris could hear me, using my diaphragm to make sure the sound passed all the way through the space between me and Johanna. "I'll come over there. You let Jamie go. You keep me instead."

She thought about that for a second. *You're not as valuable a hostage. You're a criminal.*

"I'm more likely to survive in open water, and I have no fear of heights," I said. "I will jump from that flyer without giving you any trouble over it. You're on your way faster. And at this point, Johanna?"

"What?"

"We're running out of time to get this done where we all walk away. Take the deal. The flyer is on its way."

"Fine. Small steps," she yelled. "No tricks."

So I took small steps, a dozen, then two dozen, one slow, small step after the other. I was being an idiot, my mind informed me, while my heart beat too fast. It didn't have to be me on the other end of that knife.

Too late to change your mind now, I told myself. *Too late.*

Jamie was watching me, carefully, carefully. Small step after small step. Johanna was actively reading me now. Small step. Small step.

At four feet away I asked, *How do you want to do this?*

She looked at me, at Jamie, and thought. "Come up here on the bench."

So there I was when she let Jamie go. There I was, empty, afraid.

And in the moment Jamie was far enough away, the moment that horrible knife came in my direction, I took the moment.

I slipped inside Johanna's defenses like a flea under a blanket, small burrowing crawls too small to be noticed. Planning to wait for the right moment.

Her arm dragged me toward her, or tried—she wasn't

that strong, but she used what she had ruthlessly. Her knife came down in front of me; she couldn't reach my throat comfortably, settled for my side.

The flyer settles behind us in the air, she projected to whoever was listening.

And then I saw the glint across the way, from a high-up building in the Guild skyscraper. Rifle. Sharpshooter.

Johanna saw what I saw. *It wouldn't shoot. It wouldn't shoot,* her mind said. She hadn't seen a vision. Things were changing so fast, but she hadn't seen a vision.

Jamie was nearly to Captain Harris.

I had my moment. I slipped in, to the back of her mind. . . .

I found myself in an endless empty plain, cold. Frozen grass extended as far as the eye could see. In the distance, high ragged mountains. My breath froze in front of my face. Not a picture of her mind, not a true seeming, but a defense. A real, deep defense the likes of which I'd never seen.

I ran, forward, in the quick lope I used to move through Mindspace quickly. No matter how much I ran, the endless plain extended in front of me. There had to be a way out. There had to be.

I kept moving, my speed slowing as the cold moved into my bones. I kept moving, kept looking for the way out.

After an unknowable time, on a random step, my foot broke through, into a burrow that snapped in, imprisoning my foot before I could get away.

I pulled. Again. Again.

Behind me, a low, dangerous growl that crawled up my spine. *Run,* my instincts screamed. *Run.* But no matter how I pulled against the ground, my foot was stuck.

The growl again. I turned—bending my body uncomfortably, my foot caught.

It was a leopard, a white leopard with tufted ears and

long teeth, a leopard impossibly big, ten feet tall or more, thousands of pounds. Moreover, it wore Johanna's mental scent.

My gut fell out of me.

"Nice of you to fall into my trap," the leopard said with Johanna's voice.

I pulled harder against the trap, and felt the ground stretch, stretch like taffy . . .

The leopard placed its paws. It leaped—

Something snapped in my leg. I screamed. Pressure, pressure—I was crushed. Its head looked straight into my eyes.

Prey, she thought. And I got my first true look at Johanna's soul. At the thing that lived where human emotion should be. It was cold, cold like the plains, and hungry. So hungry, for power, for respect, for status. It had killed before, and would kill again, with no more thought than a leopard hunting a rabbit, with the same fierce joy.

Let me go, I said, knowing it was futile.

No. The leopard opened her mouth. . . .

Her breath smelled like flowers. Like flowers. The little detail gave me pause as the teeth came down.

In the space between one second and another, I did the one thing, the critical thing we taught middle school children to do first, before any other training. I let go of everything but *me* and turned *in*. I let all of it go . . .

. . . and found myself back in my body. Heart racing. Terror drenching me in sweat. But I was in my own body, my mind ragged but in one piece.

In front of me, Stone had a gun trained on both of us. I looked down. The knife was drooping, inches from my side.

I reached down, grabbed her wrist. She was slow, slow, still stuck in the place in her own mind. I forced the button. Hit the button to turn the blade off and threw myself forward, to the deck. The limp vibroblade hit me as Johanna woke up, angry. But it was just cord now, just cord.

"Take one more move and I will shoot you where you stand," Stone said in a voice colder than the plain I'd found myself in.

I crawled to the side, away from the line of fire. I stood up, wary. Maybe I should run. Maybe I should push her over the edge. There had been something in the leopard's eyes . . . something terrifying. Something that was an all-too-true representation of the thing that lived inside Johanna.

Then she moved.

Crack. The gun went off.

She was moving—to me, to me. The vibroblade *whined.*

My body reacted before my mind had a chance. Hand up to strike the blade away. Body twisting—the judo flip Cherabino had drilled me on again and again—my hands, my body changing her momentum.

The blade scored my leg—pain, pain. I cried out.

She was up and moving again.

And then the world shattered, Mindspace disappearing under the weight of unimaginable tsunami force. The curving lights overhead exploded. The glass office building went dark, top to bottom. My ears popped as I fell to the floor, Stone falling too.

Jamie stood in the center of the wind, force in her hands.

Johanna was still on her knees. "You will not—"

Another tsunami rose and crushed the world. I blacked out.

CHAPTER 24

I woke up in the Guild infirmary, a tiled area that stretched over half of a skyscraper floor. Rows of beds with pulled-back curtains were filled with occupants, some sleeping, some awake. Gustolf was there, and Stone, and others. Opposite were various monitoring devices and a nurses' station. Across the room, you could just see doctors making their rounds. The lights felt too bright, and Mindspace distant, and I had a low throbbing at the base of my skull.

Two people stopped by Stone's bedside, a woman about his age with a kind smile, and a boy about ten years old. His family.

He'd gotten through it, and made the Guild better, for his family.

"Ah, you're awake," a cheerful woman with a medic patch said then. She came over, pulling out a flashlight. "Look up for me."

I complied.

She smiled and put the flashlight back in a lab coat pocket. "Now the mental flex. Stretch your mind up—" She put her fingers on my temples and looked abstracted.

I stretched my mind upward, then around, then down, while she watched.

"Any lingering pain?" she asked, removing her hands.

"Some," I said. "Feels like aftershock."

She nodded. "That should decrease steadily for a couple of days. It never feels good to have your brain-box override the Abled center, but it saves your life, so we don't complain. Much." She smiled. "I'd rest up and try not to do any active reads. If the pain gets worse, you come back here immediately."

"Thanks," I said.

"No problem," she replied. "We've got a lot of these today. She took out the electrical system and half the minds in the professional building."

I processed that for a moment.

"Captain Harris, the neutral non-Guild guy? I assume he's fine?" I asked. His brain wouldn't have been affected much by the Mindspace tsunami, maybe. Although he did have the Link to Jamic. . . .

"He's fine, though he's left the Guild for now."

"How is Jamie?" I asked.

"Tired," Jamie's voice came from ten feet away as she walked toward me. Deep circles were under her eyes, and a bandage was around her arm. *I'm okay,* she said. Underneath the words was gratitude . . . and hesitancy. She was never quite comfortable with the full use of her gift.

"We did it," I said. "We found the killer and saved the day."

"You did it," she said uncomfortably. "Johanna was quite . . . She influenced the fear. I could see her doing it, but I couldn't stop it. The fear was so . . . I couldn't do anything. I am profoundly sorry."

"You finished it, given the chance." I paused, realizing I was suddenly in the role of teacher here. "The lizard brain is hard to fight. Even policemen and women freeze up when they encounter real danger the first few times. It's the nervous system. It's not you. And she'd been manipulating so many people, I'm betting she was real good at stoking that fear." In fact, that's probably what she did with Meyers, that and plant the idea of suicide for his future-sense to play with.

Jamie looked down, not meeting my eyes.

"You did what you had to do at the moment, and you did it well," I said. "It's a win in my book. The police department might even give you a medal."

"I still thank you," she said. "You saved my life. You . . . you may not be what you were, or as strong as you were. But you've become a good man. You've built skills that make a difference in this world for the better. I'm sorry for my harshness earlier. I didn't understand. I do, now."

I took a moment and soaked in the warm feeling. She had been one of the most important teachers I'd ever had. "That really means a lot," I said.

"Good."

Awkwardness crept into the silence, so I asked, "What will happen to Johanna?"

Jamie shrugged, some of her confidence settling back. "She's with the deep-scanner now and the Council will convene tomorrow. If she is responsible for as much as I believe, she will be executed or mind-wiped the day after."

"She'll be gone. The person that she was will be gone either way."

"Yes." There was no sympathy in Jamie. "The flyer crash killed friends, and they found her fingerprint on one of the tampered parts. They found another device in the gymnasium, what they think mimicked madness and started the spread of the illness. Four people died from that alone. She deserves to answer for what she did."

"I suppose she does." It still seemed a waste.

Jamie shifted and changed the subject, firmly. "The Chenoa and Erikson-Meyer clans have accepted appointments to the ruling body. I was involved in the selection.

We will be working out our differences together, at least for now. You averted a war, Adam. The Guild will be much better for your visit."

"Then why do I feel fatalism from you?"

She looked at me for a moment, then finally said, "If you're able to walk, Diaz and Hawk wish to see you now. I have already given my testimony on your behalf and my belief that you saved my life. I said I'd come down to tell you personally."

"Oh," I said. Then I stood. "I can walk. Um, can I ask you a question?"

"At this point, you've earned any question I could possibly answer."

Oddly, the vision from earlier came back, nagging. "I had . . . a vision. It seemed very certain, and Cherabino experienced it through some spillover with a Link. She thought the boy in danger was a relative of hers. I . . . Now that I've had a chance to think about it, I don't believe it is. I knew the boy in the vision, but I don't know him now."

Jamie stopped. "What are you asking?"

"Nothing has happened yet, nothing remotely like that vision. Did our actions change it? Is it just one of the ones that appears and disappears?"

"You know I can't answer that, Adam. The future is unknown. You know that."

I sighed. "Yeah."

The female court official showed up in the infirmary then. "Adam Ward?" she called. "You're overdue."

"Will you come with me?" I asked Jamie.

She shook her head sadly. "I can't. I'm sorry." *I will always remember what you've done for me. Always. I am so deeply sorry I could not do it myself.*

Nobody's perfect, Jamie.

I left, with the unsteady and fatalist feel of my old mentor—and my own self—ringing in my head.

Now it was time to face the Council.

Diaz stood in an empty Council chamber, Rex and Hawk on either side, neither happy. Diaz looked out onto the now-graying cloudy day through the floor-to-ceiling windows, the soft light kind to his heavily wrinkled face. Darting cars moved down the skylanes. Skyscrapers started to light up with the approach of darkness.

"I'm here," I said, unable to keep myself from getting cranky. "Unless you're going to throw me out on the street like you did Captain Harris, I'd suggest we get to it."

Diaz turned, looked at me critically. "Perhaps you were right. Strength is not all that matters. The Guild . . . the Guild has been too complacent. You showed me that today. We need new skills. We need new perspectives."

"If you're offering me a job . . ."

He held up a hand. *Let me finish.* "We need new perspectives. We need . . . information. We need new blood. It came to my attention during the trial process that you have been linked to a certain young Jacob. He is strong, and by rights belongs to the Guild."

Hell of a change of subject, and everything Cherabino and I had been working to avoid for such a long time. I supposed it was inevitable, but I still chose my words carefully. "It would be a mistake to remove him from his family without due consideration. They have political and police contacts who will fight. Hell, I'll fight you. It's a mistake to target the boy when what you want is me. You know that. Hell, everybody here knows that."

"No one is targeting a boy," Hawk said then, quietly. "The Guild does not use children as bargaining chips."

"If he has the strength, he belongs to the Guild by right," Rex said. He had his mind very, very controlled. But his face—that look was disgust. The emotion that fueled violence. "Further, Ward is a criminal for concealing a potential Guild member from us. No matter how strong or weak the boy is, that needs to be addressed."

I stood a little straighter. "It would be a mistake to take him from his family," I said again. "He has an ongoing severe medical issue, and I don't believe the Guild will be able to address his needs. Furthermore—" I cut off Rex's protests. "Furthermore, I don't believe he will survive the pressures of the Guild program at this age. It would be a shame to destroy such a promising Ability to prove a point. He has allies in the police force. And he has me. This is not about Jacob, or it shouldn't be. If you're going to punish me for my sins, go ahead. I'm here. But leave him out of it. He's just a boy."

"Let's leave the boy for now and move to you." Diaz's mind leaked certainty, and respect, and sad decision. "At the beginning of today's events, the Council took a vote to remove your Ability but keep your mind and memories intact. This would protect the Guild—as Rex has argued so heavily in favor of—and yet still allow you to pursue this life you have among the normals."

I swallowed. Losing my telepathy—well, I'd lived through it once. But it was like losing a leg, or a testicle. It wasn't dying, though. It wasn't dying and it wasn't losing Cherabino or Swartz. "And now, after I've saved the life of one of the rarest telepaths?" I asked. "After I've saved your Council from a sociopath?"

Diaz shook his head. "It looks like Rex was right all along. Your . . . skills, unethical as I might find them, uncovered a snake in our midst. You risked your own life to save a Guild treasure. It's time to talk about debts."

"Where are you going with this?" I asked, cautious, not quite daring to hope.

"As head of the Council, I am overruling the vote, as is my right," Diaz said, in a flat tone. "You have paid for your accusation. You have paid, many times over, for the lapses in courtesy you have committed. I am also forgiving half of the debt you have incurred for using our medics—half."

"Thank you," I said, automatically, not knowing what else to say. "What does that mean exactly?"

"The balance sheet is accounted for. But understand, Adam Ward, I don't like you. I don't like your ethical choices. I'm asking you not to come to the Guild here—or in any other office—for any reason, unless you are called. If I find you here, you will find yourself in a cell and in considerable pain. I don't like surprises in my territory," Diaz said.

"I will be the one administering the pain," Rex said. "Consider that a promise."

I should have been scared at that. But the maelstrom of emotions I'd been through in the last several hours had left me numb and unimpressed. "Fine," I said. "I've paid off part of the debt, you forgive me, we part ways, and I stay away. I can do that. But about Jacob—you leave him alone. You want me to cooperate, that's my condition."

"No deal," Rex said.

Hawk faced the others. "The boy comes to the Guild for twice-weekly lessons with experts. We monitor any home tutoring he receives in his Ability as well. When he reaches his Level and Skills test, he will have the choice to join the Guild . . . or our support in pursuing membership at another, qualified Guild. He is a boy, not a pawn," he said roughly.

Private messages flew from him to the other two, and back, for several minutes. Hawk seemed brittle and angry, and stood his ground.

"Fine," Rex finally said, his mouth twisting like he'd bitten into a lemon. "Fine. But he fails to show and Ward pays double the use-price for the boy's talent, to be added to his debt or taken out on his hide."

Hawk paused, and I felt the decision not to argue.

"So it is," Diaz said.

I looked at him. He looked at me.

"Is that it?" I asked, a sense of relief waiting in the wings while I moved carefully, oh so carefully out of this.

"You should leave now," Rex said, that disgust back in his voice.

I nodded and walked away.

Captain Harris drove me home in total silence, the air flyer's engine and air noise the only thing I heard other than the screaming of my own mind. Relief and anger fought by stages, relief and anger and hope and fear.

Finally I couldn't take it anymore.

Now that I had escaped losing . . . well, everything, I needed to know. "Am I still employed?"

Harris glanced at me, and I felt a thin, weak burst of exhaustion escape into Mindspace. "Aren't you going to ask me if the Guild's secrets are safe now? That's usually what you people ask me at this point."

I blinked at him. "I'm not really 'you people' anymore. I don't really care if you keep their secrets or not, so long as I don't have to deal with the Council for, I don't know, approximately forever. You want to hold a press conference, you knock yourself out. I'll hold the camera and cheer." I looked out the window. Tried to figure out how soon I could ask the job question again.

He took a right turn, then a left. A few minutes later, about the time I was going to ask again, he spoke. "I haven't kept my pass by being indiscreet. Neither, I suspect, have you. You did well, for what it's worth. Focusing the anger at the third party was . . . an unusual choice, but I think it worked. Johanna certainly reacted in a way that supported that decision and made your accusations seem credible."

"They won't have a war or anything for right now, at least," I said. "That much was a lie, you know. Johanna wasn't behind it *all*. They did a lot of the stuff themselves, out of fear. The quarantines, the Tech. The fear that spread like wildfire. They engineered a large portion of their own downfalls. Even if Johanna helped. A lot. She admitted to the illegal devices, you know."

He sat with that a minute. Then: "You can lie to suspects, Ward. It's legal. And the Guild . . . well, a few lies that keep the peace may be the way to go. You handled the suspect; she's in custody. You united the Guild against her and prevented a civil war. You found the rotten apple in the TCO and solved an ax murder. I'm not unhappy with the outcome of this week."

After a moment, I couldn't wait anymore. "Do I have a job?"

"That's up to Bransen. I'll mention your performance here, however. Come in tomorrow."

"Yes, sir."

"And, Ward?"

"Yes, sir?"

"You leave me in the middle of the Guild hallways while you deal with suspects on your own again and I will chew you out so bad your ears will ring a month from now. Are we clear?"

"Yes, sir."

CHAPTER 25

Cherabino was sitting on my couch when I opened the apartment door. Her mind was worn, weary, worried sick with stress.

She looked up and put her head in her hands, a burst of relief coming through Mindspace. Her shoulders shook, and suddenly I realized she was crying.

I closed the door behind me, locked it. Then I stood there, not sure what to do. I mean, we were dating, right? I needed to do something. But Cherabino didn't cry. She just . . . Cherabino didn't cry.

I went over there, sat next to her. Put my arm around her. She pulled away. "Don't touch me right now."

"Okay," I said uncertainly. I got up to get her a tissue.

She took it, her mouth set. "I can't believe you scared me like that! You went off without even telling me where you were going. And when I showed up here . . . when I showed up here, you were gone." Her face was blotchy and red from the crying, and now the anger. She thought about punching me, decided against it. "Don't you *ever*. Not *ever*, okay?"

"I won't do that again," I agreed. And then I realized, as scared and angry as she'd been . . . I hadn't felt her. I went inside, to the place where the Link was, and it was a thin vaporous bridge, nothing that would hold any weight. Nothing that would transmit emotions without specific intention.

A huge sense of loss hit me.

"What?" she asked, blotting her face with the tissue.

I looked up. "Your greatest wish has come true. I promised you the Link would fade, and, well, it has, damn it." I crossed my arms. "I hope you're happy."

She put her hand on my shoulder, and her mind came into focus. A focus it didn't have without the contact. "Adam . . ." But she was happy, in that moment, relieved and happy and just a touch of sad and angry left over. "I guess I didn't believe you were telling the truth. I'm sorry." She paused. "What happened in there?"

"I caught a killer," I said, turning, her hand falling off my shoulder. "I caught a killer and I survived."

And then I was kissing her, kissing her as if she were the air and the sun and everything good in the world. And she was in my arms, kissing me back, the saltiness of her tears flavoring everything.

I'm sorry, I said quietly, with no idea if she heard me or not.

I pulled her down onto the couch, into my lap, and we kissed for a long, long time, me slowing her down when she tried to escalate, me drawing out the moment, just the moment, no more, no less. Finally I pulled away, panting.

I wanted to tell her I loved her. I wanted it so, so bad. I looked her in the eye, everything in me wanting to say it.

She pulled away, like she always did, and I forced myself back.

Silence rang in the room as I tried to put the lid back on the box. As I tried desperately to figure out what I'd do without the feel of her in the back of my head.

"I wish this was easier," I finally said. It was true, and I could say it, and for all the things rolling around in my head I had to say something. "I really wish this was easier."

She stood. "You'll come back into the office tomorrow and we'll figure it out, okay? I filled out a fraternization report. You can sign it and we can tell Michael and we can figure it out." She cleared her throat. "Sex is off the table for now?"

I looked up at her. "That one's up to you. As long as you want to walk away free and clear, then yeah, sex is off the table. You make up your mind to make this long-term, a lot of things go on the table," I said, unable to keep my heart away from my eyes.

She looked away. "Okay."

"Okay?"

"Okay. Sex is off the table. You're buying me better dinners to make up for it." She needed more time, she thought. Her mind flashed an image of her dead husband, and some very strong feelings of loss and a squirrelly unwillingness to lose again, before she pushed both aside.

"Okay." It was an actual effort not to respond to what I'd seen. Finally I offered, "You're not going to sleep at my place again, are you?"

She laughed, and some of the tension was gone. "Not unless you get a bigger bed, no. You're welcome at mine, but if you leave beard hairs in the sink I will kick your ass."

"Understood," I said. And a small, critical part of me relaxed. "Will you stay while I eat at least?"

"Dehydrated microwave crap?" she asked.

"Well, yeah. It's what I've got."

"Make one for me too." Her hunger flavored the space.

I called Swartz while the microwave was going, to let him know I was okay.

He was silent a long time, then finally said, "We meeting on Tuesday morning?"

I closed my eyes. "Yeah. Tuesday's great."

"Good," he said gruffly.

We talked inconsequentials for a moment before Selah made him hang up the phone. But I stood there for a long minute, looking at the phone, before Cherabino pulled me away to dinner.

The food was wretched and flavorless, but her complaining was amusing enough to make up for it, and at least the stuff was filling. And we talked about work, and life, and stupid stuff. I hadn't been so happy in a long, long time. It didn't really matter what we talked about.

She asked me about what had happened at the Guild. I told her, glossing over anything personal or private, keeping myself from reliving the emotions. Plenty of time for that in the next few weeks. Plenty of time to work through it with Swartz at the meetings. I'd have an army of listeners there. Here, now, I'd rather be with her; I was exhausted, and blocking off so much of what had happened into the back of my head would catch up later, but this one moment might never happen again.

We talked about work. Some of her current cases. Michael's first one he took on as primary. Ruffins's motives for killing Wright, and the case against him. He was in holding, coming up before the Grand Jury in January. Cherabino—Isabella—thought he'd be prosecuted. The Fiske case was stalled for now, but she had Michael working on compiling what they had outside Ruffins's influence. The inquiry into her actions was scheduled with IA in January as well.

"You think you'll be able to pull together a case against Fiske from scratch?" I asked.

She waved her fork at me. "With everything that man has been up to, if we can't pull together an airtight case from scratch, we don't deserve the badges. It'll take a while, but we'll do it." Lingering regret and worry ate at her about the trip to Fiske's house, but she pushed it aside and concentrated on the now.

"Awesome." I poked around at the bottom of my bowl for the last piece of tough pasta, and ate it with some of the limp broccoli. Got a hot pepper in there too, which woke up my sinuses. At least that was some flavor.

"How's Jacob?" I asked without thinking. She liked it when I asked about her family.

"They seem to be okay, but I'm worried," she said. "About Fiske and what I saw. About the Guild finding out. I don't know what she'll do if they try to take him away from her. We may end up leaving the country."

"You don't need to do that," I said, then realized what I'd said. "Well, probably not."

Her cop's mind turned on. "What are you talking about?"

I had a choice then. I could lie or I could tell the truth. Lying might get me the rest of this dinner, the rest of the night. Might get me a little comfort, which I needed.

But this was Isabella. "I talked to the Guild Council about Jacob. You don't have to worry about them taking him away. Twice-a-week lessons there, monitoring, and he'll get to choose what he wants when he's old enough. It's a good deal."

Fury poured from her like a tidal wave. Her voice was dangerously, dangerously quiet. "You talked to the Guild about Jacob without me?"

I pushed the bowl away from me on the coffee table. Looked at her. "It came up. I didn't let them threaten him."

"They *threatened him?*" She sputtered for a second, like she really couldn't believe what she was hearing. "They *threatened him* and you made a deal? Without talking to me. Without a single phone call to my sister or me or *anybody* who might have an actual fucking stake in what happens to Jacob. You just made a deal. All by your lonesome self."

"That's not exactly . . ." I trailed off. "Listen, it keeps him under their protection! It gets him much more training faster. And it gives him some place to go if he gets threatened. He's a teleporter, Cherabino. He Jumps away from danger into the Guild and nobody—nobody—can hurt him. It keeps him safe, damn it!" Now I was angry.

We huffed at each other for a good long minute.

Finally she said, "You might have a point."

"Really?"

"Yes. Don't rub it in. And I'm still not happy, understand? But you might have a point."

A long silence reigned.

"Are you leaving now?" I asked, when the nervousness got too much to bear.

"Are you kicking me out?" she asked, right back.

"Well, no."

She huffed and some of the anger dissipated. "Then . . . then I guess I'm staying until I get tired. I'm not sleeping on your puny cot again. I'm lucky I didn't throw out my back the first time." She paused, looked at the dishes again. "On second thought, I have ice cream at my place."

"Is that an invitation?"

"Do you want it to be?"

Oh, what the hell. "Sure."

"Then it's an invitation. Next time I'm cooking, though. This stuff is crap." She picked up the bowls and moved them to the sink, noisily washing dishes, taking out her energy on soapy water.

I picked up a towel and went to help.

"I'm still mad," she said.

"I know," I replied.

The next morning, bright and early, Bransen looked up. "My door was closed," he said in a dangerously quiet voice.

"When my door is closed, it means I do not want to be disturbed."

I looked at him. I looked at the door. "I can come back later."

"You've already disturbed me. What do you want?"

I stood, half in, half out of the door. "I just wanted to know whether I have a job."

He put down the pen he was holding. "The captain gave me a call last night."

"Ah," I said noncommittally.

"You go over my head again and you're out on the street," he said, with fire. Then: "Part-time, like we talked about, trial basis. You only get benefits because the Guild pays for them. No coddling. And I will be monitoring the close rates for the detectives you work with. You're with Freeman today."

"Not . . . not Cherabino?" I asked, gut roiling with mixed emotions.

"You work where I tell you to work. That a problem?" He peered at me.

"No, sir." Another detective might be good for everyone. Especially since Cherabino and I were dating. Plus I wasn't in a position to be picky. "Am I going to work with her eventually?"

"I'll let you know. Now get going."

After a hard day with the grumpy and hard-driving Freeman, I picked up my mail from the mailroom. Frances, the file clerk, who was now doing mail in addition to filing, had said there was something for me.

There in the mail room, I stared at the box sitting on top of a pile of my mail. The box was the size of a thick book, and the return address said PI LICENSING BOARD. I lifted it. It was just heavy enough to have a badge inside. A small thrill went up my spine.

I opened the thing. Inside, as suspected, was my PI license, a small shield that looked official but not police official. I picked it up; the weight of the metal in my hand felt like an affirmation. I'd done it.

On the way back, I tripped over an uneven tile in front of the elevator, barely staying upright. My mail fell out of my hand, bills and junk mail scattering across the lobby floor, my new PI badge landing on the floor with a bounce.

Michael came by then and grabbed several of the bills to hand to me. "Is it true you're not working in the interview rooms anymore?" he asked reluctantly.

I nodded. "For now, it's just Homicide. Not full-time."

His hand found the badge. "You going to be a PI?"

"Who knows?" I said. "But right now I'm working here."

His mind made a passing inquiry about the Guild that he suppressed. He settled for "It's good to have you back."

"Thanks," I said.

ABOUT THE AUTHOR

Alex has written since early childhood, and loves great stories in any form, including sci-fi, fantasy, and mystery. Over the years, Alex has lived in many neighborhoods of the sprawling metro Atlanta area. Decatur, the neighborhood on which *Marked* is centered, was Alex's college home.

R0153

ALSO AVAILABLE FROM

Alex Hughes

SHARP
A Mindspace Investigations Novel

Parts for illegal Tech are being hijacked all over the city,
the same parts used to bring the world to its knees in the
Tech Wars sixty years ago. Plus a cop-killer is on the loose
with a vengeance. It falls to a telepath to close both cases
and prove his worth, once and for all...

"A fun blend of *Chinatown* and *Blade Runner*."
—James Knapp, author of *State of Decay*

Available wherever books are sold or at
penguin.com

facebook.com/acerocbooks